Scarlett Bailey has loved wri[...]
Before writing novels she worked as a waitress, cinema
usherette and bookseller. Passionate about old movies,
Scarlett loves nothing more than spending a wet
Sunday afternoon watching her favourite films back-
to-back with large quantities of chocolate.

Scarlett also writes novels under her real name
Rowan Coleman. Currently she lives in Hertfordshire
with her husband, five children and a very large
collection of beautiful shoes.

To find out more, visit her website at:
www.rowancoleman.co.uk,
Facebook or Twitter:
@rowancoleman and @scarlettbailey

Praise for Scarlett Bailey

'A delicious Christmas read!' Trisha Ashley

'I LOVE it! It was funny, romantic and the
perfect book to snuggle up with – Scarlett Bailey
does it again!' Miranda Dickinson

'Endearing and funny, we loved this gorgeously
Christmassy romcom' Closer

'A light, fun and fast-paced chunk of
chortlesome chick-lit' Heat

Also by Scarlett Bailey:

The Night before Christmas
Married by Christmas
Santa Maybe

As Rowan Coleman:

Growing Up Twice
After Ever After
River Deep
The Accidental Mother
The Baby Group
The Accidental Wife
The Accidental Family
The Happy Home for Broken Hearts
Lessons in Laughing Out Loud
Quick Reads:
A Woman Walks into a Bar

Just for Christmas

Scarlett Bailey

EBURY
PRESS

1 3 5 7 9 10 8 6 4 2

First published in 2013 by Ebury Press, an imprint of Ebury Publishing
A Random House Group Company

The Random House Group Limited Reg. No. 954009

Addresses for companies within the Random House Group can be found at:
www.randomhouse.co.uk

A CIP catalogue record for this book is
available from the British Library

Penguin Random House is committed to a sustainable future for
our business, our readers and our planet. This book is made from
Forest Stewardship Council® certified paper.

Printed and bound in Great Britain by Clays Ltd, St Ives plc

ISBN 9781785037818

To buy books by your favourite authors and register for offers visit:
www.randomhouse.co.uk

For Adam, always

Chapter One

It took a few seconds after she killed the lights and switched off the engine, for Alex Munro's eyes to adjust to the dark.

This was proper dark, nothing like the night times back home, in Grangemouth, where the streets were spangled with orange street lamps, and the roads lined with neon signs, where the towering cranes crowded the docks, and the floodlights that enabled a twenty-four hour operation always kept the stars at bay. So for a moment after she switched off the lights and turned off the engine, Alex just sat there behind the wheel of her car in the pitch black, and wondered what on earth she was doing here, a few weeks before Christmas, in a place where no one knew her and she knew no one, and about as far away from her home country as she could get without actually having to use her passport. Which wasn't to say she hadn't thought about it.

'You're running away,' she reminded herself, out loud, her voice a soft whisper, because anything louder would have seemed unseemly in the perfect quiet. 'That's what you are doing, Alex. A new year is on its way, and you are making a new start. Now, get out of the car and get on with it, you big Jessie.'

Now that she'd had a moment for her eyes to adjust to the dark, Alex could see the faint orange glow behind the curtain in the window of what was to be her new home, A tiny, squat and decidedly lopsided-looking cottage, which could be no more than two up, two down, its white-washed exterior a ghostly dark grey in the darkness.

The mayor of Poldore, Mr Godolphin, who wasn't her new boss exactly, but would be her point of liaison with the town, said he'd be there to greet her when she arrived, although she hadn't really believed he meant it. She had carefully explained via a very detailed email that the drive down to Cornwall from Scotland would take several hours, she had no idea what time of the day or night she might arrive, and now it was almost ten. Mr Godolphin had told her there was a key in a flowerpot by the door, not that she'd need it because he'd be there to greet her and, anyway, no one locked their doors in Poldore. Might as well be there as anywhere, he'd said. Alex hadn't believed that either. After all it was Cornwall she'd decided on a whim to move to, not the Middle Ages.

After climbing out of the car, Alex grabbed her overnight bag, planning to come back for the rest of her stuff later, when a sound, so alien, so terrifying, stopped her dead in her tracks, raising prickles along the back of her neck.

It took two seconds more for Alex to realise it was a snarl, no, more of a vicious growl. She was being growled at by a thing, a quite big thing, with eyes that glowed in the dark, its terrible teeth glinting in the moonlight.

'Shit,' Alex whispered out loud, dimly remembering that if you were attacked by a bear you were supposed to stand tall and try to look bigger than it, but this wasn't a bear, this was Cornwall after all, so what the hell was it then?

The Beast of Bodmin, that was it. Alex's heart pounded furiously. Bodmin Moor was pretty close to Poldore, maybe only ten or so miles away. It was just her luck that she'd run away from Scotland, a broken heart and a lying father, to end up coming face to face with the Beast of Bodmin.

So this was how it would all end. Maybe they'd never find her body, maybe her disappearance would always be a mystery and then Marcus would be sorry. He'd be weeping in despair as he walked up the aisle to marry another woman, with her hair and her push-up bra and obvious tan. Alex raised an eyebrow, she was quite warming to the Beast of Bodmin scenario.

And then it growled again, lower this time and full of intent, an intent that Alex was fairly certain involved dinner. Alex squeaked, just a little, as the Beast began to advance slowly on her, low on its haunches, the gleam of bared teeth sparkling, darkly.

'Oh shit,' Alex said, feeling her knees actually quake, which up until that point she hadn't realised was a real thing, and then it crept into a shaft of moonlight. 'Oh you're only a wee dog!'

The animal, now illuminated in silvery light, had, it turned out, been mostly made up of shadows. In fact it was a reasonably small, very dirty, exceptionally smelly dog, covered in matted hair, and scarcely beastly in appearance at all. Although none of these facts seemed to matter to the hound. The hound still seemed intent on ripping Alex's throat out and then possibly eating her alive, although she wasn't sure what would kill her first – the blood loss, or the halitosis.

'Now, now, little doggy,' she said, reaching slowly into her bag for half a Twix, which was the lone survivor of her junk food driving picnic. 'Oh you're a poor wee little thing, aren't you? A little stray doggy, what you need is a lovely, lovely snack . . .' Alex grappled for the half-melted finger of chocolate, pulled it out and threw it over the dog's head. The animal chased after it at once, disappearing into the undergrowth, where it sounded as if it was ferociously killing the chocolate, and Alex took her chance, bolting for the cottage door in the hope that Mr Godolphin was as good as his word and it would indeed be open.

She tumbled into a tiny front room, where a fire

burned merrily in the grate, and landed on a large, round, red-faced, silver-haired gentleman, who had been dozing peacefully in an aged, overstuffed chair by the fire. That was until Alex landed on his lap.

'What the . . .?' He sat up, his arm instinctively encircling Alex's waist. 'Oh, oh my, beg your pardon, miss!'

Alex leapt up, followed by, who she could only assume was Mr Godolphin, the Mayor of Poldore.

'There's this rabid dog out there,' she told him, pointing in the direction of the open door. 'It's a vicious animal. It was about to maul me! We need to call someone, the police, the army. Who is it who takes care of rabid animals? The RSPCA?'

At which point the stinking, mostly grey, matted animal in question trotted meekly through the door, carrying half a Twix delicately in its jaws and settled down in front of the fire, with a deeply satisfied sigh.

'What, Buoy?' Eddie Godolphin said, looking perplexed. 'Buoy won't do you no harm, he's all mouth and trousers is Buoy, and well . . . Buoy lives here.'

'I don't care if he's a boy or a girl, he's got to go!' Alex said. 'I live here now.'

Eddie chuckled deeply, shaking his head; he didn't seem to get the gravity of the situation at all.

'No, no,' he said, smiling fondly at the fetid creature. 'B. U. O. Y. As in a life buoy. Clever, isn't it? Although Buoy is a boy, for the record. He's got about twenty or so pups attributed to him in Poldore, something of a rake in his heyday he was, getting on a bit now, though, aren't you Buoy? Buoy is your new housemate.'

'What?' Alex asked him, as the animal eyed up a pile of scones that sat on a small gate-leg dining table. 'What are you talking about?'

'Buoy!' Eddie looked like he might be a bit worried that she wasn't keeping up so well. 'Your new housemate. Our harbour master before last, Alf Waybridge, he picked Buoy up as a puppy, some rotter chucked him out when he was tiny, him and the rest of a litter. Alf found Buoy, the only one left alive in the sack. Took him in and the two of them were thick as thieves. Then when old Alf passed on Buoy didn't. He didn't fancy moving, you see? We tried rehoming him a few times, but he doesn't get on with people, a bit like old Alf, really. So the town looks after him now, and when he does want a roof over his head, when it's getting cold, this is where he comes. It's his home, you see, and he's getting on now, must be at least eleven.'

Alex stared down at the creature for a long, desperate moment. Maybe she'd go back to Scotland and watch the love of her life marry a bimbo after all, maybe that would be what she would do. Or move. Or build a new house.

'So anyway.' Eddie grinned, clearly feeling that the subject of the sitting tenant was closed. 'Hello to you. I didn't know he was bringing a young lady with him.

That's nice, isn't it? He won't be starting out here alone.'

Alex blinked at him. 'What?'

'Your man, the new harbour master, Mr Alex Munro.' Eddie grinned again, and Alex noticed he had very white teeth, teeth that a dentist had spent serious time on, and a thick gold chain around his neck. He'd told her in their email exchange that he was also the landlord of Poldore's busiest pub the Silent Man, as well as being mayor, and Alex thought he looked much more suited to that role than the one he was here for. For starters he was talking total nonsense. 'If he'd told me he was bringing his young lady, I'd have got some flowers in or something. Maybe given old Buoy here a spray with the Febreze.'

'I'm Alex Munro,' Alex told him, holding out a hand.

'Munro's young lady, yes I worked that much out.' He winked at her.

'No, I mean I'm actually Alex Munro,' she said again.

'I'm Spartacus!' he said jovially, until finally the deadly serious look on Alex's face began to sink in. 'I'm sorry, love?'

'I am Alex Munro, Poldore's new harbour master,' Alex said slowly and deliberately as understanding dawned. 'Did no one tell you I was a woman?'

Chapter Two

'Well now, that's a turn-up,' Eddie Godolphin said, settling himself back into the only comfortable chair in the minuscule room. He picked up the plate of scones and stuffed one whole into his mouth. 'That's a real turn-up for the books.'

Or at least that was what Alex thought he said; it was hard to tell through the crumbs, cream and jam. The dog eyed her with the single amber eye that was visible through his unruly coat. He definitely had a look of a pirate about him, and now that the chocolate bar was gone he looked hungry again.

'Well, I don't know why you didn't know,' Alex said. 'I did three Skype interviews with the Port Authority people, they saw my face, and I know I'm not exactly a girly girl, but I think it's pretty clear I'm a woman.'

Eddie nodded as he looked her up and down. 'Oh yes, you are all woman,' he said, cheerfully.

Alex scowled. She was fairly sure you couldn't discern her shape under her deliberately shapeless and chunky cable knit jumper, but still the comment, as benign as it was, unsettled her. She'd grown up in a world of men, working in the male-dominated industry of shipping since she'd left school at sixteen. She'd learned very young that the second a man noticed you had breasts he stopped taking you seriously. In her line of work it was best to keep everything feminine hidden away.

'Well, anyway,' she told him, raising her chin and lowering her voice, 'the Port Authority interviewed me, checked my credentials, experience and references, and gave me the job. So you can't take it away again because I'm a woman, that would be illegal.'

'Oh I know that, love,' Eddie said, stuffing another scone into his mouth before offering Alex the plate.

She would dearly have loved to eat at least three of them, but her pride would not let her take one. It didn't seem to be tactically sensible to eat scones with this man, not while she felt that her new life, her new start, was suddenly at stake because of her ovaries.

'And it's not like we aren't a forward-thinking town,' he said. 'We are very modern in Poldore you know, we've got all sorts here.'

'What men and women?' Alex asked him a little sarcastically,

'It's, well, thing is, it's tradition, isn't it?' Eddie said, rather apologetically. 'Boats and women, they don't mix, do they? Or at least that's the superstition. I don't mind it myself. But then again, I don't like boats, never have. Sheer coincidence that I live by the sea.'

Alex huffed crossly. 'I've guided several hundred

super tankers in and out of port back in Grangemouth,' she told him sternly. 'And I've never crashed one.'

'Ah, yes,' Eddie said. 'But have you ever dealt with a good old-fashioned Cornish fisherman? Or woman? Being harbour master in Poldore isn't just about parking boats, it's about being at the heart of the community, knowing everyone who comes in and goes out. It's caring for the very thing that makes us us.'

'I know that, and, as I said in my interview with the Port Authority, I have excellent interpersonal skills and am able to work well under my own initiative as well as part of a team,' Alex said, so stridently that she thought Eddie Godolphin looked a little bit scared. 'And anyway, it's about time good old-fashioned Cornish fisherpeople dragged themselves into the twenty-first century!'

Suddenly she felt exhausted – the eight-hour drive, the near mauling by the foul-breath mutt, the confusion over her sex all caught up with her and she sat down heavily on the only other seat available, a rickety old wooden chair that was tucked under the narrow gate-leg table. Both had seen better days, a very long time ago.

Eddie put the plate of scones down on the table.

'My Becky baked them,' he said. 'You won't taste any better. Go on, you must be famished.'

Alex shrugged and took a scone from the plate. She took a bite; it was utterly delicious.

'Look.' Eddie leaned forwards in his chair and smiled at her kindly. 'You're a lady . . .'

'Woman,' Alex told him sternly.

'A lady woman,' Eddie went on. 'And you are our new harbour master, appointed by the Port Authority, and I might be the mayor, but they are the only ones who could un-appoint you. A few of the old sea dogs are going to grumble, and I suppose you have to work twice as hard as a man to prove you are up to the job but . . .' Eddie stood up, and grinned. 'Our last harbour master was a drunk, so you're one up on him already. Unless you are also a drunk, that is.'

'So you aren't going to try and hound me out of town?' Alex asked him. 'With pitchforks, and ferocious dogs, maybe set fire to me in a wicker man?'

Eddie chuckled, and Alex noticed he seemed to be in a permanent state of amusement. 'Darling, Poldore is like the Cannes of Cornwall, you'll soon find that out. We've got more pop stars, novelists, film stars and millionaires round here than we know what to do with, and besides, I think you'll find all that pagan stuff happened just north of where you came from. I'll leave you to it, let you get spruced up a bit and I'll see you over in the pub in about half an hour for your welcome do.'

'My what?' Alex spluttered through a mouthful of crumbs.

'We're a *community*, Alex,' Eddie told her, emphasising

the word as if it might be one that she'd never heard before. 'And you will become a key part of it. Everyone's waiting to meet you, Becky will feed you, my daughter, Lucy, will serve you wine, or a pint!' he added to make sure he didn't sound sexist. 'All on me. The Silent Man, right across the river. There's a brand new dinghy moored for you at the back of the cottage. Take a torch though, steps down to the mooring can be a bit tricky, and we don't want you drowning on your first day, do we?'

Eddie picked up his coat and was almost at the door before Alex realised he was leaving something behind.

'The dog!' she said, pointing at the mutt, who was watching her with the one yellow eye, his chin on his paws, just the hint of his yellowing teeth exposed under one black lip. 'Take the dog with you!'

'I thought I told you, the dog lives here.' Eddie shook his head, slightly bemused. 'Remember? He's your dog now. Or, more likely, you are his human.'

'But I don't like dogs!' Alex told him. 'I'm not a dog person.'

'You should get along just fine then.' Eddie looked at the animal that now lay, snoring peacefully on the rug. 'Because he's not a people person at all.'

Chapter Three

As exciting new beginnings go, this one hadn't exactly gone according to plan, Alex thought as she explored her new home. Thankfully there weren't any more unwanted pets. Not unless you counted the spider in the bath that Alex thought might measure a foot in diameter. Well, a good three inches anyway. As predicted there wasn't much to the cottage. Downstairs, there was the living room and a sort of kitchenette – little more than a cupboard really – that led off from it, with a cooker, an ancient fridge, a sink – with a curtained off recess underneath it – and another door that led into the back garden. She could see little in the dark but the garden appeared to comprise about three square feet of grass and a sheer cliff face of rock, soaring upwards. Upstairs there was an old but working bathroom and one bedroom, containing a largish double bed and a very old wardrobe.

'It's not so bad,' Alex told her reflection in the dusty wardrobe mirror as she emerged, shuddering, a little while later, from a freezing cold shower, which the spider had stubbornly stayed in situ for, only ambling off down the overflow after she'd stepped out of the ancient bathtub. There was another tiny radiator in the bedroom, but this one was stone cold and so Alex had turned on a very small and inefficient electric heater, which was doing an excellent job at keeping her left big toe lukewarm. 'It's not so different from what you were expecting. Although to be fair you weren't expecting everything to be at a forty-five degree angle.'

It was hard to tell in the dark, but Alex thought that in the next five to ten years the cottage would have slipped off of the edge of the ledge it was perched on entirely.

She rooted around in the bottom of her bag until she found her hairbrush and pulled it through her long black hair. Hair as black as a raven's wing, her dad used to say as he brushed it out for her every Sunday night before school, and then that would be it. No more brushing for the rest of the week; Alex hated it. And even her stern and strict father couldn't do a thing to change her mind about it. By Wednesday, she'd have a distinct air of the cave girl about her, but by Friday she looked positively feral. Now she was twenty-eight, Alex knew about conditioner, and it helped keep her hair tangle free and smooth. But in her motherless household, it had taken Alex and her father at least two decades to work that out, and if it was up to Ian Munro, she'd still be washing her hair with hand soap.

Thick and refusing to dry, her damp mane sat heavily on her shoulders, as she reached for her sensible white bra and pants, jeans and a loose white shirt, which she pulled a deep green sweater over. As Alex looked at the pale heart-shaped face that peered out from between the two dark curtains of hair, parted carefully in the middle, her blue eyes suddenly brimmed with unshed tears.

'Shut up, Alexandra,' she told herself. 'Shut up and stop being such a woman. You are here; you have a new life, a new job, and a new house with a new . . . dog. Things are going to work out, because they have to. There is no way you are going back home with your tail between your legs, is there?' Alex shook her head in response to her own question. 'So you are going to get up, go downstairs, somehow get past the rabid beast in the living room and go and meet your new neighbours, aren't you?' Alex shook her head again.

'Yes, you are,' Alex told herself, getting up and pulling on her Timberland boots. 'And for God's sake, don't let them see that you are petrified.'

Buoy got up as Alex came down the steep set of creaking stairs and snarled at her.

'I've got to go out,' Alex told him. She had no idea about how to communicate with dogs, so she thought she might as well approach it as if he understood English. 'You heard Eddie? He told me I had to go to this welcome do. It sounds like a nightmare, so you can keep me pinned to the bottom step all night if you like, but that means it will just be me and you. Up to you.'

Buoy sat down, a little stiffly and regarded her, as if he was considering the options.

'Wouldn't you like to live in a nice animal shelter?' Alex asked him. 'Or get adopted by a granny? Maybe a blind old granny with no sense of smell?'

Buoy growled again.

'Right, well, Eddie didn't say anything about you having a track record of murdering people, so I'm betting your growl is worse than your bite, and I'm just bloody going out. And I'll deal with you tomorrow.'

Buoy raised one bushy brow and gave her a decidedly sceptical look.

'I'm not scared of an old mutt!' Alex told him firmly. She ran all the way to the door nevertheless.

It was cold outside, and Alex was glad that she'd taken her dad's old greatcoat off the peg on her way out. She wrapped it around her body, pointing the torch at the ground as she edged her way along the stone path that was cut into her small garden towards the cliff edge, where she assumed the steps that Eddie had referred to must be. It was cold, but not the same sort of cold that she was used to back home in Grangemouth, which was hard and bitter, and sometimes tasted of iron. Here the cold seemed softer, more enveloping and, well, sort of warm. Alex caught her breath as she reached a rotten picket fence, leaning outwards at a suicidal angle, bisected by a gate swinging on rusty hinges, which seemed to mark the end of the world.

Edging closer, Alex took in another sharp breath as she realised that this was where the path dropped off the edge of a cliff and became a steep set of steps roughly cut out of the rock. At the bottom of perhaps a twenty-foot drop, Alex could just make out where the water lapped against a small stony beach and her new boat moored at the end of short quay. As soon as Alex saw it, glowing like a new moon in the water, she smiled. It was only a very basic motorised dinghy, true, but to Alex it was freedom. Her eyes travelled upwards, drawn to the coloured lights that bobbed in the water, and she looked across the mouth of the river for the first time and saw her new home, Poldore, in all its glory.

Rising sharply up the hillside, the town glittered in the crisp night, a thousand lights in windows shining bravely. Poldore was set, like a jewel, right on the edge of the sea, mirroring the sky above it that blazed with countless stars. Alex stood stock still on the edge of the cliff, enveloped in the warm cold of a Cornish December, looked at the crescent moon shining above, and the one that awaited her at the bottom of the steps and she thought, Yes, *this* is what a new beginning feels like.

Which was when Buoy barged past her, trotted nimbly down the stone steps and climbed into the boat.

*

It didn't take long to make it across the harbour to the town, which was lucky as Alex was holding her breath the entire way to try to avoid the dog's distinctive scent. The man from the Port Authority said there was a reason the harbour master's cottage was built on the other side of the estuary, some sort of local tradition to do with witches, smugglers, or maybe pirates, he couldn't remember exactly, but Alex didn't mind in the least. She liked being on her own, she liked the idea of her lonely bolthole away from the hustle and bustle of the little town, and she couldn't have loved the commute any more if she'd tried.

Buoy, who was completely indifferent to the odour he brought with him, sat in the prow of the boat, gazing wisely out to sea, and just as Alex pulled up alongside her mooring, he hopped out of the boat and went on his business without so much as a second glance in her direction, for which Alex was oddly grateful.

After mooring her dinghy, tying it with great care, using the sailors' knots she'd learnt from a book as soon as she discovered she had the job, Alex heaved herself up onto the harbour wall, where she was greeted by a small square, surrounded on two sides by shops and restaurants, and a large Victorian redbrick town hall. Festooned in Christmas lights of all colours, which ran from building to building, the square was fairly busy with people, and Alex could hear the chatter coming from the restaurants, and the Silent Man, which stood slightly elevated above the other buildings, a little further up the steep incline.

In the centre of the square, a tall, strong-looking spruce took pride of place, positively bristling with Christmas decorations. Pop a couple of carollers in Victorian dress in and it would make a perfect Christmas card: a thought which gave Alex a tight feeling in her chest. This would be the first Christmas ever that she would spend away from her home, her dad, Marcus, her friends and everyone she knew. And yet it was the way it had to be, there was no going back now. Home was a very, very long way away, and so was the life she had left behind.

Taking a deep breath, Alex tied her hair into a knot at the base of her neck, squared her shoulders and headed into the pub.

Chapter Four

Alex had thought that pubs falling silent while everyone stared at you only happened in old Hammer horror movies, but no, the second she walked in the door of the Silent Man everyone stopped talking and looked at her, which instantly turned Alex's pale skin a ruddy shade of pink, made her hunch her shoulders and hide behind her hair. If there was one thing that Alex hated it was being the centre of attention, particularly when she wasn't at all sure that the attention was friendly. However, it was too late to escape, firstly because they'd all notice her leaving, and secondly because a lady who she guessed was Becky Godolphin, was marching towards her, arms outstretched.

'There you are!'

Alex fixed her gaze on the smiling face of a pretty blonde, rounder and older than Alex, perhaps in her early fifties, wearing a tight electric blue dress that accentuated all of her many curves and bulges. For a moment Alex thought Mrs Godolphin might be about to hug her, a thought that made her die a tiny bit inside, but instead she took her hand and led her to the bar, past a host of curious onlookers. 'I'm Becky,

I'm Eddie's wife, landlady at the Silent Man. We're all so pleased to hear you arrived safe and sound. And you're a girl too, girl power!' She shook her fist, several golden bangles jangling on her wrist, and growled a bit. 'We'll show the chauvinist pigs!'

'Um . . . well, I just do my job really,' Alex said.

'Good for you, socking it to the Man!' Becky beamed as she all but lifted Alex onto a stool at the bar, before calling over the barmaid, a tall, slender young woman, whose long blonde hair looked like spun gold. She had enough of a look of her parents about her to make Alex sure that this was Becky and Eddie's daughter, although she also had a sort of ethereal grace that neither parent possessed in obvious quantities.

'This is Lucy, our barmaid,' Becky said. Lucy smiled from behind a curtain of her hair, as Becky added after a fraction of hesitation, 'Lucy's my daughter.'

'Hello,' Alex greeted her quietly. New people were never her best thing, new people en masse were officially her worst thing. She tried quite hard to concentrate just on Lucy and Becky and forget all the other people that were unashamedly gawping at her. Lucy, she guessed, was about her age, somewhere in her late twenties, with silky blonde hair that fell to just below her shoulders, and fine delicate features that Alex thought must have come from her mother's side. She was the polar opposite to Alex who wore boys' clothes and boots, didn't know the first thing about make-up, and had literally no idea what was fashionable. Lucy, on the other hand, was impeccably made-up, just enough for a weekday evening, and working a sparkly silver top over jeans, teamed with low-heeled pumps. She looked effortless lovely, but the language of style was one that Alex didn't really know how to interpret. She had two dresses, both black, which she wore to parties and funerals, whichever the occasion required. And yet she envied Lucy's easy attitude to her femininity. Perhaps if she'd known what to do with eyeliner then maybe Marcus would have noticed she'd been in love with him all of her life.

'What can I get you?' Lucy asked.

'It's all on the house for you tonight!' Becky told her. 'Although best not get too drunk; you don't want to start your first day on the job with a hangover.'

'I'll just have a lemonade, thanks,' Alex said, feeling excruciatingly scrutinised by the rest of the pub. Although now talking in murmurs, she just knew that they all had their eyes still fixed on her back.

'And some fish and chips. That'll set you up,' Becky said.

'Oh well . . .' Alex, who had eaten precisely three and a half Twix bars, two packets of Pringles and a doughnut on her epic journey down to Cornwall, plus the scones with Eddie, attempted to refuse the offer, not because she wasn't hungry, but because she found it excruciatingly difficult to know how to respond to people being kind to her. She failed at once.

'Tell Sam to make it an extra large portion, Lucy,' Becky said. 'And stick a vodka in the lemonade. The girl needs a stiffener with this lot treating her like a monkey in a zoo.' She turned around and narrowed her eyes at the customers, who all pretended to be doing something else for a moment.

'Thank you,' Alex said.

'Not a problem,' Becky said, squeezing her arm. Leaning in a little closer, she added, 'They aren't so bad once you get to know them. Promise.'

Becky drew another stool beside her and Lucy put two sparkling clear drinks in tall glasses in front of them.

'Where's Eddie?' Alex asked. 'Did he have to lie down from the shock? I don't think he expected me to be female.'

'No, it takes more than a female harbour master to shock Eddie, even a young female harbour master, trust me.' Becky's smile wavered a little as she watched her daughter serve two new customers. They looked like tourists, Alex decided. They had an air of money about them. Even their casual clothes looked like they'd originated in some high-end exclusive boutique. 'Eddie's just sorting out the cellar, that's all. We had a barrel of bitter explode. He'll be up in a minute.'

'This looks like a very busy pub.' Alex was quite proud of that conversational gambit.

'It is, busiest and best in Poldore. There's the Ship

down the road, and the Smugglers Inn on the way out of town. Both crap.' Becky cocked her head to one side, as she examined Alex. 'So tell me what was it about Poldore that made you want to come and live here?'

Alex took a sip of her drink, grateful for the shot of vodka now. She could tell Becky that it was to escape her broken heart, and her spurned love, or that she'd been looking at the Port Authority website for situations vacant and made a snap decision, partly fuelled by Pinot Grigio, and partly by pure mortification and horror, that had somehow brought her here. Or that she actually knew nothing about the town, except that it had a busy harbour and she was now its master, or mistress, except that she was still a master even though she was a woman. The Port Authority had told her with some delight when she'd been offered the position that she was the UK's second ever woman in the job, the first one living up in Orkney. They'd talked about some publicity, and newspaper articles, about sending a photographer down, but Alex had said very politely that really she only wanted to do her job, and she didn't see what difference it made that she was a woman. What really brought Alex to Poldore was a sudden overwhelming urge to be alone to lick her wounds for a while. So far, that part of the plan wasn't going very well.

'I just thought it was so . . . pretty,' Alex said, rather inanely, thinking of the twinkling lights that had melded with the starry sky above as she had made her way over the river mouth. 'And it looked like, well, like it might be good for the soul.'

'Well, it is pretty and that is for sure,' Becky said, scrutinising Alex as if she could read her thoughts. 'There's been a human settlement at Poldore since the Iron Age for certain – there are burial sites not far out of town, overlooking the cliffs – and maybe even before that. And it was a fort for a long time, which is why we still have Castle House, the house that looks like a castle, right in the middle of the town. It started out being a real fort, but over the centuries it got built on, burnt down, rebuilt and nowadays it's more Victorian than anything, turned into one big folly – though don't you tell Sue Montaigne that I told you that.' Becky nodded over to the end of the bar where a compact-looking woman, with auburn curls cut into an efficient-looking bob was pretending to have a conversation with the man she was sitting next to, a shortish, plumpish man, with thinning sandy hair, but a kind looking face, all the while keeping her eagle eye on Alex. Alex got the distinct impression that the woman was just waiting for her to be exposed, and alone, and then she would swoop in and eat her. Or talk to her, which would be worse. 'The Montaignes have lived in Castle House for eight hundred years continuously. The family line has never once been broken. That's why when Sue got married she kept her name, and her husband changed his!' Becky chuckled into her drink which she then downed in one. She set it on the bar where it was immediately replaced with another by Lucy, plus another drink for Alex who'd barely touched her first one yet. 'Mind you he's a writer, or claims to be, although he's never finished a book yet as far as we know. His name used to be Rory Frogget so I don't suppose he minded changing it too much. There's barely any fishing here any more, although we have the regatta in the summer, and plenty of private boats, boat tours . . . You'll have been told about our cruise liner which comes in every few months. That's always good for business. Like you say, Poldore is pretty, it's beautiful, but the harbour still is the life blood of the town. Over the years we've come to rely more and more on the tourists. We love the tourists, but more than that we got the rich folk coming in now. Building their big million-pound houses high up on the cliff, they've bought up most of the seafront. We got film stars, movie directors, comics, writers, models, rock stars – quite a few of those as there's a world famous recording studios in the woods. I bet you didn't know that?'

Alex shook her head. Suddenly Poldore didn't sound quite like the backwater retreat from the world she had in mind.

'Oh yes, Brian Rogers – have you heard of him?'

Alex nodded. Her dad owned all of his albums, both the stuff he'd recorded in the seventies with his band FireSea and his solo stuff since. Alex couldn't call herself a fan of his music, but she'd heard enough about him to know that at the height of his career he'd sold several million records around the world, and was cited as a major influence for many new artists. If her dad knew that Brian Rogers lived here he would be so excited. Music was one of the rare things he got emotional about and ... Alex felt a burst of pleasure at the thought of being able to share the news with her father, but then she remembered that they weren't talking when she left. And that the way she felt at the moment she wasn't at all sure she'd feel like talking to him ever again.

'So what we do,' Becky went on, oblivious to Alex's dip in morale, 'me and Eddie, and almost everyone in this pub, is we try to keep Poldore, Poldore. We take the cash off the incomers, we welcome them, but we fight to keep this town the way it's always been, to keep the sense of tradition and community alive at the heart of it all.'

'Which is why we have the Christmas pageant.' Sue Montaigne had seen her opportunity and swooped in, her neat, beak-shaped nose and bright, intent eyes doing nothing to alter Alex's impression of her as a bird of prey. 'Becky will tell you that the Poldore pageant has been at the heart of Poldore's history since the Middle Ages, maybe before.'

Lucy put a large glass of red wine down in front of Sue who nodded in thanks.

'Sue Montaigne, meet our new harbour master, Alex

Munro,' Becky said, winking at Alex. 'Sue is our local aristocracy.'

'If only that were true.' Sue grinned, her tight red curls bouncing around her face. Sue was a well-kept woman in her late forties, wearing tight black jeans, black leather boots and green belted sweater dress. She positively bristled with energy, as if everything she said, or thought or did, even taking a sip from her glass of wine, was terribly important, vital even. 'If I'm aristocracy, it's impoverished. What I do do is keep Castle House afloat – we hold weddings; sometimes I lecture on medieval history; I breed dogs, miniature poodles and also children!' She gave a snort. 'I have three of them. And along with everyone else I do what I can for the town, which is why I took it upon myself to keep the Christmas pageant going.'

'She's just got in through the door!' Becky exclaimed, shaking her head and grinning fondly at Sue. 'At least let her settle in for five minutes before you rope her in.'

'Alex, to be part of the town you need to be part of the pageant,' Sue said, ignoring Becky, just as Lucy put a steaming hot plate of fish and chips in front of Alex.

Alex realised that she was starving hungry. Unable to wait, she put one far-too-hot chip in her mouth and spent the next few seconds nodding politely at Sue while attempting not to spit it out.

'So can I put you down to help? You could either have a role in the nativity, you'd make a lovely angel, not Gabriel, I play Gabriel, or there is still the back of the donkey that needs filling . . .'

'I'm not a . . .' Alex swallowed. 'I'm not very good at . . . showing off.'

'We don't call it showing off,' Sue said firmly. 'We call it performing. But if you're more of a back stage girl, that's fine, I'll put you down for set and float painting. Jackson Withers is in charge of that. He's a fellow of the Royal Academy you know, painted the Queen a few years back. Anyway, the next meeting is at my house on Sunday, ten a.m. You'll be able to find my house quite easily, it's the one that's a castle.' She gave another snort of laughter at that.

'Becky!' Alex recognised Eddie's voice, calling from somewhere behind the bar. 'Come down here, love! I can't loosen this valve on the new barrel!'

'Men.' Becky rolled her eyes. 'I don't need to tell you who wears the trousers in the household. In a town where the landlady of the pub changes all the barrels, I'm sure we can take a woman harbour master in our stride.'

Alex exchanged glances with Lucy, who smiled at her.

'Well.' Sue smiled at Alex. 'I'm very pleased to meet you and to get you on board for the pageant. There's so much to do and only a couple of weeks to go. You will be invaluable. I can see you've got your supper to eat and that there are a lot of people who want to talk to you, so I'll leave you to it.' Sue gestured towards the bar where the man with thick sandy hair and a large brandy in his hand was in deep conversation with a sophisticated brunette of about Alex's own age. 'If you need rescuing, wave, I'll be over there with my husband Rory and my PA Marissa. Daughter of friends of the family, caused a scandal in certain circles, became rather persona non grata. Nice enough girl, but the organisational skills of a brick. I'm waiting until the New Year, by which time I will have done my duty by employing her and then I'll send her back from whence she came. Toodle-pip!'

Alex watched Sue bustle off, feeling a little bereft.

'So tell me –' an older man slid into the space that Sue vacated at once '– what does a young slip of a thing like you know about boats?'

'Now then, Jago.' Eddie reappeared from behind the bar, his shirt soaked through with beer, and stinking of bitter. 'Alex hasn't just been given the job out of the blue. The Port Authority people interviewed her and checked her out. She's been working in Grangemouth, controlling super tankers.'

'Super tankers aren't boats,' Jago said with a sniff, and narrowed his eyes as he scrutinised Alex. 'And the weather up there isn't the weather down here. This isn't shoe shopping or cake baking we're talking about. It's lives, so, you lady, you tell me everything you know about boats, and we'll see.'

Alex sighed inwardly. Really all she wanted to do

was be left alone to eat her fish and chips, or, failing that, to go home to a preferably dogless house, fall into that creaky old bed and sleep. Not in a million years had it occurred to her that she would meet resistance in her new job simply because of her gender, although to be fair so far it was only this Jago character who was outwardly resistant and he looked so old he might have been a boy when Sue Montaigne's relatives first moved into town. Still, if her father had taught her one thing, it was respect your elders and so there was nothing else for it, she was going to have to show this old codger that she knew more about boats than him, and every other sailor in this pub put together, which, fortunately for Alex, happened to be true.

It was almost closing time, and Alex and Jago were still talking about her in-depth knowledge of navigational safety procedure and protocol, when Sue's scandalous PA left her position, seated between Rory and Sue, who appeared to be engaged in a heated debate about halos and how best to construct them, and made her way over to Alex.

'Jago, give it a rest, the poor woman's driven eight hundred miles today. I think she's pretty much proved she knows what she's doing, don't you?' Her smile was charming, her tone warm and just flirtatious enough to turn the old man's head. She was well spoken, Alex noticed, and, because of her well-educated accent and polish, she made Alex ever so slightly uneasy. And, like Lucy, she was well dressed – everything she had on was designed to make the most of her slim figure. The only difference between the two women was whereas Lucy had obviously made an effort to look nice, Marissa had made an effort to look like she hadn't made an effort – her dark glossy hair looked unkempt and tousled, but Alex could see it was immaculately cut and styled that way. Her dark eyes were ringed with kohl, and her lips were painted a dark ruby red.

'I'm Marissa,' the girl said and smiled at Alex. She then glanced at the pub door and her expensive-looking watch, seconds apart – she was obviously waiting for someone. 'I'm new here too, sort of. I've been here about six months. I came down from London to help Sue out. She was in a terrible fix, couldn't organise her way out of paper bag, so you know, I came in like the cavalry to save the day!'

'That's good of you,' Alex said, thinking of Sue's conflicting report and wondering which one of them had it right.

'Well, you know . . . It makes a nice change down here. London can be so oppressive – do you know what I mean?' Marissa glanced at the pub door once again, and then again at her watch.

'Yes,' Alex said, reluctant to admit she had never actually been to London, unless the drive around the M25 counted. 'I know.'

'So nice to have another girl to hang out with, because I am a girls' girl. I love being with women. I'm always around for a drink if you want one.'

'Oh, are you friends with Lucy then?' Alex asked her.

Marissa raised a brow and lowered her voice as Lucy served a customer at the other end of the bar. 'Well, darling, let's put it this way, we just don't have as much in common as you might think.' She winked at Alex, and Alex got the distinct feeling that Marissa was expecting her to ask her what she meant, so she could reveal some secret, but she would be disappointed.

Alex did not gossip, she did not pry, she did not bother to get involved with other people's lives unless it really was unavoidable, or they were a permanent fixture already. Alex made her five friends when she was five years old, and she saw no particular reason to expand on that social group, even though she'd just left them all in Scotland and one of them was the man that had spurned her.

'I'm living up at the Castle with Sue at the moment, got my own turret, it's hysterical,' Marissa assured her. 'So tacky.'

Alex didn't really know how to keep the conversation going and so she just kept eating the apple pie that had miraculously appeared after the fish and chips until Marissa got bored with attempting to engage her. She wished she was better at fitting in, at being friendly and open or even simply smiling but it was a skill that she had not learnt from her father, and one she hadn't needed so much back at home.

'Right-oh then.' Marissa grinned brightly, as she finally ran out of steam. 'Bye!'

She took up a new position at the end of the bar opposite the door, and Alex watched as she carefully arranged herself to present her cleavage and hair in the best possible light. Whatever old Jago still might think, boats weren't a mystery to Alex, but that sort of stuff, girls-looking-their-best stuff always completely foxed her. Not only the how, but the why. Seriously, what was the point? If a man liked you for you then it didn't matter if you had a push-up bra on, did it? Although saying that the only man that Alex had ever liked, loved actually, and who also happened to coincidentally be her best friend, was marrying a girl who was mostly breasts and hair extensions – and orange. And, most relevantly, a girl who was not her.

'It's all a bit overwhelming, isn't it?' Lucy interrupted her thoughts, leaning over the bar. 'Being new, everyone looking at you, wanting to ask you a load of questions. It can do your head in, especially if you aren't the outgoing type like some.'

She didn't look at Marissa, but Alex knew who she was talking about.

'Haven't you lived here all your life though?' Alex asked her. 'I thought Eddie said he was born here.'

'I sort of have,' Lucy said. 'I mean I grew up in the town, but I . . . I went away and came back . . . and I'd changed . . . a bit. It took people a while to adjust to the new me, at least until they realised the new me was the old me. It could have been awful, but I'm lucky. Poldore people are the perfect combination of caring about what matters and not caring about what doesn't, which is why you being a woman harbour master will be old news by tomorrow lunch time, take it from me.'

'That's good.' Alex smiled, then because of all the people she had met so far Lucy seemed the easiest to talk to, she added, 'I'm sorry, I'm terrible at small talk. I hate meeting people and chatting about stuff. I'm shy, I suppose. That's the polite way of looking at it. Marcus, my . . . my friend always says that I basically don't like people. Which isn't true. I do like people. I just like the people I like, that's all. I mean, I will get to know everyone here, eventually. I'm just not good at doing so in one go.'

Lucy smiled. 'It's OK. I think you are doing really well. You impressed Jago, and that's hard to do. And anyway, you might find that you aren't the same person down here as you were up there.'

'Might I?' Alex sounded sceptical.

'Poldore seems to have that effect on people,' Lucy said. 'I don't know if it's something in the air, or the water, or nothing at all. But you ask most people who've lived down here for a while, or come back after a time away like me. This place has a knack of getting under your skin.'

Alex found it difficult to imagine feeling at home anywhere that wasn't the house that she grew up in, the house where she'd left her dad, after an unhappy goodbye. And yet that house didn't feel like home any more, either.

'So, everyone who comes to Cornwall is running away from something, what is it with you? A broken heart, a secret or a scandal?'

'None of those.' Alex sat back on her stool. There was something about Lucy that Alex couldn't put her finger on, something in her eyes that made Alex think she'd been through a lot in her life, despite her relative youth. There was also something about her that Alex instinctively liked, and trusted, and, as she was very far away from home and her five, or possibly four, remaining friends, she went out on something of a limb and opened up, with just the tiniest chink. 'Or maybe all of them.'

But before Alex could say more the door of the pub slammed open and with it came a blast of cold, wet air and a very wet man, dripping from head to foot, carrying a sopping jacket trailing water in one hand, and a pair of sodden boots in the other. For one heady moment Alex wondered if she was looking at a real-life merman. His longish black hair was plastered against his face and his now nearly see-through shirt clung to his very well-proportioned chest, as water pooled around his bare feet.

'Where the hell is that bloody new harbour master? I'm going to kill him!' he said.

Everyone turned to look at Alex.

Chapter Five

'Oh my God, what happened?' Marissa asked, leaping from her seat, and Alex realised at once that this very tall, very wet, very well-built and angry man in the nearly see-through shirt was who Marissa had been waiting for all night.

'I tell you what happened –' the man stalked to the bar, all but ignoring Marissa, leaving a small stream behind him '– I was coming in, in the *Minerva*, on my own, thank God, and I got cut up by a bloody great big flipping yacht. No one told him I was there, he couldn't see me, he had no idea! One minute I'm puttering along, the next this bloody massive hull comes out of nowhere, far too fast I might add, and I had to jump out of the boat. I could have been killed! It didn't even notice that it hit the boat.'

'Told you women and boats don't mix,' Jago said. The angry wet man looked up and Jago nodded at Alex, whose eyes widened as she became the subject of his attention. 'This is your new harbour master, right there. A *girl*.'

'What the . . .' The man stormed towards her and,

resisting the impulse to scramble off the back of her stool, Alex, whose second life lesson from her father was never, not ever to allow herself to be intimidated by any man, stood up instead and squared her shoulders.

'What the hell are you doing in a pub getting drunk on your first day?' he bellowed in her face. 'This is people's lives we're talking about here, it's not a bloody hobby. You're not on flipping holiday!'

'I know that,' Alex said, firmly and calmly. 'I . . .'

'And it's not just my life that could have been lost, my boat went down. I've lost her, and I can't afford a loss like that.'

'Hopefully you're insured . . .' Alex began

'Hopefully? Hopefully I am insured – is that what you are going to say to the next poor bugger's family who you actually drown with your incompetence?'

'Step back now there, Ruan.' Eddie's large hand planted itself firmly in the centre of the man's chest and pushed him back a step or two. 'No need to get in the girl's face, remember who you are talking to.'

The man – Ruan, Alex thought Eddie had called him – blinked, and then he looked at her again, and she saw him close his eyes briefly, as he realised the way he had spoken to her.

Eddie continued calmly, 'Alex here doesn't officially take up her position until the morning so you are shouting at the wrong man, or woman.'

Alex watched Eddie's words sink in, she watched

the clenched jaw, the tightened fists and the set shoulders ease just for a fraction, and then with a new target in mind he was off again.

'Right,' he said, turning abruptly on his heel, leaving Alex showered with the droplets of icy water that spun out from his hair. 'No point in wasting my time on her then!'

Alex's jaw dropped open as the very tall, very wet, very rude man in the nearly see-through shirt strode out of the pub.

'Alex, you might want to come too,' Eddie told her. 'I've got a feeling he's about to pay our outgoing temporary harbour master a visit, and it might not be pretty. Ruan Thorne isn't one to lose his temper, but I've never seen him this angry before.'

Alex quite happily followed him, glad to be out of the hot air of the pub and into the cold crisp night, but more importantly she was looking forward to telling this awful man exactly what she thought of him.

Annoyingly, she had to run a little to keep up with this Ruan as he strode across the square to the white-painted building that was the harbour master's office. Eddie was also a little out of breath as he attempted to keep up with her. Then she almost ran into the back of the pompous idiot when, instead going into the office, Ruan stopped abruptly, bracing himself in the doorway. Alex halted a nose breadth from impacting right between his shoulder blades.

'Has he killed him?' Eddie asked, bringing up the rear, huffing and puffing.

'No need to,' Ruan said, obscuring Alex's view. 'He's dead. Well dead drunk anyway. . .'

'Excuse me.' Alex ducked under Ruan's arm and over the former harbour master slumbering on the floor, who muttered something about someone called Elsie, before rolling over and beginning to noisily suck his thumb. Settling herself at the desk, Alex clicked on the computer, which displayed the satellite and radar information, and picked up the radio headset.

'What are you doing?' Ruan asked her.

'My job,' she told him, coolly turning her back on him as she got to work. 'Maybe you two could remove the drunk man.'

Alex set to work on the radio, contacting every vessel that she could see on the radar, making sure they knew of each other's movements in and out of the harbour, that everyone was settled for the night, and that no new vessels were due to arrive until the morning. She checked the weather, which seemed clement, and gave each person she contacted a brief weather report, asking them to check in with any movement before leaving port. And finally she tracked down the yacht that had sunk Ruan's boat and told them in no uncertain terms that speeding in the harbour was not only dangerous, but illegal and that the Port Authority had the right to impose a fine of up to £1,000, which she guessed was about half a day's wages for the boat's owner. But as the harbour master at the time had been comatose on the floor, Alex gave them a stiff warning, not sure that she'd be able to enforce a fine anyway if the full facts came to light.

Above all, as Alex sat at the desk making sense of the equipment that to most other people would seem impenetrable, she was back in her comfort zone. This was the world that she knew and understood. A world where she didn't have to talk to people, know what to say or how to look at them. For Alex, who on dry land waddled and floundered inexpertly like the penguins she'd watched at the zoo one time, this was her chance to spin and whirl, weightless in her own deep water. Here was her chance to be graceful, purposeful and precise and, best of all, in control of the entire universe, at least the one that was displayed on the radar.

It was more than half an hour before Alex was satisfied that all was organised and safe in the harbour and, when she emerged, she found the temporary harbour master's slumbering form had been tidied away somewhere, and Ruan and Eddie were standing behind her, both leaning on the thick stone sill of the window, both with their arms crossed as they watched her.

'Don't think we need to worry about you not being up to the job,' Eddie said, grinning at her, so that Alex blushed at once to be under such intense scrutiny. 'Eh, Ruan?'

'Yes, good job. For a woman,' Ruan said, and then immediately flushed a deep shade of red, which Alex couldn't help but notice extended to underneath his still slightly opaque shirt. 'I mean, that's not what I mean. I don't mean that you did a good job for a woman, what I mean is that you did a really good job, and you are a woman. And you know –' he ran his fingers through his damp hair '– that's OK.'

'Well, thank you,' Alex said. 'Now at last I have the validation I've been seeking all my life.'

'Oh, she can be feisty when she wants to be,' Eddie chuckled. 'Properly put you in your place, Ruan.'

'Fine, I'm really sorry I behaved like an utter plank,' Ruan said, suddenly shivering, which reminded Alex that he had been wet, cold, almost died and lost what might have been his livelihood in the space of an hour or so, and really it was hardly surprising that he was so furious.

'It was just about understandable,' she replied stiffly, dropping her defiant gaze to one that was preferable, which was to not look people who made her feel uncomfortable in the eye. 'Look, there's a couple of oilskins on the back of the door there. I don't know who they belong to, but why don't you take one for tonight and bring it back tomorrow. You'll freeze to death otherwise. And perhaps you should get checked out by a doctor.'

'Thanks,' Ruan said, looking suddenly tired as the

last of the adrenalin drained from his body. 'I'll take the oilskin, but I don't need a doctor. The only thing I need is my bed.'

'Shall I see you home, Alex?' Eddie asked her, as Alex took the keys that the now comatose Phil Potts had left on the desk and locked up the office.

'Oh no, I'm fine,' Alex said. 'I can find my way across the harbour OK!'

'Still, we'll walk you back to your boat,' Eddie said, waving away Alex's protest before she could voice it. 'Yes, I know you are a modern independent woman, but I'm an old-fashioned sort of father and I've . . . I've got a daughter myself. So on behalf of your dad, I'll treat you the same way that I'd want my daughter treated if she was spending her first night far away from home, OK?'

'OK,' Alex relented, picturing the last time she saw her father, sitting at the kitchen table reading his paper, refusing to say goodbye to her because he did not agree with her going. Ian Munro was a very different kind of father to Eddie, just as loving, just as strong, and protective, but he'd never ever let the world, let alone his daughter, see the emotion he kept so tightly locked away. Alex had always believed that despite his outward remoteness he loved her, she believed it right up until the moment she left for Poldore and he hadn't gotten up from the table to say goodbye.

Still, Eddie was being kind and, more to the point,

he was right – Alex did feel far away and lonely in this new place. The offer was one she accepted gratefully, if quietly.

Ruan walked two or three steps behind them as they made their way back across the square. The pubs had closed, but the town was no less busy – restaurants bustled, teenagers hung out on the quay, boys hanging dangerously over the railings in order to impress the screeching, giggling girls, who sounded exactly like a flock of hungry seagulls, after scraps of food. Couples strolled hand in hand along the light-strewn cobbled streets, which bent steeply up towards the turrets and spires of what Alex guessed must be Castle House, its fanciful outline dominating the skyline, and the wind rolled off the sea and across the square, chiming the little golden bells that hung on the town's Christmas tree, playing its own particular carol.

Every step that Alex took had a dreamlike quality to it. She could hardly believe that she was really here, when this morning she'd been packing her bags in the yellow-painted room that she'd grown up in. Had she really changed her life so completely and so quickly? If it all turned out to be a dream and she woke up in bed at home any second, she wouldn't have been at all surprised. And yet the wind blew off the Atlantic, sweeping her hair back from her face, and penetrating the tiny holes in her sweater, and Alex knew that she was very much awake.

'So is Lucy your only daughter?' she asked Eddie as they approached her mooring.

'Oh, um, yes. Lucy is our only child,' Eddie said, a little crossly, Alex thought. 'She used to live with us, before she went away, but since she came back she prefers her independence, so she rents a little cottage up the road now. I still worry about her, not that she thanks me for interfering. It's what she's been through, you see. What I've seen her go through makes me a bit overprotective of her. And all young ladies, whether they like it or not, and that includes you.'

'That does sound like something my dad would say.' Alex smiled fondly for a moment before she remembered.

'You're a daddy's girl then?' Eddie asked her, as Ruan continued to skulk behind them.

'Well, sort of. I didn't have much choice really. My mother left my dad and me when I was three. So it's always been me and him.' Alex smiled, seeing the discomfort on Eddie's face. 'Oh, it's fine, really it is. I've had a long time to get used to it. I don't even remember her, really. But yes, me and Dad, we were very close.'

'And what does your dad think about you coming all the way down here?' Eddie asked her.

'Oh he . . .' Alex paused. She liked Eddie, but she barely knew him. Now was not the time to tell a virtual stranger of all the mistakes she and her father had made, or the mess that she had left behind rather than face. 'He thinks it's great!'

'Well, here I am,' Alex said, as she stopped at where she'd moored the dinghy. She looked at Ruan, who was kicking small pebbles into the water, one after the other – plop, plop, plop. He looked like a sulky little boy in his oversized oilskin, and this turned out to be strangely endearing. 'Are you OK? I mean can I give you a lift as your boat went down?'

'I've got more than one boat,' Ruan said, affronted. 'I've got ten actually. I own the largest tourist boat rental business in Poldore.'

'And also the only one,' Eddie reminded him gently.

'OK, well, goodnight then.' Alex knelt down to where her boat should have been moored but it was not there. No, correction, it *was* there, or at least something was at the end of the rope, which plunged deeply into the water. And then at exactly the same moment as Eddie and Ruan began chuckling behind her, Alex felt a wash of shame drench her as she realised what she had done. The tide had been low when she came into shore. She'd tied the dinghy up, with meticulous care, on a rope that was far too short. And now the tide had come in the boat had been unable to rise with it, and sunk.

'Oops,' Ruan said, his dark eyes twinkling with barely suppressed mirth.

'Oh dear,' Eddie chuckled. 'Oh dear, oh dear. Still, easily done.'

'Not by the town's harbour master!' Ruan chuckled to himself. 'The tourists are going to love this.'

'What do you mean?' Alex asked him, horrified.

'They love local colour, and local characters. I give them the low-down when I take them out. And you have provided some brilliant material on your first day here.'

Alex was going to be cross and standoffish, but then something strange and unexpected happened. Seeing Ruan's repressed smile blossom into laughter was surprisingly infectious, and she found herself laughing too, even as she covered her face with her hands.

'I'll never live it down!' she said, chuckling, as Eddie put a hand on her shoulder, joining in with the laughter. 'No one will take me seriously now.'

'Tell you what,' Ruan said, 'I'll keep the story under wraps until you are established in the harbour master's office, say until the spring. And I'll give you a lift home now in one of my other boats.' Ruan glanced at Eddie, who rolled his eyes. 'I live in the old lighthouse round the peninsula, so it's sort of on my way anyway.'

'It's sort of in the opposite direction,' Eddie observed with interest.

'And first thing in the morning when the tide is out, I'll pull up your boat and leave it out to dry. The engine might need some work, but it'll be fixable.'

'Thank you,' Alex said, pausing for a moment as she took in the unexpected offer of help. 'I'm sorry if we got off on the wrong foot.'

'No skin off my nose,' Ruan said. 'I'll be back in a bit with the boat.'

'He's a good lad, really,' Eddie told her, as she watched Ruan jog off a few paces to where a number of motor cruisers were moored. 'Don't judge him too harshly on first impressions. In truth, that boy's as soft as a lamb, he just had it worse than most, that's all.'

Before Alex could ask more, Ruan motored a new boat alongside, and offered up a hand to Alex, who took it and stepped down into the boat, at once self-conscious about where would be an appropriate place to sit on the rows of seats. If she took the seat next to him, he might think she was being overfamiliar, or if she chose the seat too far away that might mean something else all together. Alex didn't have a clear idea on what the meaning of either choice might be, but she was inexplicably worried about there being one. So after a moment's deliberation she went and sat on her own in the middle of the boat.

Ruan looked at her for a moment as he pulled the boat out into open water, shrugged and then turned back to the rudder.

'So did you say you live in a lighthouse?' Alex said, realising as she raised her voice to get his attention that sitting in the middle of the boat was ridiculous. She got up and moved two rows nearer to him, hoping he might not notice her impromptu performance of musical chairs.

'Former lighthouse,' he said. 'It was decommissioned after World War Two, and was basically a ruin when I bought it. I've been renovating it for years now, but I think it's nearly done. People keep trying to buy it off me, offering me really silly money, so I take that as a good sign.'

'Wow,' Alex said in a rare unguarded moment, finding herself sharing more words than she usually did with a perfect stranger. 'It must be wonderful to live in a lighthouse, looking right out to sea all the time. You must feel like you are living in the clouds sometimes.'

She felt Ruan appraising her, which didn't take too long, as her knotted hair and large sweater didn't offer up much to appraise, but even a few seconds of direct attention from anyone was enough to send her right back into her shell.

As they made their way up river towards her cottage, Alex tried to remember the last time she was alone with any man who wasn't her father or Marcus, or the many men she used to work with, none of whom counted, because most of them had either never noticed that she was a girl in the first place or refrained from doing so ever again after one look from her father. It had been a long, long time.

'Look.' Ruan broke her train of thought. 'I shouldn't have flown off the handle the way I did, after the accident. That boat, it meant a lot to me, which is stupid, I know. It's just a boat. But I'd had it since I was a kid, and it wasn't insured. I've barely got enough money to keep my commercial boats insured at the moment. For all the rich people that come to this town, my business is still suffering. Maybe because they all come in their own yachts.'

'I'm really sorry – sorry you lost your boat, and sorry you were put in such danger,' Alex said. 'It's no wonder you were shaken up. I mean it could have been serious. You could have been killed.'

Ruan kept his eyes focused ahead. 'I wasn't shaken up.'

Alex looked up as they passed alongside a small ketch, sitting pretty under the moon, its rigging webbed against the sky, studded with stars. She'd spoken briefly to the captain earlier, or rather the head of the household, and discovered that a young family lived on-board, which seemed like the perfect childhood to Alex.

'Yachts are much prettier to look at than the tankers and container ships I'm used to,' she said out loud. 'Poldore is incredibly beautiful, and I've only seen it in the dark so far.'

'It is,' Ruan said. 'That's why I've never left. Friends, the people I grew up with, people I've . . . known all my life, they go. They assume what's out there is better, bigger, faster, richer. But it's not. How can anywhere be better than here? I'll never leave Poldore, I'll be here until I'm old and grey and have got a great big beard and an eye patch.' Alex smiled, her face washed in moonlight. 'Anyway I'm not really that person, who marched into the pub and had a go at you. I hope we can start again? After all, we are going to be seeing a lot of each other.'

'Yes, of course,' Alex said, struggling to say more, because after what Ruan had said, she felt she must. 'I'm, well, I'm a bit of a fish out of water, I suppose. A bit shy at the best of times. Sometimes I just don't really see the point of people.'

Ruan laughed, and then so did Alex after a moment, when she realised exactly what she'd said. 'I'm not a people person,' she explained. 'Like that flipping dog.'

'Oh Buoy!' Ruan chuckled. 'Buoy's a local hero. You're going to have to love Buoy if you want the town to love you. And watch out for Sue Montaigne. My sister Cordelia nannies for her. She's a lovely woman at heart, but she's not happy unless she's organising people, preferably into a bit of fancy dress.'

'Oh God,' Alex groaned. 'She put my name on a clipboard! I should have hidden in the cellar with Eddie.'

'Eddie's a good man,' Ruan said. 'Loves his family, would do anything for them. Eddie will always see you right.'

Alex wanted to ask about Lucy, about the difficulty that Eddie had alluded to on the walk to the dinghy, but she was such a private person herself that the idea of actively prying into another person's life appalled her, and, besides, she was still new here, still an incomer. Best to keep quiet.

Ruan killed the engine as he brought the boat alongside Alex's mooring.

'I'll get your boat, and moor it for you in the morning,' he said, as he took her hand and helped her up onto the rickety jetty. 'This could do with a bit of work too. If I've got time at the weekend, I'll see what wood I can find lying about and have a look at it.'

'Thanks, that really is very nice,' Alex said.

'Not nice, just what we do around here. We take care of each other.'

'Oh, well, thanks anyway.' Alex faltered, not sure of how or what the best way to say goodbye to Ruan was. Obviously there was the simple 'Goodbye' option, but she didn't want to be accidentally rude again, not when they'd just about made up and he'd been so kind.

'So,' she said, suddenly remembering spotting an ancient little tumble dryer under the stairs in the cottage, and thinking she'd attempt some Poldore kindness herself, 'if you like, you could come in, take your clothes off and I could . . .?'

'Um, no thanks,' Ruan said, looking immediately alarmed and then anxious. 'I hardly know you.'

'Oh, I didn't mean—' Alex clapped her hand over her mouth and Ruan pushed the boat off and was already reversing into the estuary.

'I wasn't inviting you in for sex!' Alex called after him, before she could stop the words spilling out of her mouth, thankful that Ruan was in such a hurry to get away from her that he probably did hear her. 'I've not ever really had sex,' she said conversationally to herself. 'Or even actually, if you want to be precise.'

Sighing, Alex turned around to find Buoy sitting on the bottom stone step, eyeing her with that one visible amber eye, growling softly.

'I don't care if you are the Beast of Bodmin,' Alex told him sternly, wondering how he had got home before her, 'you are not getting into my bed.'

She attempted to bolt past him and up the stone steps and succeeded at first, as the old dog was stiff and slow for a few seconds, but before they reached the top of the steep flight, Alex's thighs were screaming and Buoy trotted past her cheerfully, casting her one tongue-lolling glance over his shoulder as he headed towards the house, and shouldered the unlocked door open.

When Alex finally made it up the narrow stairs and into the bedroom, the dog was sprawled out in the middle of the bed on his back, his legs in the air, his yellowing teeth slightly bared with every snore.

Alex decided to spend the night in the chair.

Chapter Six

It turned out to be almost a week before Alex saw Ruan again and she had to confess to being rather glad of it. There were far too many other things to think about, she didn't need to dwell on accidentally propositioning a virtual stranger. So even though they spoke every day over the radio, it was purely formal, although perfectly pleasant. They might has well have been separated by the entire Atlantic, not just the few feet that ran between Ruan's ticket office and Alex's desk.

Instead she spent the intervening days between their first and second meetings getting to grips with her new life in Poldore.

The first thing that Alex learned with any certainty was that when it came down to a choice of either her or the dog, the dog always won. Alex's experience with pets was limited – her dad never believed in them – but she had been sucked into the falsehood that dogs were gentle, loyal, giving creatures who'd do anything to make their humans happy. Granted she was not Buoy's human, not by a long stretch, but he was also about as far from Woman's Best Friend as any hound could be. Even within those parameters, Alex and the dog operated on a highly dysfunctional, passive aggressive and, in the dog's case, just aggressive level.

Buoy did not want to be Alex's pet, and Alex did not want a pet of any description, especially one who had laid claim to the cottage's only bed. This, she had decided on that first morning after sleeping in a chair, was her new life, she had to own it, not just fit in around the hound. However, Alex was not well versed in dog psychology, all she knew about animals came from watching *Lassie* as a child, and an article she'd read in *Cosmopolitan* about how to get the man in your life to see you as an equal. Well, Buoy was not a man, but he was a male, and frankly it was the best resource that Alex had, and, as she was highly unlikely to need the advice when it came to a relationship with a human, she thought it couldn't hurt to try applying the basic principles to the dog.

Except it wasn't going exactly to plan. Alex had tried looking the dog in the eye, but he just stared her out, until it was Alex who always looked away first. And she'd tried staking a claim on the cottage and making it hers. She unpacked her clothes, and left out her toothbrush in the bathroom, which she later found Buoy had chewed into a naked stump, spitting out the bristles as he went. The only tiny inroad Alex had made into owning her life so far had been negotiating a tiny corner of her bed to sleep in, fashioning nose plugs out of cotton wool so as not to be overpowered by the smell, and she was fairly sure she was only allowed that much space because Buoy did not like to sleep alone.

So Alex wasn't so much owning her life, rather just about clinging on to the tiniest corner of it and occasionally sleeping on the cold, dusty floor next to it.

At least life in the harbour master's office was a tranquil one that she'd slipped into with ease and not a small amount of aplomb. After only a few days in the job, word went quickly around, accompanied by raised eyebrows and mildly surprised tones, that the new girl was actually really good at her job. And before the first week was up, it didn't matter a jot to anyone what sex she was, which was a relief to Alex. She had never been very good at being a girl, and to be famous, albeit briefly, for just that was not something she had enjoyed.

Lucy had been right when she'd suggested that Alex must be running away from something. Alex had run away to Poldore to forget herself, to blend into the background of another life, where no one would notice her again, hopefully for good this time. Because the last time she had let her emotions get the better of her, and stuck her head just slightly above the parapet in a bid to be seen, not only it had all gone horribly wrong but she'd uncovered secrets that she had never wanted to learn.

Her mobile phone network had very little coverage in Poldore, and she didn't have a phone in the cottage. The only place anyone from her old life could contact her would be on her private email, or by phoning the office and Alex had been careful not to give out that number, although she supposed a bit of mild sleuthing could discover it almost at once. And yet during her first week no one from back home attempted to contact her, and, although sometimes Alex felt lonely or homesick, she reminded herself that that was how she wanted it, not even calling her father at all, even to say she had arrived safely, because she didn't want to have exactly the same argument with him again, or worse, for him to say nothing at all.

A total break was what she needed, Alex was convinced, to live her life standing on her own two feet for the first time ever. And so it was with a sense of renewed purpose that during her break on the one week anniversary of her arriving in Poldore Alex made her way along the waterfront to ask Eddie about finding a new home for Buoy.

Even in late December, when the sky and the sea were one leaden shade of grey, the town still bustled with life. And still it didn't feel cold to Alex, who was happy to make the short walk in her outsized sludge-colour sweater that hung down to the knees of her jeans, which she'd tucked into her Timberland boots. If she'd been back at home right now, she'd have been wrapped up in at least five layers, including thermals and two pairs of gloves; the wind that came in off the North Sea was always so bitter. So although many of the fashionable people who strolled down the cobbled streets sported matching hat and gloves sets, for Alex it was positively balmy.

The Silent Man was packed, not only with the faces of the local people that were slowly becoming familiar to Alex, because they smiled and nodded whenever they saw her, but also the tourists and the part-time dwellers who owned the big modernist houses on the cliff top, most of them literally dripping with money. It had to be odd if you'd always lived here, Alex thought, as she manoeuvred her way to the bar with a well-placed shoulder shove or elbow poke, like Eddie or Lucy. To be surrounded by so much very showy money, so many people who were all about being looked at, to live in a place that had somehow been declared fashionable by the people in the know, but which for you was simply home.

'Hello!' Lucy greeted her warmly, as she pulled a pint for a man of around fifty, who was wearing a gold-trimmed blazer and actual captain's hat, although he didn't look like the sort of person who drove his own boat. Alex envied Lucy's effortless style – a white, waisted shirt, which contrasted well with her honey blonde hair, a little make-up and large hooped earrings, which swung when she talked or laughed, flirting with the pretend captain and his guests who'd stopped by for a traditional pub lunch. Behind the bar was obviously where Lucy felt safe, sparkling and laughing, just as Alex did behind her desk, only without the laughing or the sparkling. 'Dad's out the back, do you want him?'

'If that's OK?' Alex felt the press of more people arriving behind her. 'Is it OK if I go through?'

'Go for it.' Lucy winked at the young man she handed a bottle of beer to. 'I've got this rabble under control in here, at least for now!'

Pushing her way through the frosted glass door, with the word 'Private' etched into it, Alex followed a narrow corridor that led into the heart of the pub, to where she could hear Eddie's booming voice in conversation with someone else. It was only as she approached the slightly ajar door that she realised who it was he was talking to, it was Ruan.

'You know what she's like, Eddie,' Alex heard Ruan say. 'She's never known what's good for her, and now I can see her getting herself into real trouble. I don't know how to make her see. Whatever I say to her, she does the opposite.'

'She's a young woman,' Eddie replied. 'Over the age of twenty-one. And you're her brother, not her dad. Maybe you should just let her get on with it.'

'I know, but . . .' Ruan stopped. 'Who else has she

got? And I'm not sure that he can be trusted.'

'What, old Brian? What's he going to do to her?' Eddie chuckled. 'He might have been a rock god in his day, bedded more women than you or I ever will, but he's seventy at least, even if he does still wear eyeliner. Shouldn't think he'd be able to catch her if she put on a fast stroll.'

'I know,' Ruan said, 'but he fills her head with ideas, ambitions. And the kind of people that come down to work with him, they are not . . . normal people. Flashy flipping musicians with their . . . fashion and their . . . hair. And Cordelia is very impressionable.'

'You know your trouble, Ruan,' Eddie said. 'You worry too much. You have done, ever since . . . Well, you know. You've got to let Cordy find her way in the world, like your other sisters, they are out there living the life, aren't they? I know Cordelia is the baby, but still you've got to let her go, like I did with Lucy. If there is one thing that Becky and I have learned it's that you've got to let a person be who they are. Anything is better than watching them wither away and die from unhappiness in front of your very eyes.'

'Even if it means them getting hurt?' Ruan asked, his tone so soft, so concerned and anxious that Alex felt the almost irrepressible urge to go through the door and hug him, which considering she barely hugged her own father was quite something.

'Even then,' Eddie told him. 'Just look at Lucy now,

out there, queen of the pub, holding court. You'd never know what she went through to get there. And Cordelia will be the same, because if she is anything like the rest of you Thornes she will come back even stronger, just like you did.'

'I'm not stronger,' Ruan said. 'That is the last thing I am . . .'

Just at moment something very smelly and hairy brushed past Alex's thighs and nosed the living room door open, leaving Alex exposed, caught in the act of eavesdropping in the hallway.

It seemed that Buoy had decided to attend the meeting on his own fate at exactly the wrong moment.

'Um . . . oh hello there!' Alex said, as if *she* was surprised to see *them*.

'How long have you been out there?' Ruan asked her, his sweet vulnerable side vanishing in an instant.

'Not long, I was just . . .' Alex looked around to try and conjure up an excuse and quickly gave up. 'It seemed rude to interrupt.'

'So you thought you'd listen in instead?' Ruan coloured and turned his face away from her. He wasn't angry, Alex realised. He was embarrassed and that made her feel a thousand times worse for intruding.

'Well, don't stand there looking like a loon,' Eddie said, attempting to diffuse the situation. 'Come on in, tell us how you are getting on. I see you and Buoy are bonding.'

'Er, no,' Alex said. 'We are not bonding. He is just stalking me. Actually I think he might be hunting me.'

'Dogs don't stalk people,' Ruan said defensively, rubbing his hand on the top of Buoy's head and then the back of his jeans. Buoy sat down in the front of the fire and looked at each of them in turn, as if waiting for the meeting to begin.

'I can't live with him,' Alex said, when it became apparent that Ruan wasn't leaving. 'I don't have anything against him as such. And I get that my cottage comes with the job and he comes with the cottage. I know it used to be his house, a long time ago, when his owner lived there. But it's just not working. I am not a dog person, or even a pet person. I had a stick insect once, and I trod on it. He's old and smells really bad, and he needs a proper home, living with someone who has a spare bedroom they don't mind turning into a fleapit . . . and who will care for him, properly. Like he deserves.'

Alex was prepared for Eddie to resist her pleas, and for Ruan to be resentful, but she was not prepared for either of them to look so sad. Even Buoy's ears dropped, his matted fringe covering both eyes for a moment.

'Ah well,' Eddie said, patting Buoy hard on the head. 'We tried, old feller.'

'He's had a good innings, I suppose,' Ruan said. 'He was loved.'

'What?' Alex exclaimed, as with a deep groan Buoy

collapsed onto the rug, like he was giving up the ghost right at that moment. 'I said I can't live with him, not that you should put him down! Rehome him, that's what I mean. Get him adopted, something!'

'The thing is,' Eddie said, 'we've done that a hundred times. He always comes back to the cottage, no matter where you take him. I even drove him up to Devon once, lovely farm. Lots of pretty little sheepdogs. Month later he's back on the doorstep. Thin as a rake, bit of a cut on his leg, but right as rain to be home.'

'And Sue took him in a couple of years back,' Ruan added. 'Apart from her poodles, she's taken in a few stray dogs up there, but Buoy didn't fit in at all, not even with his own wing to roam in. All he did was impregnate her prize poodle and defecate in the living room. I'm not sure what it was that Sue was more angry about . . . but those pups all went to a good home, so there was no harm done in the end.'

'And even then,' Eddie added, 'Sue didn't have to throw Buoy out. Once he was done with the poodle, he dug his way out under the wall, an act of extremely dogged defiance and symbolism, as the gate was open and he could have just left.'

'He was telling us that we can't fence him in,' Ruan added for extra emphasis.

'He's a dog,' Alex reiterated, feeling the point was getting somewhat lost. 'I can't sleep in my own bed because there is a dog in it!'

'Alex, look at him. He's old,' Eddie said, 'he's ugly and he stinks. He's not friendly or playful, he doesn't give a toss about any human. Who will take him? And even if we found someone, he wouldn't stay. No, if you can't live with him then . . . it's the knacker's yard for old Buoy of Poldore.'

'But—'

Before Alex could answer a loud crash sounded from the bar, followed by screams and shouts. Nearest to the door, Alex ran to the bar first, with Eddie, Ruan and Buoy hard on her heels. She flung open the door to see the very last thing she expected. The older man, with the captain's hat, had Lucy by the hair and was dragging her over the bar, his fist poised to punch her in the face.

Alex didn't think, she just acted, launching herself at his back, and caught him with enough force to knock him off the stool, freeing Lucy from his grasp, bar a few strands of hair still in his fist. Alex landed hard on his back, and caught her breath as she realised she had the man, his stupid hat now trampled on the wooden floor, pinned face down against the wooden boards.

Alex had absolutely no idea what to do next, and she sensed that if he realised that he'd be able to throw her off like she was nothing, and begin his attack again.

'Has someone called the police?' she asked, as she looked around to a sea of stunned faces.

'Call the bloody police,' the man mumbled, his breath

reeking of beer. 'Someone should arrest that pervert. It's not right, it's not natural. Trying to trap men into . . . !' Alex wasn't sure what he was going to say next, but whatever it was she didn't want to hear it, so she ground the toe of her boot into his inner thigh, and the man howled furiously into the floor.

'Right that's enough!' Eddie shouted, ringing the bell. 'The police are on their way. Alex, you can get up. You are not going to cause any more trouble are you . . . 'sir'?'

'I'll bloody well . . .' He looked at the circle of feet, belonging to the pub's regulars, that surrounded him and thought better of what he was going to say.

'Are you OK?' Ruan asked Alex, offering her a hand, which she gladly took, relieved not to be touching the odious man any more. Dimly it occurred to her that it could well be him pressing charges against her, and that she hadn't given the consequences of her actions any thought at all. Alex had never known until that moment that she was the sort of person who would get involved in the middle of a fight.

'Why wouldn't I be? It's not me we should worry about, what about Lucy?'

'Lucy,' the man spat her name, and Alex accidentally trod on his little finger. Why was he so angry with the barmaid; what on earth could she have done to him that had enraged him to this point?

Lucy was in Becky's arms, her head buried in her

mother's shoulder as she wept, and Alex watched as Becky guided her out the back, perhaps to the living quarters above the pub.

Alex smoothed her wild hair out of her eyes and straightened her jumper by giving it a tug. Now the adrenalin surge that had somehow taken her over the bar and knocked the man off his stool was rapidly receding and she found that she was trembling. Fake Captain climbed to his feet, dusted himself down, scowling at her and Eddie. To give them credit, the people he'd arrived with were nowhere to be seen, perhaps not keen to be associated with him.

'Now,' Eddie said, barely able to repress the fury that simmered beneath the surface of every word. 'You're lucky that it was this slip of girl that knocked you to the ground and not me, because if I'd have gotten to you first you would not have got off so lightly. But as I am not normally a violent man, you've got two minutes to get out of here quickly and quietly, without making a fuss, and I'll tell the police it was a misunderstanding, no harm done.'

'It wasn't a misunderstanding, and there was a lot of harm done, that . . . that *thing* tried to come on to me, and it nearly had me too.' The man shuddered and Alex saw Eddie clench his fists. Instinctively, she reached out and put a calming hand on his arm.

'That thing is my daughter,' Eddie said steadily. 'And this is my pub and you will leave here in the next two minutes or it will be me who is being charged with assault.'

The man looked around the room and, seeing a group of people united against him, he picked up his stupid hat and walked out the door.

'And don't come back again!' Alex shouted after him, after which Eddie turned around and picked her up in the most enormous bear hug, from which she never expected to emerge alive.

When eventually Eddie released her, he set Alex down, stood back and waited. Alex knew what he was waiting for. He was waiting for her to ask him the question, what the hell that was all about? To ask him why that man had attacked Lucy, and what he'd been talking about when he'd said those dreadful things about her. And Alex knew that almost everyone else in the pub, everyone who was now slowly returning to their drinks, or discreetly leaving, already knew and that in this matter she was the outsider. But as she looked into Eddie's eyes, she saw the hurt and anxiety there, as he braced himself to explain it all to Alex the moment she asked him the question. Which was when she knew she couldn't ask it, because knowing didn't matter as much to her as did not hurting this kind man and good father any more. So instead she asked another question.

'Is Lucy OK?'

Eddie's eyes filled with tears. 'She will be,' he said. 'Look, Alex—'

Instead of letting him finish Alex did something quite unlike herself. She put her arms around his thick middle, pressed her cheek into his chest and hugged him, briefly, but just as hard as he had hugged her.

'I've got to get back to work.' Alex smiled at him reassuringly. 'Tell Lucy . . . well, tell her I hope she's OK and I'll see her later.'

'Alex.' Eddie stopped her just as she was at the door. 'Thank you.'

And Alex knew it wasn't her half-baked, accidental stint as a super hero he was thanking her for, he was thanking her for not asking the question.

Chapter Seven

The thing about her job that Alex most enjoyed was the patterns, looking at the screen of radar blips, and the motion of the weather fronts on the satellite and seeing how to make sense of it all to keep the harbour safe. Outside, the sea rolled in, the wind whipped the tops of the waves into white peaks, sails billowed and deflated, and made them all dance for her. That was good, it was simple, she understood it so much more than she understood life.

Not for the first time Alex wondered what it was about her that meant she so often didn't see what other people did, understand what other people understood. Perhaps it was the lack of a female influence. Certainly, her dad had brought her up in a particularly masculine way, not entirely sure how to teach a girl to be a boy, so teaching her to be a very boy-like girl indeed. Alex barely remembered her mother, except for fuzzy memories of being held by someone warm and soft. A voice and sometimes a particularly floral scent would make her think of that person who once must have meant everything to her. But whatever pain her mother's departure had caused her as a child, Alex had buried it very deeply now, and she rarely thought of her missing mother at all.

From the first time she skinned her knee, to the excruciatingly awful conversation she and her dad had to battle their way through the first time she needed money for sanitary towels, or to go and get fitted for a bra, Alex just accepted that this was the way it was for her. She was destined to discover the secrets of womanhood mostly via rumour, magazines and trial and error. Sometimes though, Alex wondered if growing up motherless, a tomboy, and being raised by a man who knew how to be a man better than he knew how to be a dad was why sometimes she found it so hard to reach out to people and why, after Eddie had released her from his death grip, a little while ago in the pub, she had simply said goodbye and come back to the office.

And Alex was always the last person to see things coming – just look at what happened with Marcus.

Marcus had become her best friend on the very first morning they'd met and he'd dared her to put glue on the other children's seats at break. Alex had done it, and had immediately been caught, as her and Marcus's were the only chairs left unglued. From that moment a firm friendship, based mostly on Marcus getting her into a series of scrapes, had ensued. Marcus was her best friend at primary school that time she'd let the school guinea pigs out in the nature reserve and a fox had got them, her best buddy at secondary school when Alex had been persuaded by Marcus to smuggle in cider to the fifth form leavers' disco. It had been Marcus that she would hang out with at break, letting him eat her packed lunch every day, who she would ask girls out for, and who she helped cheat in his exams. Marcus, who never let anyone say a bad word about Alex, who once fought six boys twice his size behind Tesco for calling her a 'prozzy', although Alex had no idea what that was at the time, and won. Marcus, who could have played rugby for Scotland, but preferred the drinking part to the training part. Marcus, who used to text her all day every day from his day job in an insurance call centre, who never failed to include her in all of his social plans, even when he had a new girlfriend on the go, which was always. It was Marcus who was pretty much her best friend in all the world.

And Alex had not realised that she was in love with him until it was far too late. Or until, six short weeks ago, he'd told her he was getting engaged to his latest girlfriend. And then it had hit her like a truck driving at speed through the centre of her chest. And the first thing she had thought was, of course you are in love with him, you knob, you always have been. That's what that ache has been in the centre of your chest for the last few years, you've been pining for him.

Which had been something of a blow, but wasn't

the killer stroke, the one that had sent her to this moment in time, hundreds of miles away in Poldore. No, that had been at the engagement party.

Bracing herself, Alex was preparing to relive the most agonising moment of her life once more when she heard the office door open and, turning around, saw Lucy standing in the doorway, utterly composed, her hair brushed, her make-up perfect.

'Lucy!' Alex smiled, happy to see the young woman looking herself again. 'I'm sorry I haven't been to see you. I'm not very good at knowing what to say to people, and anyway you looked like you might need a moment.'

'I just came to say thank you,' Lucy said, her voice small, the confident sparkle that had been so present at lunchtime in the pub now gone. 'You were like Wonder Woman, or something.'

'Oh.' Alex waved her hand away. 'I don't know, I just reacted. Really stupid probably, he could easily have flattened me if he thought about it.' Alex thought about exactly how close Lucy had come to that happening to her and cringed. 'Sorry, I'm an idiot.'

'Not to me,' Lucy said. 'I think you're epic.'

They both stood there for a long minute, Alex not wanting to ask the question and Lucy seemingly determined to answer it.

'I'm transsexual,' Lucy said. She waited for a moment, and when Alex didn't speak or move, she closed the office door behind her and went and sat in the chair opposite her.

'I was born a boy, physically. But inside, I was always me . . . always the person I am now. I didn't find the courage to talk about it until I was nearly twenty, but it was always there, for anyone to see if they'd bothered looking. And then I woke up one morning and I knew that if I didn't change the outside to match the inside then I wouldn't make it, I wouldn't be able to go on for that much longer. Trying to hide the person I was was killing me. That's when I talked to my parents. It was a huge shock for them, but Dad got me right away. He said that as soon as I told him how it felt, everything fell in to place, it made sense to him. It took Mum a bit longer. She's still adjusting, I think. It's a long process, a difficult one. I was lucky to have my family on my side; a lot of people don't . . .

'And after the surgery I decided it would be easier on Mum and Dad if I didn't come back here. I tried living in London, and Bristol, and a few other places. It would be all right for a while and then people would find out, and even if some of them were OK about it, there was always one person who wanted to . . . hurt me. Like the man in the pub yesterday, one of the locals must have mentioned it, I've no idea who, and just the idea of me made him so angry. It was hardest for Mum when I came home. Dad, he told everyone the truth and that was the way it was now, and they could either accept that or drink somewhere else, but Mum, poor Mum . . . She cried and cried, not for herself, but for me. Because life was going to be so awful for me. But it wasn't, it just wasn't. I mean it took a while for people to remember that my name is Lucy, and there were a few people who didn't come into the pub for a few weeks, but that was the worst of it. And living here, it's like being a bubble. Most people know and don't care, and most of the people coming in and out never know. I'm protected. Dad makes it that way, the whole town makes it that way. I'm so lucky, it's not like that for most people, out there.' She nodded at the window. 'It's like it was for me in the pub today, it's a life where people hate you just for existing.

'So,' Lucy said, 'now you know. Thanks for listening. I hope you will still drink in the pub . . .'

'Of course I will,' Alex said, sensing that now wasn't a time to hold back. 'I saw another woman being attacked by a man, and that was all I cared about. Thank you for trusting me with your story, Lucy. But look, you are just you to me, you are the person I see sitting there right now, a girl who's gone out of her way to help me feel at home. You helped me, and I helped you and . . . well, I could really use a friend around here, so how about we just do that – be friends?'

'I'd like that,' Lucy said, pausing for a second as she looked at Alex, still dishevelled from the fight. 'You do look like you could use a friend.'

'Cheek!' Alex laughed. 'Are you going back to work this evening, or do you have some time off?'

'I've got the evening off,' Lucy said. 'I was going to have a hot bath and an early night . . .'

'Actually . . . Your dad and Ruan say that if I don't let that mutt live in the cottage, he will have to be put down, and I can't live with his blood on my hands so . . .'

'Yes,' Lucy said uncertainly.

'Will you help me give Buoy a bath?'

They decided early on that it was best that Buoy didn't know about the bath until it was too late, so, after work, Alex headed for the chemist's in search of some dog shampoo. She had almost made it, when she heard her name being called from a short distance behind, and Alex didn't have to turn round to know it was Sue Montaigne wondering why she hadn't turned up to the Christmas pageant meeting that she had been all but ordered to. Sue couldn't know that to Alex the thought of any kind of meeting appalled her, or that for most of the last week she'd spent her down time battling a dog for a few inches of mattress, and perhaps if she did know she would understand, but Alex just didn't feel like explaining it to her.

'I hear you've been fighting.' Jago clapped her on the back as he came out of the chemist's. 'Now, tell me, are you a trained wrestler, or was it natural instinct? A well-built lass like you, you could have a career in it.'

'Um. . .' Alex chanced a look over her shoulder and saw Sue bearing down on her with frightening speed. 'The thing is I have to go the chemist, urgently.'

'Piles is it?' Jago asked her. 'It's always piles with me, if it's urgent. It's the fierce itching, isn't it? Keeps you up all night, itching and scratching . . .'

'So anyway, bye!' Alex said brightly, ducking into the door of Mr Figg's, an old-fashioned chemist's, as it turned out, where most of the contents of the shop were kept behind the glass-topped counters. Which meant that there was nowhere to hide.

'There you are!' Sue arrived in the doorway. 'You know I think you should get your ears tested, I was calling out your name all the way down the street.'

'Oh.' Alex's shoulders slumped. There was no way out.

'Anyway, sorry you didn't make the meeting, obviously you had things to do as it was your first week. Just make sure you are at the next one, time is running out, no room for slacking now.'

'Sue,' Alex said, 'thanks so much for asking me, it's just that I don't . . .'

'Marvellous,' Sue said as she left. 'I'll see you then.'

'You don't say no to a Montaigne,' Mr Figg said from behind the counter. 'The last person who said no to a Montaigne was beheaded.'

'To be honest,' Alex said, 'that option seems pretty attractive right now.'

Mr Figg did not sell dog shampoo, but he did have baby shampoo, which they both agreed at least couldn't do Buoy any harm, even if it was probably too mild to cut through the build-up of muck and grease on his fur. So she took two bottles for good measure and headed back down to the quay where she was due to meet Lucy.

Sitting right by where her boat was moored, munching his way through a most likely stolen pasty, Alex found Buoy and she wouldn't have put it past him to have somehow found out what was going to happen and try to foil her plan to make the cottage less stinky.

'Well,' she said loudly and to no one in particular, unless you counted the life-sized automated Santa that Ruan had put by the boat tour ticket shed. 'I'm going to the pub tonight, and definitely won't be going home till really late.'

Buoy finished his pasty and licked his lips, and then, catching sight of one of Ruan's tour boats, hopped down the quay steps and made the short leap into the boat, which he knew would drop him at least near enough to the cottage for him to swim ashore.

Lucy appeared at her side as she watched Buoy intimidate one of the boat's paying passengers with his terrible breath.

'He has no idea what is coming his way,' she said, showing Alex an assortment of brushes and cleaning cloths she'd raided from the pub's cleaning stores.

'And yet,' Alex said, as they headed for her boat, 'why do I get the distinct feeling that this is all going to go horribly wrong?'

'You need a Christmas tree,' was the first thing that Lucy whispered as they crept into the cottage, hoping to catch Buoy unawares and somehow compel him up the stairs and into the bath in some imaginative way they had deliberately not dwelled on yet. 'Something to brighten this old place up.'

'I know,' Alex sighed, keeping her voice low as she scanned the tiny ground floor for the dog, knowing that if she couldn't see him he wasn't there. He had to be having a nap upstairs already, which meant whispering was redundant. If he came down the stairs, they could just grab him, but if he stayed up there it would just be a short wrestle to the bath. 'It's just the thought of Christmas this year, makes me feel . . . tired. I was sort of hoping to skip it altogether. All the joy, and goodwill. And presents.'

Lucy chuckled. 'You've come to the wrong town to avoid Christmas, Alex. We practically are Christmas here. We've had "Hark the Herald Angels Sing" playing in the gift shop since September, and Sue's pageant . . .'

Holding towels as makeshift nets, Alex and Lucy crept up the stairs, silent for a moment as they hoped to catch the dog catnapping. Alex flattened her back against the wall just the other side of the door and then burst in, but the bedroom was empty. Wherever Buoy had been heading on that boat, it wasn't home.

'Oh well,' Alex said, 'he's bound to come back sooner or later and when he does we can pounce on him. And I'm not doing the pageant. I'm no good at that sort of thing. Painting, sewing, dressing up. I am going to tell Sue, I'm just not sure when. January maybe.'

'Did Sue put you on a list?' Lucy asked, as they walked back down the stairs. Alex nodded. 'Then you are doing the pageant. No one ever says no to Sue Montaigne. The last person who said no to a Montaigne got—'

'Yes, beheaded, I know.'

There was a knock at the door and the two women looked at each other.

'Well, I don't think it's Buoy,' Alex said.

'So answer it then?' Lucy suggested.

The knocking was repeated, and then, 'Hello, Alex? Luce? I can hear you talking, you know,' Ruan said through the thick oak door.

'What does he want?' Alex muttered under her breath, remembering her hair, her torn sweater at exactly the same moment as she hated herself for caring about it.

She opened the door, and found Ruan holding a bottle of wine.

'Oh.' Alex looked at it. 'Hello.'

'Oh, Becky sent it,' Ruan said hurriedly. 'Nothing to

do with me. I just said I'd bring it over as I was sort of passing.' He looked over his shoulder in the opposite direction, where the top of his lighthouse could just be seen against the midnight blue sky. 'It only takes a minute, and also I wanted to say that . . . I've never seen a girl handle herself like that, like you did today. It was . . . scary. And impressive. And well done. And remind me never to get on the wrong side of you. Marissa said you looked like the incredible hulk – a she-hulk.'

Alex had not remembered seeing Marissa there in all the excitement, she must have been somewhere on the edges of the fray, and, briefly, Alex wondered if she had been waiting for Ruan again. Still, nice description. A crazy woman, who turned into a deranged monster when she was angry was exactly the way that Alex wanted to come across in her new home. She must thank Marissa for that, and then maybe push her off the first available cliff.

'Um, thanks, for that,' Alex said, opening the door a little wider to take the wine.

'Hi, Ruan,' Lucy waved at him. 'Come in and have a drink, we're waiting for Buoy.'

'What, are you going to clobber him over the head with a cleaver?' Ruan asked, taking Lucy at her word and walking past Alex and into the tiny living room, which suddenly seemed very small indeed once he was standing in it.

'God, I haven't been in here since I was a lad.' Ruan grinned. 'I was always up here as a boy, bothering Dom, when he used to live out here. Seems like another world out there. But this place is still exactly the same.'

'We're not murdering Buoy,' Lucy said, grabbing the wine and taking it into the kitchen. 'We're laying in wait for him so that when he finally turns up we can ambush him into the bath.'

Alex watched as Lucy twisted the top off the bottle of wine and filled three mugs to the top.

'Good luck with that. That dog hasn't had a bath since two thousand and four,' Ruan said. 'There's no way you will get him in a bath.'

'Did you see Ninja Alex in action today?' Lucy laughed, nodding at Alex who was now awkwardly standing by the fireplace wondering what to say next. 'But if you don't think we are up to it then stay and help us.'

'I'm not sure I'm up-to-date with my tetanus,' Ruan said, and Lucy laughed and Alex stood. Awkwardly. Praying for any sort of distraction that would mean she wouldn't have to keep up the awkward standing thing. Just at that moment the textbook creak of the door swinging open sounded. Turning their heads, they saw Buoy standing there, eyeing them for a moment. As he looked at the peculiar gathering, Alex knew exactly what lay in store for him, because he turned on his heel and bolted like a very smelly bolt of lightning.

Alex wasn't sure how she came to be in hot pursuit of the nimble little animal until she was, following closely on Ruan's heels, Lucy giving up at the garden gate, as she didn't have the right shoes on for chasing a dog, she called out, her voice become very distant very fast.

Instead of heading down towards the coast, Buoy was making his way into the thick forest behind the cottage, which instead of building upwards to the peak of the hill, as you might expect if looking at it from a great distance away, plummeted down into a steep hidden valley. One minute Alex was reasonably sure-footed, finding her way along the trails that led through the woods, and the next she was half running, half falling down a steep hillside, the moonlight all that was lighting her way, the odd bark and flash of greyish white amongst the trees the only clues to where she was heading. But it didn't matter, because for a few glorious moments Alex forgot why she was running full pelt down a hillside in the dark, and just knew that she was having tremendous fun.

And then she ran smack bang into the back of Ruan, knocking him into a tree, which his forehead bounced off with an audible thud.

'Christ,' he coughed, grasping his forehead. 'How many men do you usually beat the crap out of in one day?'

'Why have we stopped?' Alex asked him, looking

around. They had to be near the bottom of the valley now. It was very dark, beneath the reach of the silver fingers of moonlight, which had only managed to fight their way through the tightly laced branches of the tops of the trees so far. It was eerily quiet, except for the sounds of their laboured breathing.

Vaguely, Alex thought she remembered reading about some poor murdered maiden being dumped down here, long ago, in what was called locally the Devil's Cauldron, and how her ghostly white image could be seen floating through the trees on a full moon. Or was that a werewolf, she couldn't remember.

'We'll get lost if we don't stop now,' Ruan said. 'Especially in the dark, and I don't want the headline of the next issue of the Poldore *Echo* to be "LOCAL MAN DIES CHASING A DOG".'

'But what about Buoy?' Alex asked him. 'Won't he get lost out here all on his own?'

'You're worried about him now, are you?' Ruan asked her, and even in the dark, Alex could tell he was smirking. 'I knew he'd win you round in the end.'

'I'm not worried about the toxic scent that comes with him,' Alex said firmly as they began to make their way more or less back the way they had come. 'And if he's going to be my lodger then I am going to have to insist on him not smelling like a dung heap.'

'You don't want to rehome him then?' Ruan asked her, as he began feeling his way up the steep incline, pulling himself up by the saplings that grew on it, stretching up towards the stars.

'Well, you made it sound like a matter of life and death . . .' Alex said, following him.

'It is, and, well, Poldore wouldn't be the same without Buoy in it.' Ruan stopped, holding a hand out to her, which Alex pushed aside, preferring instead to clamber off the rock herself, however inelegantly.

'Well, if you love him that much, you have him,' Alex grumbled but not too seriously. Even though her hands and jeans were covered in mud, her damp hair clung to her ruddy cheeks and she was a little cold now she'd stopped running, being out here, in the quiet of the woods, the sound of the sea a distant rhythmic roar, was quite restful. It didn't even occur to Alex that she was spending time with another person, who was also a man – two of the things that most often filled her with dread.

'What I mean is,' Ruan said, pausing for a moment to catch his breath, 'that everything around here changes all the time. And every year it changes more quickly. I grew up here and when I was a kid, no one cared about Poldore. We'd get tourists in the summer, but not the constant year-round circus it is now. My dad was a fisherman, his dad was fisherman. It was a small town, and a small life, and I liked it. Then everyone wanted to leave, get away, start life somewhere where everything was supposed to be more exciting.

My sisters, Tamsyn and Keira, they couldn't wait to get away, and Cordy – she thinks she's going to be a rock star.' He sighed. 'Like that's ever going to happen. Houses where I used to knock for my mates now belong to people who show up once a year, and paid a million quid for them. There are more stupid gift shops in the high street than you can shake a stick at, and twenty quid for some fish and chips? The world has gone mad. But Buoy, well, although he's only eleven, it feels like he's been around forever. I'd miss his stinky, matted little face, strutting about like he owns the town.'

Alex smiled at the soft fondness in his voice. This Ruan, whose face was shrouded in shadows, as they climbed their way back to the top of the valley, much more slowly and with a good deal more effort, than they had run down it, seemed completely different to the one she'd met on that first night. Perhaps it helped that she couldn't see his face, and he couldn't see her, because she felt less self-conscious and embarrassed to be near to him, she could enjoy listening to him without worrying what he was thinking about her.

'Eddie, Becky and Lucy, they're still here,' Alex said as they began the final march again. 'Jago and Mr Figg, the chemist. And Sue and her family, they've always been here. Perhaps not as much has changed as you think. When I decided to come here, it was to live, forever.'

'That's true,' Ruan said. He grabbed her hand

without asking for permission this time, and helped her scramble off a final rocky outcrop, until they emerged onto the scrubland, just above her cottage roof. A thin stream of smoke snaked out of the lopsided chimney – Lucy must have got a fire going. 'It's nice when someone comes here, and is serious about being here. When they treat it as a home and not one big holiday cottage. It's a big decision to make. What made you decide to come here?'

Alex turned towards the sea, peaceful and calm, glittering in the moonlight, the town across the harbour sparkling, its own little constellation.

'Well,' she said. 'Honestly? It feels like here, I could be anyone.' Suddenly self-conscious about saying so much at once, Alex smiled at her boots, thrusting her hands into her pockets and hunching up her shoulders. 'We'd better go in, Lucy's probably about to call out search and rescue.'

'Before we do –' Ruan took a step closer to her, stooping a little so that he could look at her face '– I just wanted to say, you were brilliant today. Not only sorting that prick out, but also Lucy told me the way you handled what she told you. Not everyone would have been as cool about it as you were, and by that I mean hardly anyone. I've known Lucy all my life, I've always known her. Even when she looked different, she was still the same person. But for a lot of people . . . they just don't get it. So what I'm saying is, well, thanks,

I suppose. For being a friend to my friend. I appreciate it.'

'Two thank yous in one night,' Alex said, noticing that Ruan had a dimple just under his bottom lip, where the stubble grew a little darker. 'I'm on a roll.'

'We're a family in Poldore,' Ruan said, abruptly taking a few steps back from her. 'We look out for each other, and all I'm saying is, you made a good start at fitting in.'

Alex tucked her chin into the neck of her sweater and smiled to herself as she followed Ruan back down the steep dirt path that led into the cottage. She had been here almost a week and already she had one, maybe two, new friends. Perhaps life on her own, without Marcus or even her dad in it, was possible after all.

Ruan pushed open the cottage door, and stopped dead.

'Where the bloody hell have you been?' A young woman stood alone in the living room, and everything about her demeanour was angry. For a second Alex thought she might have been attacked and dragged around by her backcombed hair, as her black make-up was spread halfway down her pale cheeks and her tights were laddered and torn. And then she realised it was a look. The girl chose to look like she was an apocalypse survivor, which made Alex, who never gave the way she looked a single thought, smile.

'What are you on about, Cordy?' Ruan said. 'You're twenty-four, I don't need to read you a bedtime story.'

Cordy, his youngest sister Cordelia, Alex assumed, the girl who wants to be rock star and spends too much time hanging out with Brian Rogers.

'It was my gig tonight. My acoustic set at the Lobster Pot, from four to six o'clock. Mussels and Music, don't you remember? You said you were going to be there, Ruan. You said you would come and hear me sing for once. But where were you? Here, delivering wine in the opposite direction from where the gig is, and for someone whose actual daughter is already here. What the actual fuck, Ruan?'

'Er, hello,' Alex said, walking past Ruan and holding out her hand. 'I'm Alex. This is my living room you are standing in, shouting.'

'Hardly your living room, you've only been here five minutes,' Cordy said, giving Alex's hand a scathing look. 'Everyone else was there, *everyone*, except for you and Lucy. And Lucy had a good excuse, what with that psycho wailing on her . . .'

'It was Alex here who stepped in and sorted him out,' Ruan said.

'Big wow, she's a decent human being, stop the press! Ruan, you are *my* brother, my only family in this dump. And you said, you promised, that you were going to be there. Maybe you want me to waste my life being a nanny, and then marry some loser local and get fat and have loads of kids, but I don't want that. Don't you see, I'm good at this? Proper people, professional people think I've got talent. If you would come and hear me sing you would see it too.'

'What, Brian Rogers?' Ruan barked a single, mirthless laugh. 'Cordy, he's taken so many drugs since the seventies he thinks Buoy's got talent.'

'Where is Lucy, actually?' Alex said, hearing a heavy thud and then a small shriek from upstairs.

'No!' Cordelia stamped her heavily booted foot. 'No, that's not true. He's had a past, but he's got all his marbles. He knows what he's talking about and he knows people in the business, loads of famous acts come and record at the Studio in the Wood, loads. And he's setting me up a showcase for record labels. So, Ruan, do you want to be the last one to know that your sister is a major international singing artiste?'

'I just don't want you to be hurt when this whole pipe dream fails,' Ruan said, wearily. 'I'm trying to protect you.'

'How would you know?' Cordelia shouted, making Alex want to go back to the Devil's Cauldron again. And then there was a definite yelp from upstairs, that could have been dog or human, she wasn't sure. Looking up, she noticed a small dark patch of damp growing on the ceiling, just about where the bathroom was.

'You never come to see me sing. If you came you would know I could do it.'

'I hear you sing all bloody day long. I'm not saying you don't have a nice voice, but . . .' Ruan looked at Alex, remembering where he was. 'Look, let's go home. I'll cook.'

'I'm going out,' Cordelia said. 'To celebrate. With my friends. About what a great gig I had.'

She slammed out of the cottage with all the fury and drama of a practised diva.

Ruan watched her go, disappearing down the stone steps at speed.

'I'd better go after her,' Ruan said. 'See you, Alex.'

'Hold on, wait for me.' Lucy ran after him, slipping her jacket on as she went. A quick inspection revealed that her jeans and top were damp and covered in dog hair. 'I need a lift in your boat, and about six hundred showers.'

'What happened?' Alex called after her. 'Did Buoy come back? Did you get him in the bath?'

'You'll see,' Lucy called back. She grinned and waved before she went down the steps.

Alex watched her go, feeling the first fine mist of cold rain on her face before she finally closed the aged door. Looking up at the ceiling, she wondered what was waiting for her up there and hoped that whatever it was at least it smelled less bad. It had been a long and very tiring day, and although it wasn't quite nine yet, all she wanted to do was to climb into bed. Wearily, she hauled herself up the narrow stairs and turned gratefully into the bedroom, where Buoy was lying on her bed.

Or at least Alex thought it had to be Buoy, because she didn't think another sparkling white and dove-grey hound, his hair combed out into a ball of soft fluff, would have sneaked in and got on the bed.

'Lucy gave you a wash and blow-dry!' Alex exclaimed in wonder. She had no idea how Lucy had managed to get the animal into the bath, or to stay still for the hairdryer, but she had, and it was nothing short of miraculous. 'You look gorgeous, actually!'

The dog raised his head to look at her. Both of his amber eyes were now visible since Lucy had trimmed him a fringe. He look utterly miserable about his present fragrant state and, for a moment, Alex almost felt sorry for him. Almost.

Going into the bathroom, Alex discovered the scene of the crime: the bath was still filled with black water, which also pooled on the floor and was seeping into the ceiling below, the towels were ruined beyond saving and the two bottles of baby shampoo lay empty on the floor.

Returning to the bedroom, she saw that her hairdryer and a brush that no one would ever use again were also discarded on the floor.

The miserable dog had curled himself into a tight sweet-smelling ball of shame.

'You smell lovely,' Alex told him as she sat down on her bed.

Buoy didn't take it as a compliment, ignoring Alex as she changed into her pyjamas, and took her new toothbrush out of its secret hiding place to clean her teeth. Eventually, when she climbed into bed, she noticed that Lucy had even put fresh sheets on for her, something she was deeply grateful for as she stretched her tired legs out against the cool linen.

'You can sleep here tonight as you smell of flowers and have a very bruised ego,' Alex told Buoy, although he clearly wasn't seeking permission. 'But going forward you are going to learn to sleep on the floor or a dog bed or something. And somehow we will learn to live with one another, because everyone in this town loves you, so we are stuck together.'

Discovering she was too tired to read, she lay back on the pillow and tentatively reached out to stroke Buoy's head, which instead of being matted and oily was silky and smooth. After a moment, Buoy leaned into her hand, made a contented noise in his throat which Alex supposed must be something like a dog purr, and she thought, as she drifted off to sleep feeling the rise and fall of his breathing against her leg, that, actually, as long as he was clean he was tolerable.

Although she changed her mind at 3 a.m. when she was unceremoniously dumped onto the freezing floor, and growled at every time she tried to get back near the bed.

Chapter Eight

21 December

'There you are!' Sue was sitting at Alex's desk as she opened the office door.

'How did you get in?' Alex asked, her own bunch of keys redundant in her hand.

'Oh, I don't know.' Sue grinned. 'My family used to own the town, so there is usually a key for something or other in the kitchen drawer.'

'Right.' Alex stood by the doorway, wondering if she could get away with pulling a sicky.

'Don't think I don't know that you've been hiding from me.' Sue spun the chair round, springing out of it like a Jack-in-the-box, making Alex start slightly. 'Or that I didn't notice you were trying to run away from me yesterday afternoon.'

'I haven't, I wasn't,' Alex said, looking longingly out to sea and seriously considering a spontaneous career as a sailor.

'It's OK.' Sue smiled at her, as she pointed at Alex's chair, clearly directing her to sit. 'I know I have a reputation for being a bit "full on" sometimes. I forget that people need time to warm up to an idea.' She smiled again. 'I don't have serfs any more, sadly. But you've had a week, and I just want to make sure that from this point onwards you are fully committed to your role on the pageant.'

Alex didn't even dare look at the kitchen, which was normally her first destination when she arrived to make a much-needed cuppa.

'Oooh, two sugars please' Sue said, somehow reading her mind.

'Oh, I would,' Alex said. 'But, you know, the boats need me. Don't want anyone to drown, do we?'

'Of course not,' Sue said brightly, deciding not to take a hint even if it appeared in neon flashing lights before her very eyes. 'Tell you what, you get on with your work, Master of the Harbour, and I'll make us some tea.'

Alex sighed and checked the radar, trying not to hear Sue whistling 'Hark the Herald Angels Sing' behind her as the kettle boiled.

'So,' Sue said, setting a cup of too weak tea down by Alex, so that a little of it slopped onto her charts. Alex took a breath. 'You will be at the next meeting this afternoon, at my place, it's the one with the portcullis, then we'll set you to work. Originally, I was thinking costumes and set design, but you don't look like the type to sew, no offence, so I'm thinking scenery and float painting and decoration. We only do a traditional nativity here in Poldore. No "rock operas" or "Jesus in the Future" nonsense, like they get up to over in St Ives. No, here we stick to the rules.'

'What are the rules?' Alex asked, regretting speaking out loud at once.

'Bethlehem, a donkey, sheep, shepherds, angels, led by me, a Virgin Mary, a Joseph, some wise men, although they can be hard to come by round here, and of course the Baby Jesus. We process through the town, stop at the church for a blessing, end up at the town hall for a carol concert, and it all takes place on Christmas Eve, so not long to go now! All hands on deck!'

'Sue,' Alex said. 'I'm not really that artistic and also I'm . . .'

'Don't tell me you're busy, I know you aren't busy.'

'How do you know I'm not busy?' Alex asked her, forgetting to double bluff.

'I took a wild guess,' Sue said, snapping on a smile. 'Mine, at four, don't be late. And don't bring that bloody Casanova of a dog of yours – Duchess is still attending a support group after their star-crossed love affair, which by the way cost me thousands of pounds in vet's bills and lost revenue. And, I'm pretty sure she's coming into season any moment, but this time she'll be keeping her pants firmly on.'

'It's just that . . .' But Sue was gone, just as suddenly as she had been there, and Alex was left finally understanding what everyone else had been trying to tell her. No one says no to Sue Montaigne.

As Alex left the office just after four, the little square outside was packed with families – a children's choir from the local school was grouped around the tree, singing carols, and their parents, grandparents and siblings had turned out in force to see them. Although she was already late for the meeting, Alex stood for a moment on the periphery of the crowd, basking in the affectionate warmth of families united. Her family of two had not been a big one, but it had been a solid unit. Perhaps Alex hadn't had the show of affection or pride that these children were getting from their parents as they sang their hearts out, their faces shining with excitement as the big day drew nearer, but she had always known that Ian Munro was on her side, that he would always stick up for her, and have her back if she needed it. And although he had never said out loud that he was proud of her, it was implied, the way she worked her way up, earning respect and appreciation from her peers. Alex had known that he was. Yes, there had been a lot between them that was known and not said, and Alex thought that that was all there was. It had hurt her, perhaps even more than Marcus getting married to someone else, to find out that her father had been keeping a secret from her for her entire life. Marcus not being in love with her was hardly a surprise. It was painful, but Alex could learn to live with it. But her dad lying to her almost every single day? That was the one thing that Alex had not been able to bear, because it changed everything that she thought she knew.

Still she couldn't help but feel a pang when she imagined their little red-brick terraced house, empty and bare, as it certainly would be, because Dad would never bother to put up Christmas decorations just for himself, and he had no idea how to heat up a can of soup never mind cook a turkey. Not that he'd be on his own this Christmas. No he wouldn't be, would he? Perhaps her dad wouldn't be missing her at all.

Alex took a deep breath and looked away from the families and out to sea, waiting for her heart rate to calm down to meet the rhythm of the waves. It wasn't that her dad had someone special in his life; she wasn't that petty or cruel. Often as she'd grown up she'd wished for him to have someone to hold hands with on a walk on the front, or to go out to dinner with on a Friday night. But Dad had never seemed interested, and she wasn't the pushy type, the type to try to set him up. What she couldn't understand or forgive was that for every one of those years that she had been wishing that her father had someone, he had been having a secret love affair with their next-door neighbour, Mrs O'Dowd, and for some reason, a reason that Alex simply could not understand, he didn't ever tell her. She had found out in the worst possible way, at the worst possible moment.

'You going up to Sue's, aren't you? I'm late too.' Ruan appeared at her side and, sniffing, Alex turned her face away from him. She coughed, trying to cover up the fact that she had been on the verge of tears. 'Oh, sorry, I didn't mean to disturb you. Are you OK?'

'You weren't disturbing me,' Alex said, hoping he didn't notice her rubbing her eyes with the sleeve of her jumper. 'The wind, you know, it makes your eyes water.'

'Oh yes,' Ruan said. 'The wind can do that. And to be honest the thought of going up to Sue's to be bossed around for the foreseeable makes me want to cry too.'

Alex sniffed, and then smiled, feeling a little better. 'I'm not crying.'

'Oh well, by the end of this meeting, you will be,' Ruan said.

And as she slowly turned and began the trudge up the hillside towards Castle Hill, Alex silently fell into step beside him.

'Thank God you are here,' Sue said, almost before Alex had come under the portcullis and long before she had a chance to get over the 'Oh my God, I'm walking under an actual portcullis into someone's front garden' moment.

'Really?' Alex said, as several animals of all shapes

and sizes, some of them dogs, some of them children, were suddenly launching what seemed like a co-ordinated shock and awe attack around her feet in the floodlit courtyard. 'Because like I said, I am terrible at drawing . . .'

'Petal, Forest, Pugwash, Duchess, Meadow, stand still, right now!' Sue snapped the names, which could have been children's or dogs' or both, with frightening authority, but she was entirely ignored by the rebellious horde, who continued to engage in a chaotic game of chase around her feet. Ruan picked up what Alex was reasonably sure was a little flame-haired girl and whirled her around in a shrieking blur, resulting in even more clamouring and barking, and demands of 'Me next, me next!'

Sue grabbed her hand and dragged her out of the fray, talking all the while, although it wasn't until they were in a sort of boots, dog leads and coats anteroom, the door firmly closed on the rabble, that Alex could actually make out what she was saying.

'So I said, take it out, and she said no, and I said well you have to, and she said you can't make me, and it turns out that actually I can't, it would be classed as assault . . .'

Alex had no idea what she was talking about, as Ruan rushed in through the door, then closed it behind him and leaned against it for good measure, just in case the zombies outside tried to get in.

'Where's Cordelia?' he asked Sue.

'Good question,' Sue said. 'Back soon, I hope. She is one of the few people who can tame the rabble, which really is the only reason I haven't fired her yet, she's very insubordinate, you know.'

'Tell me about it,' Ruan commiserated.

'And then,' Sue continued, leading them through another door, this one painted a duck egg green, into a red-brick part of the house that Alex thought might be Tudor. Large flagstones lay on the floor and a huge empty fireplace, which a person could stand in, gaped like an open mouth as they walked by. 'I had a brainwave. I thought Alex will make the perfect Virgin.'

'I beg your pardon?' Alex said, just as Sue led them into the biggest kitchen Alex had ever seen, to find several familiar faces seated around a long, ancient-looking kitchen table, including Lucy, Becky, Rory and Marissa.

'You,' Sue said, slowly and loudly, as if she were talking to an idiot. 'You would make a lovely Virgin.'

Acutely aware of Ruan standing beside her, Alex's face super-heated to several thousand degrees, and if it hadn't been for the horde outside that was marginally more frightening than the Christmas pageant committee she would have bolted.

'A Virgin Mary in the pageant,' Sue reiterated. 'Were you not listening to me, Alex?'

'I heard the Virgin bit,' Alex said, finding her voice. 'The noise . . .'

'Oh, that lot. I tune it out.' Sue waved a dismissive hand. 'So, Kerry Mortlock, you don't know her, she's the butcher's girl, friends with Cordelia, I think, she was down to be the Virgin Mary, such a sweet-looking girl, even though she's a punk rocker, or something akin to that. And then she calmly turns up this morning for her special Virgin Mary coaching session with me, with her lip pierced three times, *three*! Well, I think we can all agree that Mary was *not* a Goth. And she can't take them out or else they will close up and I couldn't make her. I did try and there was a scuffle and one of the cats was slightly trodden on, but no. She wouldn't see reason. Even threatened to call the police, would you believe.' Sue sighed. 'There was a time when my family *was* the police in this town . . .'

Alex stared at her, frowning deeply. 'And what have I got to do with this?'

'Well, look at you,' Sue said, marching up to her. 'Look at your milky white complexion, and those cornflower-blue eyes and the hair!' Without any thought to personal boundaries, Sue removed the biro that had been holding Alex's hair in a loose knot and fluffed it around her shoulders. 'I've never seen a more virginal-looking Mary.'

'Oh my God.' Alex decided it was preferable if the dogs and children ate her and headed for the door.

'Wait.' Ruan put his hand on her arm, nodding reassuringly. 'Don't rush off. Sue, when will you learn that you can't manhandle humans like they are one of your prize pigs? You've terrified the poor woman.'

'Alex, come and sit down,' Lucy beckoned to her. 'You don't have to agree to anything you don't want to. Come and sit down and let me pour you a cup of tea.'

'And here's some lemon drizzle cake,' Becky added. 'I baked it myself.'

Tea and cake was enough to persuade Alex to sit, perched on the edge of the chair nearest to the exit, and find out a little bit more, although she already knew the answer.

'Oh, was I being a bit much?' Sue's face fell. 'Oh dear, Alex, I do apologise. I do get carried away sometimes, and forget that people have free will. Yes, have some lovely tea and cakes. I can tell from those thighs you're not a girl who is afraid of cake.'

Dimly aware that Sue was trying to be kind, and frankly too paralysed with horror to be able to do anything else, Alex took a bite from the cake. It was sublime.

'What my wife is *trying* to ask you,' Rory said sweetly, 'is will you please step up and be Mary for the pageant? We wouldn't normally put you on the spot like this, but believe it or not you are actually our last hope. We'd already been through the entire town when we gave the job to Kerry.'

Alex shook her head, preferring to let the deliciously lemony cake melt in her mouth rather than say actual words, although several pairs of eyes were waiting for her to do just that.

'No,' she said finally. 'No, I'm not . . . I don't do that sort of thing, acting or anything that means . . . being the centre of attention. I hate it. I really hate people looking at me.'

'Such a shame, because you are quite beautiful,' Rory told her gently.

Alex took another bite of cake and then tied her hair into an elastic band that happened to be around her wrist.

'I mean what about Lucy, or Marissa?' she suggested. 'They are much more beautiful than me, and I know that Lucy is great at being in the limelight. I've seen her behind the bar. She'd be perfect.'

Lucy smiled, and Becky nodded in agreement.

'But I am the wardrobe mistress,' Lucy said. 'I've got to adapt and alter the costumes, and help everyone get in and out of them at the right time. No one else can do that except for me.'

'It's true,' Sue said. 'Lucy is a demon with a needle, and much too valuable back stage, I'm afraid.'

'I don't mind doing it,' Marissa volunteered. 'After all, I've got the looks and, besides, I don't hate who's playing Joseph.' She winked at Ruan, who grinned back at her. 'I've been opposite worse leading men in my time.'

Alex watched Marissa flirt effortlessly with Ruan,

in awe, fascinated to see how Ruan smiled back at her, obviously pleased by the attention. And then it sunk in that Ruan was playing Joseph, and Alex was even more determined to say no.

'No, no, no, that won't do at all,' Sue said. 'Marissa, you are in charge of the publicity and the admin. We need you co-ordinating the final push. You don't have time to find your inner virgin, darling. From what your mother said, there may never be enough time for that.'

Marissa eyes widened in obvious shock, and hurt, which Sue, to her credit, felt bad about at once.

'I'm sorry, I don't mean . . . oh honestly, you know what I mean,' Sue said a little crossly. 'No, Alex here is perfect to take on the role.'

'Alex,' Rory said, gently. 'You poor thing. It's written all over your face that you don't want to take a lead role in the pageant, but I promise you, actually Mary is quite a small part. It is all about standing and sitting, next to Ruan here, for the pageant itself, and then there is a tiny bit of a nativity play followed by a concert in the town hall.' He paused for a moment, smiling reassuringly. 'And, well, Alex, this puts you right at the centre of the town's most ancient and treasured tradition. It's a great honour that you've been asked really, because it shows you that even after a couple of weeks we think of you as one of us.'

'She doesn't need to be a virgin to be one of us,' Lucy said, a little naughtily. 'Alex, there is no pressure to say yes. I'm sure we can find a suitable Virgin in this town if we look hard enough.'

'Actually there is a massive pressure to say yes,' Sue said. 'I'm sorry but there is. Time is running out, we need to rehearse, dress rehearse. And, honestly, if Alex says no, I might as I well take myself up to the top of the High Tower and throw myself off of it, just like my ancestor Lady Anwen Montaigne did in fourteen thirty-four.'

'The High Tower wasn't built until eighteen twenty-nine,' Rory reminded her.

'Yes, but she doesn't know that,' Sue hissed.

'OK,' Alex said quietly, so quietly that she wasn't at all sure the thought had articulated itself out loud.

'Beg pardon?' Sue said.

'OK.' Alex took a breath. 'Yes, fine, I will do it. I came here to be different, different from the way I was at home, and at home . . . there would be no way on earth. But, here . . .?' Alex looked at Lucy, who nodded encouragingly. 'Well, go on then. As long as there are no lines.'

'Marvellous!' Sue leaped up from her chair. 'There is so much to do! Put that cake down at once! Ruan, Alex, you are with me and Marissa for the photo shoot for the local rag. Rory, Becky and Lucy, the paint's in the garage, your painting and sewing army will be here any minute. Let's get started!'

'After you,' Ruan said, opening the door for the ladies,

which Alex followed Sue and Marissa through, although she walked a little behind the group so she could stop and take in the incredible wood-panelled corridor, which had a genuine knight in armour standing on a plinth, under an ancient-looking portrait of a very cross-looking lady, who bore a distinct resemblance to Sue. Even so, she couldn't help noticing as they walked ahead that Marissa and Ruan looked very much a couple as they whispered and laughed, their heads close together. As Alex watched, Ruan said something inaudible, and Marissa knocked into him with a sway of her hip. And, just for a moment, he placed the palm of his hand on the small of her back.

Alex wondered what it would be like to have the sort of ease in her own skin that Marissa obviously had. It wasn't something that she'd ever had, not even as a little girl, when she'd always been all legs and arms and hair, but her awkwardness had grown tenfold as she matured into a woman. It wasn't that she suddenly wanted to be a girly girl, not at all. It was just about knowing who you were, and feeling good about it. Like Lucy knew who she was, and so did Marissa obviously. Alex was still trying to find that out, and maybe taking a bigger role in the pageant would help.

Still there was one thing she didn't have worry about. She didn't have to worry about acting like a virgin, not as she actually was one.

*

'Well, stand closer together then. I know it was an immaculate conception, but still at least look like you might be capable of a traditional one,' Sue directed them as Marissa took photos. Their official costumes were almost ready, so Ruan was wearing a simple collarless white shirt and a makeshift headdress, and Sue had found a white sheet which she draped over Alex's hair and around her shoulders.

'No, dear.' Sue pointed at her. 'That is not how you hold the Baby Jesus. The Baby Jesus must be held head up, not by the legs like he is a chicken. This is a general rule of thumb for holding all babies, not just the Son of God.'

'It's just when I hold him up the other way he wees on me,' Alex said, causing Marissa to snort with laughter. She caught Ruan's eye and bit a glossed lip, as she flirted with him from behind the camera.

'I told Meadow she was to empty it out for the dress rehearsal. I told her, the trouble with that child is that she never listens.'

'The trouble with her is that she is three.' Cordelia arrived at the door, with three very dirty, exhausted-looking children in tow. She crossed her arms as she regarded her older brother with a finely tuned mixture of disgust and pity.

'What's so sad is how happy you are to be part of all of this nonsense,' she told him.

'Where have you been?' Sue asked her. 'The children

were more or less dismantling the place, and not even the Vikings could do that.'

'I was here,' Cordelia told her. 'I had it all under control, like I always do. And now I'm taking them all for a bath before bed. Kids, go and say goodnight to your mother.'

Alex watched as the three children went and suffered a kiss from Sue, before wearily heading towards the huge wooden staircase in what would have traditionally been the entrance hall.

'Don't do anything stupid,' Cordelia told her brother as she exited, looking Marissa up and down in a way that clearly indicated that the woman was the stupid thing she was talking about.

'After you've bathed them, if you could just dunk a couple of dogs in the water, especially Pugwash, she's been at the chicken droppings again.'

'Er, washing shit off stupid-looking dogs is not in my job description,' Cordelia told her.

'I'll pay you!' Sue pleaded. 'Honestly, Cordy, you are a marvel, the only one that the children and dogs listen to.'

'The only one that beats them you mean,' Cordy said, peeling herself off the wall and slouching towards the stairs. 'Joke! I'm joking!' she called after her.

'She's a lovely girl, and a great nanny,' Sue said once Cordelia was gone, 'but honestly, Ruan, the manners of an alley cat.'

'Yeah, well, you know,' Ruan said, 'we didn't really have parents for a lot of our childhood, and it was hardest on Cordy.'

Alex stayed silent, carefully holding Baby Jesus the right way up as Marissa suddenly came in very close, snapping off shots right in their faces, probably trying to catch the look of sadness that passed over them.

'Well, it wouldn't have hurt Tamsyn or Keira to hang around for a bit longer, and help out with her.'

'We're all right, me and Cordy,' Ruan says. 'Even if she is the reason I'm going grey before I'm thirty.'

'There's nothing wrong with a bit of grey in your stubble,' Marissa said, running the flat of her palm along his cheek. 'Very sexy.'

'Can we focus, please,' Sue said. 'We've got ten minutes to get the shots in the bag, Marissa. I've booked a conference call with the fake snow people and I need to get all my facts organised. Don't want another debacle like last year when I ordered in kilos instead of tons and we ended up with barely enough snow to dust a lamb with.' She smiled at Alex. 'Do you know, Alex, that it hasn't snowed at Christmas in Poldore since seventeen forty-three.'

'Or in Bethlehem, ever, probably,' Alex said, which made Marissa giggle, and Sue stop dead for a second.

'This isn't a documentary, Alex,' she said sternly. 'We aren't trying to recreate the actual birth of our Lord. No, this is all about the showbiz, the Christmas experience, the pizzazz, if you will. You give the people what they want, and the people want snow. And snow they shall have. Good news is that Oscar-winning film director Kurt Peterson has just moved into town, so I popped round there this morning, dazzled him with my heritage, and put him charge of special effects.'

'You just put a Hollywood A-lister in charge of fake snow?' Alex asked her. Even she had heard of Kurt Peterson and she'd had hardly heard of anyone.

'He's just a man like any other, darling,' Sue assured her. 'They are all available to be conquered one way or another.'

'I beg your pardon,' Ruan said. 'Nobody's conquering me.'

'Really,' Marissa purred. 'I wouldn't be so sure about that.'

'Honestly, Marissa. You are worse than a bitch on heat,' Sue said, rather cruelly, making Marissa at once look uncomfortable and at odds with herself for since the first time that Alex had laid eyes on her, suddenly she looked belittled and fragile. 'Focus will you. Ruan, put your arm around Alex's waist. Alex, lean your head on his chest, cradle the baby against that ample bosom and . . . take it, take it!'

Marissa followed orders mutely, suddenly incredibly quiet and Alex felt for her. She was sure Sue didn't mean to be quite so brutal, but nevertheless it was no fun being on the wrong end of her attention.

'There, that's in the can. You two make the perfect couple,' Sue said. 'Looks like Marissa could have a bit of competition for his affections!'

'There's no competition for my affections' Ruan said, suddenly not in the least bit amused. 'There is no nothing. I'm not interested in anything like that, with *anyone*.'

With that Ruan pulled his headdress off and marched out of the wood-panelled room, picking up his leather jacket as he left.

'Oh dear,' Sue said, unhappily. 'Oh dear, I am such a fool sometimes.'

'You should know, Sue,' Marissa said, coolly. 'Ruan isn't the sort of man who likes being teased, especially about his private life.'

'Oh my dear,' Sue said, taking the camera from her, 'that just goes to show you don't know him at all.'

Chapter Nine

'Wait up!' Alex considered pretending not to hear Marissa calling her name as she wound her scarf around and over her lips, but Marissa called out again, this time out of breath. And, judging by the click-clack of her heels on the cobbles, she was running to catch up with her. 'Alex!'

Alex stopped and sighed, looking out across the estuary at her little cottage, gleaming in the dark, and reconciled herself to the fact that she wasn't going to get home to it for a little while longer.

'Fancy a cheeky glass of wine in the pub?' Marissa asked, as she caught up. 'We out-of-towners have to stick together, don't we?'

'Do we?' Alex said, and then realised how rude she sounded. 'I mean . . . I'm sorry, it's just that, well, look at you and look at me.' Alex gestured at Marissa's grey lambswool poncho, her skinny black jeans laced into black knee-high heeled boots and then at herself in another outsized jumper over baggy joggers, topped off by an anorak and accessorised with her battered Timberlands, the only pair of shoes she owned now, since her party-slash-funeral shoes wouldn't fit in her case.

'Goodness, I'm not so shallow that I can only drink with fashionably dressed people, what must you think of me?' Marissa smiled. 'Or are you too shallow to drink with a silly insecure girl who does worry what she looks like all the time, and still hates it no matter how much effort she puts in?'

'Of course not,' Alex said, feeling a little chastened.

'Come on then, have a drink with me, please,' Marissa pleaded. 'I need a pick-me-up after a couple of hours with that old dragon. Honestly, she doesn't care whose feelings she hurts – yours, mine, even Ruan's. He was so embarrassed by her ravings.'

'I don't think she means anything by it,' Alex said as Marissa led her into the pub, where Eddie was standing behind the bar, not talking to Ruan who was sitting in silence, staring into a pint.

'Well,' Marissa said, nodding at Ruan, 'whether she means it or not it hurts people. She wants to be careful; one day someone will hurt her back.'

'Ladies,' Lucy said as she and Becky arrived back. 'How was the photo shoot?'

'Dramatic,' Marissa said. 'Ruan, would you like to join us for a drink?'

Ruan shot them a dark scowl down the length of the bar, got up and stalked off into the night.

'I'll take that as a no then,' Marissa said, shrugging.

And then she yawned. 'Actually, you know what, I am suddenly so tired I think I'll go home after all. See you around.'

Alex opened her mouth to say something, but the pub door was swinging shut behind Marissa before she could think of anything.

'She's not a woman who's that much into sisterhood, I'm guessing,' Lucy said, leaning on the bar.

'No, and I didn't even want a drink,' Alex said. 'No offence.'

'So what put Ruan in such a mood?' Lucy asked her. 'Was it Marissa throwing herself at him non-stop?'

'I don't think it was actually,' Alex said thoughtfully. 'He seemed to be having a quite a laugh with her. Then Sue said something about girls competing for his affection and he just got really moody and stormed off. Men, eh?' Alex rested her chin on the bar and watched the bubble in the drink float upwards. 'They are so complicated.'

'Sounds like there's more to that statement than just a stroppy Ruan,' Lucy said. 'Look, I'm not working tonight, want to come round to mine for dinner? Nothing fancy, some pasta, probably. We can nick a bottle of wine, and you can tell me why you ran away to Cornwall.'

'I told you, I didn't run away,' Alex insisted, weakly.

'Everyone who moves here is running away from something,' Lucy assured her. 'Come on, what do you say?'

'Fine,' Alex said. 'I mean, thank you. Thank you, yes, dinner would be nice.'

'So was it a man?' Lucy waited until the plate of pasta was sitting in front of her to get to point, which Alex thought was reasonably restrained. Lucy's cottage was a nice one, similar to hers, but cosier, and properly decorated and lit. While hers felt cold and impersonal, except with a lit fire and the overhead light off, Lucy's little living room was warm and inviting. On the mantel there were family photos – Eddie, Becky and a child, who Alex assumed was Lucy. Shy looking, awkward, uncertain. A world away from the woman who sat opposite her now.

'Do I really have to tell you?' Alex said, sticking her fork into the penne like she meant it. 'Really?'

'Well, no, but if you tell me then I can discreetly tell everyone who keeps asking me what you are doing here the edited version approved by you.'

'What?' Alex looked shocked. 'Why does anyone care what I am doing?'

'Everyone cares about everything round here, haven't you got that yet?' Lucy said, spooning healthy amounts of parmesan onto her pasta, and topping up the wine.

'And yet, I don't know anyone else's secrets,' Alex said. 'I'm not the sort of person to pry.'

'Did he cheat on you?' Lucy tried again.

Alex took a sip of wine. 'No, not exactly. Not at all actually.'

'Go on.' Lucy nodded enthusiastically.

'Fine.' Alex took a breath. 'I fell in love with my best friend Marcus when I was about twelve, although I only really realised it recently. We've known each other since we were six and he never looked at me like a girl, and I thought I never thought about him that way. We did all the same stuff together – climbed trees, went fishing, shoplifted from Tesco, you know – and I never guessed once that the reason I would do anything for him was because I was in love with him. Even when he started going out with girls, and talking to me about girls that he liked, and asking me for advice on girls, which went on for years . . . Even then it didn't click.'

'Good God, didn't you have any boyfriends in the meantime?' Lucy asked her, appalled. 'I mean look at you. Anyone can see that under all the baggy knitwear you would scrub up nicely.'

'Why thank you,' Alex said, pursing her lips. 'Yes, I had a few boyfriends, maybe three, but none of them that serious. One of them I quite liked – Matty, his name was. He was nice, he was a really good kisser and he made me laugh. And then things started to get a bit serious and he wanted me to . . .' Alex was not ready to share all of her secrets with Lucy. 'Commit, and I thought about it, and I thought well if I was ever ready to commit, it wouldn't be with him and I didn't want to just commit for the sake of it, you know, as a practice run, I wanted it to mean something . . . So I said no, and we broke up.'

'And you never said anything to this Marcus, not in all of those years and he never noticed how you felt about him?'

'No, because I still didn't really know it myself and, as much I love him, he really is very stupid,' Alex said. 'And anyway he had loads of girlfriends, loads of them, and none of them mattered that much. Until one of them did.'

'Then what happened?' Lucy asked her, topping up the wine glasses again.

Alex, who wasn't a big drinker, felt a little giddy and determined to eat more pasta to mop up alcohol. Except that every time she went to take a mouthful, Lucy asked her a question.

'This new girlfriend happened. Milly. A nice enough girl, I suppose, but all boobs and eyelashes and hair extensions and orange all year round. I thought, oh, she'll be another passing phase, I just have to grin and bear it for a little bit and then, a couple of months ago, he gets me to one side, all secret like. We were on a normal Friday night out, and Milly was with us too, on the dance floor doing something called a "slut drop". He whispers in my ear that he's got something to tell me. And I don't know, but at that second, that's when it dawned on me that I loved him, that I had always loved him, and in my own stupid, silly little head, I thought, This is it, this is the moment that he looks into my eyes, tucks a stray strand of hair behind my ear and tell me he loves me too. I think I had been waiting all my life for him to whisper that he had something to tell me in my ear.

'So I go away from the dance floor with him and just as he was about to speak, I was overwhelmed with emotion, because I thought, like a moron, that this was going to be it! It was like all the puzzle pieces had just slipped into place and I understood that we were meant to be together. So I kissed him. Right there, in the nightclub, behind a pillar outside the gents.' Alex stopped for a moment, picked up her wine glass and took a deep draught, forgetting the pasta once again. 'Well, he didn't kiss me back, he fought me off in fact, laughed at me, told me what a joker I was, trying to catch him out like that. Said that was the best practical joke I'd ever played on him, and I thought, well, either I kill myself right now or I pretend that was exactly what I was doing, pulling a prank on him. And that's when he said I'd throw the best stag night ever, and I said, what are you talking about and he said he was just about to propose to Milly. Then it all went quiet on the dance floor. I heard the DJ calling out his name. I followed him onto the stupid light-up disco floor. Someone gave him a mike and he got down on his knees in front of Milly and asked her to marry him.

Within about three minutes of me realising that he was the only man for me.'

'Oh my God.' Lucy looked appalled. 'That's bad, that's a rejection so bad that it easily merits a life-changing move to Poldore.'

'Oh no, it wasn't that that did it. If I'd left it at that, I probably would have just stayed there, pining away quietly for the next twenty or so years, happy just to be near him, while I kept house for my dad and worked at the port,' Alex said, warming to her subject as the wine warmed her insides. 'But I read this book, or rather the back of this book, that said you are never happy unless you go for the things you want in life. And I am not the sort of person to try to "go for it", or "make it happen". But, in this one thing, this thing that was so important to me, I decided to make a stand. To tell him, in words that even he could understand, that I loved him. And that maybe he should think about if he loved me too, because I was sure that if he did, he would realise that he felt the same way. And I decided the best place to do that would be at his engagement party. After most of a bottle of champagne.'

'Oh,' Lucy said, her forkful of pasta stopping dead halfway to her mouth.

'Oh,' Alex repeated. 'So I waited for the right moment. She's dancing in her stripper's outfit to Beyonce, with all her friends, slut dropping like flies, so I drag him outside for some air. He's laughing around, joking.

"'Can you believe it, Al," he says. "I'm getting married.'"

Alex stopped, pressing her lips together. 'He's always called me Al. Al, like a boy.'

'And?' Lucy leaned forwards.

'I was really brave, and eloquent. I mean I was *so* romantic,' Alex said, sadly. "'Don't marry her," I said. "She doesn't understand you, she doesn't even really know you, or love you, the way I do. That would be impossible. She won't go out in the middle of the night to look at stars with you, she won't come and watch shoot 'em up action flicks with you, and eat Chinese, because she is always on a diet. She won't hold your head when you are throwing up after too many pints, or come down to the police station and talk the custody sergeant into letting you go home after a big night out with the rugby club that ended in a small amount of criminal damage. Don't marry her," I said. "Marry me, because I love you. I love you, Marcus, I think I always have."'

'Oh wow,' Lucy said. 'That was just like in a film!'

'I know, right?' Alex's eyes widened. 'And he just stared at me for what felt like the longest time and, for a moment, for a split second, I thought he might be about to say, Yes, yes I see it now, you are the only woman for me, or something . . . but he didn't.'

'What did he say?' Lucy asked, appalled.

'He ruffled my hair, and said, "Nice try, Al, you almost had me for a moment there." And then he went back into the party.'

'Fuuuuuuuck,' Lucy said, extending the expletive to underline her horror. 'So what, you decided to go then?'

'No, at that moment I thought I would probably go home, go to bed and never get up again,' Alex said. 'I lived with my dad, which might seem a bit sad at my age, but my mum left him when I was three, so it's always just been us two. And I knew I'd go home and not tell him about what had happened, and he would know something was up and would ask me about it, but maybe we'd watch a bit of TV or he'd challenge me to a game of chess or something, to make me feel better. He's never one for giving advice or saying anything very much, but you know that he knows, you know?'

'No.' Lucy shook her head. 'My dad never stops giving me advice.'

'Well, anyway, there I was, feeling truly horrible, and I get home, and I can't find Dad. But I do find his shoes on the stairs, like one on the bottom stair and one a few steps up . . . and then I find a pair of tights entwined around the top banister.'

'Uh-oh.' Lucy's eyes widened, her fingers creeping over her mouth.

'And *then* his pants on the landing, and then . . .

there's a bra hanging off the bedroom door.' Alex finished her drink in one gulp. 'Well, to cut a long story short, he was in bed with our neighbour Mrs O'Dowd.'

'Oh my God, he was having an affair!' Lucy howled.

'Well, not exactly. She's a widow, has been almost since she was married, and he's been single for twenty-five years.'

'Oh, so sort of sweet if a bit icky then?' Lucy said. 'Not a reason to fall out?'

Alex sighed heavily, pushing her plate away. 'Well, I mean, OK, so I wasn't in the right place for seeing my dad having sex with my neighbour, and perhaps I would never have been in the right place for that moment but . . . well. I went downstairs and a few minutes later down they come. And they explain that they are in love.'

'Oh!' Lucy exclaimed. 'Well, that's sort of lovely, right?'

'And they have been for the past thirty years,' Alex went on.

'Oh my God, they've been secretly in love all this time and now they are just getting together, that's actually romantic, when you think about it, isn't it?'

'No, well, I mean, yes. Except they've also been secretly carrying on for all of those thirty years too. Without telling me. Which I get, when I was a little kid, or a stroppy teen even, but I'm twenty-eight now.

I've been an adult for ten years. And Dad still kept it from me.'

'Oh, well maybe that was off, but maybe . . .'

'That's not the worst of it,' Alex told her, emptying the last of the bottle of wine as she remembered the moment her dad told her about the love of his life. He had his pyjama bottoms on backwards, and Mrs O'Dowd had dressed hastily, with the buttons of her shirt done up all wrong. It would have been funny, except . . . 'They've been having an affair for thirty years.'

'You said.' Lucy frowned.

'My mum left him twenty-five years ago. When I was three years old. That's when it hit me. My mum left home because he was having an affair.'

'Oh,' Lucy said.

'He was having an affair with the neighbour before they even got married, he was having an affair with her when my mum had me. And when she left, without me, he was having an affair then, and every single day afterwards. So that's why I ran away to Poldore, Lucy. Because I'm in love my best friend who calls me Al and is getting married to a beautician, and because everything I thought I knew about my life, my family, my relationship with my dad, has been a lie.' Alex's voice faltered as she tried to down the rising swell of emotion with another glass of wine. 'I wish I'd never told Marcus how I felt about him, I wish he'd never treated me and my feelings as a joke, and I wish I'd never found out about my dad's secret life, and I really wish I'd never seen him in bed with the neighbour. But I did, and I can't get my head round any of those things, no matter how much I try. And I can't be at home any more, because it doesn't feel like home now. And for most of my life everything I have ever done has been about pleasing Dad or Marcus. So I came down here. I thought I'd please myself for a change.'

Lucy said nothing for a moment as she watched Alex across the table.

'So what I'm going to say if anyone asks is that you wanted to break the glass ceiling in harbour management, and came down here to strike a blow for feminism.'

'Really?' Alex said. 'You'll keep all that to yourself?'

'Listen,' Lucy said. 'I know what it's like to be in love with someone who will never love you back. I've been in love with a man for ages now, a good, decent, kind man I think. But he won't ever love me back, because . . . well, you know.'

'How do you know?' Alex asked her, wiping a thumb under each eye and sniffing noisily.

'Because he doesn't know about me,' Lucy said. 'He's crew on the ocean liner that docks here every few months, an engineer. We email when he's not here and, when he is, we meet up out of town for a drink or coffee. We've only ever talked, and we write to each other all the time. He's so sweet, so gentle . . . ' Lucy looked sad. 'But he won't understand about me. And one day someone will tell him. Just like whoever it was who told that tourist in the pub yesterday.'

'Then why don't you take control and tell him?' Alex asked her. 'How do you know he won't understand if you don't give him the chance to.'

'The thing is I am safe in Poldore,' Lucy told her. 'This whole town is my family, they protect me, they care about me, just like they do everyone else local, that is except for the person that decided to tell that tourist about me, and I have my suspicions about who that was, but on the whole here I know I am accepted. On the outside though, out there, Alex –' she paused, examining her shell-pink nails '– people are cruel, and scared, and they don't understand that I am just a person. Just a woman.'

'But I get it, and I haven't always known and I'm not a part of the Poldore family,' Alex protested.

'I think you actually sort of are, already,' Lucy said. 'Everyone likes you a lot.'

'Do they?' Alex smiled. 'That's nice. I was never the popular girl at home. At work I was the . . . tomboy. At school, Marcus's sidekick. I was always the tomboy.'

'Everyone always knew you one way, that's why,' Lucy said. 'And when they know you one way, they don't want you to change. That's the trouble with growing up with people who have known you all your life.'

'But you changed.' Alex sat back in her chair and looked at the self-assured woman opposite her. 'You changed about as much as it is possible for a person to change.'

'No.' Lucy smiled. 'I didn't change, I was always me. I just changed my body to match my heart, to match what was on the inside. And everyone close to me understood that – well, Mum still has a bit of a problem with it now and then. She misses him.' Lucy nodded at a picture of a skinny little boy sitting cross-legged on a rock, the sea in the background, his eyes squinting against the sun. 'She had hopes and dreams for him, you see, a version of his future that was never going to happen. And she's still sad about that. But we are getting to know each other again, slowly. The thing that makes her the most sad is that she can't imagine any hopes or dreams for me now, she can't see how I will ever live a normal life, or have a normal future, and to be honest sometimes, neither can I.'

'And I can't see a way to be friends with my best friend again, or even know who my dad is any more, or me, for that matter,' Alex said thoughtfully. 'Because for years I was defined by being a devoted daughter and the perfect best mate, I put everything into that and now . . . I've run away to Poldore. One thing I envy about you, Lucy, you know who you are, maybe better than anyone else I've ever met.'

'Well, that's true,' Lucy said. 'But I don't know what

sort of future is possible for me, or if I will always be stuck in Poldore, because this is the only place I feel safe, living a sort of half-life.'

'So I came here to hide, and you stay here to hide,' Alex said.

'And that's what everyone expects of us,' Lucy added.

'Well, you know what we've got to do then,' Alex said, looking her new best friend in the eye. 'We've got to surprise them all.'

Chapter Ten

The moon was high in a cloudless sky as Alex made her way, a little haphazardly, up the stone steps to her cottage, but nevertheless with a spring in her step. There were a lot of things that she had never expected when she came to Poldore – the sheer pleasure of working in a place that was so beautiful, to be welcomed so completely and so quickly by the locals, to gain a pet, at least by association, but most of all she hadn't expected to find someone who she so easily fell into a friendship with, and yet that had happened. What did it mean that Alex, stubborn, shy Alex, the girl who had her people and never particularly felt the need to extend her tiny circle of friends, had made her first new friend since she was eleven years old? Had perhaps her old life in Grangemouth been holding her back? Alex had always thought her father had taught her how to cope with anything that life might throw at her, but he had missed out an important component – as strong, and as determined, and as competent as she was at her work, Alex had never learned how to be social. But look at her now, accepted in Poldore, with at least one new proper friend to call on. The prospect of Christmas didn't seem so terrible to her any more, even if it did involve her dressing up and holding a plastic baby that weed on her, because she was part of something, at the heart of something. Alex Munro wasn't on the periphery any more.

'Ha,' she said to Buoy, who came hurtling out of the darkness. 'I'll show them, the bastards.'

Buoy didn't seem interested in her epiphany; instead he was dancing around her feet, growling and barking, running back into the dark, where Alex now realised he was snarling at something, and then back to her heels. He was trying to tell her there was something lurking in the shadows.

The warm wine fuzz that had stayed with Alex from the moment that she left Lucy's cottage was gone in an instant, as Buoy stayed by her feet growling at the darkness. It was impossible to see anything, but Alex knew they weren't alone.

'My dog's ferocious,' she warned whoever it was. 'He'll rip your throat out.'

'When the hell did you start liking dogs anyway?' A voice sounded out of the gloom, at the exact moment a shadowy figure loomed and Buoy pounced, a terrible growl ripping from his throat.

'Fuck, Al, call the mutt off will you!' Marcus said, as Buoy went to work in earnest on his trouser leg.

Alex said nothing for several seconds. *Marcus. Marcus is here.*

'Al, I'm serious, he's gumming at my leg, it's gross.'

'Buoy, it's OK, stand down.' Alex called the dog's name for want of knowing what else to do, and no one was more surprised than her when Buoy let go of Marcus's leg and trotted back to her side, sitting on her foot with a kind of possessive quality that Alex found unexpectedly comforting. Marcus was standing outside her door.

'What are you doing here?' she asked him.

'No, Al,' he said. 'What are *you* doing here? Mate, you more or less disappeared overnight and no one knows why.'

Alex smarted. Really? Did he really mean that he didn't know why she went or was he pretending to save face? If he really had no idea why she left town then she might as well go and throw herself down the steep stone steps now. Except, no. Except that she was making a life here that didn't revolve around her crush on him, Alex reminded herself sternly.

'I wouldn't exactly say that,' she said. 'I had a leaving do, they bought me a six-foot inflatable banana for no apparent reason. I handed in my notice. You knew what I was doing. You knew I was leaving.'

'Sure,' Marcus said. 'Sure I knew you were leaving, but I didn't know what it would be like until you'd actually gone, and suddenly I'm wondering . . . What are you doing here, Al?'

Alex sighed heavily: it seemed it wasn't as easy to

leave her past behind as she had hoped. 'I suppose you'd better come in.'

Marcus filled up the tiny living room in a way that made Alex excruciatingly uncomfortable. He'd been a giant since primary school, towering over all the other kids in a decade and more of school photographs. Alex hadn't forgotten, but more put out of her mind, exactly what a big man he was. Tall, broad, muscular, he'd been told for much of his life that if he'd applied himself he had enough natural talent to play rugby for Scotland. Marcus had never been one to worry about applying himself though. He lived life for fun, and he'd worry about next week when it came. The drinks after a match were always his favourite part of a rugby match, the prettiest girl in the room always the one he honed in on. He was always the one in Alex's small group of friends to think up the next fun thing to do. And Alex had never been sorry that Marcus was so content with his small, uncomplicated life in Grangemouth, not if it meant he stuck around and kept calling her every day, opening each conversation with something like, 'Hey, Al, I'm bored, what shall we get up to tonight?'

Yes, Alex thought as she made tea in the kitchenette, attempting not to let him know she was looking at him, he always was a big man. The only man that made tall, lumpy, ungainly Alex feel . . . well, womanly. Not that he ever noticed that about her.

Buoy sat on the worn rug in front of Marcus, staring

at him, and growling on a low level loop. It amused Alex to see how uncomfortable the little, aged mongrel made Marcus feel, and it felt like she had an ally, a small, still reasonably flowery-scented four-legged knight in fur, protecting her. Albeit mainly from herself and her stupid heart.

'Nice place,' Marcus said, as Alex handed him a mug of milky tea, four sugars, just the way he liked it. She sat on the only other chair at the rickety table, and Buoy relocated from his position in front of Marcus to her side, where he sat his bony backside on her booted foot, and leaned into her thigh, resting his head on her knee until she placed the palm of her hand on his head. Alex found that she appreciated his show of solidarity much more than she expected.

'Well, it's barely more than a hovel right now,' Alex said. 'I've not had time to think about where I'm living since I got here, but maybe after Christmas I can start making it feel more like home.'

'So, it is home now?' Marcus asked her.

'Yes, Marcus. I left my job, I moved out of the country, to the furthest away part of England. It was never going to be just for the weekend, was it?'

Marcus said nothing for a moment, staring into the fire that Alex had expertly built while the kettle had been boiling.

'I saw your dad,' he said.

'Did you?' Alex fingers wound more tightly into

Buoy's fur and he pressed the top of his head further into her palm in response.

'He feels like shite,' Marcus said.

'Does he?' Alex pressed her lips together. It wasn't a phrase that her father would have ever used. Marcus was summarising in his own unique way.

'Come on, Al.' Marcus leaned forwards in the chair suddenly, eliciting a low warning growl deep in Buoy's throat, which made him sit back again. 'This isn't something you can do a typical Al over, and pretend you don't care when you do. I know you, remember? I know you're not the tough chick you like everyone to think you are, not really.'

'Do you?' Alex said. 'Do you really know me?'

'He told me everything, Al,' Marcus said. 'About you finding him and Mrs O'Dowd, about their relationship . . . everything. He feels bad, Al. He feels terrible. He just wants to talk to you. I mean seriously, I don't blame you for legging it, that is one hell of a head fuck, but you know. Give your dad a break, he's your dad, man.'

'Well, he had twenty-eight years to talk to me,' Alex said simply. 'Years to tell me the truth about him and my mother, and her. Maybe I spent too long letting the people I care about take me for granted. Good old Al, dependable Al, you can walk all over her, Al. Lie to her for all of her life, treat her like a piece of crap, and she won't mind. Not Al. Break her heart and she'll still make you a cup of tea.'

Alex stopped herself, she was dangerously close to saying too much, and she didn't want to go through Marcus rejecting her again.

'Al . . .' Marcus trailed off. 'Alex, Alexandra. I miss you, woman.'

Alex looked up at him, determined not to let the tears that were obscuring her vision spill.

'You miss me,' she repeated quietly. 'Really?'

"Course I do.' Marcus smiled, that same sweet smile that always made Alex's heart do a triple double flip. 'I think I've seen you almost every day of my life since we were four. You're like . . . It's like, you know, when you have the radio on all the time and you get used to it, and then someone turns it off and suddenly it's too quiet?'

'You're comparing me to background noise?' Alex said, a smile tugging at her mouth, failing not to be touched.

'No, I'm comparing you to my best friend,' Marcus said. 'My person, my most important person. Look, all this business with your dad, you need to sort that out sooner or later. But I'm not here for him, I'm here for me. I need you, Al. I . . . I'm not good at touchy feely stuff, but . . . I know I did something wrong, I just don't exactly know what it was. One minute you were telling me you love me, and I was about to ask you to be my best man, and then . . . you'd gone. I tried phoning you, you never pick up.'

Marcus dropped his head, running his fingers through his thick red hair.

'I've got no service here,' Alex said. 'I'll get it changed sooner or later.'

'Look, I can be a bit of a prick, and I was really drunk at the engagement do. Maybe I said something, did something to offend you, but I can't remember it, Al, not all of it. Will you tell me so I can say sorry and we can go back to being friends?'

Alex tried to stop it, the well of love and affection that surged upwards through her body, as she listened to Marcus saying perhaps the most words he had ever said in one go in his entire life.

Don't be in love with him, she told herself. He's telling you he was either too drunk or too mortified to want to acknowledge what you said to him at the engagement party, even if he is saying it in the sweetest, loveliest way ever. He's hoping you can reset back to being just good friends, and he will get everything he wants, you and Milly, and a wedding, and you, you will be a tortured soul for ever and ever. Don't do it, Alex, don't do it.

But it was too late, because Alex had always loved him hopelessly, and it turned out that even moving to the other end of England didn't change that.

'You want me to be your best man?' Alex asked him.

'Yeah, well, woman. You can wear a dress. Millie said she wanted to choose what you wore, but I said, sod off, you are in charge of the bridesmaids, not my lot. So you can wear what you like.'

Alex chuckled. 'Milly should be in charge of what I wear, what if I turned up in a great big wedding dress?'

The smile on her face quickly faded as she considered the possibility, quite seriously for a second.

'Are you saying yes? You'll come back and be my best man? Woman, I mean?'

Alex looked into his sandy-coloured eyes and felt her heart breaking all over again, just as it did with every heartbeat that she was around Marcus.

'I'll come back for the wedding, Marcus, to support you. But I live here now, I love it here.'

Marcus nodded. 'I'll take that. I've still got time to persuade you to come back for good.'

'Why do you want me to come back for good?' Alex asked him. 'You'll be married, sitting on the sofa, holding hands, watching TV every night, little ones on the way before you know it.'

Marcus frowned, knotting his fingers together. 'So can I stay here then?'

'Here, here?' Alex asked him.

'Yeah, I've got a few days' leave I had to take, so I booked them all off. Thought you and me could hang out, you know. Pub every night. What's the clubbing like round here?'

'What does Milly think about you being down here,

just before Christmas? Clubbing? With me. Not that there are any nightclubs.'

'She's fine about it, why wouldn't she be?' Marcus asked, which for some reason hurt Alex more than she expected. 'Can I stay, meet the locals? It will be a laugh. Oh, go on Alex. I promise I won't embarrass you.'

'Well, that's a promise you can't keep,' Alex said. 'And besides there's only one bedroom, and one bed.'

'Well, we can share, can't we? We've done it before!' Marcus grinned and, for one wild moment, Alex imagined herself in bed with him, in his arms, his fingers entwined in her hair, as he feverishly kissed her neck, her soft yielding flesh pressed into his hard, taut body and . . . she knew it was going to be a long, sleepless night.

'You didn't mention the mutt,' Marcus said in the darkness after several moments of silence punctuated only by Buoy's snoring.

'He lived here before me,' Alex whispered, on the other side of the dog, who, instead of taking his usual place towards the bottom of the bed, had positioned himself in-between them, his head on the pillow pointing in the direction of Marcus, who was benefiting from his less than fragrant breath. 'So really he is sharing his bed with us.'

'Fuck,' Marcus said, rolling over.

He obviously wasn't that disturbed though, because

after a few more minutes Alex heard his breathing level out and he began to snore. Marcus was here, in Poldore, in her bed. And, yes, there was a dog guarding her honour, stretched out between them, preventing any chance of them touching in the night. And yet Alex couldn't help thinking that this was just about the happiest moment of her life.

Chapter Eleven

22 December

Alex was humming at her desk the next morning, feeling ridiculously happy at the thought of Marcus stretched out to his full height and breadth in her bed, now that Buoy had left it, and still sleeping. Just the idea of him being there made her ridiculously happy. It went back on everything, everything that she had agreed with Lucy only last night, but that was different. Lucy had a real quest, a proper journey to go on. Alex couldn't fight something as inevitable and as permanent as the actual love of her life. And he was here, in her bed. Not in Scotland with Milly, but here. Maybe Marcus himself didn't know what that meant yet, but Alex thought that just by being here his heart was telling him something that that thick skull of his hadn't processed yet.

'Morning.' Ruan appeared in the doorway, with a hesitant smile, pausing to look at her. 'Did I behave like a bit of idiot last night?'

'If you are referring to storming out of the pageant

rehearsal because Sue mentioned something about Marissa liking you,' Alex said cheerfully. 'Then, yes.'

'I'm sorry.' Ruan walked into the office and sat down on the chair on the other side of the desk. 'Cordy says I'm too moody for my own good. She says I've got to stop wandering around stuck in my own Daphne du Maurier novel and start lightening up a bit. It's this time of year, Christmas, you know. It makes me . . .'

He paused, struggling to describe what Christmas made him feel, but Alex understood the mix of emotions that the season of goodwill brought with it without him having to. Even before the mess with Marcus and her dad had happened, it had been a difficult time of year for her. Another year gone when she had no idea where her mother was, what she was doing, or if she ever thought of her. And yet another year stretching ahead when everything would be exactly the same as it had always been.

'To be fair,' Alex said with a smile, 'Cordelia wasn't exactly a bag of laughs last night either. She seems quite possessive of her big brother.'

'Not possessive,' Ruan said. 'Protective. We lost our parents early. My dad got sick, cancer. Died when I was fourteen, and Cordy just eight. Mum never got over it, couldn't bear living here without him so . . .'

'Oh no.' Alex looked appalled. 'She killed herself?'

'She moved to Suffolk,' Ruan said, with a wry smile. 'Not until a few years after. I was eighteen, and I wanted to stay because . . . I had a lot to want to stay for. Cordy was settled in school, and we decided she would stay with us, with me at least until she finished school. Which she did, but Suffolk seemed even less exciting to her than here, so she stayed. My eldest sister, Keira, she lives near Mum now. My middle sister, Tamsyn, she lives in Paris doing fashion. Keira, her family and Mum are out there with her this Christmas, have a Bon Noel, or something. So Cordy looks after me, and I look after her. Although she's nigh on impossible to look after, and I'm a moody pain in the arse . . . especially at this time of year. You must think I'm a prat.'

'I don't,' Alex chuckled. 'Christmas is always supposed to be so happy and jolly, when a lot of the time it just makes everyone feel worse. It's like Valentine's Day times a hundred.'

'Is it?' Ruan said, tipping his head to one side, as he watched her. 'I never pay much attention to either, myself.'

Alex found that it was rather disconcerting to have his full attention, those dark eyes lingering on her face for a moment, as if he were really looking at her for the first time, although Alex couldn't think of a good reason why. She looked just as scruffy as she always did. 'Anyway, it was Marissa who was the one who was really put out. Did she find you last night?'

'Yep.' Ruan nodded once. 'She found me.'

Alex didn't have time to consider what that rather

cryptic statement might mean, as she turned back to the radio for a moment, communicating with a yacht that was coming into harbour, giving them bearings. She was supposing that it had probably involved some sort of secret assignation when she became aware that Ruan hadn't left, but was watching her closely.

'What?' she asked as soon as she had finished.

'You've got a spring in your step this morning,' he said. 'You look sort of shiny.'

'Do I?' Alex touched her face.

'I don't mean literally,' Ruan laughed. 'I mean you are shining, from the inside out. It suits you. You're all peaches and cream.'

'Oh!' Alex was so taken aback by the unexpected compliment that she laughed.

'Fine, maybe I mean you have roses in your cheeks then,' Ruan said. 'A sparkle in those blue, blue eyes.'

'Oh.' Alex felt her cheeks flush. When had Ruan noticed what colour her eyes were? 'An old friend has come to stay that's all.'

'That's nice,' Ruan said. 'You've probably been homesick, it's good to have a friend come and cheer you up a bit. You should bring her to the pub.'

'Oh well . . .'

'Anyway, I need to talk to you about my new tour.'

'A new tour?' Alex blinked; the small talk, and any more observations about her, were obviously over.

'Yeah, I'm losing money hand over fist. People don't

care about long-dead writers' houses any more, or castles, or smugglers' caves. There are a load of world famous celebrities living up there on the cliff, so I'm starting a coastal tour, complete with a set of binoculars for every punter. I'll take them along Millionaires' Row and they can see if they can spot a celebrity. First tour this afternoon.'

'You can't do that!' Alex was appalled. 'That's invasion of privacy, that's organised peeping Tomery!'

'They do it in Hollywood all the time, only on buses,' Ruan protested. 'And, anyway, they come down here, invade my town. Turn it into a flipping playground for the rich and famous. There's no money in fishing here any more, hasn't been for years. The lads that still do it scrape by, no more. They've all but shut down the clay works because it's cheaper to do it in China.' Ruan stood up abruptly. 'This is my home, Alex. I was born here, my family goes back just as far as the Montaignes even if we don't have a big fancy castle to show for it. I have more right to be here than film stars living in glass boxes do, and I will do what it takes to stay here.'

'But just because they are rich, and famous, and can afford to live here, it doesn't mean they don't deserve some privacy in their own homes!' Alex argued. 'You're exploiting them, and maybe they do have a lot of money, but they are pouring it into this town, keeping it going when it could be dying on its feet.'

'What would you know anyway?' Ruan said, marching

to the door and flinging it open. 'You don't know anything about living round here. I wasn't coming in here asking for your permission, I was informing you of what I was doing. I'll keep you up-to-date about the times and my movements in the harbour, and that is really all you need to know.'

'Ruan!' Alex stood up as he stormed out, and stamped her foot in fury as he slammed the door on her. 'Oh bloody hell!' she told the closed door. 'Just flipping shut up, you smug git!'

And Alex didn't know why a disagreement with a virtual stranger eclipsed her good mood and unsettled her for the rest of the day, but it did.

'Good day?' Lucy asked as Alex arrived in the Silent Man to meet Marcus. 'How's your end of Operation "Get a Life" going, well?'

'Yes and no,' Alex said. 'Or possibly just no. When I got home Marcus was sitting on my doorstep.'

Lucy eyes widened. 'He came to tell you it was you he loves all along? Oh that's wonderful!'

'No, not exactly. Well, not at all actually. He came to ask me to be his best man,' Alex admitted. 'But he came, all this way for me, which has to mean something, right?'

'Maybe,' Lucy said uncertainly. 'But I'm not sure that it counts towards moving on with your life, in any way whatsoever.'

'It doesn't,' Alex agreed. 'Except as soon as I saw him, everything came back, not that it ever really went away. All the feelings I had been trying to pretend I don't have for him just burst out of me. And he is *here*. Because he missed *me*. And, like I said, that has to mean something. It's my second chance to try to make it happen between us.'

'But he's getting married!' Lucy said, through a fixed grin, keeping her voice low so that no one else at the bar would hear their conversation.

'I know,' Alex said. 'But . . . what if I spend the rest of my life wondering what could have been?'

She glanced over to the corner where Ruan was sitting, nursing a pint while another drink in a clear, tall glass fizzed at his side; perhaps Marissa was in the ladies.

'And *he's* been a right pig today too,' Alex scowled. 'I don't know why he finds it so hard just to be pleasant. I disagreed with him over this new tour he's got lined up and it was like World War Three. He totally went nuclear on me. I mean, touchy or what, what's wrong with him?'

'December the twenty-second,' Lucy said, watching Ruan for a moment. 'That's what's wrong with him.'

'What?' Alex looked confused.

'It's not for me to say,' Lucy said. 'You know me, I don't gossip.'

'Why is he sitting on his own there, looking like the

world's about to end? It can't just be because we had words over his stupid tour. And why is everyone in the town that takes care of its own ignoring him?'

Lucy looked thoughtful. 'Because everyone knows that he likes to be on his own today. Today is a day for remembering.'

'Well, I don't know,' Alex said, feeling suddenly infuriated with Ruan for sitting there, looking so sad, and with Lucy for not telling her what was going on. 'And if you won't tell me I'll have to ask him myself.'

'Alex, come back!' Lucy pleaded, but Alex ignored her as she went and sat down at Ruan's table. She was aware of the hush that followed her, and the exchanged glances as she took her seat.

She nodded at the spare drink. 'Am I interrupting something?' Her voice was tight, clipped and cross. She couldn't work out what exactly it was about him that exasperated her so much. What business was it of hers if he wanted to sit on his own and mope, what difference did it make to her? And yet she couldn't leave him alone.

'Yes,' he said. 'Please, Alex. Just leave it.'

'But why?' Alex demanded. 'Seriously, Ruan, I get it. I get that you are worried about your business and annoyed with me because I don't happen to agree that snooping on people is a good way to earn a living, but can't we just disagree? Does it always have to be war if we don't see eye to eye?'

Alex was surprising herself more as every second went by, this was most unlike her, and she found she quite liked being direct and saying it like it was.

'This is not about you,' Ruan said. 'Alex, please go away.'

Alex heard the pub fall into virtual silence behind her, as everyone was listening to their conversation, even if they were pretending not to. What *was* she doing trying to force this man to engage in a conversation with her that he clearly didn't want? Normally, she would be happy to retreat, to let him go his way, without a second glance. Alex told herself to get up, go back to the bar and leave him alone. But her feet didn't move. The trouble was she cared about him, she realised. She didn't like to see him sad.

'What is it?' she asked him, more gently this time. 'Is your business really in that much trouble?'

When Ruan looked up at her, his expression was one that was so full of pain that it sat Alex back in her chair.

'Please, Alex, I'm sorry about earlier. Just . . . please.'

He got up, leaving both drinks, and walked out of the pub. Alex thought for the briefest of moments and then she went after him, whispered murmurs following her out of the pub. The poor man was in pain, and she couldn't just pretend she didn't know that, no matter how much he might want her to. He was not difficult to find, he hadn't gone very far. She found him at the quay, looking out towards the mouth of the estuary and the sea beyond. It looked choppy and rough, white-peaked waves rushing inland. The sea didn't look like a friendly place tonight. Ruan turned away from her as she approached.

'Oh, Ruan . . .' Alex was caught in a moment of indecision. Talking to people about feelings was absolutely not her area of expertise. She had no idea why she had persisted in harassing Ruan to this moment as it was, other than she just knew she couldn't leave him sitting on his own that way.

'I'm so sorry, I don't know what's wrong with me,' she said. 'Here I am banging on about privacy and I'm practically stalking you, trying to make you talk about your feelings. I've turned into my worst nightmare. Look, my friend will be here in a minute, so I'll go back inside, tell everyone I'm sorry for being awful. You can come back in and we can pretend like this never happened and start again . . . again?'

Alex waited for a second for a response, but when Ruan remained silent, she turned and began to walk back to the pub.

'Don't go,' Ruan said, so quietly that for a moment she thought she might not have heard him correctly. 'Stay, please.'

Alex took the three or four steps required to stand beside him, and sensed that now would not be a good time to look at his face.

'It's four years ago today since my girlfriend, my fiancée, went missing, presumed drowned,' Ruan told her, quite calmly. 'They wouldn't let me go out and look for her that night. I had to wait here. I waited and waited. I sat at the bar with her usual gin and tonic for her, for when they brought her home. They found our boat, but they never found her. Every year on this day, I buy her a drink. I think maybe one year she will come and get it.'

Alex closed her eyes. She'd been hounding a grieving man, a lost man, who wanted a few moments to himself, and the realisation horrified her.

'I don't know what to say.' Alex stared at the toes of her boots, battered and worn, the wind picking up suddenly, dragging at her hair, teasing it out of its knot, strand by strand. 'I'm so sorry.'

'I'd known Merryn since we were kids,' Ruan told her. 'Fell in love with her when I was sixteen and she was the May Queen. She was like the perfect summer in a person, yellow hair, skin that glowed. Never stopped laughing, I loved how much she laughed. Took me almost a year to get her to go out with me. She used to say, "I'm not going to go out with you unless you promise to love me forever, Ruan Thorne." I promised and I promised and eventually she let me take her for a picnic. It was . . . the perfect afternoon, lying in the long grass on the cliff top, the sun so hot, the only thing in the sky a couple of swallows.'

Alex dared not move, or scarcely breathe, as Ruan conjured up a summer's afternoon, on this sharp December evening. The wind was rattling the Christmas lights strung above their heads, the temperature suddenly dropping as the sea rushed in to meet the shore.

'We were together always from that moment on,' he said. 'Merryn was part of the reason I didn't leave with my mum. We got engaged when we were eighteen, we started the tour business together. We bought a little cottage, where the three of us lived. We were a family. Cordelia worshipped her, I adored her. Our lives revolved around her. I loved her. So much.'

Alex felt the raw emotion in his voice vibrate in the centre of her chest.

'December the twenty-second,' Ruan said. 'It was mild, the sea was flat, the sky was blue. We were getting ready for the pageant. Merryn was helping, painting the floats, she was going to play Mary. We met for lunch, we . . . we argued. We argued a lot, as much as we laughed, it was just the way we were. We'd been together for so long, since we were so young. Nothing scared us about each other, we fought, we made up. We always knew we would make up. So when she stormed off and took a boat out, I didn't think twice about it. I thought we'd make up later. Only she never came back.'

A sudden gush of wind rushed a tide right up the quay, so the freezing spray showered them with salty drops. Alex shuddered, but she didn't move.

'The storm came out of nowhere; some choppy weather was forecast, but nowhere near as bad as it was. She sent off a distress signal, two flares went up. The lifeboat went out, helicopter. Risked their lives for her. She never came back.'

'I'm sorry I made you tell me,' Alex said, lifting a freezing hand, thinking perhaps of touching his arm and then deciding against it.

'You didn't make me,' Ruan said. 'I decided to tell you. To be honest it's sort of nice that you seem to care.'

He turned to look at her. 'It's difficult, when you meet new people. You can't just suddenly tell them everything about you, or why you are the way you are sometimes. But I wanted you to know, because . . . I like you, Alex. I like the fact that you say what you think, and don't fuss about the way you look. You seem like a decent person to me. I like you. A lot.'

'Thank you, I think.' Alex smiled tentatively. 'You must miss her.'

'I do,' Ruan said. 'I do, and I'm angry with her, and I'd like her to walk back up the slipway now so that we could make up. If I had to lose her then I would just have liked to have known that she knew what she meant to me. I'd like to have been able to tell her that I was sorry, I was being an idiot and that she was right, because she was always right.'

Alex shuddered as the wind really began to bite, the

tips of her fingers humming in the cold.

'Come back in and have a drink?' Alex asked him, tentatively tucking her arm into his. 'Come and sit in the corner of the pub, and I promise to leave you alone.'

'Or,' Ruan said, 'you could have a drink with me? Maybe now is the time to stop being alone and to be with friends—'

'There you are!' Marcus appeared out of nowhere, suddenly big and brash and far too loud for the moment. 'I drove the long way round, there didn't seem to be a ferry over, and I've no idea what to do with a boat. It took me *ages*! There are no street lights or signposts round here, what is it a secret or something?' He stopped and looked at Alex's arm in Ruan's. 'All right, mate.'

'Marcus.' Alex didn't really have time to ponder on why she suddenly felt so awkward to be caught with her arm looped through Ruan's. 'Um, this is my friend, Ruan. Ruan, this is my friend Marcus, who I told you about.'

'Not exactly what I was expecting,' Ruan said. He was a tall man, a head's height taller than Alex, but even he looked short next to Marcus.

'Ruan sounds like a girl's name,' Marcus replied. 'Anyway I'm the man in Alex's life, pleased to meet you.'

'And you,' Ruan said pleasantly. But he didn't let Alex remove her arm from his, not all the way back to the pub.

*

'And then she climbed up the tree and hung her PE shorts off the highest branch like a flag!' Marcus delivered the punchline and the whole pub roared with laughter. Of course he'd charmed the entire town of Poldore – with two notable exceptions – within half an hour of arriving. One was a dog, and one was a moody tour boat operator.

'Alex, you didn't!' Lucy bit her lip, as she looked Alex up and down. 'I didn't think you were that sort of girl.'

'It was a dare,' Alex said. 'I assume everyone here understands the basic rules of a dare. You have to go through with it otherwise you lose.'

'What was it your dad used to say, eh, Al?' Marcus nudged her with his elbow. 'If he told you to jump off a cliff, would you?'

'That was it.' Alex beamed up at Marcus, enjoying the feeling of being at his side again. The two of them together made the perfect double act, him like some giant ginger Santa, blustering goodwill, all year round, and she was the straight man. The butt of his anecdotes and one-liners, setting him up with punchline after punchline.

Alex jumped as she felt something wet and cold against her hand and, looking down, found that Buoy was sitting at her feet, wedging himself between her and Marcus.

'Buoy, how did you get here?' she asked.

'Oh, he went out for a pee when I left,' Marcus said. 'I thought he had a way of getting back in the house.'

'Well, did you leave the door open?' Alex asked him.

'Er, no, Al, I locked it. What difference does it make?'

'He can't open a locked door,' Alex said, rubbing Buoy's ears vigorously. 'That was hours ago, and it's freezing. And he's old. He must have walked here the long way round, poor thing. He's got a dodgy hip, you know.'

'Well, he made it, didn't he?' Marcus lifted a hand to get Eddie's attention. 'Landlord, a pint for the dog, please, he obviously needs a drink!'

Everyone laughed again, except Alex, who hugged Buoy hard against her legs. He really was very cold.

'Hey, Buoy.' Eddie leaned over the bar. 'There's a nice fire going out the back, why don't you go through and Becky'll find you something to warm you up a bit, hey old lad?'

Buoy considered the invitation, licked Alex's hand and trotted out the back, much to the amusement of Marcus.

'That dog understands what you are saying?' He laughed. 'I wish I hadn't called him a farting old git now!'

'I tell you what though,' Eddie said, putting two fresh drinks on the bar, 'if old Buoy's come all this way to find you, Alex, that means something.'

'What?' Alex asked him. 'That he was hungry?'

'He owns you now. He's your dog. He likes you, Alex, you've got his stamp of approval. Old Buoy, he doesn't fall in love that often, but when he does it's for life.'

'There you go, Al,' Marcus said, slapping her on the back. 'I always said that there was someone out there for you, didn't I always say it?'

Marcus was in full swing when Alex escaped to the ladies. She washed her face and pulled her hair out of its clip, fluffing it around her shoulders. Milly had hair the colour of honey, and skin that was always amber. And breasts that weren't especially big, but that were perfectly round and never moved, and cost three thousand pounds the pair. She had the narrowest hips on an adult woman that Alex had ever seen, and she saw them a lot because they were permanently on display. As Alex stared at herself in the ladies mirror, she tightened the fabric of her loose sweater over her breasts and stomach, comparing herself to the tiny perfect doll that Milly was. Marcus had never looked at her the way he looked at countless other girls, and most recently Milly, with naked desire in his eyes. But she had always been waiting for him to realise what a great person she was, assuming that the physical side would come later. Maybe that was her mistake. Marcus knew full well that she was a great person and a brilliant friend. After all he missed her enough to come all this way to win her back. What he had never, ever noticed was that she was a woman, a woman who, perhaps with a little bit of help, could be desirable. Alex pulled her sweater off. Underneath she was wearing a black singlet, and under that a sensible firm support bra. It wasn't exactly femme fatale territory, but it showed off the generous curve of her bosom and her reasonably flat stomach. She had never been a shopper, but when she bought jeans, she bought them in size fourteen, and there was maybe a half a centimetre gap around her waistline, although they fitted snugly on her behind.

'Hourglass figure,' Lucy told her as she walked into the ladies. 'You are so lucky.'

'Am I?' Alex asked her, holding the top up to cover her chest.

'Yes, you've got it all going on.' She nodded at Alex's black vest. 'What's this about then? Are you getting your kit off for Marcus?'

'No,' Alex said. 'I'm a bit hot, that's all.'

'Alex, it's like minus forty degrees outside. Look, if you are going to do this, if you are going to play the tits card, then do it right. Shoulders back, chin up and thrust them out.'

'Oh my God, I don't think so!' Alex said, horrified.

'Fine, let's just spruce you up a little bit then, OK?' Lucy stood in front of Alex, turning her away from the mirror and fanned her raven black hair around her shoulders. Then she stuck her hand in her pocket and pulled out a little stubby eyeliner, putting just a touch in the far corners of Alex's eyes, and then just a tiny smear of clear lip gloss.

'There, now you look like you haven't tried at all,' she said. 'And you look great.'

'I don't think I want to try,' Alex said, staring at herself, surprised by how intense her blue eyes suddenly seemed. 'No, it feels all wrong. I don't know how to be girly, I don't know how to even walk like a girl, or what to do with these.' She patted her chest.

'Well you're not supposed to juggle them, if that's what you're thinking,' Lucy said. 'Don't *do* anything, just be you. But with a fairly tight top on.'

'Nope, I've changed my mind,' Alex said stretching the neck of the sweater to pull it back over her head. Suddenly Lucy whipped it out of her hand and bolted for the door.

'If you want your nun's habit,' she called through the door, 'you will have to come and get it. Now remember, shoulders back, thrust!'

Alex stared at the closed door and seethed for several moments, before taking a breath, and re-emerging into the bar. The crowd around Marcus was now three or four people deep, and Alex couldn't hear exactly what he was saying, but from the way everyone was laughing she guessed it had something to do with one of their escapades. The thought of pushing her way through the throng to get back to her bar stool appalled her, as she stood on the edge of the action.

'He's very . . . enthusiastic,' Ruan said, appearing at her side.

'I know,' Alex said. 'I'm sorry. This was the last thing you needed tonight. Marcus always turns every night into a party.'

'Nah,' he said. 'I can't expect the whole world to join in with me when I'm finding things . . . tricky. Are you OK with him coming down here, telling everyone all these stories about you from when you were kids?'

Yes,' Alex said, surprised that he would even ask the question. 'Yes, I think I am, I mean why not?'

'Well, because you've come here to be yourself, haven't you? Not the person that everyone is always telling you to be.'

'Oh, I hadn't thought about it like that,' Alex said.

'Want to come to my place?' Ruan said quite suddenly.

'What?' Alex said. 'To the lighthouse?'

'Yes, for a glass of wine and bit of peace and quiet. I'll take you home afterwards.'

'I'm not sure I should,' Alex said. 'I mean I've got a guest.'

'Your guest looks pretty busy,' Ruan said, glancing back at the pub. 'Look, don't worry about it, I shouldn't have asked.'

A burst of raucous laughter rocketed from the bar. Maybe it would do Marcus good if when he finally noticed that she wasn't sitting next him Alex wasn't there any more.

'Actually you know, what, yes, OK,' she said. 'Let's go.'

Ruan looked at her for a fraction longer than felt comfortable.

'You better grab your jumper though,' he said. 'You'll freeze to death if you go out in just that.'

Chapter Twelve

The sea was choppy and rough, even for Ruan's fairly substantial motor cruiser. As he took her around the headland towards the lighthouse, the moon was lost behind cloud, and Alex, who had worked around boats her whole life, was surprised by how dark it was and how remote it felt, even just a little way out to sea.

'I don't think I know enough about sailing,' she said, a spray of water drenching her. 'I know how to parallel park a container ship, but I have no idea how to handle a little boat like this all by myself.'

'I could teach you,' Ruan offered, his eyes fixed on the dark shore, only just visible against the dense night sky.

'Really, would you?' Alex asked him. 'That would be great. I'd love to know how to sail.'

'We'll start in the spring,' Ruan said, as he guided the boat into a jetty lit with a string of fairy lights, which rattled in the wind. 'When it's good and windy and freezing cold and raining all the time. Best time of year to learn.'

'Oh I can't wait.' Alex grinned; the idea that she would still be here, still know Ruan in a few months' time and be learning to sail made her feel happy. She hadn't thought about Marcus once, not since she'd climbed into the boat. It was like the further away from him, the less of a hold he had on her. Not that he knew he had this power over her, Alex thought. If he knew he'd laugh himself silly.

Ruan offered her a hand and helped her climb up onto the jetty.

'Careful, it's slippy,' he told her, letting go of her fingers and striding into the dark beyond the spangle of brave little lights. 'I'm really glad you came.'

'Are you?' Alex called after him, taking her time along the greasy surface of the jetty.

'Yes,' his voice came from the darkness. 'It's been ages since I've shown anyone the lighthouse for the first time. The first time is always the best.'

Alex found him standing at the bottom of the cliff where a metal box was set into the rock. Taking a bunch of keys from his pocket he opened the box and flicked the single red switch inside.

Suddenly a set of stone steps, cut into the rock, appeared in the darkness, every step lit with its own individual light, almost as if he had conjured up a constellation of stars out of nowhere and bent it to his will.

'Wow,' Alex breathed, smiling like a child as she

looked up the steps. 'Wow. It looks like it should lead all the way to a spaceship.'

'That's what I'm talking about,' Ruan said happily. 'And this is just the beginning. Come on, you first. Take it easy, it's a steep climb, it's broken fitter men than you.'

'Yes, well, I am a woman,' Alex reminded him as she enthusiastically embarked on the climb, like a small child desperate to get to the top of a tree.

'I had noticed,' Ruan said, the comment snatched away by the wind before it reached Alex's ear.

She wasn't so much out of breath when she got to the top as unable to even draw a single breath. She threw herself down on the wet springy grass and laughed with the sheer joy of it. Ruan stood over her, grinning.

'Told you,' he said.

'No wonder you are so fit,' Alex said, without really thinking about what she had said.

'Nice of you to mention it.' Ruan laughed. 'Come on, you're drenched.'

Alex clambered to her feet and, despite the burning in her thighs, had to stop herself from jumping for joy when she looked up at the floodlit lighthouse, painted red and white, just like it would be in a children's storybook. Even in the darkness it was enchanting.

Ruan punched a number into another metal box, and took a huge iron key out of it then flicked another switch, which turned the lights on the steps off. 'Want to do the honours?' he asked, offering Alex the key.

Delighted, Alex took it, weighing it in both of her hands. She grinned wildly as she hefted it into the ancient lock, and, after some jiggling, turned the key with a satisfying series of clunks. She caught her breath in anticipation as she pushed the heavy wooden door open, revelling in its screeching creak.

'Go on.' Ruan smiled, nodding that she should go in first. Alex laughed as she entered a perfectly round kitchen. Cornish slate gleamed gently on the floor, oak units swirled around her like warm toffee and in the middle was a handmade oak table of exactly the same colour.

'This is wonderful, it must have cost the earth!' Alex said, running the palm of her hand over the slightly uneven surface of the table.

'No, I built it myself,' Ruan said with more than a touch of pride. 'I reclaimed the wood, some of it from skips. No one wants brown furniture any more, so I just took the wood, sanded it down and remade it. All the cupboard fronts are from different cupboards.'

'Oh, Ruan, it's amazing,' Alex said, clasping her hands together. 'It must have taken you forever.'

She glanced up the open wooden spiral staircase that twisted upwards, and hopped a little bit. 'May I?'

'Yes.' He nodded, clearly taking pleasure in her pleasure.

Alex pulled off her boots and raced up the stairs.

They emerged like the twist of a shell into a living area that was lined with shelves, containing books and vinyl albums, and featured a handmade sofa, which fitted into the embrace of the wall.

'Oh my.' Alex stretched her fingers out and spun around. 'Did you build all this too?'

'Yes,' Ruan said. 'I took out most of the workings of the lighthouse. There was an old iron staircase, quite modern, so took I that out too and built a wooden one. All reclaimed. I learned to upholster to make this sofa.'

'You will make someone an excellent wife,' Alex said, flopping back into the sofa, her arms over her head, as she looked around. 'I feel like I've fallen down a rabbit hole into Narnia.'

'I'm glad you like it,' Ruan said. 'A glass of wine?'

'But we haven't been to the top yet,' Alex said, bouncing up.

'You go and explore, I'll meet you by the bulb,' he told her. 'If I get all the way up there and have to come back to get wine from the kitchen I may lose the will to live.'

Alex didn't need telling twice as she climbed the second flight of stairs.

On the second floor she found two semicircular rooms – a bathroom, with a wonderful old iron bath standing in its centre and a shower curtain suspended from the ceiling that went all the way around, and a smaller sized bedroom, which she guessed must be

Cordelia's when she was here. Someone had painted it deep purple, and an electric guitar stood on a stand in the corner of the room. The next flight of stairs took her to the master bedroom. Alex bit her lip as she looked at the room that Ruan went to bed in every night. It was a simple room, with a large, ancient-looking wardrobe, which looked as if it might grant entry to Narnia, but which Alex saw had been expertly modified to fit the curve of the wall, and an absolutely huge bed, neatly made with clean white linen. Buoy would have loved it. The room was bare, simple. No photos, or pictures anywhere, just a lamp, which stood on the floor by the bed.

'Like what you see?' Ruan asked, as he arrived with a bottle of wine and two mugs, adding apologetically, 'I keep meaning to get glasses.'

'I'm surprised you haven't blown a set yourself,' Alex said. 'This is amazing, it must have taken you years.'

'Almost four years,' Ruan said, and suddenly Alex realised what she was looking at. This was the place that Ruan had poured his grief into, all that he had loved and lost he'd tried to build into the walls of the lighthouse, and Alex couldn't help wondering if he'd bought the lighthouse so he could always keep watch for Merryn's return.

'There's one more place to see,' he said, pulling on a length of thick rope that hung from the ceiling to reveal a ladder unfolding itself.

Alex scrambled up the ladder and found herself standing next to the biggest light bulb she had ever seen, around it a panorama of glass and a few old armchairs.

'They were a bugger to get up here,' Ruan said, sinking into one and gazing out at the dark. Cradling the mugs on his lap, he poured a little wine into each of them.

Alex gazed out into the darkness. 'What happens if you switch the light on?'

'Nothing, it doesn't work any more. I keep it because I like it. And it's part of the history of the place,' Ruan said. He got up and handed Alex a mug, standing next to her.

'Thanks,' he said, as she took a sip.

'For what, coming round here, running round your house like a nutter and drinking your wine?' Alex shot him a sideways look.

'Yes,' Ruan said. 'When I started out on this old place, it felt like I had no other option. It wasn't joy, it was work, it was something to just keep me busy so that I didn't go crazy. The years went by and I kept working on it, kept busy. It wasn't until this year I realised that I love it, that it is a labour of love. And showing it to someone like you, who sees the magic in it, reminds me how lucky I am to have this.'

'Is this where you bring all the women you seduce?' Alex asked mischievously, in the millisecond before it occurred to her that that might not exactly be the most tactful thing to say.

'All the women.' Ruan raised an eyebrow; fortunately he didn't seem too offended. 'There hasn't been anyone serious, not since Merryn. Or at least . . . I don't know, I didn't think it would be possible to even want to feel that way about a person again, but recently, I think perhaps maybe it is. One day. Maybe. It suddenly seems possible again.'

Alex watched his face as he looked out to sea, and she thought about Marissa. There was certainly something going on between them, was she the someone that made him think maybe he could fall in love again? Alex felt a familiar knot of discomfort in her stomach, the same dull ache of missing something she had never really known first hand. Yes, she'd had a crush on Marcus for the longest time, so long that it had become a background hum of longing. But she had never felt loved, not truly, not passionately, by anyone. Perhaps some people were made for it, like Marissa and Milly, and perhaps she just wasn't. And as Alex stood next to Ruan in silence, sipping wine from a chipped mug and staring out to a sea shrouded in the night, she realised that the thought she might never know what it was like to be loved the way he had loved Merryn, the way Marcus loved Milly, the way her father loved Mrs O'Dowd, made her want to cry.

'I'd better get back,' Alex said suddenly, feeling foolish. 'Work in the morning.'

'Oh, right,' Ruan set down his mug. 'Come on then, I'll take you back.'

'Are you sure?' Alex asked him.

'Well, if I don't you'll either have to swim round the headland or walk about fifteen miles upriver to the next crossing.'

'Thanks,' Alex said. 'I don't mean to be a nuisance.'

'You are quite annoying,' Ruan told her. 'But the last thing you are is a nuisance.'

It was very late when Alex got in through the cottage door. Buoy was already in, sitting on the rug by the fire, clearly waiting up for her. Alex tripped over Marcus's shoes, which he had made the mistake of leaving in the middle of the living room floor and which had been thoroughly chewed. Marcus wasn't going to be pleased about that.

At least he had come back to the cottage, Alex thought, feeling guilty for abandoning him, wondering if he'd been worried about where she'd gone. Tired and feeling a little sorry for herself, Alex climbed the narrow stairs. Buoy, a few steps ahead of her, stopped in the doorway of the bedroom, standing stock still, nose pointing at the bed.

Marcus was spreadeagled face down and butt naked in the centre of the bed, his arms and legs reaching out to every corner.

Yelping, Alex covered her eyes, and then peered out from behind her fingers to look at him. He was snoring, and drooling slightly. Covering her eyes again, she turned to Buoy. 'Go on, wake him up, Buoy, go on,' she said, pointing at the bed. 'Bite him, go on, give him a bite on the bum!'

Buoy gave her a look that certainly said, *You must be joking*.

Unhappily, Alex attempted to wake Marcus by poking him with a wire coat hanger, then shaking his ankle so vigorously that his muscular buttocks quivered. Finally, in desperation, she filled the tooth mug in the bathroom with water and trickled a little bit on the back of his head.

'Fuck!' He sprang up at once, whipping over and grabbing her by the waist. Before she knew it, Alex was pinned to the bed by his massive naked frame.

'Shit, Alex,' he said, as his eyes focused on her face, 'you shouldn't sneak up on me, you know I'm army trained.'

'I wasn't sure the Boy Scouts counted as army,' Alex said, swallowing nervously.

'Where did you go?' Marcus asked her. 'One minute you were there, the next you were gone.'

'I . . . needed some air,' Alex said, wondering if she breathed in far enough she might somehow not actually have to touch him.

'Oh well, I missed you,' Marcus said, pausing to study her face.

'Marcus.' Alex squirmed beneath him.

'You look different,' he observed thoughtfully. 'With your hair all messed up.'

'Marcus, the thing is . . .' Alex paused as she felt something shift against her stomach.

'You smell great.' Marcus breathed in the scent of her hair. 'You feel great, Alex. Soft . . .'

'Marcus,' Alex said as she became aware of what exactly it was that was pressing into her abdomen. 'You are quite drunk and very naked.'

'Shit!' Marcus sprang off her and stood up, and then, noticing his own state of naked arousal, swiftly covered the offending part, with his discarded T-shirt. Which only left his muscular shoulders, and strong thighs for Alex to admire. God, she hadn't seen him naked since they were about seven, and she had to say he had improved with age. Apart from the fact that he was bright pink almost from his head to his toes, but even that she found rather fetching.

'Alex, I am so sorry,' he said. 'I just woke up, and you were there and I got confused, and . . . you know.'

'It's OK.' Alex sat up, smoothing her hair off her face, and smiled at him, feeling remarkably composed and in control considering that that was her closest encounter with anything even approaching sex for a very long time. And yet she didn't feel flustered, or nervous, or even like throwing up. 'Um, maybe put some clothes on. I'll turn around.'

She got off the bed and faced the wardrobe. As she heard Marcus shuffle around behind her, she pulled her own vest off and replaced it with an outsize T-shirt. She unhooked her bra, slid the straps off each arm and tugged it through an armhole. She slipped her jeans off and turned around to find Marcus watching her, a look in his eyes that she had never seen before.

Now Alex felt nervous and flustered and a bit like throwing up.

'OK?' she asked him, nervously thinking of the moment before when she felt at least one manifestation of passion, almost in the flesh.

'I . . . ' Marcus looked confused. 'I think I'll check into a B & B tomorrow.'

'OK,' Alex said, as she climbed into bed and drew the cover up to right underneath her chin.

'I mean you and I know this was all a silly drunken jape, but imagine if Milly heard about us, getting naked in bed.'

'You were naked,' Alex pointed out, patting the bed for Buoy, who stayed in the doorway, eyeing them suspiciously.

'You're naked under that T-shirt,' Marcus pointed out.

'I was last night too,' Alex said. 'You didn't have a problem with it then.'

'I don't think I have a problem with it now, and that's the problem.' Marcus sat on the edge of the bed.

'It feels a bit weird now, getting in bed with you. Now I've, well, you know . . .'

'Look,' Alex said, very keen not to have to talk about it any more, 'it's fine. It's just you and me. Let's get some sleep and tomorrow, if it makes you feel better, you can book into a B & B. Eddie might have a room going at the pub.'

'Right then,' Marcus said, as Alex switched off the light and turned her back on him, wondering what it was that made Buoy continue to stay in the doorway.

'Alex,' Marcus said, after a few moments of silence.

'Yes?' Alex asked him drowsily. She suddenly felt very sleepy.

'Tomorrow night, can I take you out for dinner? Somewhere nice, to say thank you, you know for being my best man. Not like a date or anything.'

'Fine,' Alex said, drifting off into a welcome sleep.

'No, certainly not like a date,' Marcus clarified, but only Buoy heard.

It was a long time before either man or dog went to sleep.

Chapter Thirteen

23 December

'*There* you are.' Sue appeared at Alex's side, as she was about to treat herself to a posh coffee for breakfast, with a decidedly lack-lustre Marissa trailing behind, looking tired and bored.

'Here I am!' Alex said, mustering a smile. It was difficult to be as relentlessly upbeat at Sue always seemed to be, and it took some effort to rise to the occasion. How did she manage it, to always be so cheerful, Alex wondered. Perhaps it came from centuries of being in charge of everyone, and no one daring to disagree with you, maybe that was it.

'I must say, you are quite elusive considering what a small town this is.' Sue peered at her with her bright, eagle eyes. 'Eddie told me you were in the Silent Man with your young man last night, but by the time I got there you'd vanished.'

'Yes, there were a couple of people missing from the pub last night,' Marissa said, eyeing Alex suspiciously. 'But the man you turned up with wasn't one of them.'

'Marcus isn't my young man,' Alex clarified, certain that Marissa couldn't be jealous of her going anywhere with Ruan. Someone like Marissa could never think that someone like Alex would be any competition for affections at all. Didn't Marissa know that Alex was always the asexual sidekick best friend? 'Anyway, I thought we were all sorted for the pageant. I put on the costume, get on the float thing, go round the town, stand by the manger, we all sing and then I go to bed?'

'Good to see you're approaching the role with the same dedication and attention to detail as Meryl Streep,' Sue said, which made Alex smile. If only Sue knew exactly how suited she was to the role. 'The big day is almost upon us and tonight is the top secret dress rehearsal. Three a.m., starting at Castle House, we do a completely silent run-through, so as not wake anyone up, and also not to ruin the magic on the real day.'

'Three a.m.?' Alex repeated the most salient detail. 'You're telling me we all get on floats in our costumes and go around the town in silence at three in the morning?'

'Yes, full dress rehearsal, except that we won't have the snow. The snow is very expensive so we have to keep it for the big day, but if a multi-award-winning Hollywood director can't muster up a bit of fake snow, what hope have we got? And keep your lips sealed, OK, we don't want any leaks!'

Alex watched as Sue turned on her booted heels and

marched back up the hill towards Castle House, her auburn curls bouncing purposefully on her shoulders.

'It's almost as if when I took the job as her PA I sold my soul to the devil,' Marissa said, pouting. 'I don't know why she doesn't put a collar round my neck and lead me around like her own private slave.'

'She's not *that* bad. I like her.' Alex looked at Marissa, who looked like she probably hadn't got a lot of sleep recently. 'I like that she's so passionate about the town and its history, and that she wants everyone to be part of everything. She is quite demanding, but I think she's got a huge heart, don't you?'

'She's got a huge arse, that's for sure,' Marissa said. 'Look at it, wobbling around like a jelly. I'm never having kids. The second you have a baby your arse volume increases by six thousand, and you might as well kiss goodbye to ever having a flat stomach again. I mean, sure, motherhood must be nice, but wearing a bikini is better, right?'

'Why *did* you take the job?' Alex asked Marissa, whose fur gilet was zipped up over dark skinny jeans, her patent leather, knee-length stiletto boots gleaming in the pale December sun. Alex wondered if Marissa's story would be the same as Sue's version.

'Working for a bone fide aristocrat seemed like fun,' Marissa said non-committally. 'And my mum went to school with her mum, and I needed to fill a gap on my CV.'

'Really?' Alex was not convinced. 'You just seem like more of a fast-paced, super-glam big city girl to me.'

'Let's just say this.' Marissa pulled her sunglasses down and peered over the top of them. 'Let's just say that everyone who comes to Cornwall is running away from something. And I was running away from something of a scandal. I had a bit too much fun, and got myself into a lot of trouble. But you know how it is, right? A girl's got to do what she's got to do to get ahead.'

'Marissa!' Sue bellowed from almost the top of the hill. 'Get your skinny backside up here now!'

'And, boy, am I paying for it.' Marissa sighed, as she began trotting up the hill after her boss. 'Seriously, twenty-five years in a hard labour camp would have been better than this!'

As Alex watched her go, she wondered about Marissa and Ruan. It wasn't that she couldn't see them together, she could. He was tall and handsome, with – Alex happened to know – a spectacularly good torso, and she was small, and pretty, with those huge almond-shaped eyes. When they stood next to each other they looked like an advert for a dating agency, or the cover of a romance novel. But when it came to being with a person, knowing them, caring about them and planning a future with them, she couldn't see how the Ruan who had showed her his lighthouse last night and the Marissa who'd just bitched about Sue could possibly be compatible. Of course, men never worried about finding a soul mate, did they? If they did then Marcus wouldn't be about to marry a girl who so patently was not his type.

It was a quiet morning, so Alex took her posh coffee and sat on the bench on the quay to drink it. From there she could see with her own eyes what boats were on the move in the harbour, and radio them on her walkie-talkie if it came to it. It was a mild and gentle day; the sun glossed the town in a coat of gold, the river sparkled like a million diamonds had been cast into it, the sails of the boats gleamed white on the horizon. Marcus had still been asleep when she got up this morning and for a little while Alex and Buoy had watched him sleep, only one of them wondering what sort of fun it would be to chew his ear.

If there had been a similar, silly drunken incident in Grangemouth, involving nudity and arousal, Marcus would have laughed it off and told everybody the hilarious story about how he accidentally fell into bed naked with his best friend, good old Al, and probably, knowing Marcus, wouldn't have left out any of the gory details. But here it was different, he was different, Alex thought. Or at least he had been last night. He hadn't laughed it off, he hadn't turned it into a joke. There had been something – a moment between them that might mean something else. And then he'd asked her out to dinner. Things were different here, Alex thought to herself, feeling a tingle of excitement rise in her chest as the slightest chink of possibility that perhaps maybe, maybe things could be the way she wanted them. *I'm different down here. Marcus sees me differently here. And tonight we are going to have dinner, like two people going on a date.* OK, so Marcus had been careful to say it wasn't a date, but even him just saying that meant it was more than just two friends hanging out, because if that was all it was, he wouldn't have needed to clarify, would he? Alex stared down at the frayed knee of her too big jeans and suddenly it occurred to her that she had nothing to wear tonight.

'Are you Alex Munro?' A man sat down on the bench next to her. He was in his thirties, with greyish blond hair and ice blue eyes that crinkled as he smiled at her. Normally, this was exactly the sort of random occurrence that would have caused Alex to instantly clam up, go red and run for the nearest darkened room, but she was different today, she noticed. Today she was totally fine about a handsome man she'd never met before knowing her name.

'I am.' She smiled at him. 'Can I help you?'

'David Tyler, Port Authority. I'm popping by for a spot check on our newest and most famous employee.'

'Oh hello.' Alex offered him her hand, wondering who this woman was who wasn't remotely fazed by this unexpected visitor. 'I was watching the boats from out here for a few minutes. Obviously, I can track it all on the computer, but it helps, I think, to take a look at the real world now and again, don't you?'

'I do,' David said. 'Especially on such a pretty day like this. So, tell me, how you are settling in?'

As they talked, Alex could see Ruan come into view, returning from one of his boat trips up the estuary towards the China Works, and sitting at the helm, his red hair glowing in the morning sun, was Marcus. He must have hitched a lift when he saw Ruan going by, Alex guessed. Seeing the two of them together gave Alex a feeling of mild discomfort, and she realised she didn't want Marcus to know that she had been with Ruan at the lighthouse, and she certainly didn't want Ruan to know that last night she'd seen a lot more of Marcus than she'd bargained for.

'Alex?' David interrupted her.

'Oh sorry.' Alex smiled. 'Could you repeat that question, please?'

'It wasn't a question, it was a well done,' David said. 'This is a busy harbour and it hasn't been so well managed in years, you're doing a great job.'

'Thank you.' Alex beamed at him, before looking again at the approaching boat. 'I must say there is a lot to love here.'

'That's very true.' David returned the smile, turning up his serious levels of handsome in one fell swoop. 'I have to say I don't really want to leave.'

'Well, come back any time,' Alex said, as Ruan moored the boat more or less at her feet.

'I wonder, it's a little bit . . . unconventional, but perhaps I could take you out sometime?'

'To talk about work, sure.' Alex nodded. 'Office hours are nine to five, and every other Saturday.'

'Well.' David Tyler smiled. 'I was thinking more as in a date? I mean unless you're taken.'

'Oh.' Alex folded her hands in her lap as Ruan and Marcus made their way up the steps and then stood there, both of them, obviously waiting for her to finish her conversation.

'Sorry.' David observed the two of them with mild amusement. 'Should I be at the back of a queue?' he asked.

'No,' Alex said, hardly believing the words that were coming out of her mouth. 'I'm not taken, actually. And yes, I think it would be nice to go out sometime. You've got my number?'

'I have.' David stood up, and nodded at the men. 'Gentlemen. See you soon, Alex.'

Alex bit her lip in an attempt not to smile, as she watched him leave. Being asked out by a handsome man in front of Marcus might have been the most exciting moment of her life.

'What was that about?' Marcus asked her, a little crossly.

'What's it to do with you?' Ruan asked him, glowering.

'A lot more than it's got to do with you,' Marcus said, squaring his shoulders. He was a good two inches taller than Ruan, although the latter probably had the edge when it came to stormy glowering. 'I look out for Alex.'

'She doesn't need you to look out for her,' Ruan said. 'Not in Poldore. No one is going to upset her here.'

'I don't need anyone to look out for me, actually,' Alex said, standing up. 'I've got to get back to work. What are you two doing loitering around here anyway? Can I help you with something?'

'I came to see you,' Marcus said, looking hurt. 'That dog has decided to really hate me. I made myself a cup of tea, and it watched my every movement, growling. I thought any second now it's going to take a chunk out of my backside.'

'I shouldn't worry,' Ruan said. 'Buoy's got better taste than that.'

Marcus ignored him. 'So I thought I'd come and hang out with you. Maybe we could chuck chips at seagulls or something?'

'I'm working.' Alex smiled. 'But I'll see you tonight. I'll meet you in the pub about eight?'

'What shall I do in the meantime?' Marcus asked her.

'I don't know, you're a grown man, go and think of something. Go for a walk or something.'

'What for fun?' Marcus asked her, confused.

'If you walk to the top of the hill, where the hotel is, that's where you'll find some mobile signal, you can call Milly.'

'And say what?' Marcus looked alarmed.

'I don't know, you are the one who's engaged to her!'

Marcus shrugged, gave Ruan something akin to a warning look, and began to slowly trudge up the hill towards Poldore Hall Hotel.

'He needs a nanny, not a fiancée,' Ruan said, watching him go. 'How did you and he ever become friends? You are so different.'

'He comes across a lot worse than he is,' Alex assured him. 'In reality he's just . . .' She found her mouth stretching into a wide grin as she thought about how to sum Marcus up. 'He just makes me laugh.'

'Oh, well, that's nice,' Ruan said. 'Anyway, I'm starting the new tour today. First one midday. And . . . well, I know I wasn't much of a laugh, but I just wanted to say thank you so much for spending time with me last night, it really helped.'

Alex smiled. 'It was brilliant fun,' she said. 'Your lighthouse is the best place I have even been in my life.'

'Really?' Ruan's tiny smile was full of pleasure. 'I'm glad you enjoyed it.'

'So, I'll see you at this silent rehearsal tonight then?' Alex asked. 'Or rather in the wee small hours,' she added, remembering the time.

'Yes.' Ruan nodded, and Alex waited for a moment or two, because it seemed like he was going to add something, but instead he simply nodded again. 'Yes, see you later. I'm looking forward to it, Alex.'

When Alex got back to the office she closed the door behind her and leaned against it for a moment. She could be wrong, of course, she'd been wrong about it so many times before, but this time it felt different. This time she felt like something was going to happen. And the most important thing was to be ready. Going to the desk, she picked up the phone and dialled Lucy's number.

'Hello you, you dark horse,' Lucy said. 'Tell me everything about you and Ruan.'

'What? We're just friends,' Alex said hurriedly. 'This is much more important than that. I'm going out with Marcus tonight, and this time something's going to happen. I'm coming over later and you, you are going to turn me into a sex bomb.'

'Dave Tyler asked you out?' Lucy repeated the question, because it was clear that she wasn't getting the sort of answer from Alex that she wanted, and she'd asked her a lot of questions since Alex had arrived at her cottage to get ready for her night out with Marcus.

'Yes, right in front of Marcus,' Alex said. 'And I think he was jealous. I think . . . Lucy I think he might be changing the way he feels about me.'

'Based on what?' Lucy said. She took dresses and shoes out of her wardrobe and laid them out on the bed as she sized Alex up. 'It's nice he's taking you out to dinner. But I wouldn't exactly call that a declaration of love. Especially as you said it's to thank you for being his best man at his wedding.'

'That's not everything . . .' Alex hesitated, not entirely sure how to describe what had happened in her bed last night. 'When I got in from Ruan's—'

'Ruan invited you round, to his actual house?' Lucy asked her. 'To the lighthouse?'

'Well, he's only got one presumably,' Alex said. 'But anyway—'

'Ruan never asks people round to his house. Cordelia is the only other person I know who's been inside and she lives there, when she's not nannying at Castle House.'

'Well, you know, he's busy I expect.' Alex smiled. 'It really is very lovely, by the way. So, anyway, I got in and Marcus was already in bed, passed out, and *naked*.'

'Am I going to need therapy for what you are about to tell me?' Lucy asked.

'Well, I needed to go to sleep, so I woke him up, and he was bit surprised, and in the commotion he kind of ended up on top of me on the bed naked and . . .' Alex hesitated again, feeling her cheeks simmer as she recalled the moment.

'And?' Lucy prompted her.

'Well, he, um, he was pleased to see me.'

'Oh my God.' Lucy covered her mouth with both hands, then her eyes and then her mouth again. 'And then what happened? Did you have sex?'

'No!' Alex was appalled. 'No, I mean we couldn't, I wouldn't. He is engaged to someone else and I'm . . .'

'What?' Lucy asked her, taking another dress out of the wardrobe. 'Because if you tell me now that you're not interested I'm going to know you are lying.'

'I'm twenty-eight,' Alex said. She picked up an open bottle of wine that Lucy had brought up to the bedroom and refilled their wine glasses.

'Not sure your age has much to do with it,' Lucy looked nonplussed.

'And, technically, I am what you would call inexperienced in the sex department.'

'So, you haven't had a ton of lovers, that's no bad thing,' Lucy said.

'No, I mean I haven't had any lovers,' Alex said. 'At all.'

'You mean you're a virgin?' Lucy said. 'Still?'

'Some people refer to it in that way, yes,' Alex said, rushing on. 'But, you know, it wasn't like I planned it this way, to stay pure, or keep myself for Marcus. I would have done it, with the right person at the right time, it's just that that hasn't happened yet.'

'Wow.' Lucy stared at her. 'I mean good for you. Oh, we should phone Sue and tell her, she can alter all the posters for the pageant, I can see it now: "Real Life Virgin Plays Mary".' Lucy clearly found herself hilarious.

'OK, OK, there's no need to tease me about it.' Alex grumbled. 'Bloody hell, you are my first proper female best friend, and I felt sure the whole point of hanging out with a girl was because they were supposed to be supportive and kind and nurturing.'

'I am, I am being kind and supportive and nurturing. And proper female friends take the mickey out of one another. I'm just not sure that building your hopes up when it comes to Marcus is the right thing to do. I think from what you said it seems like you've given him a fair few chances to realise how wonderful you are. I think . . . well, I just think it shouldn't take a man lying naked on top of you for him to realise what a great person you are, or that you are an attractive woman. And you've got this far without doing it with Mr Wrong, so it would be such a shame if you stumbled right at the last minute.'

'Marcus isn't Mr Wrong,' Alex said. 'How can he be? He's been one of the best things in my life, all of my life. And yes, he's a bit of an idiot, but he's got the kindest heart. I think the difference is this place. I think it's Poldore. I think something has happened to me since I got here. I feel more . . . like myself, or like I am supposed to be. And the funny thing is I didn't know who I was, not really, not until I found out. Do you know what I mean?'

'No.' Lucy smiled. 'I've always known who I am, but when I finally looked like me, it was a relief. I will never forget that moment, it was like "Oh, there's my reflection. It's finally in the mirror where it should be." Which makes me wonder . . .'

'What?' Alex got up and picked up a bright red sexy dress, which had been laid out on Lucy's bed next to a similar one in black, and pulled it on her over her head. Lucy was slimmer and taller than her, and technically it didn't fit her, except that it was stretchy and forgiving, showing off Alex's curves to full effect.

'Blimey.' Lucy bit her lip as she looked at Alex in her red dress. 'I'm not sure we should be doing this to you, dolling you up in dresses and make-up and shoes that will murder your feet after five minutes. You are a natural, Alex, *that's* what makes you you. Bone-china skin that doesn't need a scrap of make-up, shiny hair, jeans and T-shirt – although whoever let you buy those particular jeans should be put in prison. You are beautiful enough without all the gubbins. A man that really cared for you would see that.'

'But you wear all the gubbins,' Alex protested.

'Because that's me. I love clothes and shoes and make-up. I choose it. But, be honest, if it wasn't for your insane quest to get Marcus's attention, you would never *choose* any of this stuff, would you?'

'Yes, I think this one,' Alex said, staring at herself in the mirror, too focused on what she was convinced was going to happen later that night to really listen. 'And red nails and lips like you see on TV.'

'Oh dear Lord,' Lucy muttered to herself as she opened her make-up bag. 'The Virgin Mary has gone over to the dark side.'

Chapter Fourteen

As Alex teetered down the cobbled street towards the Silent Man, she thought two things. First of all that a strumming double bass should be accompanying her walk, plucking a sultry note with every hip-swinging step she took, and secondly that there was no way she was ever going to be able to walk again after tonight.

So far she'd travelled less than a hundred yards from Lucy's front door almost to the pub, and it felt like the soles of her feet were on fire. It didn't help that her feet were a little bigger than Lucy's, so her poor toes, which up until that moment had been cheerfully free range all of their lives, were now crammed together in unnatural agony, and protesting vehemently. And it was that horrible bewildering world of agony that Alex was still caught up in when she more or less crashed into the pub, hurling herself in the general direction of the bar, more in hope than expectation of stopping with even a modicum of grace.

'Hello, love.' Eddie half looked at her, as he fiddled with the tap on the draught lager. 'You off out somewhere?'

'Yes.' Alex looked around. There was no sign of Marcus even though she had made it her business not to leave Lucy's cottage until fifteen minutes after they were due to meet. 'Dinner with Marcus.'

'He's a fine fellow,' Eddie said, grinning to himself. 'Had us in stitches last night, right up until the minute he realised you'd gone home, and then he did look a bit sorry for himself. I dropped him and Buoy back to yours in the end. Was a bit worried he might fall off the steps so stayed with him to the top at least.'

'Thanks, Eddie,' Alex said, pleased to think of Marcus worrying about her.

'No bother, love, he's about to get married, isn't he? Can't be the man who let the groom crack his head open just a few weeks before the wedding.'

The pub door opened, and Alex looked up expecting to see Marcus bowling in. Instead it was Cordelia first, followed by Ruan.

'That's a lot of lipstick,' Cordelia said, as she sat next to Alex at the bar. 'Been ripping the throats out of innocent victims?'

'Cordy,' Ruan said, searching his pockets, presumably for some cash. 'Coming from the girl who is wearing enough eyeliner to qualify for a leading role in *Night of the Living Dead*, that's a bit rich.'

'It is a lot of lipstick,' Alex conceded, her lips feeling sticky and alien as she thought about why women felt the need to colour their faces in. 'I thought I'd give it a try, but it feels funny, you know, like someone stuck my lips together with a Pritt Stick.'

Cordelia seemed to find that sentence very funny, and even Ruan smiled.

'Drink?' He looked at her for the first time then, and tilted his head slightly to one side. 'Wow, that is red. That is the reddest red I've ever seen.'

'Does it look awful?' Alex asked him, drawing the edges of her coat further round her.

'Not awful,' Ruan said. 'You just look different that's all.'

'Like a vampire serial-killer slut,' Cordelia added.

'I'll have a large wine, please.' As Ruan continued to examine her newly enhanced face, Alex realised that she was suddenly boiling hot. Sliding off the stool she stood up and slipped Lucy's faux fur coat off her shoulders, carefully folding it on the chair.

'Better take this off,' she said. 'Otherwise I won't feel the benefit.'

When she looked up again she saw three open-mouthed faces.

'What?' Alex looked down at herself. 'Have I split something?'

'Almost split something more like,' Cordelia said. 'You work it, girlfriend.'

Alex knew at once what she was referring to. In Lucy's house the two milky half moons of her breasts surging up over the square-cut neckline hadn't seemed too exposed. Now, however, they seemed right out there and, when she came to think about it, Alex thought that the only other time she'd showed so much of herself outside of her house had been when she was a tiny baby and someone had thought it would be a good idea to photograph her nude on a rug.

'Do I look awful?' Alex asked them, anxiously. 'Shall I go home and get changed?'

'No, no, you look great,' Eddie said, busying himself by putting a lot of ice cubes in a glass for no apparent reason. 'You look a knockout, darling.'

'I wish I had a cleavage like that,' Cordelia said, peering unabashed down Alex's top. 'Have you padded that out or is it all real?'

'It's, um, all real,' Alex said, suddenly very aware that Ruan was doing his utmost best not to look at her at all.

A wash of shame and horror swept over as she realised what an idiot she'd made of herself, pouring herself into a dress that didn't really fit her, smothering her face in make-up . . .

'Oh God,' she moaned. 'I look like a slutty clown, don't I? I was trying to look womanly.'

Alex picked up the glass of wine that Eddie had handed her and downed it in one. 'Lucy said I should go more understated and less make-up. But no I was all "I want to wear a dress, I'm picking one that makes me look like a harlot!"'

'You don't look like a harlot,' Ruan said, being very careful to look only at her eyes. 'You look . . . amazing.'

'I'm here!' Marcus announced himself as he swung open the door. 'I didn't mean to be late, thought I'd have nap and then . . . Wowzers! Alex, get a load of you! Jeez, you look stunning.'

'I do?' Alex said uncertainly, with a very small smile, feeling ever so slightly better. 'You don't think that maybe I've gone a bit over the top for a meal out with a mate? It was, you know, an experiment. I'm experimenting with a new look.'

Alex squirmed, as she waited for Marcus to answer her. Normally, he always looked at her face. Tonight though his gaze was several inches south of there.

'Good result,' he said, nodding several times to emphasise his point. 'Really, really good result. Um, look the table was booked for like five minutes ago. I'll just pop to the gents' and we'll run over, yeah?'

'Oh OK,' Alex said, still waiting for him to notice her lipstick. 'Yeah, except that I don't think I can run anywhere in these shoes . . . if you can call them shoes, as they aren't really fit for purpose.' But Marcus had gone before she got to the end of her sentence.

'I think you've pulled,' Cordelia said. 'The ginger yeti has deffo got the hots for you. Or bits of you, anyway.'

'We're just friends,' Alex said, although it was clear for anyone to see that if Marcus had gone the last twenty-five years without noticing that she was a woman that wasn't going to go on for very much longer.

'I'm off home.' Ruan got up suddenly, his drink untouched on the bar.

'What?' Cordelia protested. 'You said we were going to have some brother and sister time before Sue's so-called secret dress rehearsal!'

'I know, I just remembered some . . . paperwork, needs to be done tonight,' Ruan said. He hesitated next to Alex, level with, but not looking at her.

'You don't look like a clown,' he told her. 'You look beautiful. But you don't need all of that stuff on your face, or that dress to look beautiful. You're beautiful whatever you are wearing. See you later, and Alex . . . take care.'

'Whoa.' Cordelia took in a deep, whistling breath as she watched her brother go, before turning her attention to Alex.

'Are you after him, are you after Ruan?' she asked Alex, who was still reeling from Ruan's words. No one had ever said anything like that to her before.

'No,' Alex said. 'We just get on well, we're friends.'

'Friends? You seem to have a lot of male friends.' Cordelia was suspicious. 'And anyway, I haven't seen him look at anyone the way he just looked at you, not since . . .' Cordelia downed her drink and stood up abruptly. 'I'm warning you, stay away from him, OK? He might think he's ready, but he's not. He'll never love anyone like he loved Merryn, do you understand me? So just leave him alone.'

'But I—' Alex spontaneously fell off one of Lucy's shoes, pitching her sideways, giving her a sort of Hunchback of Notre Dame stance, as Cordelia stormed out after her brother.

'You know how to clear a room, don't you?' Eddie said.

'I'm not after Ruan,' Alex told him, putting her coat on again, because it just seemed safer that way. 'I don't know where all that came from.'

'Oh, you don't mind Cordy. In a lot of ways Ruan is all she's got left, and she reckons she's a lot more tough than she is. It was Cordelia who had to try to be there for him after Merryn. I don't think she ever wants to see him like that again. No woman will ever be good enough to replace her.' Eddie smiled at Alex, lowering his voice a notch. 'I'm not sure that Ruan agrees with that thought, not at least when it comes to you.'

'He was just trying to be nice,' Alex insisted. 'In a big brother sort of way.'

'You've never had brothers, have you?' Eddie smiled. 'Look, Ruan never said anything just for the sake of it, not in his whole life. And I'm not Cordelia, granted. But I'm telling you, Alex, don't you let that young man think there is a chance if there isn't. Else it won't just be Cordelia who's after your guts. None of us want to see him hurt again.'

'I'm going out for dinner with Marcus!' Alex exclaimed just as Marcus returned, buttoning up his fly as he strode around the bar.

'Alex Munro,' he said, looking her up and down, 'who knew that you are properly fit?'

There was a little bit of Alex that wondered just why Marcus had chosen Poldore's only chain Italian restaurant in a town that was chock-full of high-end eateries, offering fresh food as good as anywhere you'd find elsewhere. The place on the quay, for example, almost had a Michelin star, Sue had told her once, as if the near miss was almost as good the real thing. Marcus, however, had chosen to go to the one place where he knew the menu would be the same from Land's End to John O' Groats, and Alex wouldn't have been at all surprised to find there were branches there too.

'Large pepperoni, mate, and a beer, cheers,' Marcus told the waitress as soon as she brought over the laminated menu. He looked expectantly at Alex.

'I haven't decided yet.' She laughed.

'You'll have a margarita and garlic bread,' he told her. 'You always do.'

'You should be on *Mr and Mrs*,' the waitress said, at once overly familiar in Alex's opinion. 'You know each other so well! Been together long?'

'Oh we're not—' Alex began to explain, but Marcus talked over her.

'Childhood sweethearts,' he said, reaching out and taking Alex's hand over the table. 'I'm the luckiest man alive.'

'I'll have the Caesar salad,' Alex said, testily, withdrawing her hand. 'And a glass of house white.'

'You've changed,' Marcus said, as Alex sat awkwardly opposite him. She had tried to retain the menu as a sort of modesty screen to cover the cleavage that she hadn't really been conscious of until Cordelia pointed it out, but the waitress had whisked it away, so instead she lay the cotton napkin out on her lap, spreading one corner as far up as was possible, not that it actually helped.

'Everyone changes,' Alex said. She was nervous, everything about this evening was making her nervous. The way that Marcus was looking at her, not at all in the same careless, effortless way that he used to. His normally happy-go-lucky blue eyes were suddenly intense, and sort of purposeful in a way that Alex was not accustomed to, not in all the years that she'd known him. At least not concerning her, because with a sudden terrifying thrill, Alex suddenly remembered when she had seen this sort of predatory behaviour in Marcus before. It was when he was on the pull.

It was finally going to happen, Alex realised. After all these years, a lifetime of yearning, the moment was here. Marcus had finally seen her the way she had always wanted him to and Alex was fairly certain that tonight could well be the night that finally her dream came true. Marcus wanted her.

Suddenly she was petrified, but not only that. In the very instant that Alex realised that her dream was within reach, every part of her that had been so certain that Marcus was the one for her was now totally and utterly unconvinced that this was a good idea. In fact, it suddenly seemed like the worst idea possible in the history of bad ideas.

It's just nerves, she told herself, as Marcus talked about an Iron Man thing he was planning to do in the New Year and she nodded and smiled.

It's just like jitters, like pre-wedding jitters. Obviously, you are just worried that it's not going to work because you've never done it before. But it will work out. This is Marcus, and not only does he suddenly really fancy you, he's your best friend. The bloke who's always been there for you. It's bound to be wonderful, it's bound to be a wonderful first kiss. And then maybe some wonderful touching of a sexual nature, and then maybe even actual . . . sex.

Alex downed her glass of wine and then ordered another one.

'So tell me about you,' Marcus said, leaning forward a little, his eyes seemingly focused on her red painted lips.

'What?' Alex frowned. 'You know everything there is to know about me.'

'I thought I did,' Marcus said. 'I thought I knew you,

but I was wrong. I never knew you were the sort of person to just jack it all in and start a whole new life on your own. I never knew you were that brave, braver than me. It never occurred to me in my life that I'd ever leave Grangemouth. I just always assumed I'd live there, get married there, have kids there, die there, probably of an alcohol-induced heart disease. But you, you just got up and changed everything about your life, and look at you. You've . . . .transformed.'

'Transformed?' Alex smiled, as that was not the sort of word she was used to Marcus saying.

'Yeah, like a butterfly or something,' Marcus said, warming to his theme. 'And seeing you this way, it's made me think about everything, it's made me question everything, Alex.'

'Has it?' Alex said, signalling for another glass of wine.

'Shall I bring you a bottle?' the waitress asked. 'It will be much cheaper, the way you're knocking them back.'

'Oh yes, a bottle, yes.' Alex nodded. Her protective napkin slipped to the floor. Just as she bent to scoop it up, Marcus got there first, and there was a long excruciating moment when his nose was more or less in her cleavage. The way he was looking at her when he finally straightened up and handed her back the napkin made Alex want to run for the door and put on flannel pjs that buttoned right up under her chin.

She reached out for the napkin, and had to tug it ever so slightly from his closed hand.

'Oh, Alex . . .' he said, just as the food arrived.

'Oh good, I'm starving,' Alex said, staring at her salad and wishing it was a pizza. 'I think I'll just pop to the ladies before I start.'

It became very apparent, very quickly, to Alex that she wasn't going to be popping anywhere, except perhaps out of the top of her dress. She wasn't able to walk in Lucy's shoes in the first place, but, after quite a substantial amount of wine, it was much worse. For what felt like an age she waited for the world to right itself on its axis, but she only had to attempt to take a step for it to tip and tilt again. Glancing back at Marcus, who was thankfully absorbed in his food with his usual gusto, she kicked the shoes off under a nearby table, and, flat-footed, managed to find her way into the ladies.

'Hello?' Lucy answered on the first ring.

'He totally wants me,' Alex told her. 'And I don't know what to do!'

'Whoa, wait a minute.' Lucy's voice was calm and serene. Alex wanted to go round to her house right now and sit down with a cold flannel on her head for twenty minutes while Lucy told her what to do, only she couldn't help but think that that might ruin the moment a little bit.

'How do you know that he wants you and when you say wants you, what do you mean?'

'I mean that he wants me, like in a sex way,' Alex hissed into the phone, leaning over the wash basin. 'And I know because he hasn't stopped looking at me like I am a very delicious cake.'

'Oh, OK. And how do you feel about that?' Lucy said. 'I mean are you ready?'

'Of course I'm bloody ready, Lucy,' Alex exclaimed. 'I'm twenty-eight! And it's Marcus, the love of my life. I love him and he wants me, it's just . . .'

'What?'

'I don't know. I don't know what it is. I mean I want this, I know I do. I've always wanted it. So this kind of gut-churning horror that I'm feeling, that's just nerves, right?'

'Or a lot of wine on an empty stomach.' Lucy sounded a little worried. 'Look, Alex, are you listening to me?'

'Yes,' Alex said, straightening up and looking in the mirror. There was only a trace of her red lipstick left now, but she still looked OK, she thought. Womanly, sexy, like a womanly, sexy, sexual woman who could easily do sex and it would be no big deal whatsoever, as it's just sex.

'Alex, you only get to do this once,' Lucy said. 'You only get to have your first time once. I know you've waited a long time for it, I know that you have, but please, babe, please be sure. Because this moment won't ever come again, and it's not the end of the world if it's disappointing, you'll get over it eventually. But it is a huge, huge deal if the person you choose ends up hurting you, and I don't want that to happen to you, OK. I just want you to be sure. There's no rush, a few more weeks won't make any difference.'

'There's no rush,' Alex repeated, before adding, 'oh my God, I need to sober up if I'm going to have sex.'

'Alex, remember what I said?' Lucy repeated. 'There's no rush.'

'No, there is no rush, except I've got to be the Virgin Mary at three a.m.'

Hanging up, Alex took a deep breath. The tipsiness brought on by too many glasses of wine in quick succession had calmed her down a little. All she needed to do was to get back to the table, eat her depressing salad, a lot of bread, maybe some cheesecake, drink lots of water and then she'd be absolutely fine. It was a pity really that she was wearing these control tights.

As Alex opened the door, Marcus was leaning against the red-painted wall, waiting for her.

'You were a long time,' he said. 'I was worried. You were knocking back the wines.' He grinned. 'Your salad is getting cold.'

'I'm fine,' Alex said. 'You should have started without me.'

'Oh, I did, I've finished without you too.'

'Oh, so come on then. I think I might get some garlic bread after all.'

'Alex.' Marcus took her by the arm, stilling her. 'I feel weird.'

'Maybe the pepperoni was off,' Alex said.

'I don't mean that, and you know it,' Marcus said. 'I thought I'd be OK when you left. I thought, good for Alex, and I'm getting married. And I'll see you at Christmas, you know? I didn't realise what an impact it would have on me, not having you around.'

'Well, you've got Milly,' Alex said. 'You've got her around as much as you want, all the time, in fact. For all eternity.'

'I know,' Marcus said. 'And Milly is a great girl, fit and a nice person. But she doesn't make me laugh, not like you do. Don't get me wrong, she laughs at my jokes, she thinks I'm hilarious, but she doesn't make me laugh great big belly shakers, not like you.'

'Because she doesn't let you talk her into all sorts of nonsense,' Alex said, daring herself to look up into Marcus's eyes.

'I saw you again, and you were different. I don't mean the way you look tonight, although how you look tonight should probably be against the law. I mean the way you were, the way you are in yourself, now. You look happy, content.'

'I am,' Alex said. 'Or at least I was until you came back and reminded me.'

'Reminded you of what?' Marcus asked her.

'Do you really not remember?' Alex asked him

carefully, her voice low. 'At your engagement party? The things I said to you?'

'I don't,' Marcus admitted. 'I was leathered.'

'Marcus.' Alex shook her head. 'I didn't just come down here because I fell out with Dad over his affair with Mrs O'Dowd. I came down here because, on the night of your engagement, I told you, Marcus Duffy, that I, Alex Munro, was in love with you. That I had always been in love with you, and that you shouldn't marry Milly, you should marry me. It took me every single ounce of courage to say that, and you don't remember it?'

Turning on her stockinged feet, Alex headed back towards the restaurant only knowing that she didn't want to have that conversation standing outside a toilet, tears stinging at her eyes as she remembered the humiliation of Marcus brushing her off like some annoying kid sister.

She went back to the table, and then, deciding she couldn't face her salad, picked up a bread roll and shoved it in her mouth, scooped Lucy's shoes up from under the table, and walked out of the front door, with Marcus not far behind. Alex wasn't sure what was worse, the freezing cobbles beneath her feet or the prospect of putting the shoes on. The smooth, damp cold beneath the burning soles of her feet won out as she headed towards the quay. The streets were busy, packed with Friday night revellers. Christmas hats bobbed up and down, girls in skimpy dresses stood outside bars, the coloured lights strung across the narrow streets swung in the wind, as snippets of Slade could be heard through doors opening and closing.

'Alex!' Marcus caught up with her just as she rounded the corner into the town square, the glow from the tree bathing her face in a rainbow of lights.

Alex stopped and sat down on a bench opposite the tree, on the end of which a couple were engaged in some serious kissing. Alex watched them for a moment. To them it all seemed so natural. So easy that they could show each other exactly how much they liked each other in a very public place and not think twice about it.

'I'm sorry,' Marcus said, sitting down next to her. 'I'm really sorry that I didn't hear you say those things. Except that maybe, in a way, I did. Because then you went, and I missed you and I knew that everything was wrong, because things weren't right between us.'

'Oh well,' Alex said. 'It doesn't matter now, does it? I'm down here, and I'm happy actually. I like it. And you will get married to Milly, and have seven kids, and I will be their cool aunty.'

'I'm an idiot.' Marcus took her hand in his, turned it over and kissed the palm. It was such an unexpectedly sweet gesture, and so romantic, that it quite took Alex's breath away.

'I thought I knew what I wanted, Alex,' Marcus said.

'But seeing you has muddled everything up, and I don't know what I want any more. I don't know what's right. I only know one thing, and that's that I want to kiss you right now.'

Alex didn't have a chance to respond before Marcus's lips were on hers, his arm snaking around her waist as he pressed her body hard against his. Somewhere Alex could hear an enthusiastic chorus of partygoers singing, 'Hark the Herald Angel, something, something newborn King.' She could hear the shouts from a group of teenagers across the square and behind her closed eyes she could sense the glare of the star on top of the tree.

What are you doing? she asked herself crossly as Marcus's tongue enthusiastically explored her mouth. This is Marcus, kissing you at last, and you're trying to remember the words to a Christmas carol. Concentrate. Forget the words.

Alex relaxed into the kiss, feeling Marcus's fingers tighten on her waist. Hesitantly, she allowed her fingers to flutter upwards to his face and she kissed him back, which seemed to encourage his ardour even more, as the hand that had been gripping her thigh suddenly found its way to her bosom.

'Oh,' Alex said, breaking the kiss as Marcus's fingers enclosed her soft flesh. 'Um, bit public . . .'

'Sorry, of course.'

Alex waited and, after a moment, Marcus removed his hand. ' Look, there's a few hours until you're due for your rehearsal right?' Alex nodded, still waiting for her heart to catch up to everything else. 'Shall we go back to the cottage? Where it's not public?'

Alex nodded. This was it, it was really it. The moment had come.

As they got up and headed towards the boat hand in hand, she felt a prickle on the back of her neck and turned round expecting to see someone watching her, but there was no one. No one except a lone shadowy figure walking hurriedly up towards Castle House, his hands thrust in his pockets. Now wasn't the time to worry about him though, Alex told herself. Now the time had finally arrived. Tonight was the night, and if things went to plan, by the time she put on her Virgin costume she wouldn't be quite so typecast any more.

Chapter Fifteen

Buoy wasn't at all keen on the idea of Alex having sex.

As soon as they had walked in through the door, Marcus had grabbed her again, kissing her standing up this time, grinding his hips into hers, and Buoy hadn't been the least bit amused about that, growling, low on his haunches as if he might actually pounce.

'Passion killer.' Marcus laughed, loosening his grip on Alex for a moment. 'He's going to have to go out.'

'Oh.' Alex bit her lip. 'It's cold outside. We can't do that to him.'

'But if we go upstairs he'll come with us!' Marcus said. 'And it's you I want to be stroking, not a dog.'

'Or we could have a cup of tea?' Alex suggested, screeching inwardly.

'Tea? What are you talking about, woman?' Marcus kissed her again, and Alex noticed that he kissed with gusto, much like he did everything else in life. There were no stages, or gears. It was either KISSING or NOT KISSING. You had to applaud him for his commitment. 'No, come on, you get up the stairs and I'll rig up a barrier to keep him down here.' Alex cast one last look at Buoy before going up the stairs, hearing a series of bangs and barks as she went into the bedroom, and wondered about climbing out of the window. There were so many reasons not to go through with this – what about poor Milly, who trusted Marcus with her, who even now might be sitting down and looking at wedding dresses, or her father, who'd told her that she should always trust her instincts when it came to big decisions, because all you have to do to know what is right is to stop for a moment and think. But Alex didn't want to stop. Alex felt like her whole life right up until this moment had been one big full stop, and now was her chance, perhaps her only chance, to write herself a new chapter.

It was now or never, and stopping to think was the last thing she should be doing.

'There,' Marcus said, appearing in the doorway. 'I have contained the dog.'

Alex said nothing, because she knew if she opened her mouth all she would do would be to laugh like a loon, and that didn't seem very sexy to her.

'Come here you,' Marcus said. 'Let's get you out of that dress.'

'Marcus,' Alex said, stopping him as his hand reached behind her back to look for a zip, 'I'm a bit . . . nervous.'

'Me too,' Marcus said, finding the zip and undoing it with one long sweep. He stepped back, and looked at her. 'Go on.'

Her heart pounding, Alex stripped the dress off, first one shoulder and then the other, letting it pool on the floor around her ankles.

'Alex.' Marcus looked at her standing there in her bra and control top tights. Quickly, he lifted his shirt off over his head, without bothering to undo the buttons, displaying that washboard stomach, and those muscular arms. 'I like this game. Your turn.' He crossed his arms and waited.

Alex bit her lip as she put her thumbs in the top of her tights and pulled them down, struggling slightly as she tried to get them off her feet. It didn't seem to bother Marcus though, his gaze sweeping her from head to foot as she stood there in her underwear. There had to be a moment, one that came really soon, when she could tell him that she hadn't exactly done the whole sex thing before, so that he would know not to expect too much, but when would that be? Now, before she took off her bra or afterwards?

'Oh God, Alex,' Marcus said, undoing his trousers, 'you look so good.'

'Marcus, the thing is . . .' Alex tried to think of the right words.

'Bra.' Marcus said the word, with some difficulty, and Alex realised he probably wasn't in the mood to talk much. Maybe she didn't have to tell him, maybe it didn't matter if he didn't know, perhaps it would just be fine to go ahead and do it and he would be none the wiser and then it would be done, no big deal. 'Bra off, now.'

Alex supposed that she should probably feel a lot sexier than she did just at that moment as she reached around and unhooked the back of her bra. The way that Marcus was looking at her, so full of desire and quite obvious attraction, should have made her feel like an all-powerful siren, invincible and irresistible. Instead there was something, something nagging at the back of her mind that unsettled her. And it wasn't just the thought of poor Millie, Marcus's actual girlfriend waiting back in Scotland for him.

Slowly, she eased the straps off her shoulders, and then, still holding the cups to her breasts, she realised what was wrong.

'Marcus, what will happened afterwards?' she asked.

'What do you mean?' Marcus asked her, blinking as if just snapping out of a trance. 'Not exactly the moment to talk about it, Alex, although you would win prizes for striptease. I don't know, a cup of tea, maybe a bit of a snooze. Oh and a cuddle.'

'No, I don't mean right afterwards,' Alex said, a little exasperated. 'I mean you and me. We do this tonight, and then what? When do you tell Milly? Where do we live? Do you want me to come back to Grangemouth? Or would you think about coming down here?'

And suddenly everything in the room changed.

'I wasn't really thinking about that just yet,' Marcus

said. 'I was thinking about you and me, and tonight. And now.' He smiled and it was so sweet and boyish. He looked just like he used to when he was proposing one of his mad schemes destined to get her into terrible trouble.

'But you would tell Milly, right,' Alex said. 'I know she'll be upset but it's better for her to know sooner rather than later. And this would be the two of us together at last, wouldn't it? This would be the start of us, right?'

Marcus looked at a loss. 'I don't know, Alex,' he said finally. 'I don't know what would happen next. How can I know until after this?'

A wave of sadness hit Alex all at once, followed very quickly by something that was almost anger. She let her hands fall, her bra falling it with, and stood in front of Marcus for a moment, as she looked at him aghast.

'Marcus, we've been friends all these years, and you'd just risk it all for some sex, that might not lead to anything? You'd throw it all away to get a look at my breasts? Well, here they are. Is it worth it?'

Marcus, blushed, dropping his gaze. 'Alex, I don't know what's going to happen, I just know that I've got these feelings for you, and right now all I can think about is you and how much I want to touch you. I'm not going to lie to you, or lead you on. I would never do that. I just wanted . . . I want *you*, Alex. Right now.'

Alex stood there for a moment, as all of the little

doubts and uncertainties clicked into place. 'Take a good look at them, Marcus,' she said, gesturing at her breasts. 'Drink them in, because this is as near as you are going to get to them, tonight, or ever.'

'Alex!' Marcus looked distraught. 'I'm sorry, I thought you wanted this.'

'I thought I wanted it too,' Alex said, grabbing a jumper off the floor and pulling it on over her head. 'The difference is, I wanted it to mean something, not just to me, but to you too. I wanted this to be our beginning, but it can't be. Maybe it might even be our end.'

'Alex, please . . . we can still be friends.' Marcus took a step nearer, just as there was a huge crash from downstairs and then Buoy scrambled up the stairs, inserting himself between Alex and the impostor.

'Tonight would have been my first time,' Alex told him bluntly. 'Which you might think is funny, something to take the piss out of. But I would have shared my first time with you, and you would have gotten in your car and gone back off to Milly and to you this would have meant nothing. I see it now. We can't be lovers, Marcus. I'm not all together sure we can be friends any more.'

'But . . .'

'Look, I'm going to get some sleep before the pageant rehearsal,' Alex said, realising she was trembling. 'So please would you go. Go and see Eddie; there will be a room in the pub. You'll have to drive the long way; I need the boat. If you go now, you'll make it before closing.'

'Alex, I don't want to leave it like this,' Marcus said. 'I mean maybe I am meant to be with you, maybe it's not Milly, I just don't know.'

'If you don't know,' Alex said, 'then you've got no business being in my bedroom.'

Marcus hesitated for a moment longer and, as Alex turned her back on him, he hastily dressed before heading down the stairs. Alex waited until she heard the front door close, and then she curled up on the bed with Buoy and began to cry.

Right up until the moment that she'd dragged herself out of bed and got dressed again, Alex hadn't been planning to turn up to Sue Montaigne's early-hours secret dress rehearsal for the pageant. The very thought of it was too much, after everything she'd been through. To get so close to being in that very place she had always dreamt of being with Marcus, only to realise at the last minute that it hadn't been her he cared about; not the her that he'd grown up with, shared his deepest secrets with, led on more foolish escapades than she cared to count. No, all he had cared about was the body in the red dress and the high heels. And then, the idea that she had to get out of her very own personal dog-inhabited pit of despondency to go and pretend to be history's most famous virgin was just about the straw that broke the camel's back. So Alex had curled up under her duvet, with Buoy's warm weight leaning against her feet, and decided that tomorrow she would start again, somewhere else perhaps. She didn't have Wi-Fi in the cottage, but maybe there was another job, in another port. Perhaps this time she could change her name, too. And never, ever have to see anyone she'd once known ever again.

For a moment Alex missed her dad fiercely. She hadn't got to tell him what had happened between her and Marcus back in Scotland, and there would never be an appropriate moment for her to tell him what had happened tonight, how she had made such a terrible fool of herself chasing a man who really deep down she'd never actually ever expected to want her back. Perhaps she never even wanted him to? He'd been a safe bet, a secure option. Maybe, deep down, she'd been pretending to herself to be hopelessly in love with him and then it didn't matter that she'd got to the age of twenty-eight without ever really connecting to any other human being, or letting anyone know the real her. That wasn't strictly true, Alex conceded. She did love Marcus, she loved him as a friend. Shame he didn't seem to feel the same way about her. Alex would have liked nothing more than to have spoken to her dad just then. Not for words of comfort, or advice, just to hear his gruff, monosyllabic tones telling her about some business at the port would have been soothing enough. And if she had had any signal on her mobile phone that that point, she might well have called him, even though it was the early hours of the morning. Because she knew that he wouldn't for one moment acknowledge the time she had called, or what had passed between them. He would simply act like nothing had happened, and Alex found that rather appealing.

But she didn't have a mobile signal and Alex found she could not sink into the refuge of sleep. So at two forty-five, she got up, washed her face clean of every last trace of alien make-up, and, wrapping herself up against the blustery wind, went out into the night. Alex had been pleased, even a little moved, when Buoy, stiff and weary, picked his way down the slippery stone steps to join her in the boat. Alex welcomed his reassuring presence, as he sat in the prow of boat, looking out to sea, his eyes closed against the handfuls of needle-fine rain that the wind threw into their faces.

'You are late,' Sue exclaimed when Alex, her dark hair plastered to her face, arrived with Buoy. 'And that dog's not coming in here. He's a cad and a bounder.'

'More of a bouncer, really,' Rory said, winking at Alex, who smiled wanly, though neither she nor Buoy budged.

'Well, I suppose he could double up as a sheep,' Sue said, noticing that Alex had been crying. 'As long as he keeps his you-know-what in his trousers. And that's quite enough chatting, come on, everyone, follow Lucy, it's time to get your costumes on.'

'You made it then,' Ruan said, falling into step alongside Alex as they followed Lucy down a dark and shadowy medieval corridor – all that was missing were torches burning brightly on the wall to complete the effect. His tone was off hand, carefully uncaring.

'Yes,' Alex said, keeping her eyes on the floor. Ruan had seen her kissing Marcus. He knew what had happened. What he didn't know was what an idiot she had made of herself. 'Why wouldn't I?'

'You looked busy the last time I saw you,' Ruan said. 'I thought you might be a bit occupied.'

'Oh that.' Alex shuddered at the memory. 'That was nothing.'

'Right,' Ruan said. 'I didn't take you for the sort of person who was so laid-back about these things.'

It was only as they walked into what Alex could only describe as a great hall, lined with dark wood panels and floor-to-ceiling tapestries, and a gallery that was only missing a band of minstrels, that Ruan's words finally sunk in.

'What do you mean?' Alex looked at him, but before he could say more Lucy clapped her hands to get their attention.

'Right then,' Lucy said. 'Shepherds, you are under the gallery, angels by the swords, and Inn Keeper, Virgin

Mary and Joseph you are over here. Just grab your costumes and pop 'em on over your clothes.'

'Where is Marissa?' Sue enquired, suddenly appearing on the balcony. 'That bloody girl! She is supposed to be here taking preparation photos of you getting dressed for the *Gazette*! Rory? Rory! Where is my bloody husband? Seriously, why do I keep a dog and bark myself?'

Sue took out her phone and started snapping away as Lucy helped Alex into her white shift, topped off with a standard-issue blue sash, and then a veil that covered her head.

'How did it go?' she whispered as she pinned the veil to Alex's head.

'Really, really terribly,' Alex told her. 'Imagine the worst possible outcome and then times it by about seven million.'

'Oh no, you had sex!' Lucy looked appalled.

'No, we didn't have sex!' Alex said, rather too loudly, so that the shepherds and angels all looked over at her. It was only Joseph that studiously ignored what she had said.

'Thank God,' Lucy said, with genuine relief. 'I was hoping you would come to your senses before it all went too far.'

'But if you thought it was a terrible idea, why didn't you say something?' Alex asked her. 'Why did you lend me that dress?'

'Because, well, because I never for a moment thought you would let it go that far,' Lucy said. 'And because I think you see yourself in this one way, and it's not that it isn't a good way, it's a great way to be, but you underestimate yourself, Alex. It's almost like you are living in your own shadow.'

'Nope.' Alex shook her head. 'No idea what you are on about.'

'Come on!' Sue clapped her hands together smartly. 'I swear to God if Rory doesn't come out from whatever rock he's been hiding under in the next three seconds I'm going to—'

'Here I am, darling. Sorry, call of nature,' Rory said. He turned to the assembled players. 'Sorry, sorry, for my tardiness. We are walking the route tonight because we don't want to wake residents. There are a fleet of umbrellas at the door, please do take one and I hope you've got your thermal knickers on, it's brass monkeys out there.'

'I bet the real Virgin Mary never nearly froze her toes off,' Marissa said, appearing at Alex's side, and handing her the prop baby.

'Where were you? Sue was very annoyed with you,' Alex told her, attempting to cradle the baby convincingly once or twice before tucking it under her arm as if it were a rugby ball.

'It's three a.m. on Christmas Eve, and I'm knackered. I haven't been to bed at all. She was making me redesign the sodding website for ages, like anyone ever looks at it. I went for a catnap in the laundry room while I could. I'm sure the world hasn't ended in my absence.' Marissa cocked her head to one side, and Alex had to admire how perfectly well turned out she looked after such a long day, her skin smooth and shiny, her hair fashionably tousled, her lips naturally ruddy. 'I say, Ruan, you are the sexiest Joseph I have seen.'

'I think that might slightly be blasphemy,' Alex said.

Ruan grinned. 'I admit, I wear a tea towel well,' Ruan said, smiling at Marissa, as Sue opened the door and a blast of freezing, soaking air swept in, engulfing them in chills.

'This is my worst fucking nightmare,' Marissa said. 'I have no idea why we are doing this.'

'Cheer up,' Ruan said. 'At least tomorrow we can have a bit of a lie-in.'

'Oh, that sounds like an invitation.'

'Maybe it is . . .'

Alex bit her lip as she listened to Marissa and Ruan flirting, and was grateful when Sue handed out their route and a thoroughly detailed itinerary of who did what, where and when. Fortunately, Alex didn't seem to have to do very much except look virginal, which sort of came naturally to her.

'Hang on!' Lucy appeared at her side.

'No, no, no,' she said, removing the baby and rather unceremoniously shoving a cushion up Alex's stomach, securing with a belt. 'You don't get to hold the baby until we reach the town hall. You are preggers all the way there.'

'What?' Alex looked down at her newly formed bump in horror.

'Ooh pregnancy suits you,' Marissa giggled. 'It's because you have one of those figure that carries weight well. Child-bearing hips and all that.'

'Yes,' Ruan said. 'You make a beautiful pregnant woman.'

Neither Alex nor Marissa responded; neither one of them knew how to.

A freezing ramble in the dead of night, in near silence, up and down the steep, sharply rising streets of Poldore wasn't something that Alex expected to enjoy, but actually it was bizarrely entertaining and the best distraction from her near miss with Marcus that she could have hoped for. Poldore was exceptionally pretty in the small, dark hours, although the moon was all but lost behind the silver-edged rain clouds, the soaking-wet streets shone and the strings of fairy lights that decorated every street were haloed in fine mist.

Sue's edict that there must be silence actually made the process even better, firstly because Alex didn't have to think of anything to say to Ruan, who spent the entire time at her side, at the head of the procession, and also because Alex found herself unexpectedly charmed by the silent pantomime that was going on around her. At certain stages they would stop on a street corner, read their instructions for that location and stealthily act them out.

Alex had done nothing more strange in her entire life than pretend to be visited by a mute angel, perhaps the first time ever that she had spent more than five seconds in Sue's company without Sue actually saying anything. Or silently trek out of Nazareth, which was really Linda Leighton's grocery shop but which later on would be fronted with painted chipboard that made it look more like a Middle Eastern town from long ago. When the time came, Alex would be sitting atop what she hoped was a robust model of a donkey, built on the base of gymnastic horse, but for now she walked silently, side by side with Ruan, as they headed towards the town hall, which soon would be a snowy Bethlehem, the star on top of the square's tree acting as *the* star. Somehow the cold and the wet didn't matter as, serenaded by the odd muffled cough and occasional sneeze, or swiftly stifled fit of giggles, Alex and Ruan pretended to knock on various doors, only to be told with a shake of a solemn head that there was no room at the inn. Finally, the innkeeper with a stable, played by Brian Davies, invited her into the town hall. As soon as they were inside, where the nativity set was already waiting, there was a rush of giggles and chatter, like a group of naughty children who snuck out after bedtime for a midnight feast. Ruan and Alex smiled at each other in the hubbub, which was soon silenced by Sue.

'The Baby Jesus hasn't even been born yet!' she shouted through a megaphone, which she must have been itching to use up until this point. 'Focus, please! Stay in character! Wise men, if that's beer you've brought along, Eddie, it's not too late for me to fire you.'

The hall slowly subsided into something like silence.

'Now, Joseph, Mary, please come on stage.'

Alex began the awkward walk up the aisle at Ruan's side, when Sue barked an order through the megaphone making her jump. 'Honestly you two, you are supposed to be in love. Mary, you are expecting your first baby, and not only your first baby, but *the* baby! You are full of wonder and amazement, and, Joseph, you are escorting this precious, precious cargo. Put your arm around her, gaze at her adoringly. Alex, nuzzle into him.'

'Sue,' Ruan said, awkwardly, 'I'm a tour-boat operator, not Robert de Niro.'

'If only,' Sue said, looking momentarily wistful. 'Well, you're a man, aren't you? And Alex is a pretty young woman. I'm sure it can't take too much effort to look like you at least fancy her.'

'This is ridiculous,' Ruan muttered, putting an arm around Alex's waist.

'I'm sorry,' Alex said, too tired and still rather hungover to be bothered to be polite, especially now that they were inside and the electric lights were glaring down at them. 'I had no idea that I was so repellent.'

'Oh for God's sake.' Ruan rolled his eyes. As they went up to the stage, his fingers felt tense and unnatural on her hip. 'You weren't doing much to repel Marcus earlier on.'

'Very nice,' Alex said. 'Very nice language in the middle of a nativity.'

'You are impossible,' Ruan hissed at her, as they passed behind the painted scenery of hay bales and a tree, and Lucy whipped Alex's cushion out from under her robe and handed her the plastic doll. 'Why are you taking offence?'

'I don't know,' Alex snapped back. 'Is it because you are treating me like some sort of plague victim?'

'So you want me to be all over you, do you,' Ruan asked, 'just like that idiot Marcus, pawing at you for everyone to see? Is that what you like?'

'Oh my God!' Alex said. 'What business is it of yours what I like and don't like? I don't go prying into your little secrets, do I?'

'Guys.' Alex vaguely registered Lucy speaking, but it wasn't until she raised her voice by quite a few notches that she actually stopped talking.

Lucy nodded at the other side of the hay bale, where

there was complete silence, and raised an eyebrow. Half the town had listened to their argument,

'If you've quite finished your little exercise in unresolved sexual tension,' Sue said, 'perhaps we can get on and finish this farce before dawn?'

And so it was a darkly glowering Joseph and a sulky red-faced Mary that held court to the now slightly drunk three kings, which was actually two kings, since Harry Forsythe had gone to the gents' and never came back, and a rabble of shepherds, one of whom had his iPod resolutely plugged in.

As they completed the final tableau, at which point on the actual night the carol singing would be due to start, Alex scowled down at the plastic baby and wished she had stayed under her duvet instead. The second that Sue shouted out 'and scene' she dumped the doll in the manger, and stormed off stage, where she found Lucy waiting for her.

'Hey, what's up?' Lucy asked her, as Alex struggled to get out of the stupid tunic, caught for too many hideous seconds in its awful white folds, before Lucy finally pulled her free. 'What happened out there? One minute you were the sweetest-looking couple in the world and the next you were at each other's throats.'

'We are not a couple,' Alex snapped. 'What would make you think that there is anything between me and Ruan when I was practically stark naked with another man in my bedroom earlier?'

Inevitably, Lucy's eyes travelled over her shoulder, and Alex knew that Ruan was standing behind her. She closed her eyes and he brushed past her, dumping his costume in Lucy's arms as he went by.

'Well, that put him his place,' Lucy said carefully folding the costume. 'If that was what you wanted,' she added as she left Alex standing there.

It was still pitch black as Alex opened the unlocked door to the cottage, the little lamp shining bravely behind the orange curtain. She was glad to be home, looking forward to a precious day off.

At first, when a lady in a full-length fur coat, Chanel sunglasses perched on the top of her platinum-blonde hair, stood up from the armchair, Alex thought that a combination of exhaustion, tiredness and the remnants of a hangover were making her hallucinate, and then when Buoy growled at the woman, she thought she must be an unlikely ghost, whose unfeasibly glamorous spirit was somehow trapped in this tiny cottage.

'Hello, darling,' the 'ghost' said, smiling. 'It's me, your mother.'

Chapter Sixteen

Christmas Eve

'I beg your pardon?' Alex spat the words out, pinching her left arm hard in the hope that it would bring her to her senses. 'Ouch!'

'I know it's probably a bit of a shock that here I am, sitting in your cottage, in the middle of the night . . . but—'

'I'm calling the police,' Alex told the stranger. 'This is breaking and entering.'

'I don't think it is,' the woman said pleasantly. 'Your door wasn't locked, you see.'

'Who *are* you?' Alex asked her. 'Why are you picking on me? Have you escaped from somewhere, an asylum or something? Prison? Are you an escaped mass murderer?'

The woman chuckled. 'Even when you were a very little girl you had the most vivid imagination. Remember your imaginary friend, Rebecca Constantinople? Once, you insisted that I drive you round to her house for tea, insisted. Even though she didn't have a house, and didn't exist at all, but no, you were going to her house for tea come hell or high water. I had to drive around and around for hours until you eventually fell asleep. When you woke up I told you about what a wonderful time we had, and you remembered it all!'

Alex stared at the woman in amazement. Rebecca Constantinople was a real imaginary person. She was Alex's real imaginary person, and she had thought, right up until this point, that there were only two people in the whole world who knew about her – Alex and her father. She'd not even told Marcus.

'How do you know that?' Alex asked.

'Because I am your mother, Alex,' the woman said, and somewhere behind the transatlantic twang Alex thought that she might be able to detect the slight hint of a Scottish accent. Just maybe.

'You can't be,' Alex's voice faltered, as Buoy still rumbled away his disapproval at her side. 'I haven't seen or heard from my mother in twenty-five years. You can't be her. She knows nothing about me – not how I grew up, not what exam results I got, not what I do for a job, and certainly not that I have moved to Cornwall.'

The woman thought for a moment.

'You grew up a decent, hard-working girl, following in your father's footsteps, working in shipping, and conquering a man's world without barely a backward glance,' she said. 'You got excellent grades, all level 1s except for maths and history, which you would have got 1s in but you had stomach flu the day before, and you weren't quite yourself. You got two 2s. You worked alongside your father in Grangemouth for a very long time, and then, a few months ago, for reasons that I don't know, you came here and became Cornwall's first ever female harbour master.'

'How do you know all that?' Alex asked her, stunned. She felt almost frozen, as if all the emotional upheaval that she should have been feeling was waiting, somewhere to suddenly break through and wash her away.

'I may have left, Alex, but I never stopped thinking about you,' the woman said, her voice suddenly strained. 'I have someone . . . a friend of the family. She's kept me up-to-date all these years. You know her.'

'Who?' Alex demanded. 'We don't have family friends, me and Dad. It was always just us, some blokes from work and their families and . . . You mean Mrs O'Dowd, don't you?'

'Yes, Eleanor.' The woman nodded. 'Your father doesn't know, but we've kept in touch all these years.

'But she . . .'

'Yes, she's the love of his life,' the woman said calmly, though Alex thought she could detect a wistful sadness behind her words. 'I know. I found out about it soon after you turned three. She'd been married when he fell for her, so he married me, the next best thing. He never thought that perhaps it would be a good idea to move to a house that wasn't situated right next door to the woman he couldn't have. But that was your father all over, he was always such a practical man. And I expect he thought he could bear it. After all, he is an expert at hiding his feelings, as you know. And then Mr O'Dowd passed on. I don't know how long they waited after she buried her husband, but I suspect it wasn't very long.'

She smiled briefly. 'Now, you are a sensible, logical girl, Alex. I think you can accept that I am your mother now, yes? It's almost morning, and you look exhausted and I have to admit I am rather tired too. Go to bed. I'll sleep in this chair, by the fire, and we can talk some more when you wake up.'

Alex did not move, staring at the woman who was her mother, in her fur coat and improbable sunglasses. So many questions and thoughts were running through her head. Why had her mother chosen tonight – of all nights – to walk back into her life? Whenever she had imagined this scenario happening she had been sure she would experience a myriad of emotions – anger, betrayal, hurt – but still, none of them came. Nothing but weary exhaustion and a kind of acceptance that, of course, it had to happen like this. This way, at this time in her life, because moving to Poldore was somehow like moving to the centre of the universe, and all the moments of her life were colliding in this one place.

'OK,' she said, because she simply didn't have the energy to say more. 'Goodnight.'

Without saying another word, she went upstairs and lay on the bed, after a moment joined by Buoy who curled up against the bend of her spine. And before she could ponder for even one more moment everything that had happened, Alex was lost in a deep, dreamless sleep.

Christmas Eve day

Alex woke to the smell of bacon, and the realisation that Buoy was no longer at her side. Glancing at her alarm clock, she saw it was almost midday, so she got up and peered out of the window. Christmas Eve looked thunderous, the heavy clouds billowing with rain. The forecast had been for heavy rain and strong winds, although nothing that merited a weather warning yet. Technically, today being her day off, it was the one day when Alex didn't have to worry about the weather, but she thought she'd pop into the office the first chance she got anyway, just in case there was anything she hadn't remembered to tell Steve from St Austell, who was covering her shift. Still there was no hurry, and there was bacon. Which was when Alex remembered that her mother was the one downstairs cooking it.

She had been hoping that she had dreamed the whole thing, but no, as she made her way down the stairs, her mother was sitting at the little table, feeding Buoy bacon from between her painted fingernails. Somehow, in the hours that Alex had been asleep, everything in the tiny front room had changed. Gone was the grey and grimy rug, and the floorboards had been washed so that they glowed faintly. The dreary greying nets had been taken down, and the orange curtains tied back with two lengths of purple ribbon. There was a bunch of holly, laden with bright berries, in the measuring jug on the table, and every surface had been dusted and polished, which came as a shock to Alex because she hadn't even realised that she owned any cleaning products.

'Morning, darling,' Gloria said, as Alex took the other chair opposite her, staring at her mother in the dull light of the leaden day. 'What a rainy old Christmas Eve isn't it? There's bacon here, if this old sea dog has left you any, have you, you ikcle wickle poppet, you have, haven't you?' Buoy all but purred as Gloria tickled his ears, leaning his head into her palm in pure delight. Oddly, Alex discovered that she felt rather betrayed. Nevertheless she pulled the plate of still sizzling bacon towards her and piled it between two thick slices of bread.

'I'm quite sure I didn't have any food in,' she told Gloria.

'You didn't,' Gloria said. 'I took your little boat across to town while you were sleeping, stocked up, enough to get us through until after Boxing Day, including a lot of wine and a small turkey, which is just as well because I cleaned your oven, and it's bijou to say the least.'

As Alex munched a mouthful of her sandwich, her stomach lurched in hunger, and she realised she hadn't eaten for almost twenty-four hours. Perhaps Gloria, sitting there in an off-the-shoulder white mohair jumper and bronze leggings, was a figment of her starved imagination after all, except that Alex didn't think imaginations smelled quite so pungently of expensive perfume.

'So I don't see you for twenty-five years of my life and then you make me a bacon sandwich and er . . . Christmas lunch and we're totally fine?' Alex asked her, setting the sandwich down on the plate even though her stomach cried out for it.

'No,' Gloria said, matter-of-factly, taking a packet of cigarettes out of her pocket and tapping one on the table. 'No, of course not. You're incredibly angry with me, I'm sure. And hurt. You think you've grown up without a mother—'

'I did grow up without a mother,' Alex cut her off.

'Who cared about you,' Gloria added briskly. 'And I know this is hard to understand, Alex, but even though I went, I didn't stop caring about you, or loving you. It's difficult to explain, but I did what I did for you.'

'Did you?' Alex watched her mother toy with a heavy gold lighter. 'How kind.'

She took another bite of the sandwich, unashamedly

taking in her mother's face in the unflattering light. She was almost sixty, Alex worked out, and her skin had clearly had professional attention. Not so long ago, someone had smoothed out the lines of her forehead, and her complexion bore none of the blemishes of sun damage or smoking that you might expect in a woman of a certain age who was clearly rather tanned, not to mention clearly addicted to nicotine, even if it was the expensive kind. There were crinkles around her eyes – brown eyes, utterly unlike Alex's, a sort of rich dark toffee and her hair was burnished gold, most likely from a bottle, although there were no visible roots for Alex to check. There was nothing in Gloria's face that reminded Alex of herself, and she wondered absently if that was the reason she hadn't taken her, because she was her father's daughter through and through.

'Why did you come here?' Alex asked. 'In the middle of the night, it's like you were sneaking in.'

'I just separated from my current husband,' Gloria admitted, as she placed the unlit cigarette between her lips, and left it dangling from the corner. 'We were on his yacht. The plan was to spend Christmas in Cannes, however, he didn't see the funny side of my liaison with the first cabin boy, and now our short-lived union is soon to be over, which makes me wish I had never signed that goddamn pre-nup. I honestly thought this one was the one.'

Alex said nothing, only waited.

'Well, he threatened to put me out at sea, without so much as a lifeboat, but we compromised on Plymouth. What really smarted is that the cabin boy kept his job. I was the one that got fired. So I arrived in Plymouth very late, with only the cash I managed to smuggle out of his safe, and I thought of you. Cornwall is only a hop, skip and a jump from Plymouth after all and I thought, this is fate. Alexandra is so close, and it's almost Christmas. This year I finally get to spend it with you.'

'And you thought it was going to be that easy?' Alex asked the question, not in anger, more in wonder at the sheer front of her mother.

'Well, I'm sitting here and we're having breakfast, aren't we?' Gloria said, with a shrug, finally lighting the cigarette.

Alex allowed her one long drag, before taking it from between her lips and stubbing it out in the dregs of tea in the saucer of Gloria's cup. 'If you want to smoke, do it outside.'

'But I can stay?' Gloria asked, taking another cigarette. 'I mean are you really going to throw me out, penniless into the world on Christmas Eve, with nothing but the suitcase of cash I took from his safe, when you could take a chance and see if you like me even just a little bit? I know we can never be the closest mother and daughter in the world, but perhaps, just perhaps, we might be friends?'

'The only place to sleep is on that chair,' Alex said. 'And it's not very comfortable.'

'It's not so bad when you have a faux fur leopard skin to keep you warm at night,' Gloria told her. 'And I put my feet up on the stool, so it was quite comfy.'

'I thought you were used to five-star luxury yachts?' Alex asked.

Gloria smiled. 'It hasn't always been that way for me,' she said. 'That was a recent development, one that's now over, it seems. I doubt I'll have the pulling power to bag myself another millionaire any more, not when there are so many younger, firmer prospects than me.'

Alex said nothing.

'I'm not proposing that I move in,' Gloria said. 'But what if I stay tonight and spend Christmas Day with you? I could do that at least.'

'I have plans for tomorrow,' Alex told her, although she did not.

'Oh, are you working? Well, I can pack up Christmas lunch and bring it to you,' Gloria said cheerfully.

'And tonight I'm in the Christmas pageant.'

'Are you?' Gloria looked delighted, clapping her hands together like a little girl. 'I only ever saw you do one play, when you were at nursery, and you were so freaked out by everyone looking at you that you pulled your Santa hat right down over your face and never came out again. What part do you play?'

'Mary,' Alex said begrudgingly, remembering her strange and very public spat with Ruan last night, which in turn made her remember what had happened with Marcus a few hours earlier, which in its own way made her want to go out to the end of the garden and jump off the cliff.

'Mary! The lead! I am so proud, maybe you are a bit like me after all,' Gloria said. 'I don't suppose your father told you I was an actress slash model did he? I did three commercials before I married him, and there was talk of a walk-on part in *Coronation Street*. I gave it all up for love sadly, which considering the outcome perhaps wasn't the best move I ever made.'

'You can stay,' Alex said. 'Until Boxing Day.'

Gloria beamed, and Alex was unexpectedly caught up in a perfumed hug.

'Thank you, darling, thank you. You won't regret it.' Gloria got up and slipped on her giant coat, then slipped her cigarettes into one of the deep pockets.

'Come on, boy,' she said to Buoy, opening the door and producing from behind a large suitcase a bright pink umbrella edged with frills in triplicate.

'Where are you going?' Alex asked, taken by surprise by a sudden feeling of panic at the prospect of her leaving.

'Well, seeing as you are making me smoke outside, I might as well take this handsome boy with me while I do it, right? Don't fret, we'll be right back.'

'I wasn't fretting,' Alex lied, because, oddly, she had been.

'I tell you what, in that bag –' she indicated a matching carry-on suitcase '– there is the biggest box of the finest chocolates that you will ever eat in your life. Why don't you crack them open while we're gone. They are the best thing for a hangover next to bacon.'

Alex waited for the door to close behind Gloria before she finally breathed out, letting go of all the tension in her body which had kept her huddled in the chair. What kind of woman was her mother? she wondered. All she could come up with right now was a sort of fusion of Joan Collins and Mary Poppins.

Chapter Seventeen

'Well, if you're what Santa is putting in my stocking this year then I must have been a *very* good girl,' Gloria said as she opened the front door, a gale of laughter caught up in an actual gale that blew freezing air into the cosy cottage. At first Alex thought that perhaps she might have been talking to a soaking wet Buoy, but it was Marcus that followed Gloria in out of the rain.

'Look what a handsome hunk I found on the road, looking like a drowned rat,' Gloria said. 'And it turns out he is little Marcus Duffy who you used to beat up at nursery. It's so sweet that you two have stayed friends – some would say, even romantic.'

Gloria winked at Alex.

'Has Marcus told you he is getting married?' Alex asked.

'Oh, he did,' Gloria said. 'But you know what they say, "It's not over until the fat lady sings." I shall give you some space.' She hesitated for a moment. 'Come on dog, you and I are going for another walk.'

Buoy, who was now making a small puddle in front

of the banked fire, gave her a look that said quite clearly, *Not on your Nelly*, and firmly closed his eyes.

'Go upstairs,' Alex said. 'There are some books in my bedroom.'

'Or, I could look through your wardrobe, see if I can't find something that might brighten you up a bit.'

'Funnily enough,' Alex said, noticing how Marcus was looking everywhere in the tiny room to avoid looking at her, 'I think I've had enough of makeovers to last me a lifetime.'

'I see,' Gloria said. 'Well, have fun, darling, don't do anything . . . oh never mind.'

Alex waited until she heard the creak of footsteps overhead.

'I think under the circumstances,' she said, 'that I shouldn't be your best man. And I think that perhaps we need a break from being friends at all.' She paused, fighting the wave of horror as she involuntarily recalled what had passed between them last night. 'I just find it sort of hard to think of you the way I did before. So you know, Happy Christmas and all that. Be in touch, see you around and all that jazz.'

'I'm not going to marry Milly,' Marcus said.

'What do you mean you aren't going to marry Milly?' Alex said. 'I mean I know what we did was stupid and selfish and mean, actually, and yes, we saw each other naked, and yes, we touched each other in places where we probably shouldn't have, but we didn't actually do "it", so I think you can still marry Milly with a relatively clear conscience.'

'Maybe,' Marcus said. 'But I can't marry her when I'm in love with another woman.'

'What other woman?' Alex asked, frustrated.

'You, Alex,' Marcus said. 'I'm in love with you, you idiot.'

'No, you are not,' Alex said, advancing on him, furiously. 'You are not in love with me.' She shoved him hard in the middle of his chest and, in his shock, he stumbled back a step or two. 'Oh my God, this is so typical of you. You get an erection and you assume it's love.' Alex pushed him again, advancing him another inch towards the door. 'And you think it's fine to just mess around with me, mess around with our friendship like it's some sort of toy you can pick up when you feel like it. And you want to call it love?' She gave him another shove. 'You are not in love with me, Marcus.'

'How do you know if I am in love with you or not?' Marcus asked, bracing himself at last, so that the last push achieved nothing at all. 'How do you know what's in my head or my heart, or how confused I am, and how when I got to the pub last night I lay awake all night thinking about you, Alex, about how much I just want you. You can tell me that you don't love me, but you can't tell me I don't love you. That's for me to know.'

'I can't deal with this,' Alex said. 'I can't. I've got to

be the Virgin Mary in a few hours, and there's a storm coming. I need to get into character!'

They stared at each other for a few seconds, and then a smile tugged at the corner of Marcus's mouth.

'Don't you dare laugh,' Alex threatened him, but her voice was shaky with unexpected laughter. 'It's not funny!'

'It is a bit funny,' Marcus said.

Alex shook her head, smiling as she sat on the armchair. Maybe they could still be friends, if they could still laugh with one another?

'OK, maybe it's a bit funny, but I am right about one thing, I can't deal with this now.'

'Why can't you?' Marcus asked her. 'Haven't you been waiting for me to fall in love with you for all of our lives? Well, it's happened, Alex, it's happening now.'

'You really are spectacularly arrogant,' Alex said. 'And you're right, I have been waiting for you to fall in love with me all of my life. I'm just . . .' Alex shrugged. 'I'm not sure it didn't happen a bit too late.'

'You mean you don't feel the same way any more?' Marcus asked her.

'I don't know what I feel,' Alex said. 'And I don't want to think about it. Did you see that woman that just went up the stairs, Marcus? That's my mother. You know, the mother that I haven't seen for most of my life? She just turned up out of the blue and you haven't asked me about her once.'

'But not because I don't care,' Marcus said. 'Of course I care, and of course I know that you must be freaking right the fuck out right now, but I came here to say I love you. I've been practising it all night, and when I saw you I had to get it out before I lost my bottle. Because I love you, Alex. What the fuck is your mother doing here?'

'I don't really know,' Alex said. 'And I just . . . I need to deal with that for now. Shouldn't you go back? Shouldn't you be with Milly? It's Christmas Day tomorrow!'

'I'm not marrying Milly, I told you. And I'm not going anywhere until you give me an answer.'

'An answer to what?' Alex asked. 'You haven't exactly asked me a question.'

'Come back with me, Alex, come back to Scotland. I'll explain everything to Milly, and we'll fix things up with your dad. We'll be together and we'll get married one day and have a ton of babies. Come back with me.'

Alex felt her eyes fill with tears. For so many years those had been the words that she'd longed to hear, but now? Marcus had probably said something almost identical to Milly not so long ago, Milly who even now was choosing flowers for her dream wedding in blissful ignorance as to what her fiancé was getting up to.

'I just can't deal with this, what with the pageant and Christmas to get through.'

'OK, you need some time. That's cool. I'll wait. They

do this Christmas lunch in the pub that anyone can come to for thirty quid. Eddie said he could squeeze me in, you too. I'll book us tickets.'

'I'm working, and I'm having a working lunch with my mother,' Alex told him. 'Go back to Milly.'

'I'm not going back,' Marcus said. 'I'm waiting. I'll see you later at the pageant, OK?'

Alex shrugged and, as soon as the door was closed, she sank onto the rug, buried her face in Buoy's wet fur and wept.

Chapter Eighteen

It was after three when Alex finally escaped the cottage, and Gloria, who, despite her protestations of innocence, had, after all, laid out some of Alex's clothes on the bed but put by far the greater majority in a bin bag by the door.

'You can't come in here and throw away my clothes!' Alex protested.

'Darling, I can and I have,' Gloria told her. 'I must. I may not have dressed you as a child but it's my duty to you as an adult; after all I worked in fashion, darling. Even if you weren't my daughter I couldn't let you go on dressing all wrong. These jeans are a size too big, this bra is clearly a size too big on the back and two sizes too small in the cup. You're a disaster!'

'I'm just not that sort of a person,' Alex tried to tell her. 'I don't like dressing up. I dressed up last night and it just made me feel stupid, and . . . well, like a piece of meat.'

'I assume you are referring to this *garment*.' Gloria had uttered the word with distaste. 'Yes, darling, this would rather put all your wares on display. It's really made for a slighter, flatter-chested woman than you.'

Alex thought of Lucy, with her subtle curves and tall elegance, and supposed she had been more than kidding herself when she thought she could fit into one of her dresses and carry it off. She had poured herself into it more like, and quite a lot of her had spilled out.

'I can see you like classic chic,' Gloria said. 'You just don't know how to do it. Now, you are about the same size as me in the hip, a bit bigger on top so . . .' Gloria had returned a few minutes later with a pair of black skinny jeans, and a soft grey lambswool sweater with a deep V neckline.

'I don't wear hipster jeans,' Alex said, looking at the trousers as if they might bite her.

'But why not?' said Gloria.

'Er, because I've got hips?' Alex protested. 'I don't want to go round with one of those horrid muffin tops.'

'Oh my God, what do you see when you look in the mirror!' Gloria asked her, appalled. 'Here, put this on under the top. I bought it in my usual size, but it came up pretty big so I think it will fit you a treat.'

Alex took a black lace, under-wired bra. 'Sexy underwear just gets me into trouble,' she said like a sulky teen.

'Darling, that's exactly what's it's for,' Gloria chuckled. 'Well, go on then.'

Not ready to get stripped down in front of her

mother, Alex scooped up the offerings and went into the bathroom, where she reluctantly complied with Gloria's wishes. Perhaps if she let her dress her up like a doll, she would be able to escape and go and call in on St Austell Steve in the office. The weather outside was awful, and all Alex could hope for was a lull in the storm for her debut in the pageant.

She pulled on the jeans, surprised that they fitted quite comfortably around her hips and that she could do them up. The bra also didn't seem too bad when she fastened it. It certainly contained her bosom a good deal more efficiently than the one that Lucy had lent her. The sweater was soft, and pleasant to wear at least. Alex stomped back into the bedroom, where Gloria was sitting on the bed looking out at the rain. For a second she looked so sad that Alex almost wanted to put her arms around her, but then she remembered that Gloria was all but a stranger, and she never had been the sort of person who hugged a stranger. Not even in Poldore.

'Good.' Her mother nodded, and patted the bed.

A little warily, Alex went and sat next to her, and Gloria put her hand under her chin and tilted her face towards her.

'Look up,' she instructed, not knowing that Alex was caught unawares by her mother's touch. Suddenly twenty-five years melted away in a moment, and Alex was sitting on the grass with this fabulously beautiful blonde-haired woman, who was holding a buttercup under her chin, checking to see if she liked butter.

'Now, you are lucky,' Gloria said, unaware of the wave of emotion that such a fleeting memory had triggered, holding Alex in its wake. 'Your skin is flawless, and that's because you don't spend too much time in the sun. All you need really is a little bit of eyeliner to make those blue eyes pop, and perhaps just a dash of mascara.'

Alex waited until her mother had finished ministering to her, and then, to her shock, Gloria cupped her cheek in her hand.

'You are so beautiful, she said. 'I've lost so many years.'

Alex wanted to say something then, because, while her mother was touching her, she felt this unexpected connection, going all the way back to sitting in that field of buttercups when she was very little, and there was suddenly so much that she wanted to say, wanted to ask and to understand, but, most surprising of all, Alex realised perhaps for the first time that for years now, years, she had missed her mother's touch.

'Go and look in the mirror,' Gloria said, sliding away from her and gesturing towards the ancient and foxed long oval mirror that was set in the middle of the wardrobe. Alex stood up and looked. She had to admit that her reflection was a lot easier to assess now that her mother had swept away the film of dust that had settled on the glass long before even Alex's residency. Which was when she noticed her reflection. Gloria had been right – the clothes fitted her perfectly, accentuating the generous curves of her hips, and the swell of her breasts, and, with her curtain of dark hair brushed off her face, Alex was surprised to notice that her bright blue eyes seemed to positively shine in the gloom of the afternoon.

'What do you think?' Gloria asked her.

'I . . . well, I like it,' Alex said, amazed.

'Now then, we'd better get off to your office and the pageant, hadn't we, darling?' Gloria asked her. 'I'll just pop into something suitably festive, won't take me a tick.'

'You can't come with me,' Alex said dismayed. 'Imagine all the explaining I will have to do.'

'Well, I can't stay here either,' Gloria said. 'I need to get over to Poldore tonight, and I don't fancy my chances in that little dinghy on my own – not in the dark. I'm coming over with you, and I'll pop to the pub, meet a few locals. Marcus was telling there is a fair bit of money here – you never know I might bag myself a decrepit millionaire yet.'

Alex couldn't help smiling to herself, as Gloria disappeared behind the open wardrobe door, and her bronze leggings appeared over the top, followed by the fluffy jumper.

'Can I ask you a question?'

'Of course,' Gloria replied from inside whatever it was she was putting on.

'Why did you marry Dad? I mean you were this model, this beauty. What did you see in Dad, especially when he must have been in love with Mrs O'Dowd when you met?'

'Well, he hid that well,' Gloria said thoughtfully. 'And he had this way with me, Alexandra, this way that no other man had ever had. He was so gentle, respectful. He held me like I was cut glass. He listened to me, he cared what I thought about things. Before him no one had ever seen past my hair or my legs . . . I loved him so much. I thought we'd have a little family, and I'd be the perfect wife and mother. It came as something of a shock that I couldn't live up to that old frump Eleanor O'Dowd, Dowdy indeed! But there you are, love is blind it seems.'

Gloria appeared from behind the open door and did a twirl. 'Now, tell me, what do you think?

Alex thought two things.

Firstly, that her mother looked fabulous.

And, secondly, that she was wearing Lucy's red dress.

'Well,' Gloria said, 'if it got you into so much trouble, perhaps it will do the same trick for me.'

Alex didn't have high hopes for either of them staying dry as they made their way across the river in her boat, which bobbed and dipped, struggling to master the tide that surged like Alex had never seen it do since she'd arrived. Even Buoy had declined to come out, climbing up onto the chair, turning around three times and then settling into it, presumably for the night, Alex thought. At least she managed to persuade Gloria into a pair of wellies and one of her parkas, though Gloria had done her best to resist.

'The only fashion statement parkas make,' she said glumly, 'is that the chance of spontaneous sex is extremely small.'

So it was with some relief that Alex helped her mum out of the boat and they set foot on dry land at just before five.

She looked up into the thunderous sky, the wind whipping at her hair. 'Oh dear, I do hope the pageant isn't ruined,' Alex said, 'Sue's been planning it since January.'

'Darling, stop looking at the rain and get me out of it,' Gloria said. 'Where is the nearest pub?'

Alex dreaded to think what her mother would get up to as she dropped her off at the Silent Man, but she supposed that she hadn't known anything she'd gotten up to for the last twenty-five years so there was no point in worrying about it now. Instead she popped into the office, where she found St Austell Steve staring into the radar.

'What's it like?' she asked him.

'It's pretty dreadful,' he told her, 'but it's OK. There's

virtually no movement in the harbour, because it's Christmas Eve, and everyone is staying put for the pageant. It's more just a bit of babysitting, no big deal.'

'Any chance of a break in the weather do you think?' Alex asked him.

Steve didn't look hopeful as he watched the constantly updating screen of weather on the computer monitor. 'It depends,' he said, 'I can see a tiny little break, right in the middle that might just come our way if we're lucky, but only if God approves of fake snow at his son's birthday party though, right?'

'So you're all set?' Alex laughed.

'I'm all set, safe and warm in here. It's you who's going out there!'

'Wish me luck,' Alex said. 'And, if I don't see you beforehand, Happy Christmas!'

The wind tore the hood from her hair as Alex made her way up to Castle House, pleased when Lucy, huddled up in snood and purple coat, fell into step beside her.

'Hey,' Lucy said. 'I've got a bone to pick with you. This woman just came into the pub wearing my dress and looks better in it than either me or you!'

'Oh yeah . . . That's my mum,' Alex told her, having to raise her voice to be heard above the wind.

'But I thought you hadn't seen your mum in years?' Lucy bellowed back.

'I know, she just showed up,' Alex shouted. 'I don't know what it is about this place, it's almost as if as soon as I arrived all of my unresolved issues were magically resolved.'

'You aren't the first to say that about Poldore,' Lucy said, suddenly sounding too loud as the wind dropped unexpectedly. 'Long, long ago before Christianity came here, it was a place of pilgrimage for the Druids, a place of healing of the mind and body. Some people still believe it. Stacey Arthur, who works in the bookshop, still goes out into the woods sometimes and does pagan-type stuff, dances about in the moonlight with her kit off, you know the sort of thing.'

'Really?' Alex said.

Amazingly there was a break in the cloud and Castle House was bathed in the yellowish sheen of the last rays of sunlight, turning the red brick bronze for a fleeting moment.

'Yes,' Lucy said. 'And then there's the other magic thing about Poldore.'

'Pixies?' Alex whispered, wide eyed.

'Better,' Lucy said. 'Never once, in six hundred years, has the pageant been called off because of the weather.' She smiled up at the suddenly benign sky, as the pair of them walked under the portcullis.

Chapter Nineteen

Walking under the portcullis was almost like walking back in time, four or five centuries ago. The courtyard was filled with people, many of them already in costume, and Sue was standing on the flatbed of a small truck, decorated to look like a horse and cart, addressing the crowd through her megaphone. For one glorious moment, as she took in Sue's halo and flowing white robes, not to mention the luxuriant false beard that stretched almost down to her navel, Alex thought Sue must have cast herself as God, which frankly made perfect sense. But then Alex saw the stiff, cardboard wings, painted gold, and she remembered that Sue was the Archangel Gabriel, which she supposed was the next best thing to God, especially as she couldn't exactly play Jesus.

'This way,' Lucy told her, leading her through a gaggle of children, many of whom actually belonged to Sue, who were dressed as various barnyard animals. The kids had not been present at the dress rehearsal, and they were clearly pushing Sue right to very edge of her heavenly limits.

256 • *Scarlett Bailey*

'Will you little buggers, SHUT IT!' Cordelia hollered at them, so fiercely that she finally subdued them. As Alex followed Lucy through an archway that she had not noticed before, she heard one small voice belonging to a lamb say, 'Cordy, I've done a wee in my fleece.'

'Is it always like this?' Alex asked Lucy, as she seemed to lead her very far away from the action and into the bowels of Castle House, which felt a little bit odd. The last time she'd put on her costume there had been about fifty other people there.

'Always,' Lucy said cheerfully. 'There's always the chaos before the calm and it always seems to work out in the end. Here you go, in here.' She opened an ancient-looking panelled oak door. 'Star dressing room.'

As Alex looked in, she discovered Ruan, his shirt off, just about to put on his first layer of Joseph's costume. The sight was one that momentarily gave her and Lucy pause. Ruan was a well-put-together example of the male species. While not quite as tall or as broad as Marcus, he had an altogether different quality, which Alex had never seen without any clothes on before. To put it simply, he was quite beautiful, from the hollow at the base of his neck to the perfectly muscled torso and arms, which looked like he could as easily have been a ballet dancer as a tour-boat operator, because in the few seconds that Alex allowed herself to dwell on his dusky complexion and the line of black curly hair that trailed all the way down to his navel and beyond she became certain, if he were so inclined, that he would be able to pick her up in his arms as if she were no more heavy than a feather and take her . . . well, he could take her anywhere really, she didn't care.

'So.' Lucy broke the lust-filled moment with a single wistful word. 'You two, you've got to make up. Get your costumes on, get yourselves ready and by the time you come out of here I want you to be the best of friends. We can't have Baby Jesus growing up traumatised, now can we?'

Lucy gave Alex a small shove into the tiny little room, which was more of a cell really, lit by one naked bulb, and closed the door. Alex and Ruan regarded each other warily as the lock clicked behind them.

'She's locked us in!' Ruan said. He was forced to brush past Alex as he went to the door and banged on it. 'You can't lock me in, I don't like small spaces. I got stuck in a treasure chest when I was kid.'

'What are you, a pirate?' Lucy called back. 'Sorry, it's Sue's instructions. I'll be just down the hall, give me a bang when you're back on track with your marriage.'

Ruan sighed, hanging his head, and turned slightly so that Alex could see his beautifully formed pectoral muscles. Her mouth suddenly felt ever so dry, and she felt the urge to sit down, but there was no seat, so she leaned against a huge old wooden chest, so old that it was almost black with years of human use.

'Was it this box you were locked in?' she asked, the

weakness she felt in her knees translating in her voice. This was new to her, this sudden physical attraction to a man. This was something she hadn't experienced before, this sort of desire of another person that made you want to, well, lick them all over frankly. Not even with Marcus had she felt this pull. Alex blushed at her own uncharacteristic immodesty, dropping her chin so that her hair fell forwards and covered her blushes. 'Feel free to put a top on at any time,' she said.

'Sorry.' Avoiding her eye, Ruan picked up the first layer of his outfit and slipped it on over his head, which was both a relief and a shame all at once.

'No,' Alex said. 'I'm sorry. I totally overreacted yesterday. I'd had a really long and confusing day, and I was tired, and a bit hungover. I mean, you were right. There was nothing in the Bible about Mary and Joseph making out, was there?'

'It's me who should be sorry,' Ruan said. 'I didn't realise until later how rude I must have seemed. It must have seemed like I'd rather chop my arm off than put it around you, and that's not how I feel at all. At all.'

There was a moment of silence as their eyes locked. Alex remained perfectly still, certain that if she so much as breathed she would scare Ruan away from what he wanted to say next.

'I didn't finish telling you about Merryn,' he said.

They weren't the words that Alex had been hoping for, although she wasn't at all sure what they would have been. Had she wanted Ruan to scoop her up into a passionate embrace, to disqualify her from her virginal status in that very moment?

No, she told herself firmly, no, of course not. She had far too much else to think about at the moment, and wasn't it only yesterday she had stopped more or less the same thing happening with Marcus? Because she realised that she wanted her first time to really mean something. By lusting after poor, grieving Ruan, she was no better than Marcus had been last night when he'd been prepared to throw away a lifetime of friendship to have sex with her. Unless, of course, Marcus really did love her, Alex thought.

'Merryn went out to sea, and she never came back – that's the part of the story that everyone knows,' he told her. 'But there is something else. Something I've never been able to tell anybody else.'

'What is it?' Alex asked, all thoughts of naked torsos and Marcus's declaration banished from her mind in an instant. She could feel that Ruan was telling her something really serious.

'Merryn had left me,' he said simply. 'That's what we were arguing about. I think I'd known it was coming for a long time. I'd fought against it, of course. I loved her, in just exactly the same way that I always had, but I stayed the same, she changed.' He glanced up at Alex, who held his gaze, encouraging him to go on. 'I love this place so much,' he continued, with such passion that it almost physically touched her. 'Everything about it – the mountains, the rocks, the grass, the sky, the waves crashing on the rocks. I love all of those things, and that doesn't even get me started on the buildings, or the people. It's like, well, it's like I am this land and it is me. That sounds so sad, doesn't it?'

'No,' Alex said, her voice a little husky. 'I think it's wonderful to feel like you belong to a place as strongly as you do.'

'I never wanted to leave,' Ruan said. 'It never even crossed my mind. Merryn had wider horizons though. She wanted to see the world, to live in a big city, have a job where she wore a suit and high-heeled shoes, like my sister Tamsyn, I suppose. But I just didn't want that. I wanted to stay here, work with boats, raise a family one day.' His small smile was so sad that Alex couldn't stop her hand from floating upwards, travelling across the small gulf between them and taking his.

Ruan didn't look at her, but he didn't remove his fingers from hers either.

'But that wasn't what Merryn wanted. So the day she took the boat out was the day she told me it was over between us. She was going up to London to stay with a friend, look for work. Try to really do something with her life. I told her she'd regret it, I told her she wouldn't make it and then she'd come back with her tail between her legs, and I wouldn't be waiting for her when she did.'

When Ruan looked up at Alex, his dark eyes were shimmering with unshed tears.

'I was horrible to her, Alex, not because I believed any of those things. I knew Merryn could do anything she wanted, she was brilliant. It was because I was heartbroken, bereft. I didn't want to lose her, not ever.'

There was a pause when he turned his face from her and Alex guessed he was waiting to compose himself before he spoke again. Still his fingers rested in hers, and she found herself stroking the back of his hand with the ball of her thumb.

'She was so angry with me, she took the boat out to calm down. It was something she did all the time, something she'd done since she was a little girl. It was a calm day, the sea was flat, so when I saw she hadn't taken a lifejacket with her, I didn't worry. It was something we both neglected to do all the time, it's like a superstition you see? Like how in the old days sailors never used to learn to swim, because they thought if they did it would mean they would go in the drink?' Finally, Ruan withdrew his hand. 'She never came back. Everyone treated me like a grieving lover, and that was what I was. I never told anyone, not even her mum and dad, about the fight. And in all the years since, they've been like a family to me, and to Cordy. Every year, on the day, when I go to Merryn's grave, I meet them there. We have lunch together. And so . . .' Ruan paused.

262 • *Scarlett Bailey*

'And so sometimes it feels like I can't ever think about moving on. About having feelings for another person, feelings so strong and so unexpected that they frighten me. It feels like if I give in to feelings like that, then I'm letting down Merryn, and I'm letting down her family.'

'I don't know Merryn's family,' Alex said, 'I don't think I've met them yet. But if they love you, and care about you, surely they are going to want you to be happy? Won't they?'

'The thing is,' Ruan told her, 'I haven't had to worry about it until recently. Until recently there's never been anyone who'd made me feel so . . . much.'

For an agonising moment Alex wondered if he was talking about Marissa, or perhaps . . . could he? Was there even the slightest chance that he might be talking about her? Or was she becoming delusional, believing now one man had declared his love for her that all of them were in her thrall? How ridiculous, Alex told herself, and a nice top and bit of eyeliner didn't change that. If it came down to a choice between her and Marissa there would be no comparison. Marissa, with all her effortless style and delicate beauty, would win every time.

'I said make up, not make love,' Lucy interrupted them, banging open the door so loudly it made them both jump. 'Bloody hell, get your kit on and get out here. Sue is going berserk!'

As if they had both been shaken from a trance, Alex and Ruan jumped into life – Alex pulling on her tunic, Ruan standing very close to her as he helped her pin her blue sash into place and then finally attach the veil to her hair with kirby grips.

'There,' he said, looking into her eyes as he put the finishing touches on. 'You're ready.'

'Good God.' Sue was outside the door when they opened it. 'You better have conquered all of your differences. The pageant is starting in ten minutes. Here, Alex, here's Jesus.'

Alex was horrified as Sue put a very well wrapped, very real and very large baby in her arms.

'Where's the doll?' she asked, holding the infant out at arm's length as if it might bite her. 'What am I supposed to do with this?'

'Him. Cradle him adoringly,' Sue said. 'Don't worry, you don't have to hold him until we get to the town hall, but I wanted you to have some time to make friends so that he didn't burst into tears when he got put in your arms later.'

'He doesn't exactly look like a newborn baby,' Alex said, eyeing the screeching child, who was struggling in her grip. 'He looks about seven.'

'Oh don't be so ridiculous,' Sue said, her beard quivering as she spoke. 'He's eight months old. We don't have a newborn in Poldore at the moment. Well, we do, Suzanne Eddy had one yesterday, but she seems to think historical accuracy comes second to the well-being of her newborn child. Honestly, first-time mothers are so fussy. Now, give the poor creature a cuddle. You've got eight minutes to bond before the pageant begins, and I want you on that goddamn donkey at precisely zero seventeen hundred hours. Now all I need to do is locate that Marissa.'

Sue, her wings in danger of flapping themselves right off the elastic, marched off with Lucy at her heels.

'Here.' Ruan chuckled, taking the baby out of Alex's arms, and cradling him against his chest. Clearly relieved to be in the hands of someone who knew what they were doing, the baby immediately relaxed against Ruan, his big blue eyes watching Alex warily. 'Babies just want to feel safe. Hold him like he is something really precious, and talk to him in a very silly, willy, ickle voice, yes. You like a silly, willy, lickle, ickle baby voice, don't you?'

The sight of tough, dark, brooding, moody Ruan talking baby talk and rocking the biggest baby that she had ever seen, was enough to make Alex laugh out loud.

'You have a go then, smart arse,' Ruan said, grinning and thrusting the baby towards her.

'I can't,' Alex said. 'I have no idea what to do with one of those.'

'It's a baby, not an alien,' Ruan said. 'Now rest most of his weight in the crook of your arm, see, and then use the other one to support his bum.'

This time, as Alex took hold of the baby, carefully following Ruan's example, she felt a little more secure, and when the baby, obviously curious about his new mode of transport, tipped his head back and looked into her eyes, she smiled instinctively.

'Hello, little lambkin pie,' she said in a sing-song voice. 'Hello, little sweetness.'

The baby smiled back at her, and it was like some sort of alchemy – Alex was instantly in love. 'Oh, you are a darling, little massive thing.'

'His name is Horatio,' Ruan told her. 'His dad is a Nelson buff.'

'Oh dear, you poor, poor little gorgeous thing, never mind, you are so, so handsome that all the girls will love you anyway, unless you like men, which is completely fine.' As the baby stared deep into her eyes, he seemed to concentrate on her with surprising focus, which at first Alex found charming and then slightly alarming as he went from a normal baby colour to a deep shade of puce. And then the smell found its way to her nose, and she realised what had happened.

'Oh God, it's done a poo,' she said, holding Horatio out at arm's length, so that he began to cry again. 'Help, it's done a poo, call someone, the police, and ambulance, someone!'

'You are funny,' Ruan said, chuckling as he took the baby. 'Come on, we've got about three minutes to get this little feller changed and back to his mum before the pageant starts. Luckily, Sue and Rory have got such a huge brood there are always nappies around. Follow me.'

The baby laughed as he jiggled on Ruan's shoulder and Alex realised as she walked in step next to man and very large baby that she was exceptionally happy. That maybe she had never felt this light or joyful or as full of laughter just brimming away beneath the surface before. What did it all mean?

'Here.' Ruan took her into what must be a playroom, because it was strewn all over with more toys than Alex had ever seen before in her entire life. In the corner there was a change station, which held a variety of nappies. Alex watched as Ruan expertly changed the little boy, making him giggle as he blew a raspberry on his tummy, before wrapping him up, ready for the cold outside.

'Here.' Alex took the considerably sweeter smelling Horatio back in her arms, pleased to see that since they had shared that special moment he was happy enough to nestle into the crook of her neck. 'If we go through here,' Ruan said. 'And cut through Sue's office, we should just about be bang on time.'

'Ruan, can I ask you something,' Alex began, as she followed him through a shadowy library, lined with books on all sides from the floor to the ceiling. 'Is it Marissa?' she asked him at last. 'Is it Marissa who makes you feel things?'

'Marissa?' Ruan said, as he opened another door and then stopped dead in his tracks. Alex didn't have to wait long to see why he had stopped, because they had done what Sue had not: they had found Marissa.

They had found Marissa perched on the edge of a large desk, her skirt pushed up to reveal the tops of her stockings, her shirt undone to reveal her small, perfect breasts, on one of which Rory Montaigne's hand was enthusiastically clamped, as his pale white bottom moved like a piston, between her thighs.

It was Marissa who saw them first.

'Rory,' she said, urgently tapping him on the shoulder. 'Rory.'

'Oh, Marissa,' he moaned in return, 'Oh yes, baby, oh yes.'

'Rory, fucking get off me!' she hissed, pushing him off her so that he stumbled backwards in his half-mast trousers, fell over a magazine rack and then tumbled onto the rug, leaving Alex with an explicit image in her mind that she could never unsee. Without thinking, she shielded Horatio's eyes.

'Ruan,' Marissa said, hurriedly trying to cover herself. 'It's not what it looks like.'

'We haven't got time for this,' Ruan said, grabbing Alex's hand. 'Come on.'

Alex was speechless as Ruan stepped over Rory and guided her out through the other door, just as the clock on the bell tower struck five precisely.

'Oh, well done.' Sue beamed at them, as a pink-faced blonde lady came and took Horatio out of Alex's arms.

Ruan then helped Alex up onto the float, lifting her into a side-saddle position on the makeshift donkey.

'Just a few words before we commence,' Sue said and the crowd groaned good-naturedly.

Alex noticed Marissa appearing out of the corner of her eye.

'Ain't you run out of words yet?' A voice came from the crowd that Alex was pretty sure belonged to Eddie. A ripple of laughter echoed round the courtyard.

'I know, I know. I have been, well, a bit of a tyrant in the last few weeks,' Sue said. 'I know that I've bossed you all about and made you do things that you would never normally do. But now is my chance to say thank you. Thank you to all of you who make Poldore such a wonderful town to live in. And for being part of this pageant, and keeping the history and tradition of Poldore alive.' She paused as the crowd cheered her, and Alex bit her lip as she saw Rory take his place at his wife's side. Delighted to see him, Sue kissed him on the cheek.

'I may have the body of weak and feeble woman,' she said, quoting Elizabeth I, who once (according to Sue, anyway) stayed the night in Castle House, 'but I have the heart and soul of a very strong-minded and bossy one, and I am so grateful to all of you for putting up with me so that we can create the magic that is the Poldore Christmas pageant.' This time the cheer was positively rowdy, and taken up by the expectant crowd outside the portcullis. 'Let the four hundred and eighty-seventh pageant begin!'

Chapter Twenty

The portcullis was hauled upwards, and Castle House's great wooden door swung open to reveal a constellation of stars beyond, just as if they had fallen down from the heavens and into the streets of Poldore.

It took Alex a moment or two to work out that the myriad of lights were, in fact, hundreds and hundreds of tiny candles, held by many of the crowd that was lining the street outside, creating a stunning sea of tiny, dancing pinpoints of light. As their float lurched into first gear, Alex almost slid off the donkey, but Ruan steadied her, putting his hands on her waist either side of the cushion bump, and keeping one arm firmly around her, shoring up her position.

In one giddy, joyful moment, Alex finally realised what this was that Sue, and everyone else, had been working so hard towards over the last few weeks and the months that had preceded her arrival in Poldore.

If the town had been decorated for the festive season before the pageant, now it seemed it had truly become Christmas. Yards and yards of lights were strung across the narrow streets, every single building along the pageant route was fronted with carefully painted scenery that transformed the small Cornish town into a Christmas card representation of Nazareth and Bethlehem. And, most wonderfully of all, as the moon sailed above the parting clouds, and their float slowly crept out of the gates of Castle House, Sue's crazy, eccentric film director supplied, as promised, fake snow, which somehow began to drift down from somewhere that Alex couldn't see – and, most miraculously of all, it seemed entirely appropriate in the circumstances.

The whole scene was fabulously mad and magical, and, for a moment, Alex was transported back to her childhood again, and remembered, in one sharp moment, how she and her father used to spray the windows with fake frost every year on the twelfth of December. When did they stop doing that? Alex wondered.

It was then that Alex caught Marissa's eye as she stepped in front of the float to take a few shots, and Alex thought if she'd been the one driving the jeep that was towing them, she would have been sorely tempted to put her foot down on the accelerator.

'We have to tell Sue,' she whispered to Ruan, her hushed tones only audible above the cheers of the packed crowd that lined the streets if she whispered right into his ear, which meant his dark curls tickled her lips. 'The first chance we get. We can't let them go on making a fool of her like that. Right under her nose, it's horrible.' She tried not to think of how Milly would feel if she knew of her own dalliance with her fiancé.

'It is, but we can't,' Ruan whispered back. This time it was his stubble grazing her cheekbone, as he spoke into her ear. 'She'll be devastated, and all of this that she's worked so hard for will be ruined. And it's Christmas Day tomorrow. There are three children in that house, Alex, who think it's the best and happiest day of the year. We can't do this to them on Christmas Eve.'

'We haven't done it.' Alex turned her face sharply, so all at once they were nose to nose, looking right into each other's eyes, which, just for a second, distracted Alex from what she was trying to say.

'Are you sure she's a virgin?' some joker called out from the crowd just outside what was usually the bakery, but was now a cluster of shivering palm trees.

Flustered, her heart feeling as if it might actually take flight, it was beating so rapidly, Alex turned away and took a second to compose herself.

'We aren't the ones who have done this,' she repeated, raising her voice above a whisper, because she felt that it was far too dangerous to have her lips that close to his again. 'We aren't the ones who've been having an affair, under her roof, in her home. It's them that have done it and we can't let them go on doing it. Imagine how she will feel when she finds out; we have to stop this now.'

Ruan was silent for a moment, tightening his grip on her as they lurched bumpily around a sharp bend. On the stairs of the old school house, the children's choir sang 'Away in a Manger', their faces lit by candles, looking so hopeful and happy. In amongst them, her fiery red curls making her easy to pick out, was Sue's eldest daughter, Petal. Where the other girls smiled angelically as they sang, each word saturated with sweetness, Petal sang with a particular kind of passion and vigour that made her robust tones stand out from the crowd, as she scowled her way through 'the little Lord Jesus asleep in the hay'. Ruan was right, Christmas would be awful if they told Sue what they had found out. It would be terrible for her and for the children, Petal included. But Marissa was due to sit down to lunch with them tomorrow as part of the family. Sue had probably picked her out a present. How much worse would it be if they all found out on Boxing Day or New Year's Day or in twenty years' time, after a lifetime of lies? If Alex knew anything, it was that the truth always came out, one way or another, and waiting to find it out only made it worse.

'We have to tell her,' she said, once again, as they left Petal and the rest of the choir behind. Alex slipped forwards on the donkey as they began the steep decline that was taking them down towards the bakery, and up again towards the church. As they travelled, the people who had been lining the street fell into step behind them, creating a long festive procession. 'If you're too afraid to then I will.'

'I can't let you do that,' Ruan said. Somehow his hand had found its way under her tunic and slipped under the belted-on cushion, so that his strong arm was encircling her waist. Alex thought that at that precise moment she might very well have actually swooned if it hadn't been for the fact that she was so angry with him. Being so unexpectedly physically attracted to Ruan wasn't going to do her any good; it was worse than having a crush on Marcus for all those years. Not only was Ruan still grieving for his lost love, he'd just found out that the woman he'd been having some sort of dalliance with was cheating on him with a man who wore mustard-coloured trousers and a Barbour jacket.

'Is it because you're upset too?' Alex asked Ruan, a tad more sharply than she intended. 'Look, I know you and Marissa had something between you, and it must sting to find out what she's been up to, but surely Sue's marriage is more important than a fling.' Alex drew a sharp inward breath as something hit her. 'Except that it was more than that, wasn't it? For you anyway, it was Marissa who was making you feel the things that you didn't think you should feel, wasn't it?'

'No!' Ruan said, horrified. 'No, is that what you thought? That I was seeing Marissa? That I was talking about Marissa when I said those things, about feelings, and stuff?'

'Well, yes,' Alex said, stiffly. 'Yes, she seemed to always leave a room when you left it, and enter one not long after you. And you flirted with her. A lot actually.'

'Did I?' Ruan looked genuinely perplexed. 'Cordy always tells me I couldn't flirt my way out of a paper bag. She says I have the romantic skills of a lump of rock. She's always worrying that some woman will take advantage of me on the one hand, but on the other she says I am so terrible at talking to them that I might as well become a monk.'

'I don't think you're terrible at talking to women,' Alex said.

'I don't think I'm terrible at talking to you,' Ruan replied. 'You're easy to talk to.'

Alex sighed inwardly; her perpetual role as tomboy sidekick/best friend had taught her how easy she was to talk to over the years, about other girls usually. Being easy to talk to was no great thing in her opinion – it clearly meant that the male in question didn't fancy you at all.

'Well, Marissa made it very clear that she fancied you,' Alex said, a little primly. 'I really thought she did, but maybe you were a decoy.'

'Well, if I was a decoy, I was a good one,' Ruan said. 'She did keep asking me to meet her. She even followed me out of the pub one night, and she was quite tipsy, so I walked her up to Castle House and . . .' Ruan coughed, as the float began creeping upwards again, the engine on the old jeep spluttering as it dragged its heavy load behind it, heading towards the church where the vicar was waiting to give the whole town a Christmas blessing. 'And, well, she sort of lunged at me, and we kissed a bit.'

'A bit,' Alex said. 'What qualifies as a bit?'

'Why? Do you care?' Ruan asked her.

'No,' Alex responded, at exactly the same moment as she realised that she cared very, very much. 'What a tart!'

Ruan laughed. 'Not sure that's appropriate language for the Mother of Jesus.'

The pageant gathered outside the Norman-built Church of Saint Piran, which was perched on the corner of three intersecting roads, one leading upwards, and two others either side, going into the heart of the town. It was one of the few areas of Poldore where so many people could fit all at once, crowding into the triangle of space the crossroads created. Slowly, the floats were surrounded by townsfolk, each one carrying a candle. As they waited outside the church, the crowd fell silent, until faintly from within its walls, Alex began to hear the sound of an altogether more tuneful choir than the one that Petal had been in.

'That's the Fisherman's Choir,' Ruan whispered in her ear. 'They rehearse with the vicar twice a week. He started it up when he arrived here last year. It's become quite a thing over the past few months. They keep trying to get me to sign up, even though I keep telling them I can't carry a tune in a bucket.'

'Gosh, it's really beautiful,' Alex said, as she listened to blended male voices singing 'In the Bleak Midwinter', voices that grew louder as the choir made a slow procession out of the church. The vicar, a surprisingly young man, led them out at their head.

Alex always thought that vicars should be old, decrepit even, certainly nothing at all like this rather good-looking young man. He was in his thirties, she guessed, with thick sandy-blond hair falling into his eyes, and a jaw line that wouldn't shame a male model.

'Nice vicar,' she said, appreciatively.

'The Reverend Jed Hayward?' Ruan chuckled. 'That's certainly what half the womenfolk of Poldore think too – the congregation has swelled quite considerably since he arrived – but our handsome young vicar's been in town for over a year, and still no lady friend.'

'He's waiting for Miss Right,' Alex said. 'There's no law that says you have to rush into a relationship. Some people like to take their time.' Like their entire lives, and still get it quite wrong, she thought to herself.

'Poldore!' The vicar was well spoken, his voice clear as it boomed out across Three Way Corner, aided by a little portable mike. 'First of all, may I wish you all a Merry Christmas and may I suggest that you wish your neighbour a Merry Christmas too. Whether you know or them not, share season's greetings with whoever is standing next to you.'

'He's very into all this touchy-feely stuff,' Ruan said, before looking deep into Alex's eyes. 'Merry Christmas, Alex.'

'Merry Christmas, Ruan,' Alex said, returning his gaze and his smile, her worries about Sue, Marcus and her parents momentarily eclipsed as he hugged her, while a chorus of 'Merry Christmasses' chimed all around them. For the briefest of moments Alex let herself lean into Ruan's beautifully sculpted body, conjuring up for just one fleeting second that image of him without his shirt on, and then she made herself pull back and take a breath of cold, calming air.

'The Poldore pageant has been telling the story of the nativity for generations,' Reverend Jed spoke again. 'Reminding us what Christmas is truly about, the birth of Jesus Christ. And for those of you who want to hear the real Christmas message you will be very welcome at our midnight service a little later on. But for now, and just in case you can't make it, I offer you this blessing.' He paused to take a deep breath. 'May the joy of the angels, the eagerness of the shepherds, the perseverance of the wise men, the obedience of Joseph and Mary, and the peace of the Christ child be yours this Christmas; and the blessing of God Almighty, the Father, the Son and the Holy Spirit be among you and remain with you always. Amen.'

'Amen,' the crowd repeated before breaking into spontaneous cheers.

'I wouldn't mind going to the midnight service,' Alex said thoughtfully.

'You and all the other single ladies,' Ruan said, a little sharply. 'That's how he gets the bums on seats.'

'There's nothing wrong with being charismatic,' Alex said, secretly smarting about being lumped in with 'all the other single ladies', as the pageant began to move again, commencing its final, slow descent towards the quay and the square. 'I thought it was really lovely.'

'Yes,' Ruan conceded. 'Yes, it was nice.'

Just as they started on the steep decline, the wind picked up again. Looking up, Alex saw that the moon was lost again behind a bank of ominous-looking clouds and she hoped that the little window of clement weather that St Austell Steve had spotted on the satellite wasn't completely over already. But even as her hope ascended upwards in something like a prayer, the first heavy drop of rain shattered on the tip of her nose, its fellows soon joining it, turning what might have been a shower into a full on storm. A few drops quickly turned into a deluge and soon they were all soaked through, the fake snow turning to slippery mush under the wheels of the float, the crowd darting for cover wherever they could find it.

And then suddenly the jeep that had been inching its way down the steep incline slipped a little, rolling forwards so quickly that it made Alex yelp, and cling on to Ruan. And then it slipped a little bit more, as the rapidly increasing flow of rain began to rush downhill around them, beginning to turn the street into a waterfall, this time for five or six feet.

'Oh shit,' Ruan said, lifting Alex off the donkey.

'What?' Alex asked him, grabbing him around the neck as the jeep picked up speed again, pitching them both forwards against the low railing, which was all that was keeping them on the trailer.

'It looks like Bill's brakes have gone again,' Ruan said, bracing himself as the truck picked up speed.

'What do you mean "again"?' Alex asked him in horror, as it hit her that if the jeep was out of control, the only thing that was going to stop their journey was the mouth of the river.

'We're going to have to jump for it,' Ruan shouted.

The jeep had picked up considerable speed, the quay and harbour were coming up very fast. From the clunking and complaining of the engine, it sounded like Bill was doing the best he could to try to slow down the jeep, changing down the gears, but nothing was happening. Alex realised that she had good reason to be scared.

'No!' Alex screamed at Ruan. 'We'll die if we jump.'

'It's better than drowning!' Ruan said.

Alex shook her head, knowing that jumping from

the float at this speed meant broken bones at the very least, possibly even injuring some of the crowd who were already diving out of the way of the jeep, flattening themselves against houses and walls as it rushed by. And what of Bill – he couldn't jump from the jeep. And then she had a thought.

'The handbrake!' she turned to Ruan. 'The handbrake!'

There was a beat of amazement on Ruan's face as he realised that Alex's suggestion was by far the better one. In the few seconds that they had left he tried everything to get Bill's attention, but the driver was intent on trying not to kill anyone, dramatically steering his vehicle away from pedestrians, as it gathered momentum.

With only a few seconds to spare, Ruan reached across the short distance and gripped the jeep's roof, and bridged the gap between the trailer and the jeep. Somehow he managed to slide through the thankfully unglazed back window, much to Bill's surprise, and forced the handbrake on. Alex was flung forwards off her feet as the jeep slowed to a screeching halt, the steering locked and the trailer crashed into its back end. Alex rolled forwards onto the railing and clung on for dear life as finally the world around her slowed down and stopped. As Alex lay there on her back, the rain pouring down, she looked up at the Christmas star on top of the tree and said her own private little prayer of thanks.

'Alex?' She heard Ruan calling her name, as he climbed up into the trailer. 'Alex?'

'I'm here, I'm fine.' She raised a rather limp hand and, a second later, Ruan leaped over the railing and scooped her up in his arms, as if she were in fact as light as a feather. And Alex, who couldn't remember why she was cross with him, and who did happen to have a good excuse to feel faint anyway, swooned into unconsciousness.

A few moments later, she woke up inside the town hall, dimly recognising the red and gold carpet in the foyer, as well as the sea of concerned faces all around her.

'Oh God, how embarrassing,' Alex said, sitting up. 'I'm fine honestly.'

'This is because you don't eat enough.' Gloria appeared at her side, sounding exactly how a mother should. She knelt on the floor and started robustly towelling her dry.

'Mum, get off me.' Alex batted her ministrations away. Although, secretly, she felt a pang at her mother's care for her, she was also acutely aware that Ruan was kneeling the other side of her.

'This is your mum?' he said, surprised.

'Hard to believe, I know.' Gloria winked at him. 'I do look more like her sister, it's true. And who are you? I'm hoping you're Santa come to tell me what a naughty girl I've been and spank me!'

'Mother, enough with the hideously dirty Santa comments,' Alex groaned.

'Oh, she's telling me off. She's OK,' Gloria said, smiling at Alex. 'She's fine. Thank you, young man, for saving her.'

'I'm not sure who saved who, actually,' Ruan said.

'Sorry,' a rotund silver-haired man, who Alex guessed must be Bill, mumbled. 'MOT's due next week, you see.'

'Is everyone else OK?' Alex asked. 'We didn't run anyone over?'

'Oh, there you are.' Sue appeared and all at once Alex remembered the horrible sight she had seen in Sue's office. The distraction of the car crash had actually been quite welcome. 'No one else is hurt, thank goodness for that, but the rain is bucketing down and the wind is gale force, so I think we should get on with the nativity and the carols before everyone gives up and goes home. Are you fit?' she added, as an afterthought.

'Yes, I'm fit,' Alex, said, not wanting to let Sue down, although privately she felt like she should go and check on St Austell Steve, not because she didn't think he was up to the job, but she because she had a feeling in the pit of her stomach that something wasn't quite right. She was just being foolish she told herself. Steve had said all the boats were safely in harbour, he'd said there was no traffic, nothing to worry about. He was experienced, he knew what he was doing, and yet she couldn't shake that nagging feeling of anxiety.

Sue and Gloria helped Alex to her feet, and she spotted Horatio and his mum in the small crowd. The baby gave a small squeal as he spotted his stand-in mum, and his chubby little face lit up as his real mum brought him forwards.

At the exact moment that Alex took him into her arms the power went out.

'That's it,' Sue said crossly. 'I'm having that vicar fired.' She lifted her megaphone. 'Ladies and gentlemen, if you have torches or candles that are still lit, please use them and stay where you are. There will now be a short intermission, while our illustrious mayor turns on the backup generator. Eddie! If you're drunk I'm going to hang your gold, frankincense and myrrh on my tree as decorations!'

'I'm going to pop over to the office while they get the lights back on,' Alex said, seizing her chance.

'Are you sure, darling?' Gloria said. 'It's awful out there. And you've just been in an accident – a near miss, anyway.'

'Yes, it's my job, Mum. I'll just be a minute,' Alex said. 'I'll feel better if I check.'

Alex shouldered her way through the damp crowd in the town hall foyer, and into the wildest weather she had ever experienced first-hand, even in Scotland. At once the wind tore at her clothes, cutting right through her costume, with an icy chill, and if Alex had dried off even slightly during her short time indoors, she was saturated again in the matter of seconds that it took her to get to the office.

'Hi, Steve!' Alex called out as she pushed the office door shut against the force of the wind, and pulled her costume off over her head. There was no answer, and when Alex turned around she found the office empty. Perhaps he'd popped out to get a sandwich, she thought, sitting down at her desk and examining the monitor to see the latest satellite weather updates, and the location of the boats safe in harbour. Everything seemed in order, despite the extreme weather; even Steve not being at his desk probably didn't merit the small niggle of worry that was still eating away at her. It was probably the whole awful business with Rory and Marissa, followed by the drama of the crash. That was enough to give her a whole room full of niggles. Just as Alex began to look for a notepad to leave Steve a note, the door blew open and Ruan came in.

'Everything OK?' he asked, soaking wet again. He was a man that carried the look off exceptionally well.

'Seems to be,' Alex said, returning her attention to the chaotic desk, rather than appear to be dwelling on him. 'Although Steve isn't here. He's probably popped out or something. But on the whole all quiet on the western front.'

'Good.' The room was suddenly very quiet, even as

the wind gusted and rattled the window panes outside. Ruan stood by the door, his soaking hair hanging in wet waves, his skin glistening with droplets of water. Alex sat in the chair, acutely aware of how her mother's fine grey sweater clung damply to her skin.

'Um, there's a towel, let me get you a towel,' she said, standing up and going into the little kitchen, suddenly feeling the need to put as much space as possible between the two of them.

'Feels like we've been here before,' Ruan said, following her to the kitchen doorway where he stopped to watch her take a thin and rather worn towel down from the peg.

'Oh yes,' Alex said. 'The first night we met.'

She meant to hand him the towel, that was what she meant to do, but instead she found herself rubbing his damp neck with it, and what was exposed of that magnificent chest, holding her breath with every stroke.

'That kiss with Marissa,' he said, his voice low, his mouth close to hers. 'It was nothing, and it was awful anyway, all gums and teeth. It was over in a second, and I told her right then that I wasn't interested in her that way.'

'You don't have to explain,' Alex said, watching her hand as if it were an alien creature all of its own, undo first one, then two, then three buttons of Ruan's shirt and towel him gently a little lower.

'And the reason,' Ruan went on, swallowing as Alex

continued to rub him. 'The reason I didn't want to put my arm around you at rehearsal. It wasn't because I didn't want to put my arm around you. It was because I didn't want the first time I touched you to be in front of half the town. I've thought a lot about what it would be like to touch you, Alex, and it wasn't like that.'

Alex stopped towelling, stopped breathing even, and if she'd been present enough to be able to notice, her heat skipped a single beat as she listened to him.

'It's you, Alex,' he said, softly. 'You're the girl that makes me feel things I never expected to feel ever again. Never in a hundred years. No, that's not right. The things I feel for you . . . this is the first time ever that I've felt them. And it's *you* that makes me feel that way.'

'Oh . . . I . . .' Alex wasn't exactly sure what she was planning to say, but it didn't matter, because before she could finish the sentence Ruan's lips were on hers. His arms encircled her waist, as they kissed, and Alex was lost in something entirely new to her, as wave after wave of desire ran the length of her body – along with his hands – in long delicious shudders. She kissed him back hungrily, feeling his hand grip her bottom, hearing a deep groan somewhere in his throat, as he pulled her hips tights against him, his desire answering her own.

'My God, you're perfect,' he whispered, his hand in her hair, the other gently tipping her chin back as he kissed her neck. His hands then found the hem of her sweater and pulled it up over her head. Ruan's eyes raked across her torso. 'Utterly perfect.'

'Thank you,' Alex heard herself say, ridiculously polite. 'You're pretty good yourself.'

He ran a tip of one finger along her jaw line, down her neck and over the swell of her breasts.

'Oh, Alex.' He pulled her to him and Alex caught her breath as Ruan found the catch of her bra, their eyes meeting, just as he was about to undo it. And then the door crashed open, and Ruan bundled her further into the kitchen, out of the sight of the intruder.

'Ruan, are you in here?' a male voice called.

'Yep,' Ruan said, fighting to keep his voice level, his eyes still devouring Alex.

'We're launching the lifeboat, we need you, mate!'

Alex gasped, as, shaking his head, Ruan composed himself and went out to greet the man.

Alex closed the door behind him.

'What on earth is out in this?' she heard him ask.

'Bunch of teenagers, took their dad's motor dinghy out, didn't tell the parents. They only just found out, because they went home and it was missing, along with a case of beer and a note.'

'A motor dinghy in this weather?' Ruan sounded horrified. Just then Alex noticed a wet and muddy piece of paper on the floor. She picked it up and was just able to make out the message scrawled on it in blotchy ink: 'Gone to help out some kids who've gone a bit far out to sea. Back in ten. Sx.'

'Steve's gone out too,' she said, after pushing her dignity aside to rush back into the office. She held out the note to Ruan and the man she realised was Andy from the lifeboat crew. 'He must have thought there was no one else around to help. He's already gone out after them.'

Taking the note, Ruan and Andy ran out of the door, Alex at their heels as they made their way down to the lifeboat launch. In a matter of minutes the men were wearing protective clothing and Alex watched, her heart rending in two with anxiety, as Ruan raced to the lifeboat, seconds before it was launched. All she could think was that even a lifeboat didn't look big enough to withstand the storm that was raging all around them.

'Oh no.' Eddie appeared at her side, bundled up in a huge anorak. 'Sue sent me to fetch you in case the lights came back on, but I guess there won't be any nativity now. Dear God, I hope they bring those poor souls home safe.'

'I didn't know,' Alex said. 'I didn't know that Ruan was a volunteer.'

'Oh yes,' Eddie said. 'He has been ever since he lost Merryn.'

Chapter Twenty-one

It was Eddie who insisted that Alex came back to the town hall to wait for news of the lifeboat. Alex's first instinct had been to go back to the office and listen in on the radio for any news that might come, but Eddie steered her towards the town hall, where a large proportion of the town were waiting.

'Someone needs to be in the office,' she insisted.

'News will come when it comes,' Eddie told her. 'The harbour's locked down and safe, there's nothing you can do in there. There's no good way to hear bad news,' he told her, 'but over the radio's got to be the worst way of all.'

'You think it will be bad news?' Alex asked him, her blue eyes wide with fear, anxiety overtaking the cold and exhaustion and keeping it at bay, as adrenalin kept her on her feet.

'Not at all,' Eddie. 'Not at all. Alex, there's no need to take this so personally, love. You did nothing wrong, it was Steve who was on duty, and the second he knew there were kids out there, he should have called nine nine nine and got the coastguard, not gone out there on his own. He knows that.'

'The weather was calm. He thought it would hold long enough for him to bring the kids in,' Alex said, unhappily. 'I bet it was because he knew all the lifeboat crew were involved in the pageant. He's such a nice man.'

'There, there.' Eddie guided Alex through the nearly silent throng of people to her mother, who put her arm around her shoulder and kissed her temple, a gesture of affection and reassurance that Alex felt grateful for, too worn out by the highs and the lows of the last few hours to question what right her absentee mother had to care for her.

As they sat side by side in the hall, now lit only by candles, a lone male tenor voice began to sing, not a carol, but a hymn, 'Amazing Grace'.

When Alex looked up she saw Reverend Fred, standing alone on the abandoned nativity set, his face lit only by a torch he was holding. Slowly but surely, other voices joined in – first there were three or four, then ten or more, until everyone in the hall who knew the words was singing too, and those who didn't were humming along. And, at the moment the music swelled to fill every corner of the room, Alex could bear it no longer, and she had to find a quiet place to go and cry. Standing up, she almost ran up the aisle and out into the shadowy foyer, finding her way to the empty town hall office, dimly lit by the emergency lights in the lobby.

Sinking down onto the office chair, Alex buried her head in her hands and wept.

It couldn't have been very long before Gloria arrived with a lantern she had found somewhere and set it down on the desk.

'Oh dear,' Gloria said softly, sitting opposite her. 'I do believe you've had a really very emotional time over the last couple of days. And I suppose at least part of that is my fault. I'm sorry, darling. It must all seem a bit much right now.'

Alex looked up at her, calmer now that the flood of tears that had been steadily building up within her had finally broken through. Calmer and tired, so, so tired. If only she could close her eyes, she thought, she might sleep for a thousand years.

'Actually,' Alex said, watching Gloria in the lantern light, her features changing slightly with every flicker, 'I've been sort of glad you've been here.'

Alex sounded as surprised about the fact as her mother was.

'Tell me, Alex,' Gloria said, 'is there something going on between you and your devastatingly handsome co-star? Because if the real Joseph had been that good-looking I don't think Mary would have held out for an angel.'

'Mother!' Alex laughed despite herself. Whatever else her mother wasn't, she was certainly a lot of fun.

'Well?' Gloria asked.

'I don't know.' Heat seared through Alex as she thought of the few minutes she had spent with Ruan's hands all over her in the harbour master's office, and how her hands had been so keen to explore him. Of the way he'd kissed her, and the way she'd kissed him back, for the first time in her life not worrying about what should go where, or how it should be done, not conscious of anything except her desire for him. 'I think maybe, but . . . then this happened and now he's out there, and it's really dangerous, Gloria. It really is. There's a good chance that none of them will come back.'

As Alex's voice caught, Gloria reached across the table and patted her hand. 'There, there, darling,' she said, soothingly. 'It will be all right.'

'And even if there is something between us, what does it mean? I mean what if it just means that he is a really good kisser?' Alex said. 'How do I know if it means anything?'

'Well, it was really good kissing that kept me and your father going for as long as we did,' Gloria said. 'Although in the end that wasn't enough to keep him interested in me.'

'Exactly!' Alex said. 'I mean he might be really good-looking, and kind and funny and sensitive, with a rock-hard chest . . .' She paused for a moment to compose herself. 'But what if that's it? What if it's just physical attraction that we have in common? And anyway, what am I playing at? Right up until almost now, Marcus has been the official love of my life. What sort of person am I if I decide that I love one person totally and utterly, and then change my mind based on . . .well, some snogging?'

'I can't tell you what you feel, and what you don't feel or for whom,' Gloria said. 'But I can tell you that love is a lot less complicated than you think it is. Either you are in it, or you are not. And if you stop for a second and really concentrate, you will know which one it is.'

'Were you really in love with Dad?' Alex asked her.

'Yes,' Gloria answered without hesitation. 'Yes, I really was. But I quickly realised that he was really in love with Eleanor. He did try not to be, to give him his credit. He did his best, but it was something he couldn't fight.'

'And do you hate him now?' Alex asked. 'For letting you down?'

'No.' Gloria was quiet for a moment. 'I suppose that if I stopped for a second and really concentrated, I'd say that I still loved him, even now. Perhaps that's why I do my best not to do either.' Her smile was wide, brave, but full of unexpected pain.

'Why didn't you take me with you?' Alex asked her suddenly. 'Didn't you love me enough?'

Gloria withdrew her hand, and sank back into her chair, dropping her gaze. The shadows the lantern cast seemed to stretch and lengthen her face into a theatrical mask of sorrow.

'I understand why you were hurt and angry,' Alex said. 'And why you had to leave. But why didn't you take me with you? Didn't you want me?'

'Of course I wanted you,' Gloria looked up, leaning forwards in her chair. 'You were the apple of my eye, you were my heartbeat. The only person in the world who loved me, and who I loved more than anything. Of course I wanted you, Alex. I wanted to take you with me, I just couldn't.'

'Why not, wouldn't Dad let you?' Alex asked. 'Did he keep me from you?'

'No.' Gloria shook her head. 'Your father might not ever have been able to truly love me, but he would never have been so cruel, not to me or to you. I was hurt, so hurt when I realised that he and Eleanor were together. And so I had to leave. I couldn't be with him another moment, but, Alex, I didn't have a job, or any skill that might get me a job. My modelling days were over. I didn't have a place to live, I had no idea where I was going or what I was going to do. I remember the night I packed my bag. I remember going into your bedroom, and you were sleeping, so cosily. Snuggled up with that funny little blue octopus you loved so much. An octopus! I've never seen a child with a cuddly octopus, before or since.' Alex did not mention that Oswald, now sporting only seven legs, since a rather robust encounter with Buoy, was carefully packed inside her suitcase under the bed. 'And I knew I couldn't take you out of this lovely, safe warm place into a cold, wet night with no idea of where we were headed. My plan was always to go, get settled and come back for you. I thought it would take a week or two at most, perhaps a month.'

'Instead it took you twenty-five years?' Alex said. 'And how many husbands? Surely at some time during those last twenty-five years you must have been settled enough to at least send me a postcard.'

'It took a lot longer than I thought for me to find my feet,' Gloria said, sadly. 'I was hopelessly naive. But it didn't take twenty-five years. It took a year. I came back for you after a year.'

'No, you didn't.' Alex shook her head. 'You didn't.'

'I didn't have any qualifications or practical experience other than looking pretty,' Gloria said. 'So I got a job in a shop in Edinburgh, but it paid pennies. I couldn't find a place to live that I could afford, so ended up sleeping on a friend's floor and paying her for the privilege. It took me time, time to get promoted in the fashion department, time to earn a little more. To be able to afford a room of my own. And as soon as I had a bedroom, I came for you. '

'You didn't,' Alex insisted. 'If you had we wouldn't be having this conversation.'

'I've always wondered if you remembered,' Gloria

said sadly. 'I had always hoped that you did, but it seems I was wrong. I came back for you. You were playing in the front yard, on the steps. Not much of a garden, is it? Just a few feet of concrete with a railing round. You were sitting on the front steps having a dolls' tea party. I stopped, waiting for you to see me and to run into my arms, but you didn't. You looked up, smiled and offered me a cup of tea. You didn't recognise me, and that hurt. It hurt that you had forgotten me already.'

Alex caught her breath, her fingers clenching on the edge of the desk. She didn't remember her mother coming, but she did remember the yellow lady, the sun lady. Who came to play and have tea with her once. Or rather she remembered telling her dad about her, and that still her father joked about her imaginary friends Rebecca Constantinople and the Yellow Lady who came to tea. But, what if the yellow lady had been her mother?

'You looked so happy,' Gloria said. 'You were so happy and you didn't recognise me. We played tea parties for a quite a while, and I kept expecting Ian to come out and discover us. I could hear the radio on in the house, the front door was open, but he didn't. It was Eleanor who found me. She came out the front, going to the shops or something, and caught me. I'd told you I'd be back in a minute and I went to see her.'

'She knew you'd been and she didn't tell my dad?' Alex asked, angrily.

'She begged me not to take you away. She said that Ian lived for you. That he insisted on keeping their relationship a secret to protect you. She said that if I took you away, he'd be devastated and so would you. She told me about how you loved nursery. How you played with the boys as much as the girls, how you spoke your mind even at four years old. How nothing scared you. She told me you were happy, and that, if I wanted, she would help me to talk things through with Ian, find a way to share custody. Weekends and holidays—'

'But it was none of her business!' Alex all but shouted. 'What did it have to do with her?'

'I remember thinking that she must really love Ian, to beg me not to take you. How much easier it would have been for her to have him if you weren't there. But she wanted him to be happy more than she wanted it for herself.' Gloria nodded once. 'Eleanor has always cared for you, Alex, at a distance perhaps, but that wasn't her choice. It was your father's. With his funny sets of rules and codes of conduct. It was me who decided to break the ties. You were happy, you were secure. You didn't know who I was. If I took you then, even for the weekends, it would have felt like you were going with a stranger. That's what I told myself. I told myself I was doing the right thing by not rocking the boat.' Gloria shook her head. 'The right thing for you.'

Alex stared at her. 'It's never the right thing to abandon your child.'

'I know,' Gloria said simply, suddenly looking her age. 'I know that now. I've known that for about the last twenty years, but, even then, it seemed too late.'

'I may not have known you, or remembered you on that day – I was barely four years old!' Alex went on. 'But I missed you, I've always missed you. Every single day, and the worst thing is . . . The worst thing is I didn't know it until you turned up. You even took that away from me. You took me being able to miss you away from me too.'

Alex stood up, not sure where she was going or what she planned to do, except at that moment a cheer rose up from the direction of the hall. Stumbling in her bid to run, Alex slammed her thigh into the corner of a desk and then careered into a door handle as she hurried to find out what the news was. It was the lifeboat, it was back.

'What happened?' she asked Horatio's mum, who was jiggling the baby on her hip.

'Everyone back safe,' she told Alex happily. 'The boys and Steve are spending the night in hospital, but they should be back home in time for their turkey.'

Just at that moment the lights in the hall came on and everyone cheered for the second time.

'Oh God, what a relief,' Alex said as, searching the

throng of people, she spotted Ruan's head above the crowd. She began to fight her way across the sea of celebrating people to see him, because she knew that the second she looked into his eyes, she'd know exactly what it was that was happening between them.

'Brilliant news!' Lucy said, grabbing her and kissing her on the cheek.

'Wonderful, isn't it?' Sue said, patting her firmly on the back as she edged between her and Mrs Carmichael from the Tourist Information.

'Thank God,' Reverend Jed said, clasping her hand and smiling into her eyes for a moment, before moving on to the next person.

'Alex, can we talk?' Marissa was at her elbow, which Alex accidentally on purpose slightly dug into her ribs, perhaps a tad more viciously than was required.

Still she pressed on, and Ruan was in sight, just on the other side of a little clearing of people and then the weirdest thing happened.

Marcus appeared in the centre of the space and stood right in front of her. Alex tried to look around him, but he sort of dodged from side to side until at last he had her full attention.

'Marcus, what is it?' she asked him, impatiently.

And he started to sing.

The first thing that happened was that Alex's jaw dropped, and then her ears protested, because Marcus had never been able to sing, least of all the Madonna classic, 'Like a Virgin'. But that was exactly what he was doing. He was singing, and Alex was fairly sure she wasn't hallucinating, because of the gut-wrenching horror of being suddenly the centre of so much attention, and although she couldn't see it, the sensation of Ruan's gaze burning a hole through the centre of Marcus's chest was all too real.

And then it got worse.

One by one, more male voices joined in and Alex realised that while Ruan and the other lifeboat men were out at sea, rescuing people, Marcus had been recruiting the remaining members of the choir, including Reverend Jed, into joining in with his bizarre and, in Alex's opinion, highly inappropriate song of choice, which for reasons that she did not fully understand he was singing to her, quite terribly, in front of everyone. The Fisherman's Choir assembled around her best friend, building to a crescendo, which finished with the weirdest display of jazz hands that Alex had ever seen. If this was Marcus's tact-free attempt at an apology, then all she wanted was for the madness to be over so she could go and talk to Ruan.

But then, Marcus gestured to the cheering and laughing crowd to quieten down and Alex realised, with ice-cold dread, that he was planning to say something. It was never good when Marcus said something in public, especially if he was a bit drunk. Look at that time he said that the president of the

Scottish Rugby Club's wife had really great tits when he was accepting the best newcomer award.

So Alex was ready for mortification on a grand scale. She was braced for it. But she was absolutely not prepared for what happened next.

Marcus dropped down onto his knees.

'Alex Munro,' he said, 'I've known you since you were a wee girl, who used to stick crayons up her nose. You and me, we grew up together, we know the same places, the same people, we've always been together. And you have been my best friend. Which is why I am an absolute effing idiot for not noticing that you are the fittest woman in the world, oh yes, and that I love you. So, Alex Munro, please will you marry me?'

The hall erupted into spontaneous cheers, and Alex, all colour draining from her face, looked up to see Ruan watching her, his face tight, closed and, worst of all, hurt.

'Do it! Do it! Do it! Do it!' the crowd began to chant.

Alex looked back at Marcus and saw the man she had spent most of her life dreaming about on his knees, wearing his heart on his sleeve, telling her that he loved her more than anything in the world, and she didn't know what to do. A few hours ago, in the office with Ruan, she would have known exactly what to say, but now, now the idea of hurting Marcus, her oldest friend, in front of all these people, seemed impossibly cruel.

'So, Alex,' Marcus asked her, with a hopeful shrug, 'what do you say?'

'Um . . . Marcus,' Alex said. 'I . . .' She tried desperately to think of what to say next, how to explain to Marcus how she felt. 'Marcus, I do love you . . .'

And the crowd went wild, drowning out Alex's 'but' while she was still forming the sentence that would follow.

Chapter Twenty-two

Christmas Day

Alex sat bolt upright in bed, and immediately regretted it as the room spun, her head pounded and the contents of her stomach threatened to make an unscheduled reappearance. Carefully, she lowered herself back onto the pillow and realised with a lurch of dread that the last thing she remembered from last night was seeing the back of Ruan's head, as he left the second after she had accidentally accepted Marcus's stupid proposal of marriage. Then there had been a sort of generic celebration party, and then nothing.

Alex panicked, as much as she was able to when any sudden movement was likely to make her throw up, terrified that she might have decided that last night was not only the perfect time to agree to get married to a man she wasn't all too sure she loved, but also the right time to have sex for the first time with her now fiancé. Opening her eyes against the painfully bright light, Alex worked out that at least she was in her own bed, in her own cottage. That was a good thing. Patting the bed to her side, the only sleeping body she found there was Buoy, and even he seemed not to be especially talking to her, curled up as he was facing away, not up against her feet as he usually did.

Still that meant nothing, that might just mean that Marcus was up already. Highly unlikely after a big night out, but not totally beyond the bounds of possibility. Gingerly, Alex lifted the duvet and peered beneath it. The immeasurable joy she felt at discovering she was still wearing last night's clothes almost outweighed the terrible hangover and the ever dawning realisation that last night she had made the biggest mistake of her life.

And to cap it all it was Christmas Day.

Slowly this time, she raised herself up onto her elbows and, when the world didn't end, gradually raised herself into a full sitting position. It wasn't that bad of a hangover, she thought, as hazy memories of much dancing, drinking and carousing came back to her in flashes. The townsfolk of Poldore might not have had their pageant in quite the same way as it had been for the last four hundred years, but they did have a lot to celebrate, and they were determined to do it in style. Somehow, the rescue of the teenagers and St Austell Steve, and Marcus's crazy proposal had been adopted by them all. Eddie opened up the bar in the foyer, and before long Reverend Jed was leading them in a good deal of raucous carol singing. It would have been a brilliant night if somehow she hadn't accidentally agreed to get engaged. Oddly, Alex didn't remember spending hardly any time at all with Marcus. The moment he'd heard her declaration of love, he'd picked her up in a sort of vice-like grip and kissed her firmly closed mouth, before putting her down, and now that he had safely netted her, went off to be manly with his new best friends, the Fisherman's Choir. And Alex never got her chance to say, 'But I don't want to marry you, Marcus.'

It had been her absolute intention to sit him down and talk properly about things, or, failing that, to slope quietly away and curl up in bed and die, but no one would let her. People kept stopping her, buying her drinks, hugging her, kissing her, congratulating her, and it would have been absolutely lovely if it hadn't been a really terrible mistake.

Alex experimented with putting first one and then the other foot on the floor. And when that worked out OK she stood up, very slowly. Buoy raised his head, shot her a look of pure disgust and then got up and went downstairs, as if he couldn't stand to be in the same room with her any more. And Alex didn't blame him.

One careful step at a time she made her way down the stairs, where the sight of her mother in the kitchenette, elbow deep in a turkey, made her gag. She threw open the front door and headed out into the garden. Taking deep breaths of the cool damp air, Alex looked up at the sky. It was dense and white, but looked benign. A few more steps and she could see the sea in the harbour was calm and flat, and just beyond the edge of the town the lighthouse, Ruan's lighthouse, stood tall and proud.

Christmas Day, and she was due at work, but not quite yet. Alex glanced at her watch. It was a little after ten, that wasn't too bad. If she could get into the shower, get dressed, force some toast down, then she could be in the office at eleven. That was where she needed to be this morning. She needed to be in the office, gazing at her screens and devices. Lost in a world of symbols and patterns, where real people didn't come along and make everything so complicated.

Gloria appeared at her side, wearing a sea-green dress, her nails perfectly manicured and well scrubbed after their liaison with the insides of a turkey. She even had a face of full make-up on. She might not have been the most successful mother in the world, but Alex knew it had been Gloria who'd guided her onto the boat last night, and helped her find her way safely up the steps and put her into bed, displaying unexpected sensitivity by allowing Alex to go to sleep in what she had been wearing, and not have to go through some horrible minutes wondering who it was who'd put on her pyjamas. Alex was very glad that

Gloria had been there last night, and now she smiled at her.

'Slightly bad news. I was just examining the turkey and quite a large portion of it is missing in action, presumed chewed by Buoy. I don't know how he got in that fridge, but he's definitely been at it, unless it was always a one-legged bird. I'm sorry, because I wanted to do this for you.'

Alex shrugged. 'It doesn't matter. I don't really fancy lunch at the pub, but we could just have toast and hot chocolate, that would be OK by me, as long as the awful sickening feeling of total dread that I've got goes away.'

'I don't mind what it is I eat, as long as I am with you,' Gloria said ever so gently, as Alex felt stronger with every breath of Cornish air. 'I don't want to pry – God knows I probably lost my right to, a long time ago – but I can't help feeling that not everything is quite right when a woman who has just got engaged spends her first night as a fiancée on the other side of a river from her intended.'

'I didn't know what to say,' Alex said. 'Everyone was looking!'

'You should have said no, I am not in love with you, Marcus. I've got the hots for that sexy Joseph. Fortunately, he was in no fit state to be much of a lover, and so it was easy enough to take you home without there being an awkward moment.'

'Thank you,' Alex said, the relief evident on her face.

'That's OK. Now, if sexy Joseph had been anywhere to be seen, I would have brought him home with us.'

'His name is Ruan, it means river in Cornish,' Alex said quietly, as she watched the greyish green hills emerge from the mist. 'Jago told me when he was filling me in on all the other things I needed to know to be inducted officially into the town. Next year he's going to teach me Cornish wrestling.'

'Or did you secretly Google it, because you couldn't stop thinking about him?' Gloria asked her, and Alex declined to answer.

'It's more than just fancying him. I wasn't sure until just now, when I came out of the door, and I looked across the river and I saw his lighthouse. And then I realised, I might have grown up in Grangemouth, but this is my home. This is a place that I love, and one of the reasons I love it is because he is here. And I love him. And as long as he is here I will never want to leave.'

Alex turned and looked at her mum, her eyes wide in shock and understanding. 'I've fallen in love with him, how did that happen?'

Gloria smiled. 'The usual way. Although, darling, the fact that you accepted another man's proposal in front of his very eyes might prove to be something of a fly in the ointment.'

'Oh God.' Alex buried her head in her hands. 'I am

never going to sort this mess out, am I? And I've got to go to work!'

'You must be one of the most diligent people that I have ever met,' Gloria said laughing. 'Your life is falling apart, and you're worried about managing the sleepiest Christmas Day harbour that I have ever seen. Even I know that you are not obliged to go to work today, you're just going in to avoid dealing with everything else.'

Gloria was right. As Alex looked down at the estuary, dotted with boats and ships of all sizes, it could have been a painting, it was so still and peaceful. And Alex had every right to take Christmas Day off, along with everyone else. It was her decision to work.

'Look, this is what we will do. You go and have a shower, get dressed. I hope you don't mind, but when I went to town to get the food, I picked you up a few things, as a little Christmas gift; you'll find them in your wardrobe. And then we'll all go over together, you, me and Buoy. I can sit in the office, you can tell me what to look out for and if anything happens, which I very much doubt that it will, I can come and get you. In the meantime, you can find Marcus and break off your engagement, and then find Ruan and break the buttons off his shirt as you rip it off with your teeth.'

Alex laughed, and in a quite spontaneous moment,

put her arms around her mother and hugged her. 'I'm so glad you are here,' she said. 'I'm sorry I didn't get you a present.'

'Oh,' Gloria said, hugging her back, 'you gave me my present already. You gave me a second chance.'

Chapter Twenty-three

A short time later, Alex left her mother in her office drinking tea and reading a very racy-looking novel, and seeming quite content to be where she was for now. As she walked into the middle of the square, Alex looked both ways, towards the Silent Man, where she knew Eddie and Becky would be gearing up to cook Christmas dinner for half the town, and up to Castle House were Ruan had been invited, along with Cordelia and Reverend Jed, for lunch with Sue and Rory. Marissa would be there too, opening presents and fighting over the box of chocolates with the children. The thought made Alex sick, but really, as things stood, was she any better? Milly had trusted Marcus when he came down here to see Alex, even though he was still here on Christmas Day. And during that time they had done more than enough to really hurt the poor girl, who had done no wrong other than fall in love with the great oaf. All this time and Alex had barely given her a second thought. It wasn't good enough. It all had to be sorted out now.

'Which way first, Buoy?' she asked the dog, who was

standing at her side, panting. Buoy seemed to give the question some serious consideration and then trotted a few steps towards the pub.

'You're right,' Alex said, deciding he was actually advising her in his capacity as woman's best friend, and not just because Eddie always gave him a plate of sausages. 'Once I've set things straight with Marcus, then I can go and tell Ruan how I feel about him with a clear conscience.'

'I would say that he already knows,' Marissa said, appearing at her side. 'Accepting a proposal of marriage from another man could be seen as rather conclusive.'

'Well,' Alex said, starting towards the Silent Man, 'you don't seem to have issues with exclusivity.'

'Alex, please, wait, just hear me out.' Marissa put a leather-gloved hand on her arm, which Alex shrugged off.

'What?' she asked her.

'I know what you saw looked really bad,' Marissa said. 'It was really bad, but you have to understand I love Rory, and the children. We never meant to fall in love, it just happened. We are planning to tell Sue at the right time.'

'And when is the right time to tell the person who's given you a job and a home that you've been sleeping with their husband under their own roof?'

'Well, not today, anyway,' Marissa said. 'Please, Alex. I've talked to Ruan and . . .'

Alex rolled her eyes and began walking.

'He's said if we come clean after Christmas, ourselves, then he won't say anything.'

'That's what he says is it?' Alex asked her. 'Were you attempting to kiss him at the time? And, out of interest, what does Rory think of you sneaking around back alleys kissing other men?'

'Oh, Ruan told you that I kissed him?' Marissa said, raising an eyebrow. 'Oh no, that wasn't how it was at all. Ruan kissed me. I gave him the brush off, of course. Like I said, I love Rory. It's going to be difficult for Sue, moving on. I know that. But once Castle House is sold, and Rory has his half of the money, I think she will feel happier, I truly do. I think the enormous responsibility of that place has really weighed heavily on her. I think it's one of the reasons that she is just a dreadful cow.'

Alex spent about three seconds wondering how much she would hate herself if she slapped Marissa, and decided not at all, but she somehow knew that if she gave in to the wonderful temptation, Marissa would have gained some sort of moral high ground, which she did not deserve, so instead she walked away, marching to the pub.

'So you won't say anything?' Marissa insisted on following and Alex wondered if she ordered Buoy to bite her, would he do so. She didn't think so somehow; Marissa's skinny frame wasn't nearly so appealing as a plate of bacon.

'Say anything about what?' Sue asked her, appearing from within the Silent Man, going on without waiting for an answer. 'Good, I'm glad I've found you, Alex, I was just about to come to the office. I wanted to invite you and your fiancé to Castle House for lunch. I've told Marcus, but I know what men are like, rubbish all of them, so I am double issuing the invitation. I say lunch but it probably won't be ready until about five, but do come over anytime, we have roaring fires, presents, chocolates galore, it will be wonderful! Of course your charming mother is welcome, too. Dear Brian is coming over and I noticed that the two of them were getting on quite well at the party last night.'

'Oh well, I . . .'

'I just saw Gloria going into the office with you, didn't I? I'll pop over there now and appraise her of arrangements. See you later, any time from noon!' Sue said happily. 'We've got so much to celebrate.'

Alex watched her go and then looked at Marissa. 'Well,' she said. 'Merry Christmas, Marissa.'

Alex's mind was racing as she headed into the heat and joviality of the pub. It was already packed with a mixture of locals, and tourists, Christmas weekenders, a few faces that Alex recognised from the front of gossip magazine and newspapers. The beer was flowing, and Eddie was in his element. Lucy was wearing a Miss Santa outfit, and had tinsel in her hair, and even

Becky was wearing a tiny pair of Christmas tree earrings that flashed as they dangled from her ears.

'Here she is!' Eddie shouted as soon as he caught sight of her. 'The blushing bride to be! Let's raise a drink to her shall we, everyone?'

'To Alex and Marcus!'

Alex could see Lucy digging her dad in his side and whispering something in his ear, as the pub toasted her on an engagement that wasn't real and was about to last another ten minutes, but she couldn't see what Lucy was saying as her back was turned to her. As politely as she could, Alex, smiled and thanked people for their good wishes, battling her way through a sea of festive joy, to reach the door that led to the rooms upstairs.

'He's in room four,' Lucy told her, beckoning her out into the relative quiet of the back hall with a jerk of her head. The unmistakable aroma of Christmas dinner and all the trimmings filled the back room, and Lucy could hear the chef, Mary Bramble, singing along to the *Best of Bing Crosby* with gusto in the kitchen. All around the bells were ringing out, proclaiming that it was Christmas Day, but Alex had never felt less Christmassy in her life.

'You OK?' Lucy asked her.

'Well, I am a class A, one hundred per cent idiot, who accidentally agreed to marry a man she's not in love with in front of the whole town, seriously upsetting someone else I actually am rather keen on in the process,' Alex said. 'Rather keen' was a gross understatement, but she wasn't quite ready to proclaim her true feelings to the world just yet, not when they were so new, and not to mention as likely to be doomed to failure and futility as her twenty-year devotion to Marcus had been. 'Oh and I've got a shocking hangover. But apart from that, fine.'

'You look great, anyway,' Lucy said, giving her a hug. 'I think you might have found your style.'

Alex glanced down at herself. She was wearing a pair of deep indigo skinny jeans, some super soft leather long boots and a charcoal-grey ribbed jersey top, with at least fifty hooks and eyes down the front. It was amazing that her mother, who'd known her as an adult for barely forty-eight hours, had worked out exactly what she should be wearing in no time at all, even when it was completely the opposite of anything that Gloria herself would wear. Alex did feel confident, even a little bit sexy in the outfit. She was finally learning to embrace her curves, and, she thought in passing, she rather hoped that Ruan would learn to embrace them again too.

'I didn't discover my style,' Alex said. 'My mum did.'

'It's so lovely that your mum has turned up, and that you're getting on so well.' Lucy beamed at her. 'And don't worry, I'm sure that everything will work out OK between you and your love triangle.'

'Are you drunk?' Alex asked her. 'I'm pretty sure my life is in tatters. Although granted it is strangely nice to have my mum around.'

'Shall I tell you a secret?' Lucy leaned in close to whisper to her, even though there was no one else there, and even if there was they would have been hard pressed to hear what she was saying over Mary Brambles's rendition of 'White Christmas'.

'Yes,' Alex said, sensing any other response would have been ignored anyway.

'Remember my pen pal on the cruise ship?' Lucy sad. 'Well, his ship is in tomorrow. It's the first time he's been in port for six months. We're going to meet up for a drink.'

'Oh wow,' Alex said. 'Oh wow, Lucy. Are you excited?'

'No, I'm really, really depressed about it.' Lucy rolled her eyes. 'Of course I'm bloody excited. But scared too. I think . . . I think now is the time to tell him all about me.'

'Are you sure?' Alex asked her.

'Yes, aren't you?' Lucy's wide blue eyes filled with concern. 'What do you think he'll say?'

'Look, Lucy,' Alex said gently. 'If it was me, I'd be fine about it. But I'm not an engineer on a cruise liner.'

'Well, I would ask you out, but you're spoken for, apparently,' Lucy said, some of her sparkle fading a little bit.

'Oh no, don't get down-hearted,' Alex said. 'Like you said, you've been writing to each other all this time. And talking. He knows Lucy the person. If he really cares about you, nothing else will matter.'

'That's what I'm hoping,' Lucy said. 'I'm hoping he really cares about me. Somebody's got to, haven't they? There has to be one person in this whole wide world that can love me, doesn't there? I mean aside from my folks and friends.'

'Of course there is,' Alex told her. 'Someone as wonderful, and as kind as you, deserves to be loved.'

The two women hugged for a moment, holding one another as they both silently wished each other's hopes and dreams well.

'Now tell me you are going up there to finish it with that plank?' Lucy asked.

'He's not a plank!' Alex said. 'He's my friend. He's an idiot, who thought singing "Like a Virgin" to a girl who is actually a virgin was the perfect way to woo her, and actually, yes he is a plank, but a plank who is good at heart. And yes, I am going up there to finish with him, not that I can really finish anything that I haven't technically started yet.'

'Good luck, anyway. Shall I save a leg for you?'

'Oh no, we seem to be going to Sue's for lunch . . .'

'Oh really.' Lucy raised a questioning brow that Alex didn't respond to, instead she steeled herself and headed up the stairs to face the music.

*

The door to room number four was slightly ajar and, as Alex approached, she could hear that Marcus was on the phone. Standing outside, it didn't take long for it to become apparent to Alex who he was talking to.

'I know, baby, I know,' he said, in his sweetest voice. 'Yeah, I'm gutted to be apart from you today, too. Who could have known about the storm, and those kids nearly drowning. Alex is really shaken up. I couldn't leave her, babe, she's my best mate. You understand, don't you, princess?' Alex clenched her fists as she listened, unsure whether she should be relieved or furious, and settling very quickly on both, relieved on her own behalf, and furious for Milly, who Marcus was lying to like a trooper. 'Yes, baby, yes I went to Tiffany like you asked. There's a little box under the tree just for you, wrapped in the gold paper. You can thank me properly when I get home tomorrow . . . Oh yeah, that's the perfect way to thank me.'

Alex pushed the door open, leaned on the frame and tipped her head to one side as she waited for Marcus to catch her eye. As soon as he did, the phone slipped out of his hand, like a bar of slippery soap, shooting under the bed. Alex watched as he scrabbled about on the floor, fishing it out. 'Sorry, darling, don't know what happened there. Service around here is crap. OK, OK, baby. Happy Christmas. Yeah, me too.'

Marcus ended the call, and stared for a long time at

his phone, perhaps hopeful that Alex might simply go away. And if it hadn't been for the last tattered remnant of their long friendship, she thought perhaps she might have done. But the truth was Alex Munro and Marcus Duffy might make terrible lovers, but they made brilliant friends. And Alex didn't want to give that up. Even so she wasn't going to let Marcus off the hook so easily.

'So when are you going to tell Milly that you are marrying me now?' Alex asked him. 'Or were you not going to tell her at all? Just commit a spot of bigamy, oh, or wait . . . Were we all about to move to Utah and you were planning to marry us both at the same time?'

'Al,' Marcus said. 'I got a bit carried away.'

'Oh, but you do love me, don't you, Marcus? I mean I am the *only* woman for you aren't I? The Fisherman's Choir sang to me and told me that I made you feel like a virgin, which I can tell you first-hand means that you feel quite cross and very tired, but anyway there is no way that you proposed marriage to me in front of the *whole town* by mistake, is there, Marcus?'

'This is . . . you see, the thing is this. I do love you, that's the thing,' Marcus said, struggling terribly. 'I really do. And all I could see was that you were moving away from me. You had a new life here, and new friends and men, and . . .'

'New men?' Alex scoffed. 'What, Buoy?'

'It's obvious that flipping Ruan likes you, with his brooding good looks and stubble. And I got jealous, and then you came out in that dress, the one that showed most of your . . .' He gestured at her frontage. 'And I got jealous and started thinking with my you know what. It never occurred to me to fancy you before, Alex.'

'Gee, thanks,' Alex said. 'Thanks a bunch.'

'I could tell you were getting closer to Ruan, and I thought it shouldn't be him. It should be me. I'm the one who's been your best mate all these years. I'm the one that looks out for you.'

'If you are referring to who is more qualified to take my virginity, then I'm sorry but this friendship is over,' Alex said unhappily.

'No, that's not what I'm saying, not at all . . . maybe a bit,' Marcus said. 'I never knew you were so old and still a virgin. Rob Buckley said you did it with him at the Rugby Club New Year's party, three years ago.'

'He said what?' Alex asked, momentarily distracted. 'Bastard!'

'I should have known he was lying, he told everyone he passed his driving test when he hadn't even had a lesson. I thought, that's a bloke who gets a bus a lot considering he's apparently got a Porsche in the garage.'

'Oh God!' Alex stamped her foot. 'That's it. I can't talk about this any more so let's just be clear about it, shall we?'

'OK,' Marcus said, a little uncertainly, looking rather scared.

'You love me, but not in that way, not once you sobered up and stopped thinking with your penis,' Alex said. Marcus nodded. 'And it's Milly that you want to marry, because Milly is the one you talk to like a love-sick little school boy, and as all we did was a little bit of kissing, and some nudity, I think we can both forget what we saw and never speak of it again.'

'I'm not sure I can forget everything I saw,' Marcus said, staring pointedly at her chest.

'Marcus!' Alex shouted. 'Focus!'

'Oh, yeah, I mean, yes. I will never think of your breasts again.'

'Good. And so we will not be marrying each other, we will go back to being friends and maybe I can still come up for your wedding.'

'Just for the wedding?' Marcus asked her, suddenly looking a little hangdog. 'Not for good?'

'No.' Alex shook her head. 'Life up there, it wasn't ever really mine. Not like it is down here, here is where I can be myself.'

'But what about your dad?' Marcus said. 'You can't leave things the way they are with your dad. You can't hate him for being in love.'

'Marcus,' Alex said, 'I don't hate you for being in love with Milly.'

'I wasn't talking about me,' Marcus said, hesitating

324 • *Scarlett Bailey*

for a moment. 'Promise that we are still friends. I want you to be my best man.'

Part of her marvelled that Marcus could so easily switch from viewing her as a potential bride to best man so easily, but then again, that was Marcus. He always saw life in the least complicated way; it was one of the things she had always liked about him. 'We are still friends,' Alex reassured him. 'And I know I can't leave things this way with Dad. I know I need to get in touch with him and talk about stuff. I just need to—'

'Oh shit, we're missing the pre-Christmas dinner drinking game,' Marcus said, catching sight of the digital clock by the bed. 'So we're cool, yeah, and I don't have to come to Scary Sue's for lunch, I can stay in the pub and get wasted?'

'We're cool,' Alex said. 'Drink yourself into a stupor with my blessing.'

'This beats Milly's parents' house any day of the week.' Marcus gave her a peck on the cheek as he passed by. 'Happy Christmas, Al. I was going to get you a gift, but I didn't have time – I'll buy you a pint later, though.'

Alex waited for a moment or two before she followed him downstairs. It was funny how now the years of self-inflicted torment of loving Marcus to no avail had dissipated just as quickly as a fake snowflake melting in the palm of your hand. The truth was, Alex realised, as she sat down on the bed, that for the last several years she had been doing exactly what Marcus had done in the last few days. She had felt like she ought to be in love, she had felt like her heart ought to belong to someone whether they wanted it or not, and she had enough genuine loving feelings for Marcus to make him the object of her affections. And even the fact that it had never really been love, not for all those years, didn't matter to Alex, because she realised none of those moments were wasted. Not if every one of them had led her to this moment, this decision. The moment she was going to go and find Ruan and tell him that she had fallen in love with him.

Chapter Twenty-four

Alex hooked her arm through Gloria's as they stepped through the smaller wooden door in the giant wooden door that led through to the courtyard of Castle House.

'Goodness, a real castle,' Gloria said. 'Surely there must be a millionaire somewhere in this town for me to marry.'

Alex thought privately to herself that former '70s rock legend Brian Rogers was definitely a millionaire several times over, but she decided it was best not to mention it. Instead she was determined to be focused on one thing at a time, and the next item on her list was Ruan.

Alex was sort of hoping that the news of the end of the world's shortest ever engagement might have reached him before she got to Sue's, especially as just before she left the pub, she had stepped behind the bar, rung the bell loudly and announced to everyone that she and Marcus would not, repeat not, be getting married. But as she led Gloria into a busy steam-filled kitchen, and saw Ruan, who, as an old friend of the family, had been put to duty peeling carrots and his face darkened at the sight of her, all of Alex's hopes were dashed.

'There you are!' Sue said happily, utterly in her element, and suddenly much more relaxed now that the pageant was out of the way. 'Oh, do go through to the hall. There's a massive fire roaring, and Cordy is in there with Rory and Marissa, who's been throwing herself at Brian. That girl has got no shame.'

Alex and Ruan looked at each other briefly, but his eyes were guarded and dark.

'So anyway I'm totally not marrying Marcus!' Alex said, to the room at large, but looking at Ruan as she said it.

'Oh no!' Sue looked genuinely upset. 'What happened, Alex?'

'I never wanted to marry him,' Alex said. 'And he never really wanted to marry me. He lost his senses for a little bit and I didn't know how to say no in front of all those people.' Alex was still looking at Ruan, who continued to methodically peel carrots. 'So we were never in love and it was all just a big mistake. He loves this girl back home and I . . .' She trailed off, looking at Gloria, who shrugged sympathetically.

'Come on, let me take you through. What would you like to drink? I've got Petal on waitressing duty. It's probably illegal, but she does make excellent cocktails.'

So it wasn't going to be as easy as Alex had hoped,

she realised as she followed her mother and Sue into the hall, although the sight of Castle House's great hall dressed for Christmas did quite a lot to lift her spirits. Its transformation, since Alex had used it as a makeshift changing room, was amazing. It was garlanded in fresh holly and mistletoe, with a huge fire roaring in the inglenook fireplace. At some point, between the early hours of the morning and now, an enormous tree, covered in lights and ribbons and baubles, had been erected in the stone archway that divided the spacious room, giving it a much cosier feel. Two battered but comfy-looking red sofas were arranged around the fire, and a rug that Alex was surprised to see Buoy already stretched out on, alongside Pugwash and Duchess the poodle, was covered in scraps of wrapping paper, assorted toys and children.

'Harvey Wallbanger?' Petal asked her. 'Or, I also do Snowballs, and Baileys although that isn't a cocktail but it tastes nice, a bit like ice cream, not that I've tried it.'

'Um, a Baileys, please,' Alex replied.

'Can you do me just a whisky on ice, please, darling?' Gloria added her order.

'S'pose,' Petal said, looking depressed at the lack of imagination of adults. She trotted off to the laden-down drinks cabinet, bristling with different coloured glass bottles.

'Brian,' Gloria purred at the older man who was

sitting in a chair, dressed head to foot in denim, his silver ringlets hanging down past his shoulders. 'I see you have a guitar with you, do you play?'

Alex found it hard to believe that Gloria didn't know who Brian Rogers was, but she supposed that it was possible, so while her mother allowed Brian to show her an E chord on his priceless guitar, which Alex knew from trashy gossip magazines he had made with his father when he was a little boy, she took her half pint of Baileys from Petal and sat on the floor with Meadow and Forest.

'What did Father Christmas bring you?' Alex asked Forest, whose auburn curls fell into his brown eyes. He was Sue's boy through and through.

'Some Lego, some trains, some cars and some clothes, although I don't think clothes count as presents, do they?' He screwed up his face as he looked at her.

'I think sometimes they can a bit,' Alex said, as she began to help him build a Lego castle that looked an awful lot like his actual place of residence.

'It's supposed to have a flag on top of this turret,' Forest told her, 'but Pugwash ate it, so we have to wait for it to come out of her bum.'

'Oh.' Alex nodded, wrinkling her nose up. 'Good luck with that!'

'Alex?' Alex found herself looking at a brand-new pair of tartan slippers, the price, handwritten on a little white tag, still hanging off the back. She looked upwards

330 · *Scarlett Bailey*

at Rory. 'Could I have a word? About some ... um ... research I'm doing?'

'Daddy?' Forest tugged at Rory's trouser leg. 'Daddy, are you sure that is all of the presents?'

'Yes, darling,' Rory said crouching down to look into his little boy's eyes. 'Why, did Santa forget something?'

'Yes,' Forest said, 'and I was especially careful to make sure that it went on the list, Petal promised!'

'Oh did she?' Rory glanced over at Petal who was earnestly excavating the bones of a Tyrannosaurus Rex from a block of plaster with some of the family silver. 'And what was it, darling?'

'I asked for a puppy,' Forest said. 'One that was just mine. Not Duchess, who is Mummy's or Salty who is Petal's, or Ginger, or Mutley or Pugwash who's ... just around. I want my very own little puppy, Daddy. I asked and I have been quite good, I think.'

Alex suppressed a smile and Rory nodded, very seriously.

'I don't see why we couldn't squeeze another dog in here,' Rory said. 'But you know we'll have to check with Mummy.'

'Oh.' Forest groaned and rolled his eyes. 'That's why I asked Santa. I've asked Mummy already and she said no!'

'Let me see what I can do,' Rory said. 'I just need to have a chat with Alex, and then, well, you never know ...'

Reluctantly, Alex got up, and walked past Gloria who was curled up next to Brian on one of the sofas, laughing seductively over her whisky, as Brian regaled her with tales from the road.

'And then we threw a TV out of the window . . .'

When she realised it was Sue's office that Rory had led her into, and that the last time she'd been here she'd seen rather more of him than she ever wanted to, Alex made to turn around and walk the other way, but Rory put a hand on her arm.

'Please, Alex, hear me out.'

Alex gave him a look that meant he removed his hand rather swiftly from her person.

'So what are you hoping?' she asked him. 'That Sue will let Forest have a dog to make up for the fact that his daddy is knocking off her secretary?'

'Look, I don't expect you to understand . . .' Rory began.

'I do understand,' Alex said. 'I understand that men put their penises first, above all else.'

'No, that's not it,' Rory said earnestly, and Alex could see that at least he believed that he was engaged in a great love affair of epic proportions. 'I know what this looks like from the outside. I know it looks like a pathetic older man caught up in the allure of a much younger, firm-bodied siren.'

'Oh, please.' Alex said.

'But that's not what it is,' Rory went on. 'If you will

just listen, just for a moment and let me explain. Marissa really loves me, and I really love her. And we tried, we really did try not to fall in love, but we didn't have any choice, because sometimes feelings creep up on you when you aren't looking; you must have experienced that?'

Alex nodded reluctantly. 'I suppose I have,' she conceded.

'Well, that's what it's like for me and Marissa,' Rory told her. 'So please, give us a little time, to minimise the damage. Let me tell Sue in my own time.'

'I just don't think there ever will be a good time to tell Sue,' Alex said. 'I mean, when is there going to be a good time to tell her that Castle House is going on the market, that you're going to make her sell her home – one that's been in her family for hundreds of years, and that life for her and the children is never going to be the same again, all so that you can shack up with your tart?'

'Oh no.' Rory frowned deeply. 'That will never happen. The house, the name, the land, it's all tied up in an ancient trust that means it can never ever be sold, or leave the family. It wasn't how Sue wanted it. When we married she tried to see if there was a way to break the trust, but there wasn't. It seems that those medieval lawyers knew their stuff. Which is why I took Sue's family name and why, when Marissa and I leave, I won't be taking a bean with me. We will be starting from scratch just like any young couple. I'm hoping we'll be able to rent a cottage nearby, to be near the children, and I don't expect that Sue will want to continue employing Marissa, so she'll have to look for something else local, perhaps up at the hotel. They are always looking for waiting staff. You see, that's how I know Marissa loves me, I know she's prepared to support us while I finish this novel.'

A little strangulated screech came from the far corner of the room.

'Marissa, darling?' Rory called out and Marissa emerged from the doorway that Alex and Ruan had been standing in when they first found out about Rory and Marissa's affair.

'You never told me that you wouldn't be entitled to any of the money,' Marissa told Rory, tight lipped and pale with fury.

'But you're Sue's PA,' Rory said. 'You deal with her personal affairs. I thought you knew.'

'Do you think I would have let you . . .' Marissa's expression was one of pure fury. 'I am twenty-nine years old. I am not going to be waitressing in some hotel, slaving away to keep some failed, middle-aged and frankly terrible writer, who even if he did finish a book would never in a million years be published anyway!'

Marissa turned on her heel and stormed out of the door, leaving Rory looking bewildered, hurt and lost. Alex almost wanted to reach out to him, but the urge to slap him smartly around the face was much greater, so she did neither.

'She's confused,' he told Alex. 'She's upset by the strain of it all. She'll come round. I'll just go and make sure she is all right.'

'Rory.' This time it was Alex's turn to stop him with a hand on his shoulder. 'Don't go after her. For what it's worth, I do believe you. I think you think you really are in love with her. But I don't think Marissa feels the same. Look, Sue told me, Marissa came down to Cornwall because she caused a scandal at home. She had a fling with her mother's best friend's husband.'

'I know about that,' Rory said. 'He took advantage of her, promised her things that he was never going to deliver on . . .'

'Rory,' Alex tried again, 'your beautiful family, your lovely children, are in the room next door. Your wife is in the kitchen cooking Christmas lunch. Please, please don't go after Marissa. She doesn't care a bit about what you're giving up for her, but maybe it's not too late for you to save it.'

Rory hesitated for a moment. And then he went after Marissa.

'You knew Jimi Hendrix?' Gloria was saying, wide eyed, as Alex returned to the Great Hall. Forest had fallen asleep on the rug in front of his Lego castle and Meadow was decorating his face with glitter gel pens.

'Another drink!' Petal handed Alex another half pint of Baileys, clearly not noticing that she hadn't touched the first one. 'What were you talking to Daddy about?'

'Oh, I was helping him with some research on his book,' Alex said.

Petal looked sceptical. 'What do you know about dragons? Daddy is writing a fantasy book about dragons. It's not very good but it keeps him happy, Mummy says.'

Alex wondered how many times Petal had heard that phrase.

'Well, there's a bit with boats in. I was helping him with that bit.'

'Right.' Sue appeared, still wearing a pinafore, with Cordelia and Ruan trailing behind her. 'Dinner should be about another hour, so why don't we have some entertainment while we are waiting. Charades?'

There was a deep groan from the children.

'Hide and seek,' Forest said, somehow instantly awake and not remotely fazed that his face was now mostly sparkly green.

'I don't think so,' Sue said, 'the last time we played hide and seek, Forest, we didn't find you for seven hours.'

'I know!' Gloria clapped her hands together. 'How about Brian gives us a song. He's brought his guitar!'

'Oh well.' Brian looked modest, as if he carried

around his priceless guitar in the same way he might a wallet or a mobile phone. 'I suppose perhaps, well, Cordelia, why don't you sing that song we've been working on?'

'Oh yes, why don't we?' Cordelia might well be a great singer, but, as it turned out, was a terrible actress, at least when it came to feigning spontaneity. 'That would be nice, because Ruan, my brother, has never heard me sing.'

'Surely not,' Brian said, carefully rehearsed. 'How is that even possible, when you have the voice of an angel?'

'Search me,' Cordelia said, as she crossed over to Brian's side, put her hands on her hips and offered Ruan a challenging glare. Her brother shrugged his shoulders.

'OK. I get the message. I'm sorry I haven't come to any of your gigs. I've been a bit busy.'

'Yeah, because gazing moodily out to sea is terribly time consuming,' Cordelia said, forcing Alex to suppress a smile.

'Come on then,' Sue said, sitting on the rug next to Meadow and Forest who instinctively leaned against her. 'Cordelia, Brian – we await your greatness! You too, Ruan, you can't spend all of Christmas Day standing in doorways glowering. Sit there. Best seat in the house.'

Alex wondered if Sue had directed him to the seat on the sofa right behind where she was sitting on the floor on purpose, but whatever her motivation was Ruan took up her offer, and Alex could almost feel the length of his calf brushing against her upper arm, or at least she would have been able to, if there hadn't been the faintest hair's breadth of distance between them. Oh, how she longed to lean into him, to rest her chin on his thigh, perhaps while he stroked her hair.

Alex mentally chided herself. Why on earth would you want that, she told herself. What are you – a dog?

Brian spent a few moments fiddling around, tuning his guitar, winking at Gloria as he did so, while Cordelia perched on the arm of the chair next to him. He nodded at her and began to play.

Alex wasn't sure what she had been expecting when Cordelia had begun to sing, but it wasn't the extraordinary sound that suddenly filled the room. The song was somewhere between country, folk and rock, and was about a man whose love was forever lost to him. It didn't take any prizes to guess who had inspired the poetic lyrics, and Alex could feel the initial discomfort radiate from the man sitting behind her, but then as the song soared, and Cordelia's voice – pure, beautiful and true – rose with it, there was nothing more than the beauty of the music and the moment. When it finally drew to an end Alex realised she was crying, not because she was sad, but because she was so almost happy, so nearly content, that it hurt.

The children cheered, and Rory, who must have reappeared at some point during the rendition, clapped.

'You're amazing,' Alex told Cordelia. 'Did you write that yourself?'

'Well, Brian helped me with the tune,' Cordelia admitted, flushed with pleasure, her usual angry guard slipping for once. 'But I wrote all the words. It's about how you think you might have lost your chance of happiness, but how actually you might not have, if you just pull your finger out and say what needs saying.' She stared at Ruan. 'Well? What do you think, bro?'

'I think you're an amazing singer,' Ruan said. 'Truly, Cordelia, I don't know where you get it from; no one else in the family can even carry a tune.'

'But?' Cordelia crossed her arms.

'But there are thousands of amazing singers, and most of them never make it beyond pub gigs. I just don't want you to get your hopes up.'

'Why not?' Cordelia asked him. 'Why shouldn't I get my hopes up and at least give it my best shot at making my dream come true? Isn't that better than just sitting around, scared stiff of taking a chance, even if that could be the one thing that makes you happy?'

Ruan sighed. 'Cordy, if Tamsyn and Keira were here—'

'But they aren't here, are they? They're far away living the lives that make *them* happy. Tamsyn is in Paris, designing stuff, that deluded fools pay thousands of euros for, and Keira is a happily married lady who lunches, with a BMW and a diamond on her finger the size of Castle House! You didn't try to make them stay in the same place, doing the same thing, over and over again, year after year, even though it doesn't make them happy, so why are you trying to do that to me? Is it so you won't be lonely?'

As soon as the words came out of her mouth Alex could see that Cordelia regretted them, but it was too late. The room fell silent except for the crackle of the fire, and Buoy's snoring.

'Do you know "The Wheels on the Bus go Round and Round and Round"?' Forest asked Brian and then everyone laughed, grateful to be able to gloss over the excruciatingly painful moment that had gone before.

'I know "Puff the Magic Dragon", will that do?' Brian offered.

'Are you OK?' Alex turned to ask Ruan, as Brian began to play.

'I'm fine.' He nodded, his hands resting stiffly on his knees.

'Ruan—'

Just at the moment the door opened and Reverend Jed popped his head around the door. 'Oh good, you are here!'

Sue leaped up to greet him. 'What a wonderful service it was this morning, Vicar. The way you gave thanks for the lives saved last night and paid tribute to the lifeboat crew. So moving, wasn't it, Ruan?'

Ruan nodded, and Alex had to admit she was a little surprised that he'd gone to church on Christmas morning, after being so sceptical about it the previous day.

'I am sorry about Meadow,' Sue said. 'She is awfully enthusiastic.'

'Never be sorry about enthusiasm of faith,' Jed assured Sue. 'Even if it does take the form of tap dancing down the aisle. Were we having a sing-song?'

'How about this one,' Brain said, nodding at Gloria. 'Fancy a duet?'

Brian and Gloria began to flirt outrageously, whilst duetting on 'Baby, It's Cold Outside'. What her mother lacked in talent she made up for in gusto and Alex watched part in horror, part in awe, right up until the moment they rubbed noses, and then muttered something about going to the kitchen to check on the carrots.

She was pouring herself a tall glass of water when she heard someone come into room behind her. Turning around, she hoped it was Ruan, but it wasn't. Cordelia had followed her instead.

'You have a wonderful voice,' Alex told her again.

'I know,' Cordelia said.

'I don't think Ruan wants to hold you back,' Alex

said. 'I think he's just trying, in his own way, to protect you.'

'I know that too,' Cordelia said.

'Oh, um . . . well, cup of tea?'

'You hurt him.' Cordelia told her. 'He doesn't talk to me. He doesn't tell me what's going on, he never has. Not since . . . well, not since Merryn. The day she never came back was the day he changed. He shut himself off, closed himself up. Yeah, he's still that same big brother I grew up with. Still has a laugh down the pub, poured his heart and soul into that lighthouse. But the light he used to have, here.' She gestured at her eyes. 'It had gone out. Until you came to town. You switched him back on, brighter than he's ever been before.'

Alex held on to the edge of the marble counter, unable to speak.

'I don't know what went on between you,' Cordelia continued. 'But I know my brother, and I know that whatever he said to you, it cost him. It cost him nearly everything to allow himself to reach out like that again. And you . . . you rejected him in front of the whole town.'

'But . . .'

'And it doesn't matter if the whole town doesn't know that. Ruan knows it, and he's hurt, really wounded. Closed off and angry again, and I could . . . well, I could beat you up for that if I was a violent person.'

'Are you a violent person?' Alex asked, in a small voice.

'No,' Cordelia said. 'But I think it's best that you move on. He's got a lot of healing to do. Again. You being around will just make it worse.'

'No,' Alex said. 'No, I'm not going. Because that whole thing with Marcus, it was just a stupid mistake, a ridiculous reaction to peer pressure. And it's done. It's finished. Marcus and I were never meant to be together that way.'

Cordelia shrugged. 'I don't see what difference that makes.'

'The difference is, I . . .' Alex put her hands over her heart. 'Oh God, I am really in love with your brother, Cordelia. Really and truly and madly in love with him. And if he feels that way about me, if all that is stopping us from being together is his stupid pride and very silly temper, then I am not going anywhere. I am not. Not until I make him see that we can be together. And I can be very persistent. It's one of my things. I can turn the light back on again.'

Cordelia's dark eyes scrutinised Alex for a moment, and then she smiled. 'You're actually all right,' she said.

'Am I?' Alex said, feeling a rush of relief.

'Yes, I like you,' Cordelia said. 'A little bit, and it might be a lot if you manage to make my brother happy. So you love him, you say?'

'I really do,' Alex said in wonder. 'It's sort of doing

my head in, actually. I think about touching him all the time.'

'Whoa there!' Cordelia held up her hand. 'Too much freaking information!'

'Sorry,' Alex said. 'I didn't think . . .'

'Look,' Cordelia said, 'I'm fairly sure he loves you too. Otherwise he wouldn't have such a face on.'

A timer, shaped like an egg, went off on the counter.

'Here.' Cordelia handed Alex a pile of deep red linen napkins. 'Go to the dining hall. The table is mostly laid, but it's missing the napkins and the glasses. I was going to get the kids to do it, but you'll do.' She tapped the side of her nose. 'I'll send someone else in with the glasses.'

Alex blinked at her.

'I'll send Ruan in with the glasses, you numpty. Hopeless, the pair of you.' Cordelia rolled her eyes, and left the room.

The dining room was more of a gallery, another floor up; a stone spiral staircase led from the kitchen to the back of the room, through an entrance that Alex guessed had once been for servants only. An Elizabethan addition, it was a long thin room, with a polished parquet floor, and, most stunningly of all, floor-to-ceiling diamond-paned windows set in arched stone frames. They flooded the room with light, and afforded the most wonderful view of the harbour. Still holding the pile of napkins in her arms, Alex went over and

344 • *Scarlett Bailey*

looked out at the sea, watching the waves crash over the cragged outcrop of rocks.

'Oh.' A man's voice interrupted her thoughts.

She turned around and saw Ruan arrive with a tray of glasses.

'Ruan, please . . .' Alex put the napkins down and went to him. 'I just need to—'

'Look,' Ruan cut across her. 'I was hoping to avoid this today, for Sue's sake. But, as we're alone, let's just get this over with. Last night, in the office, before the call out, when we . . .' Ruan's gaze dropped for a moment. 'I put my heart on the line then, Alex. I didn't hide a thing about how I felt. I told you how you made me feel, and how much I wanted to be with you, to touch you and . . .' He stopped again. 'Because that's just me. The sort of man I am. I don't go into things half-hearted, I can't do that. It's been a long time, a really long time, since I even dared to hope that I might feel that way about another person. And the way I felt for you, it was so strong. And, fair enough, it was mistake. I told you how I felt, right up front. And you threw it back in my face.'

'I didn't!' Alex said. 'That's the thing, I didn't. Well, I mean I sort of did, but it was a mistake, because everyone wanted me to say yes, so I tried to explain but no one was listening and . . . I didn't know what to do. But it's over now. It's done. It was a silly mistake that's been sorted.'

'Don't you see?' Ruan asked her. 'If you had felt the

same way I feel about you, with the same passion and . . . certainty, then it wouldn't have mattered who was there in the hall. You never would have gone along with it. You would have come to me, whatever.'

Ruan held out his hand.

'And so I hope we can be friends in time, although please forgive me if I keep my distance for a while.'

'Wait.' Alex took a breath. 'So you're telling me that you are shelving all the passion and certainty about how much you feel for me because I let you down, I disappointed you? You're saying that was a one time only offer, and I fell at the first hurdle and now the deal is off?' Ruan said nothing. 'Christ, Ruan, if you're going to have feelings for me, then you have to understand I'm only human, I'm not perfect. I might be a virgin, but I am not actually the Virgin Mary.'

Alex stopped, realising that she had said rather more than she intended to, to make a point. Unable to look at Ruan's face, she took a deep, steadying breath. 'I don't want to be just friends with you. And I do mind if you keep your distance. Because that's not what I want. I want to be with you, and yes, I mean really be with you. I want to take off all of your clothes and . . . kiss you, everywhere. I think. I'm not sure, I don't really have much experience in that area, but whilst I am saying the words out loud the idea does seem rather appealing. I want you. I want you in the way I wanted you in the office last night. And I want to make you laugh, and see you smile, and make you happy. What's more, Ruan, I have never felt that way about anyone, ever. And if you will just stop behaving like an enormous dickhead, and see that this isn't about me, it's about your pride and your stupid weird life code that doesn't seem to achieve anything except to stop you being happy, then you'd realise that we could be brilliant together. We could be really, really brilliant.'

Finally, Alex mustered the courage to look at him, and found him returning her gaze. For a long time they stood there, as the winter sunshine flooded in through the centuries-old glass, and as she waited Alex wondered how many more conversations, just like the one she was having, had these walls seen over the years. Hers wasn't such a unique story after all, it was just unique to her, and what Ruan said next meant everything.

'I can't do this right now,' Ruan said. 'It's too much. I'm sorry.'

Alex watched speechless as he set the tray of glasses carefully down on the table and walked out of the room. About a minute later she saw him marching across the courtyard, and let himself out of the small door in the big gate.

'Did that not go quite according to the plan?' Cordelia asked, as she joined Alex at the window.

'Well, I bared my soul to him, and he sort of freaked

out,' Alex said, her sorrow being slowly replaced, molecule by molecule, with anger. 'I mean, he stood there and told me he was an all or nothing kind of guy, and I literally gave him my all, and he . . . left.'

'He is so dumb,' Cordelia said. 'And I know what it is. He's overwhelmed. He needs to get his head straight. You just need to go after him. Go on, by the time you catch up with him, it will all have sunk in and it will be happy endings all round.'

'Do you really think so?' Alex said. 'Because, all I am saying is that so far your advice hasn't exactly been spot on.'

'Oh my God, you two will never get together.' Cordelia threw her hands up in disgust. 'And this is why Ruan doesn't get that I want to try to make a go of it as a singer, because you and him – despite what you said earlier – are the sort to just give up at the first sign of trouble. Well, all I can say is you are made for each other, not that you will ever find that out, because he is too busy storming off and you are too busy not going after him.'

Alex stood there a fraction longer and then began to run, down the small spiral staircase, through the kitchen, across the courtyard and out of the small door. She pelted down the steep road towards the quay, arriving just in time to see Ruan head out to sea in his motorboat, going back to the lighthouse she guessed.

She hesitated for a moment, the practical harbour

master in her entirely certain that her little dinghy wasn't the right kind of vessel to venture out into open water. But another part of her whispered that it was only a very little way around the headland, with its treacherous rocks and dangerous current. Just a very little way indeed, and although the wind was still strong and the sea was still churning, Alex thought it wouldn't be so bad if she stayed as close to the shoreline as possible.

'Faint heart never won grumpy, overdramatic, but really foxy man,' she told herself. After putting on her lifejacket, she was just about to jump into the boat, when Buoy appeared.

'No, Buoy, you have to go back,' Alex told him. 'You haven't got a life jacket and it's really choppy out there.' But Buoy ignored her, hopping down the steps and into the boat, taking up his usual position at the prow, where he stayed despite Alex's attempts to shoo him back onto shore.

'Fine,' she said. 'I just hope you are really good at doggy paddle.'

Chapter Twenty-five

It became clear to Alex at almost exactly the same point that it was too late to go back, that she had probably made a mistake coming out, even just this little way, in her small, inadequate boat.

The sea was much rougher out here, even than it looked, and with every jerk and jump her boat made on the big waves it took on a little more water. Which meant that as every second passed, the boat lay a little lower in the ocean. Alex looked back to the quay, the last of the day's light almost gone, and she knew that she wouldn't make it that far now without sinking. The only option was to press on round the headland and hope she could get to Ruan's private beach.

It was when the sudden swell of a huge wave knocked her and Buoy off their feet, sending her backwards in the boat, where she cracked her head against the rim of the dinghy, that Alex first felt afraid.

Suddenly she realised exactly how badly wrong this could go, that her life was in danger. Trying to steady her nerves, she scoured the horizon. It was almost dark already and her torch wasn't strong enough to illuminate more than a few metres ahead, and, even then, anything she could see changed, and changed again, every second. Alex hoped to be able to spot Ruan's boat, to be able to signal to him somehow to come back, but there was no sign of it, which worried her, because she didn't think he had that much of a head start on her. If he'd already moored his boat, and was even now heading up the lighthouse, she was in big trouble.

And then Buoy barked, and Alex saw something white caught in the beam of her torch. What was it, the top of a wave? A rock? Swallowing her fear, as Buoy barked again, Alex swept the horizon once again, and then again, on the third time catching the object once more. It was the hull of a capsized boat. And Alex didn't have to see the name painted on the side to know that it was Ruan's boat.

Fear surged through her as she did her best to direct her little boat towards the hull, although the current had very different ideas due to her inadequate engine. Every time she tried to get nearer, the waves did their best to pull her even further away.

'Pull yourself together,' Alex said out loud, making herself pause and think. 'You're the harbour master, you know what to do.'

Her fingers were numb and frozen, but she remembered the watertight emergency box in the back of the boat and took it out. Buoy cowered as she sent all the flares she had up into the air. As the dinghy sank ever lower in the water she stood up, pointed the torch at the water and searched for Ruan in the waves. Alex didn't know how many heart-stopping minutes she scoured the dark, looking for him, but she knew that she didn't have very many more of them left before she herself was going to be pitched into the freezing sea. And what if no one saw the flares, or what if they confused them with Christmas Day fireworks? What if no help was coming?

It was at that moment that Alex saw Ruan, bobbing in the water, his lifejacket keeping him upright. He was unconscious though, and Alex knew that the freezing temperature of the water might have already stopped his heart. She tried once, twice, three times to get the boat alongside him, but she knew it wasn't going to happen and, even if it did, it wouldn't be enough anyway. Ruan's beach seemed tantalisingly close. Would she be able to swim to it, against the tide, with Ruan in tow? Alex didn't know if she was a strong enough swimmer; her usual twenty laps of the local pool had never prepared her for a swim like this. The water would be freezing cold and, if she didn't get them to shore within a few minutes, the chances were that they would both freeze to death before help came. But what else could she do? She had to try. There was no alternative.

'Don't worry,' Alex told Buoy, hugging him briefly. 'Help is coming. Without my weight the boat will stay up a lot longer. Stay here, OK, you will be safe. I love you, Buoy.'

She leaped into the water, the shock of the cold taking her breath away, and for several terrifying seconds she found herself locked in a black and alien, airless world, uncertain which way was up. Then the lifejacket did its job and Alex was ejected from the chilly embrace of the water, into the freezing air again, where it took long, agonising seconds for her lungs to react and take in air. Twisting around in the water, she spotted Ruan and swam to his side. The fear that she might not make it to him at least was laid to rest. Another fear replaced it at once though as she put her arm around him. He looked bad, deathly pale, and Alex wasn't sure if he was still breathing.

Desperately, she tried to reach the shore. Again and again, she fought against the current to get them closer to land, feeling each effort draining what little was left of her energy, knowing that she didn't have very many attempts left in her. Alex paused for a moment and gazed up at the sky and at the horizon. There was no sign of a chopper, no sign of the lifeboat. She had no way of knowing if it had been seconds, minutes or hours that she had been battling the waves. Was this the place where she was going to die? When she hadn't told her dad that she still loved him.

And then she felt something brush against her, and heard a high-pitched anxious bark. Buoy was in the water with her. He clamped his jaw firmly around her lifejacket and began desperately to try to paddle towards the shore. Alex had never been more grateful, more honoured, more humbled than she was in that moment. And never more desperate to stay alive, inspired by an old dog, who wasn't going to let the sea defeat them without a fight.

'One more push, Buoy,' she cried and together they strove for the shore, pulling Ruan behind them. It seemed like aeons that Alex and her dog battled the water and the rocks and the debris of the broken hull for the beach, every stroke and kick hurting her more, the cold seeping into her body, tightening its clutch on her heart. Alex would never know how long it actually took them, but all at once she felt soft sand beneath her feet and they were in shallow water. That would have been the easiest moment to stop trying, to let the tide wash them out to sea again, but Alex fought on, dragging Ruan's weight up the beach, with Buoy's dogged help, until at last they were on dry land.

Shuddering uncontrollably, the last thing Alex heard was Buoy's frenzied barking at the sky, and the last thing she saw were lights dazzling her, and a roaring, thunderous noise. And then there was nothing.

Chapter Twenty-six

Christmas Night

Alex woke up and didn't know where she was, only that she was alive, and breathing, dry and warm. Every part of her felt bruised, stretched, pulled and battered. It hurt her to breathe in, each breath causing her lungs to burn, as they pushed against her fragile ribcage. But she wasn't dead, and not dead was definitely one up from what she expected. And then she remembered Ruan.

'Is he dead?' she said to the room at large. It was quiet, a low greyish light hummed somewhere above, and now Alex thought about it, she noticed a steady beeping to her left, which she supposed was associated with the beating of her heart.

'Darling.' Gloria's face appeared, worn, tired looking, her skin fragile and translucent without the benefit of make-up. 'Hello, my brave girl.'

'Is he dead?' Alex asked her again, with some effort. She had been hoping for a definite no right away, and her mother's failure to provide meant the beeping of the machine picked up just a little bit.

'No.' Lucy was there too, sitting on the other side of her. 'No,' she repeated, reassuringly. 'It looks like you saved his life, Alex. No one is quite sure how you did it, but you got him to shore. When the crew from the helicopter came down you were passed out, Buoy was licking at you, they said, to try to keep you warm, they think. Ruan's heart had stopped.'

Alex gasped, the action causing pain to sear through her chest, inducing a sharp fit of coughing.

'But it was OK,' Lucy reassured her. 'The chopper crew got it started again, and then they airlifted you all to hospital. Even Buoy . . .' Lucy trailed off.

'And so, he's fine. Ruan's OK.' Alex needed further clarification.

'The signs are good, darling,' Gloria soothed her. 'He got very cold, so they are keeping him asleep while they slowly warm him up. But they say that the cold might actually mean that he won't suffer any brain or organ damage. Of course, no one knows how long his heart stopped for, so we have to wait and see, a little while longer.'

'But everyone is very hopeful,' Lucy said. 'They really are. You're a hero.'

'I'm not,' Alex said. 'I couldn't have done it without Buoy. He pulled me, I pulled Ruan. I think I would have given up without him . . .' Alex caught her breath, unable to talk for a moment as the enormity of what she had survived caught up with her.

Alex saw the look that Gloria and Lucy exchanged over her head.

'What?' Alex asked. 'What happened? Where is Buoy? Oh God, is he dead?'

'He's at Vicky Carmichael's,' Lucy told her. 'Poldore's vet. He was in a bad way, Alex. He injured himself – probably on the wrecked hull or a piece of driftwood. He had a couple of bad injuries, lost a lot of blood and, of course, he's an old dog . . . the cold and the stress got to him. Vicky said that to do what he did, to swim with you to the shore, he had the biggest, most courageous heart of any animal she'd ever seen.'

'He's going to die.' Alex said the words as if they were a statement.

'Vicky's doing everything she can for him,' Lucy reassured her. 'And she's the best vet for miles around. If anyone can save him, it will be Vicky.'

'They called me, they asked me what to do,' Gloria said. 'The nice young woman seemed to think it might be kinder just to let him go, but I said no. That dog is not ready to go yet, no dog that fights so hard to stay alive can be. And besides my daughter loves him. So you get him better. Vicky said she'd try. And I'm footing the bill. No expense spared.'

Alex felt that she had to sit up, that lying in bed, looking at the ceiling, was failing Buoy somehow. She gripped the edge of the bed, determined not to ask for help, agony enflaming every move.

'What about me?' she asked her mother, repressing the urge to cry, because now wasn't the right time. She didn't seem to have any bandages or dressings, although large purple splotches covered her legs and arms.

'You're badly bruised,' Gloria told her. 'And for a while they were worried about internal bleeding, in case you hit the wreckage too. But you've been checked out, and you're fine. You just need to rest and let your body heal.'

The news that she wasn't really injured at all spurred Alex on further and she swung her feet out of bed.

'Alex!' Lucy said. 'Did you hear your mother?'

'Yes.' Alex paused to catch her breath that the exertion of moving had cost her. 'She said I was fine and I need to be with him, Lucy. Please?'

Lucy looked at Gloria who nodded.

'Right, well, you stay there, I'll get you a wheelchair.'

'I don't need a wheelchair, I'm totally fine.' Alex attempted to stand and sat down again at once as her legs gave out from under her. 'Fine, get me a wheelchair.'

Ruan's room was a little way down the corridor. It was dark and quiet. As Lucy wheeled Alex in a nurse was taking his temperature. She smiled at Alex. 'He's warmed up nicely. He should come around in the next few hours, and then we'll know more.'

Alex nodded, as Lucy wheeled her next to the bed. He lay very still, and he looked so young. Someone had shaved away his stubble, his long dark lashes swept the tops of those cheekbones, and Alex wondered if she kissed him, would he wake?

Someone entered the room and Alex looked up. It was a woman in her fifties, blonde, plump, with turquoise eyes. She stopped at the sight of Alex.

'You must be Alex,' she said, a smile spreading across her face. 'I'm Amy Sceptre. I'm—'

'Merryn's mum,' Alex said. 'I don't know why, but I knew as soon as I saw you. Is it OK if I wait with you?'

'Of course it's OK, you saved his life,' Amy said. 'In more ways than one.'

She hovered for a moment by the door, and then came and sat down next to Alex, taking her hands in hers. 'Ruan and my Merryn, they were so lovely together. So happy. And they always thought it would be the two of them, you know. Like young people do. They thought it was be forever. I knew that they would be together for as long as they were meant to be. I knew that my Merryn was thinking of going, although she hadn't found a way to tell Ruan, I don't think when . . . when the accident happened. And he's spent so many years of his life honouring her memory. Because he's a good man, and he loved her. But now it's time for him to live again. I've not met you before, Alex, but Cordelia told me she's sure you love him, and, as if we needed proof, you nearly killed yourself saving him. No, he's proud and stubborn and stupid. But I know you will make him happy. Just don't you let me down, OK?'

Alex shook her head. 'I will try my best, if he'll have me,' she said.

'If he doesn't then we will know that he's brain damaged,' Amy said, smiling fondly at Ruan. 'Come on now, Lucy, how about you and me go and find Cordy, and buy her a cup of tea?'

The second the door was closed Alex picked up Ruan's hand, squeezing his fingers gently in hers. *What if I . . . I mean would it be, considering that I have never really . . .* Alex closed her eyes and began to pray. Uncertain of how to, or even who to, nevertheless she closed her eyes, lay her cheek on the back of his hand and wished with all her might that he would come back to her just as infuriating, stupid, stubborn and ridiculously hot as he had been before.

'You saved me.' The words were so quiet, scarcely a whisper, that Alex almost thought she had imagined them. Lifting her head she looked at Ruan, his drowsy eyes trained on her. 'I got rescued by the most annoying woman I have ever met. I am never going to live this down.'

'Well, better alive and shamed, than dead,' Alex said, smiling at him in a bid not to appear over-emotional. 'Have you still got all your marbles?'

'I think I have now,' Ruan said. 'I don't think I did when I left Sue's house. After everything you said, I should have—'

'Shhh.' Alex stopped him. 'It's OK. Let's not talk about it here. Not now. Not when I'm covered in bruises and you're as weak as a kitten.'

'Never compare a man to a kitten,' Ruan told her, smiling. 'We don't like it.'

It lifted Alex's heart so much to see him smile that she couldn't hold back the tears any longer. Burying her face in the covers, she wept, her shoulders rising and falling with every sob. After a while, she felt Ruan's hand on her head, gently stroking her hair.

'It's OK,' he said. 'It's OK. We made it thanks to you.'

'And Buoy,' Alex said, 'and my lovely Buoy.'

Tearfully, she told him the story of how Buoy had leaped into the water and helped drag him to the shore, and how his impulse to save their lives would probably be the thing that killed him. Ruan reached out and wiped a tear away from under her eye with the ball of his thumb.

'Want to know a secret?' he said.

'What?' Alex said, completely unsure as to whether she did.

'Buoy isn't the kind of dog who'd give up without a fight. When I marched out of Castle House in a strop on Christmas Day? I caught him in the pantry with Duchess. Let's just say they were enjoying something of a reunion. Buoy won't give up, he's not the type.'

'Oh my God!' Cordelia arrived. 'You're awake!'

Cordelia looked like she was going to fling herself on the bed, but thought better of it just in time, embracing her brother and smothering his face in kisses instead.

'And you.' She flung her arms around Alex. 'You're my hero. I'd have lost him if it hadn't been for you. You are obviously a lucky charm. He should definitely keep you on, you're brilliant.' She looked at Ruan. 'Isn't she?'

Ruan nodded. 'As much as it pains me to say it, yes she is.'

'And you don't seem to be brain damaged,' Cordelia said, narrowing her eyes as she examined his face. 'Although to be fair it would be hard to tell the difference.'

'Ha, ha,' Ruan said.

The nurse returned, this time with a doctor.

'I'm sorry, ladies, we're going to have you ask you to step out while we conduct some tests, OK?'

'OK,' Cordelia said. 'But don't bother testing him for brain function, he never had any.'

The doctor laughed. 'Perhaps you wouldn't mind taking Miss Munro back to her room? She isn't supposed to be on her travels just yet.'

'OK.' Cordelia kissed her brother again. 'I'll be back in a minute.'

As Cordelia wheeled her back to her room, Alex could hear the loud, familiar boom of Marcus's laugh.

'Are you still here?' Alex asked him.

'Of course I am,' he said. 'I couldn't just go and leave you at death's door, could I? Now I know you are on the mend I can get away off back home.'

'Thanks, mate.' Alex smiled at him, and she had to admit to being grateful, as he helped Cordelia lift her back onto her bed, before she made a discreet exit.

'Alex.' Marcus paused. 'You're my best friend in the world, you know that don't you?'

'I do,' Alex said. 'I'm glad we sorted out all of our differences.'

'And, oh, by the way, you've got a couple more visitors, they'll be here any second.'

'Who's that?' Alex asked. But Marcus didn't need to answer as she looked over his shoulder she could see who it was. Her dad had arrived, and just behind him was Mrs O'Dowd.

Chapter Twenty-seven

'Ian.' Her mother stood up, and smiled pleasantly at Alex's dad. 'How lovely to see you.'

'Gloria.'

Alex watched her father, as he bent stiffly in the middle and kissed her mother on the cheek.

'And Eleanor.' Gloria smiled at Mrs O'Dowd, who was a good deal shorter, rounder and greyer of hair than Alex's mother, but still the love of her father's life, nonetheless.

'Gloria.'

The two women looked at each other for a moment and then hugged, and Alex realised for the first time that it was friendship that connected them, not just some deal made long ago. It was a friendship that had endured, despite her father and not because of him.

'Alexandra.' Her dad came and stood by her bedside, looking down the length of his daughter, the livid bruising on her arms and legs quite obvious. 'Are you well?'

'I am, Dad.' Alex nodded. 'I am. Well, considering I nearly drowned.'

'Aye,' he said. 'It turned out not so bad.'

After all she'd been through, Alex couldn't stop herself from laughing, and it hurt her. But even though her bruised ribs protested, and her sore lungs wheezed, she couldn't stop.

'Oh Dad,' she said. 'It's a miracle I grew up as sane as I did! With a mum who disappeared off for twenty-five years, and a dad who can't even talk about his feelings to the extent that you kept a secret mistress next door for longer than most people are married! And then I'm supposed to grow up and be normal. It's no wonder that I am anything but.'

Ian looked at Gloria who shrugged and smiled at Eleanor.

'I think you are rather wonderful,' Eleanor O'Dowd said to Alex. 'I always have done. And I've always told your father so. And your mother. And from the second your dad and I decided we had to be together, I told him, almost every day, to tell you about us. And he wouldn't. Didn't want to hurt you. And every single time Gloria got in touch, with a new address, or I told her a piece of news about you, I told her to come back and see you, and she always wanted to, but she was so afraid you wouldn't want her. Of course she will want you, I used to say. You're her mother.'

Ian had turned and was staring at Eleanor in some surprise.

'Oh yes,' Eleanor said. 'I forgot to tell you that while

I was being your secret mistress for all these years, I was also being Gloria's secret friend. I know I should say I am sorry, but I'm not. Someone had to do something for that poor girl to keep her in touch with her parents, and seeing as neither of you two were up to the job, I did what I thought was best.' She sniffed.

For the first time, Alex got a sense that Eleanor O'Dowd was also an injured party in this charade, and she found that her mousy, dowdy neighbour, who'd she'd never paid much attention to – until she'd caught her with her dad – was actually a passionate and caring woman. A woman, Alex thought, that if she took the trouble to get to know she might actually quite like.

'I do not presume to say who you should befriend,' Ian said. 'Nor have I ever.'

'Oh God, Dad,' Alex said. 'Please stop bottling everything up inside, it doesn't do any good you know. You have to let it all out, at least sometimes. You have to let the people you care about know that you care about them before you push them away, or lose them altogether. Sometimes it's not all about the way it looks, Dad, sometimes it's all about the way it *feels*.'

'I think perhaps we should go for a cup of tea, Eleanor,' Gloria said.

'I think you might be right,' Eleanor said, smiling kindly at Alex. 'You knock some sense into the stupid head for me, darling, OK?'

'Alexandra,' Ian said, standing with his hands behind

his back. 'I . . . well, I feel I must apologise for not telling you about my arrangement with Mrs . . . with Eleanor, before the evening when you came home unexpectedly . . .'

Alex shook her head. 'Dad, you aren't giving a statement in court. This is me, your daughter. Come and sit down here and talk to me.'

Ian sat down, his long legs stretched out awkwardly on the low hospital armchair.

'Alex,' he said. 'I am very sorry. I've had a lot of time to think about it since you came down here. I thought I was protecting you,when you were a little girl. You don't remember, but you missed your mummy for a very long time. For weeks after she went you cried, and cried and cried. I should have gone then and found her. I should have brought her back to you at least. Even if I couldn't love her the way she wanted, I could have kept her close to you. If I'd been better at reaching out. And if she'd been better at sticking to her guns. I thought I was doing the best thing, and then as the years went by it never seemed like a good time to tell you about me and Eleanor. It never seemed like a good time to rock the boat. You and I, we were always so close. I couldn't bear to lose you. But then you walked in on Eleanor and I, and . . . well, now you live at the other end of the country. It's not hard to see that in trying to keep you, I've lost you.'

He reached out, and covered Alex's hand with his

own. 'And now . . . when I realised how close I came to losing you forever . . .' His words trailed off and Alex knew that he couldn't say any more for the time being.

'It's OK, Dad,' she told him. 'It's fine. I've changed since I arrived in Poldore. It's the kind of place that changes people. And if there's one thing I've learned, it's that nobody is perfect. Everyone gets things wrong. You made a mistake, but it was because you love me. I get that. Mum made a mistake by staying away all of these years, telling herself it was too late to change things. But do you know what I've realised? Just because you've gone on doing something the wrong way for so many years, it doesn't mean you have to keep on doing it. You can stop, and you can put the past behind you, and you can start again. And you can be happy. And that's all I want for you, and Mum, and Mrs O'Dowd, and me. I just want us to be happy, and happy for each other.'

Ian Munro studied his daughter for a moment, and then he bent over and kissed her on the forehead. 'I don't know where this wisdom has come from,' he said softly. 'It's not from me or your mother.'

'I think that quite a lot of it came from a dog,' Alex told him, thinking of Buoy and his refusal to give up, as he had dragged Ruan and her to safety.

'Well,' Ian said, 'I should like to meet that dog someday. The dog that saved your life.'

'I hope you get the chance to,' Alex said, sadly. 'I really hope you do.'

'Alex,' Ian said, touching her cheek, 'will you come home with us?'

'I can't come back with you, Dad,' Alex told him, smiling. 'Don't you see? I am already home.'

It was some time later, after her family had left – Ian and Eleanor to a hotel, and Gloria back to the cottage to wait for news of Buoy – that Alex was able to get herself out of bed, and walk, if very stiffly, down the corridor to see Ruan again. His door was closed when she got there, and when Alex looked in he was sleeping peacefully, Cordelia, dozing in the chair next to him, nodding away to whatever was on her iPod.

'Hello,' Sue said, catching her unawares.

'Oh, Sue.' Alex smiled at her, a little sadly. 'He's sleeping. Probably best to leave him in peace.'

'Probably,' Sue said, hooking her arm through hers as Alex began the slow walk that would take her back to her room. 'Actually I didn't come to see, Ruan. I heard he was on the mend. I wanted to come and see you, and say thank you.'

'Thank me?' Alex said. 'For saving Ruan? Because I think that was mostly Buoy.'

'Well, yes, I mean, no,' Sue said. 'I wanted to thank you for talking some sense into Rory over the whole Marissa business. And for not overreacting when you found out. It would have ruined the children's Christmas if I'd been forced to confront him, and I didn't want that. As it was, he came to see me last night and told me everything, including how you pointed out to him how much he had to lose. So, thank you.'

'You seem very calm for a woman who's just found out that her husband is having an affair,' Alex said.

'Oh, my dear, I haven't just found out. I've known for weeks.' Sue steadied Alex as she lowered herself onto the bed. 'But with the pageant to organise and Christmas coming up, I just couldn't face dealing with it, not just then. And in my experience Rory normally sees sense in the nick of time.'

'In your experience?' Alex asked her.

Sue sat down on the visitor chair, looking very sad. 'We loved each other once, when we got married. We loved each other a lot. And sometimes we must still love each other a lot, otherwise we wouldn't have had quite so many children, would we? But Rory is a weak man, and a vain one. It doesn't take much to turn his head. Although I think Marissa has been the most serious threat to date. Younger, beautiful and, in her mind at least, he was a catch with his imaginary fortune. She really was so very cross when she found he didn't have one.' Sue's smile was bitter and wrought with pain. 'Well, she's gone, and he's stayed, and he's begged me to give him another chance.'

'And you are going to?' Alex asked her.

'I have to,' Sue said. 'I don't have any choice. There hasn't been a single divorce in the Montaigne family in eight hundred years, and the days when I could have had bricked him up in a tower are long gone sadly. No, there is no other choice. I must take him back.'

'I don't know how you can,' Alex said.

'Because of our children,' Sue said. 'And because I do love him, even now. He's such a silly fool, he doesn't realise that he's already got so much more than he deserves. So thank you. Thanks for keeping everything to yourself, for not letting it spoil Christmas for the children, and for putting him back on the right track. Oh, and I've been meaning to say it since you arrived and I never had a second to get round to it, on behalf of the Montaignes of Cornwall, and the people of the town, Alex – welcome to Poldore.'

Chapter Twenty-eight

New Year's Eve

It was a freezing cold, but bright morning as Alex fought her way through the beech copse that surrounded the land-bound side of the lighthouse, making her way up the rarely used single track road, delighted to have the codes that would let her into the lighthouse in her pocket, courtesy of Cordelia.

Ruan was due out of hospital today, and Cordelia, whose band was playing down in Newquay, had asked her to go to the lighthouse, to switch the heating on and make sure there was something edible in the fridge for him, and Alex was happy to do it. She'd been back to see Ruan a few times since she'd been discharged, and an easy, friendly familiarity had developed between them, as if they were somehow circling each other, each of them too bruised and battered, both literally and metaphorically, to be ready to revisit their feelings just yet. It didn't change how Alex felt about Ruan though, not in the slightest. Every second that she spent in his company, chatting or lazily messing around with a crossword puzzle, was one that confirmed she was madly in love with him. How he felt about her now, now that he had come so close to death and out the other side, she couldn't say for sure. He was always pleased to see her, and there was something about him Alex hadn't noticed before, a sort of happiness and easiness – a new kind of gentleness. And, as he recovered and she spent more time with him and Cordelia, she saw him laugh more and more. But after that first day in hospital, he never tried to touch her, or to say anything even the slightest bit romantic to her, not even when they were alone, which they had been a great deal.

And so Alex was glad to go to the lighthouse and get it ready for Ruan, because she felt that here she might feel closer to him, in a way that she hadn't been in the hospital. Just as Alex stopped at the white-painted steps that led up to the lighthouse she turned around. She'd parked her car about a few hundred yards up the road, because the vet had said Buoy need to start his rehabilitation with short, gentle walks. And that was exactly what Alex had intended for him, except that Buoy had other ideas, and as soon as he got a scent of something he was off after it. Alex whistled for him and after a while he ambled out of the bushes, now with a slight limp, which would be permanent, and one less eye, which meant he was likely to bump into things. Still he bore the lampshade collar that was strapped around his neck with surprising dignity. He was a pure pirate dog, and Alex couldn't have adored him more even if she tried.

'Come on, Long John Silver,' she said, as she punched in the code that let her into the lighthouse.

'Now.' She opened the utility room door, where Ruan kept an old blanket just for Buoy. 'I'm shutting you in here for your own good. You stay there and rest. I won't be long; there's water, and some biscuits, look. We can't have you going up and down stairs just yet.'

Buoy settled down quite gratefully, as Alex put the shopping she had brought with her into the fridge and turned the heating on. Unable to resist, she walked up two flights of stairs, until she came to Ruan's bedroom. She sat down on the bed, running her fingers over the fresh clean sheets and then lying back. Closing her eyes, she imagined what it would be like if Ruan came in right now and lay on the bed beside her. She pictured taking his shirt off, running her hands down the length of his body and then . . . She got up, went to his huge wardrobe and opened it, then took out one of his shirts. She didn't know why she slid her own top off and put Ruan's shirt on instead; it was just a very silly, foolish way to be close him, to be able to imagine a little better what it would be like to have his arms around her. She lay down on the bed again, and then after a moment wriggled out of her jeans, enjoying the feeling of the cool cotton against her naked thighs, as she settled into his duck down pillow and wondered what it would be like to kiss that beautiful six-pack—

A door slammed downstairs, and Alex sat bolt upright.

'Hello? Cordelia? Cordy?'

'Shit,' Alex whispered to herself. Ruan was back and she was not only half-naked, but wearing his shirt in his bedroom, on his bed. It was probably deal-breaking behaviour for a man as private as Ruan.

'Cordelia!' Ruan called his sister's name again. 'Have you gone out and left the place unlocked again?' When there was no response, and while Alex was standing in his bedroom holding her clothes in her hands, he answered himself. 'I'll take that as a yes.'

She had had some half-baked plan to get dressed, and come up with an excuse for being upstairs, but it was swiftly thwarted as she heard Ruan slowly make his way up the stairs. She looked around and, displaying the guile and cunning of a particularly dim-witted hedgehog, she climbed into the wardrobe and pulled the door shut. Alex closed her eyes as she heard Ruan come into the room. It would only be a matter of minutes before he opened the door and found her there and then he would think she was insane, with fairly good reason, let's face it, and everything would be lost.

But Ruan didn't open the wardrobe door. Alex heard the bed creak as he sat on it and the beep of a phone keypad as he dialled a number. After a few seconds she realised that the vibration in her jeans meant that he was calling her.

Obviously it would be here, in Ruan's wardrobe, that would be the one place in the whole of Poldore where she got any signal. As quietly as she possibly could Alex rejected the call, holding her breath all the time, and wondering how she'd explain to him that she wasn't able to take calls as she was hiding in his wardrobe.

'Hi, Alex, it's me. It's Ruan. I . . . well, I just got back to Poldore. I'm home, a bit sore, but pretty fit and I . . . well, Cordelia doesn't seem to be around, and I just wondered what you were up to? Maybe we could hang out, watch a movie . . .' In the wardrobe, Alex nodded, thinking that that sounded lovely, or it would do if she wasn't sort of stalking him. 'So anyway. You know, give me a call or something.'

Ruan ended the call and there was a beat of silence.

'You know what, mate,' Ruan said, and it took Alex a second to realise that he was talking to himself. 'You can't put it off any longer, you have to find that woman and tell her that you love her, before it's all too late.'

Which was when Alex fell out of the wardrobe.

'Fuck!' Ruan said standing up, as Alex collapsed at his feet, dressed only in his shirt and her underwear. 'What the fuck?'

'Um.' Alex pushed her hair off her face and smiled. 'Hello!'

'Why are you in my wardrobe looking so . . . Why haven't you got any clothes on?'

'Honestly?' Alex said, rushing the next words out on a single breath. 'Cordelia asked me to come round and get the place ready for you and I did that and then I came up here and I've . . . Oh, I've missed you, Ruan, and I didn't think you were going to be home for hours yet, so I thought I'd just put on one of your shirts and . . . Oh God, fine, I was fantasising about you, OK? On your bed. And then you came in, I got embarrassed and hid in your wardrobe and then you said you loved me. You did say that last part, didn't you? I wasn't fantasising that, was I?'

Ruan blinked. 'I think that might be the sexiest thing any woman has ever said to any man,' he said.

'Really?' Alex looked uncertain. 'Because I was worried that it would come across as kind of creepy.'

'You were fantasising about me?' Ruan asked, his expression of surprise intensifying gradually.

'I was,' Alex said, talking another step towards him. 'But you're probably a bit too delicate for me to do the things to you that I was thinking about, just yet.'

'I'm pretty sure I'm fine,' Ruan said, hooking his fingers between the buttons on her shirt, and drawing her near to him. 'And delicate is another of those words you shouldn't say to a man.' Slowly he began to undress her, but Alex closed her hand over his.

'Why didn't you say or do anything like this when we were in the hospital?' she asked him. 'I thought you'd gone off me again.'

'Because I didn't want a hospital to be the next place that I kissed you, or touched you,' Ruan said, gazing into her eyes.

'And just to clarify, that thing you said just now – you meant that? Not the movie part, the being in love with me part.'

'Yes, I meant it, Alex. I am in love you, very much, and since I've discovered you half-naked in my wardrobe, a little more.'

Alex caught her breath as Ruan unbuttoned the rest of the shirt, and pushed it off her shoulders, his eyes travelling slowly down her body.

'And you are sure that all this won't do you any harm?' Alex asked him. 'What with you being a bit erm "delicate"?' she teased.

'I'm sure that not doing "all this" would do me some harm,' Ruan said. 'I want you so badly, Alex.'

Alex squeaked, which wasn't the most seductive or sexy thing that she could have come up with right then, but it was all that she had.

'Are you sure that this is what you want?' he asked her. 'Because it doesn't have to be now, it could be next week, next year, whenever you are ready. I love you, Alex, I'll wait for you.'

'Oh, Ruan.' Alex smiled as she wrapped her arms around his neck and pressed his body into hers. 'I love you too, and, tell me, what is it about a half-naked woman hiding in your wardrobe, that looks like she isn't ready for everything that happens next?'

Epilogue

Easter Sunday

Daffodils danced against the newly whitewashed walls of Alex's cottage, as she and Buoy made their way to the steps that led down to her boat. As they reached the newly mended and blue-painted gate, Alex bent down and scooped up the newest tenant of the harbour master's cottage, a poodle-mutt-cross puppy, by the name of Skipper.

It turned out that Buoy's last liaison with Sue's poodle, Duchess, had not been a fruitless one, as nine weeks later, just as February drew to a close, Duchess became the proud mother of six small, curly-haired mongrel puppies, or as Sue referred to them 'Muttely-poos'. Sue had borne the scandal with reasonably good grace, especially as the news of Buoy's heroics had made the litter quite sought after in the town, and she'd got almost as much for the puppies as she would have if they'd been pure bred. And as for Buoy, he had positively shone with pride at his fecundity. Alex was certain if he could have said the words 'See, there's life in the old dog yet,' that he absolutely would have.

It hadn't taken much persuading for Alex to take Skipper, and one of the girls had gone to a delighted Forest, who had promptly named her Mike.

Buoy certainly seemed to like having the puppy around, even if most of the time he was tangled in his dad's feet or hanging off one of his ears, growling furiously. Best of all, since the little one had moved in, Buoy had even taken to sleeping in their dog bed, in the living room, in front of the fire, curled around little Skipper. Yes, Alex had noticed a definite spring in the old dog's limp, since the puppies had arrived. Maybe Buoy would see twelve and beyond after all.

The day was bright, and cold, but full of sun, the sea beyond the estuary as blue as Alex had ever seen it, sparkling with the faintest promise of summer. Alex was looking forward to the coming day, and not only because it was the day of Poldore's ancient and historic Easter passion play, when rumour had it Sue Montaigne was actually going to play God, but because today was a going to be a very special day. It was the day when everyone she cared about would be in one place for the first time ever.

No one had been more surprised than Alex when Gloria told her in early January that she was planning to use the last of the money from the suitcase to put a deposit down on a little cottage in the town and had been offered a job in a very chic little fashion boutique on Castle Place Hill.

'So you're planning to stay here for good then?' Alex had asked her, stunned.

'Yes,' Gloria had said. 'Yes, if you say that I can. Because I've missed twenty-five years of your life, and now – well, I don't want to miss any more. I mean I promise not to interfere *too* much. Or flirt with that ravishing young man you haven't been able to put down since New Year, well, not *very* much anyway. And I will admit that my "guitar lessons" with Brian are an added incentive to stay on. But I will only stay if you say that it's OK for me to be here. Because me being here is all about getting to know you.'

'Yes,' Alex had simply. 'Yes, you can stay. I'd like that, Mum.'

So it had been a surprise, but a nice one.

It had been less of a shock, when her dad had called her a couple of weeks ago to tell her that he and Eleanor would like to come down for Easter weekend. Now that all of their relationships were out in the open, Eleanor and her mother talked on the phone at least twice a week. Even Alex's dad seemed to talk to her more now than he had when she'd lived with him. The thing was, Alex realised, when they'd been in the same house together there had rarely been any need for conversation, and they'd fallen into an almost wordless side-by-side existence. Now though, when they talked on the phone, the words flowed between them like they never had before. Alex would tell her dad about her day at work, what Buoy had been up to, and even sometimes how things were going with Ruan, although she was scared stiff of jinxing her happiness by admitting to it too much to anyone. And since her dad had discovered she was now on good terms with rock legend Brian Rogers, he'd told her more and more about his love of music. So Alex wasn't even a bit worried about her parents and their respective squeezes being in the same room as her; she was actually looking forward to it.

It was when Milly called her to tell her that she and Marcus were heading down for a romantic Easter getaway that Alex had nearly decided to grab Ruan and the dogs and get on the next cruise liner leaving the harbour and never come back. Things had been fine between her and Marcus after he headed back to Scotland, and quite quickly had gone back to normal – he'd send her stupid jokes via text, they'd call each other every other week or so and he'd update her on the progress of the wedding, which had taken place, complete with a Cinderella coach and horses and the biggest princess dress that Alex had ever seen. The wedding had been fine, lovely even; never, not once, did they mention the whole naked incident debacle and Alex had barely even spoken to Milly, who divided her time between negotiating corners in her massive dress, and performing rehearsed routines with her many bridesmaids to classic disco numbers. Alex had thought the whole sorry business was behind them.

And then Milly called her out of the blue.

'Oh my God, Alex, you never said you know Riley Rivers!' was how Milly greeted her.

'I . . . er . . . who?' Alex had asked her, wondering if the name, which was vaguely familiar, had anything to do with Milly wanting to come down there and rip all of her hair out for messing with her man. Perhaps it was the name of the trained assassin that Milly had hired to whack her.

'Riley Rivers, oh my God, woman, where were you from two thousand to two thousand and two? Don't you remember Ominous, the sexiest boy band that history has ever produced? Riley Rivers was the cute one, that was until he had to go into rehab due to an uncontrollable addiction to doughnuts. I always wondered what happened to Riley, well, turns out he's an actor now, and he lives down your way and he's only playing Jesus in your Easter play! Riley Rivers, Al, you know a celebrity!'

Alex had pictured the man that was playing Jesus in her head – an amiable guy in his late thirties who Alex might have thought was very sexy had Ruan not, well, ruined her for other men. Everyone called him Lee not Riley in Poldore. 'Oh, so, you are a fan then?' Alex had asked her. 'Of Lee – I mean, Riley?'

384 • *Scarlett Bailey*

'Yes, as soon as Marcus showed me the latest Poldore blog instalment, I said "we're goin'" so yes, and me and Marcus are coming down for it. I thought it'd be nice, you know, out first married mini-break after the honeymoon. And the three of us, catching up. All together.'

'Oh yes.' Alex had tried to fake enthusiasm. 'Yes, that would be lovely. Super.'

'And I'm glad you got it out of the way, by the way.' Milly had dropped that bomb into the conversation just as Alex had begun to think she was safe.

'What would that be?' Alex had asked her, suddenly nervous.

'The almost thirty years of unresolved romantic tension between you and Marcus,' Milly had said, quite matter-of-factly.

'Um, have I told you about my boyfriend . . .'

'Look, it's OK. Well it's not OK exactly – when I finally got Marcus to admit that you and he had been playing tonsil tennis, I did *nearly* beat him to death with the Prada shoes that I made him buy me as a consolation for not being here at Christmas, but I always knew that something was brewing between you two. You've been friends for such a long time, clearly at some point you had to decide if you fancied each other, so I was glad it was before the wedding, and I was glad that the answer was no.'

'It really was very much a conclusive no,' Alex had

reassured her. 'It was a "Oh my God, this is actually making me be a bit sick in my mouth" no.'

'I'm not an angry person, Al,' Milly had gone on. 'I do my yoga, I do my Pilates. I'm a Zen sort of girl.'

'That's nice,' Alex had said. Though the word she most often applied to Milly was 'orange' rather than 'Zen'. 'I've always thought that about you, about how very Zen you are.'

'But know this, if I ever get a whiff of anything inappropriate going on between you and my husband again, I will have your eyes, do you hear me, *your eyes*. And I will parade them on the spikes of my Prada heels.'

'OK!' Alex had said brightly. 'Seems totally fair.'

'Lovely, so we'll see you in a couple of weeks then, we'll do lunch, yes? And if you can hook me up with a meeting with Riley and an autograph that would be fabulous. Laters, darling!'

And so, Alex had to admit she was a little bit nervous about seeing Milly again. Still, at least if the worst happened, Buoy had a spare eye patch he could lend her.

The Passion Play had been an enormous hit, and there were no freak storms, no trucks with failing brakes. Reverend Jed had done an excellent job of delivering the Easter Sunday sermon in the town square and Riley Rivers had manfully kept in character, even when a bus load of now rather ageing Ominous fans shrieked and screamed every time he said something. Sue had been quite brilliant as God, though, in many ways, Alex thought she was probably typecast. Best of all was watching the whole thing rather than being forced to take part, with Buoy at her feet, Skipper under one arm, and Ruan holding her other hand, pulling her close to him, so that she could rest her cheek on his shoulder as she watched the children of the town become near hysterical during the Easter egg hunt.

After most of the crowd had dispersed, Alex and Ruan, followed by her family, as well as Marcus and Milly, who was dressed a lot like a stripper, but looking stunning nevertheless, if you liked Perspex heels and hair extensions, began the walk up to Castle House where Sue had invited them for lunch.

They were almost there when Lucy appeared and, at her side, her engineer, Michael. Today was a big day for Lucy too – the day her boyfriend met her friends and family, and the poor man looked petrified.

Alex remembered only too well how Lucy had told her about their first date. It had been on the drive back from hospital. So much had happened, Alex had completely forgotten that while she and Ruan had been in a life-threatening accident, Lucy too was going through potentially life-changing events.

In the car Alex had been afraid to ask, afraid that it had all gone wrong.

'Oh bloody hell, can I tell you now?' Lucy had asked her just as they were arriving back at the cottage.

'Yes!' Alex had pleaded. 'What happened, how did he take it?'

'He was very quiet,' Lucy had said. 'Very, very quiet for a long time after I told him I used to be a boy. And I was waiting for him to be angry, or scared, or hurt, but that didn't happen. He just sat there, across the table from me, and he didn't say a word, not for ages. And so after a bit I thought, he just doesn't know what to say to me. That's the trouble. He's waiting for me to go, and I thought, well, I don't hang around when I'm not wanted, so I got up, ready to leave and then . . .' Alex would never forget the quiet smile of pure unexpected joy that appeared on Lucy's face as she remembered the moment. 'Then he held my hand.'

'Oh!' Alex had clapped her hands over her mouth.

'And he said, "Lucy, it's you that I've been writing to, talking to, dreaming about for all these months, and you're still you. So thank you for telling me, but if it's OK with you, can we carry on as before? Because . . . I think you are pretty smashing." He actually said smashing!'

'Lucy, that is the best thing ever!' Alex had hugged her friend hard, even though with her injuries it still hurt, and she'd thought of Ruan, who had still been in hospital then, and oh how her heart had ached for him to reach out and hold her hand in the same way.

And now here was Michael, getting ready to meet the good people of Poldore. Except that he looked like he was going to a lynching not a lunch. His lynching.

'Do you think Eddie will be kind to Michael?' Alex asked Ruan as he led her under the portcullis.

'I think he will do his fatherly best to scare him to death,' Ruan said. 'And then I think he will try to kill him with kindness.'

Alex had been in the dining hall helping lay the table when Ruan found her.

'Hello,' he said, watching her from the doorway. He had a large box in his hand tied with a ribbon, and Alex was rather hopeful it was chocolate. 'Remember the last time we were in this room. If only I'd kissed you, the way I wanted to so badly, then there would have been no drama, no near-death experiences, no hospital.'

'Well, you're an idiot,' Alex said, setting down the spoon she was polishing, and going over to him. 'But a very, very sexy one, so I think I can forgive you.'

'I don't know about you, but the last four months, have been . . .' He grinned and blushed at once. 'Great. I've been so happy, and I am never not going to say what I am thinking or feeling, or not do what I want to do with you ever again.'

'Oh good, how about we make mad, passionate love under Sue's seventeenth-century dining table?' Alex suggested hopefully.

'That's a good idea,' Ruan said. 'Except lunch is in fifteen minutes, and we'd need much longer than that, and I want to give you this present.'

He presented Alex with the box, which she noted at once was far too heavy to be chocolate, or shoes, or any sort of lingerie. So it was an unconventional present, which Alex didn't mind at all. She set the box down on the table, and untied the pink ribbon, letting it float to the ground. Carefully, she lifted off the lid. Nestled inside, on a bed of pink tissue paper was a very large wrought iron key.

'But . . .' Alex looked up at him. 'Is this—?'

'Yes,' Ruan said proudly. 'I had your very own key to the lighthouse made, just so you know that you're welcome there any time you like, and you can stay too, for as long as you like, whenever you like. Even perhaps, some time not too far away, forever.'

'Ruan.' Alex gazed down at the giant black key, so unwieldy and ungainly, and thought it was the loveliest present she had ever received.

'I had to get Danny to forge it for me at the smiths, he'd never made a key before, took him eleven goes! But this one works, I've tested it.'

'Thank you,' Alex said. 'I got you an Easter egg with your name on it in icing, and actually it's not your name, it's Ryan, but I ate the tail off the "y" so I was hoping you wouldn't notice.'

'So the key hasn't freaked you out then?' Ruan asked

her, winding his arms around her waist and nuzzling his cheek against hers. 'It hasn't made you want to run for the hills and end it between us? It's not too much too soon?'

'No.' Alex shook her head, turning her face to his and kissing his cheek. 'No, it's not too much too soon. In fact, if you want to know what I really think about what the future holds for you and me, then I'll tell you. I think this is only the beginning.'

Acknowledgements

Thank you to the exceptionally brilliant team at Ebury, especially my wonderful editor Gillian Green and the completely marvellous Emily Yau and Hannah Robinson.

Huge thanks to the lovely Lizzy Kremer, the world's best agent, Harriet Moore, Laura West and everyone at David Higham Associates Ltd. who look after me so well.

Thanks to readers Clare Boret, Catriona Merryweather, Michelle Powell and Adelle Hopkins for coming up with brilliant character names!

And to all the staff at the beautiful Fowey Hall Hotel, thank you so much for looking after me so wonderfully when I stayed with you to finish *Just for Christmas*.

Finally, thank you to all the people of Fowey, Cornwall who were so warm and welcoming each time I visited and helped to inspire the town and townsfolk of Poldore, but especially my good friend, Melissa Love.

Enjoyed *Just for Christmas?*
Need a little more Christmas sparkle?

Turn the page to read extracts from

THE NIGHT BEFORE CHRISTMAS

and

MARRIED BY CHRISTMAS

also by Scarlett Bailey

available now from Ebury Press

The Night before Christmas

Scarlett Bailey

EBURY
PRESS

Prologue

Lydia Grant hadn't meant to find the engagement ring intended for her, on that dank and drizzly December morning, but she had. Her boyfriend, Stephen, had got up long before the crack of dawn, leaving Lydia with the luxury of the middle of the bed. A rare treat that she relished by assuming the position of a starfish and tapping the snooze button on the alarm clock four times, dipping in and out of sleep with delicious, dozy abandon until 6.50 a.m., when she had sat bolt upright and remembered who she was.

By night, she was a serial romantic, taking every precious spare second she had to lose herself in the golden age of the Hollywood romances that she'd loved so much since she was a young girl. She could fall in love over and over again with Cary Grant or Trevor Howard; and even occasionally – but not quite so much recently – her own boyfriend.

But by day – a day that should have started at 6.30 sharp – she was Lydia Grant, Junior Barrister, a career-hungry, hard-as-nails crusader for justice. And, in just over an hour, she had to be in court representing a forty-six-year-old surgeon's wife who stood accused of credit card fraud running into tens of thousands of pounds. Having only been handed her client's brief at eight-thirty last night, Lydia needed to get a move on if she were to get to court in time to meet and talk over the case with the accused before the start of proceedings, and reassure Mrs Harris that everything would be all right. After all, if there was ever a barrister who could make a judge see that a woman needed two hundred pairs of designer shoes, it was surely Lydia Grant. Failing that, she'd go for diminished responsibility. Who hadn't gone mad lusting over a pair of shoes they could ill afford at least once in their life?

Running dangerously late, Lydia thanked her lucky stars that Stephen's Holborn flat – hers as well now, she reminded herself, though somehow, despite living together for the last six months, she couldn't stop herself calling it 'Stephen's flat' in her head – was only a fifteen-minute walk away from court. She leaped out of bed and allowed herself five minutes in the shower, before bundling her long, dark, chestnut-brown hair into a neat chignon with practised ease. Slipping into a smart white shirt and an authoritative black trouser suit that she'd set out before going to bed, she gave her lucky Gucci killer-heeled boots a quick polish. Taking a moment for a quick glance in the hall mirror – and pulling a face at her reflection – she told herself out loud that today she needed to be a strong, confident and capable woman; a woman who was never in doubt, not even for one second, that she'd show the judge and jury how ridiculous the charges were, and that her client was the true victim in this case, a victim of a wealthy husband who refused to buy her sufficient shoes.

It didn't help that Lydia couldn't find any black socks in the drawer Stephen had ceremoniously cleared out for her when he'd invited her to move in. 'After all, Lydia,' he'd told her when he'd casually handed her the key to his flat, 'it's about time we moved things along, don't you think?' Perhaps it hadn't been the most romantic moment in Lydia's life, but it was a benchmark, nevertheless. A step towards commitment that, until quite recently, she would never have thought possible, even if it was commitment that afforded her just one drawer.

She could find training socks, pop socks, a pair of pink glittery socks that her eleven-year-old step-sister, from her father's third marriage, had got her for her birthday, plus a quantity of tights all tangled up in one big bundle, but no suitable socks to go under her lucky boots. Verging precariously on the edge of acceptable lateness, Lydia had done what any strong, capable, confident woman would. She'd decided to borrow a pair of her boyfriend's socks, yanking open his top drawer only to find the shock of her life sitting there, right on top of his neatly paired socks, blatantly out in the open, without even a minimal effort to hide it.

It was a small, square box in unmistakable pale greenish turquoise, with the words *Tiffany & Co* printed in black on the lid.

Without even thinking about what it might mean, Lydia grabbed the box and opened it, like a greedy child ripping open a packet of sweets. And there it was, winking at her in the electric light required on the dark, winter morning.

A one-carat, platinum-set, Tiffany Bezet princess-cut diamond engagement ring. Lydia sucked in a long breath. It was perfect. It was beautiful. And most importantly, it was exactly the ring she'd always dreamed of, chosen by a man who had taken some considerable time and care to discover her taste exactly. A man who knew that she always carried a battered and dog-eared copy of *Breakfast at Tiffany's* in her briefcase, and that since her early teens, her idea of the pinnacle of romance was to receive just such a ring, presented in that wonderfully distinctive box. It was a ring chosen by a man who cared enough about her to get it exactly right. By a man Lydia was now certain must love her very much to get it *so* right, and who knew that proposing to her at this special time of year would make another dream come true for her, because finally Lydia would get to have her own happy Christmas.

Which was why the second thought to pop into Lydia Grant's head that morning, as she stared at the ring, was rather surprising.

Lydia Grant wasn't at all sure that she wanted to get married.

Chapter One

21 December

Lydia glanced sideways at Stephen, who had been finger tapping the steering wheel since the last service station.

'Looks like we're going to beat the worst of the weather, anyway,' she said, briefly squinting out of the car window at the voluminous leaden clouds, hanging low over the horizon, pregnant with the promise of snow. 'The forecast said dangerous driving conditions, snow, snow and more snow – but look, it's only just started to come down.' Lydia nodded at the windscreen, where the first few delicate flakes of snow that had begun to waft down were settling briefly before being brutally wiped away in an instant.

Stephen said nothing in reply.

'So are you going to sulk about this for the whole three hundred miles?' Lydia asked him impatiently. 'God, I said I'd pay the toll on the M6.'

'It's not that and you know it,' Stephen said, keeping his eyes on the road. 'This is our first Christmas.'

'No, it's not.' Lydia sighed. 'It's our second Christmas,

or wasn't that you drunk and wearing a Santa hat at my mum's last year?'

Lydia grimaced as she remembered their actual first Christmas together; her mother, who had started on the Baileys at breakfast, sitting on her step-father's lap, chewing his face off while the Queen gave a speech in the background and Stephen worked his way through an overcooked turkey and undercooked potatoes.

'It is, it *was*, going to be our first Christmas alone,' Stephen said. 'No family this year, you said. No trekking from Kent to Birmingham in the space of forty-eight hours just to make sure that you see all of your various parents and multitude of step-siblings. This year, I distinctly remember you saying, we're going to do as we please, by which you obviously meant do as you please. Silly me.'

'Various parents?' Lydia complained. 'You make me sound like a Mormon or the child of some sort of hippy commune. It's called a blended family these days, Stephen, which you of all people should know, Mr Family Law.'

'You know what I mean. What was it last year? Your mum and Greg on Christmas Day, practically having sex on your gran's reclining easy-up chair. And then we had to get up first thing on Boxing Day to make it to your dad and Janie's in time for lunch, where you have so many half siblings, and half-half siblings, it's like visiting a crèche. I mean, how old is your dad? How does he have the energy?'

'I don't know, perhaps you should ask him,' Lydia muttered under her breath. 'You know what my family's like.'

Lydia's childhood had been far from perfect, something she'd been at pains to express to Stephen since they'd first started getting serious, knowing that sooner or later he'd have to meet them. And love them as she did – most of the time – they weren't exactly the sort of family a girl looked forward to introducing to her most serious boyfriend ever.

Her parents had had a whirlwind courtship – marrying a month after they'd first met, and only discovering once they'd conceived Lydia that they hated each other's guts. The Christmases of her childhood were far removed from her beloved screen versions, where it always snowed, everyone always loved each other and it always turned out all right in the end. Lydia's childhood Christmases had a nightmare soundtrack of angry words, bitter recriminations and slammed doors, until Lydia was twelve and her father had walked out on her and her mum for good on Christmas Day. It had easily been the worst out of a lifetime of disappointing Christmases, and for the next few years she'd become a bargaining chip in the increasingly spiteful war between her parents, alternating holidays between the two of them and not feeling at home anywhere.

Since then, her mother had remarried, perhaps a little too happily for Lydia's liking, given the incident last Christmas, and her father seemed to be competing in some world record challenge for most-married man.

'Dad's got issues. He's been having a midlife crisis all his life. At least you met him in the Janie phase. I actually quite like her. His second wife was a proper cow. She always used to call me "the girl". Never used my name, just "the girl", with a sort of bad smell expression. I used to dread it when it was their turn to have me for Christmas . . .'

Lydia always did her best not to blame her dad for the Karen years – for leaving her alone in the living room in front of the telly for Christmas lunch, for never remembering to get her a gift, even though he always spent every penny he didn't have on Karen. And for agreeing, as soon as Karen demanded it, that Lydia did not have to come at Christmas at all, or Easter, or at any time, for that matter. Lydia resolved not to blame her dad for letting Karen edge her almost completely out of his life, because after all, he had left the witch before it was too late. And after that, he'd made a token effort to rebuild their relationship. At least he had until he'd taken up with the very buxom, though far more personable, Janie. Either way, Lydia was glad that Karen was gone. Janie made her dad happy, and she always remembered to get her some smellies from Lush, which was something.

Noticing Stephen's expression softening slightly, Lydia reached over and rested her hand on his thigh for a moment. 'Anyway, it's not as if we're doing family, is it? We're not trekking from Broadstairs to Birmingham. We *are* having a proper grown-up Christmas in the stunning surrounds of the Lake District, just the two of us.'

'Just the two of us *and* all of your friends,' Stephen muttered. 'I told my mum we weren't going to hers this year because we were doing our own thing, because . . .' Stephen stopped himself from saying more, and Lydia, hearing alarm bells in the vicinity of her heart, thought it best not to press him further. Having met his mother on a number of occasions now, she could honestly say that she'd rather gouge out her own eyes with a rusty nail than have to endure any more of the those 'you'll-never-be good-enough-for-my-only-son' looks again, something that would be tricky if she married Stephen. Mentally, Lydia added 'Stephen's Mum' to her list of pros and cons for marrying him, slotting it very firmly under 'con'. His dad was nice, though, in that quiet, unassuming, had-all-the-life-and-joy-sucked-out-of-him-by-the-cow-he'd-married sort of way, which, all things considered, Lydia didn't think could be counted as a 'pro'.

'Look, I'm sorry I said yes to Christmas at Katy and Jim's without exactly running it past you,' Lydia apologised, not for the first time. 'The thing is, when Katy phoned, she was all over the place. It's been six months since she and Jim and the kids bought the hotel, and . . . well, reading between the lines, I think it's been a bit of a money pit. I don't know what possessed them . . . After all, Jim used to be an investment banker, and the nearest Katy's ever previously come to running a boutique hotel in the middle of nowhere is making us all toast after a big night out when we were students. They've poured every single penny they have into Heron's Pike. If it doesn't work out, they're stuffed. Katy said that they're fully booked for New Year's Eve and she needs to practise on someone. Who better than her three oldest friends and their lovely, handsome, sexy men?'

Stephen said nothing, keeping his eyes on the road as the falling snow began to thicken. Lydia turned to look out of the window, a shiver of anticipation running down her spine as she thought of the photos of the house Katy had sent her. Heron's Pike looked like the setting for a perfect Christmas. 'Besides, think of it, Stephen,' she continued, 'it's the Lake District, and Heron's Pike is a beautiful Victorian manor house, a stone's throw from Derwentwater Lake. It's got its own little boathouse and Katy says the village down the road looks like a picture postcard.' Lydia sighed. 'It will be just like the bit in *Holiday Inn* when Bing sings "White Christmas" and I always cry. And, look – it's going to be a white Christmas, too, a real one with snow, and open fires, and food, and wine, and people that actually like each other, for once. I, for one, can't wait to spend it with you and my best friends. I just wish you loved them as much as I do.'

'It's not that I don't like your friends,' Stephen began, carefully. 'Alex is great, although she is quite possibly the most frightening woman I've ever met, especially now she's pregnant. And David's okay if you don't mind talking about Romans or Normans, or whatever it is he lectures in. I've only met Katy and Jim at Alex's wedding, and I didn't get to talk to them too much because – if you remember – Katy got over-excited by the free champagne, burst into tears and then passed out in her dessert. But I'm sure they are a lovely couple. Just as I'm certain that their kids and their grandparents are charming. But Christmas with Joanna Summers? The queen of TV shopping? I'm sorry, Lydia, that is so low down my Christmas wish list that it comes below being stranded on a desert island and forced to eat my own legs to survive.'

'Harsh!' Lydia chuckled, despite herself. 'I know Joanna is an acquired taste, but the four of us have been friends since we met at university, and she's been a good friend to me, the best.' The four girls had met in the first week of their first term, thrown into the random mix of being on the same corridor in their hall of residence. And sharing a house in their final two years – through boys, exams, assorted family dramas and one very real tragedy – had cemented their friend-ships for life. 'Besides,' added Lydia now, 'if Joanna hadn't let me live with her rent free while I was studying for the bar, then I'd have been sunk.'

'She's just so up herself, strutting around like she owns the place.'

'That's her TV image, not what she's really like. She's had to be tough.' Of all of them, Joanna had found it easiest to adapt to student life and living away from home for the first time. She might joke about having been raised by wolves but, in truth, she'd been dumped by her parents in various boarding schools from the age of seven. She'd had to cope. 'You need a lot of guts to do her job. All that drama and confidence, that's more about keeping up a front than anything else.'

'She's so superficial,' Stephen snapped back. 'She sells cheap tat to people who can't afford it on a shopping channel, Lydia,' he added. 'How does blathering on incessantly about how you can own a genuine fake diamond ring for forty-nine ninety-nine, in two easy instalments, require guts?'

'God, you are such a snob,' Lydia retorted as the snow began to fall in earnest, and the last motorway sign flashed up a new fifty mile per hour speed limit. 'Not everyone can charge about saving the world like you, you know.'

'No, but *some* people could do a little more to try,' Stephen said, glancing pointedly at Lydia. Lydia bit her lip. She did her best to keep up with him, his charity work, all the legal aid stuff and the weekend volunteering, but it never seemed to be enough to please him. He forgot that, while he was at a comfortable, secure stage in his career, she was really still only starting out in hers. She had to do the work that chambers gave her, when it came in, and that barely left her time to breathe let alone spend every spare minute doing good, in the relentless way Stephen did.

'Besides' – Lydia decided to ignore his jibe – 'I'd like to see *you* present live TV. She has to think on her feet all the time. That's why she's the best at what she does, not just because she's beautiful. Sometimes, if I've got a case I'm particularly nervous about, I think of her, and that gives me courage.'

'Who knew that flogging crap could be so inspiring,' Stephen muttered under his breath, but again Lydia let it pass. While she loved Joanna to the depths of her shallows, and would defend her to the hilt, secretly she was rather glad Stephen hadn't instantly been utterly charmed by her stunning, long-legged, titian-haired friend. A fair few of her past boyfriends had rather let her down in that respect, and although Lydia knew that Joanna would never, ever break the golden rule when it came to pinching a friend's beau, she had not been quite so certain of some of her ex-boyfriends. Lydia did sort of take after her parents when it came to bad romances. In the past, she'd fallen in love at the drop of a hat, and her eternal romantic optimism had seen her disappointed in love more than her fair share. That was until she met sensible, stable Stephen. After a moment's reflection, Lydia added, 'Did not fall for Joanna' to her mental list of pros.

'What I'm intrigued by is this latest guy Joanna's bringing along,' Lydia went on. 'Alex says she's mad about him, she says he's definitely the one she's going to marry.'

'Definitely the one she's going to marry until after she's collected a big, expensive engagement ring that most certainly hasn't been purchased on BuyIt! TV,' Stephen said, cynically. 'Then I'm sure he'll go the way of her other short-lived fiancés, and she'll simply have another obscenely large diamond to add to her collection.'

Lydia wriggled in her seat, yanking at the seatbelt that, after too many hours sitting in one position, had started to grate on her neck. The conversation was also beginning to sail just a little too close to the wind for her peace of mind. For the last two weeks, Lydia had felt the presence of the engagement ring in Stephen's top drawer like a ticking bomb in a bad B-movie. But Stephen had proven himself an expert at keeping his plans to propose to her a secret. Even when she'd dashed his suggestion of a country cottage hideaway just for the two of them, begging him to let them spend Christmas with her friends instead, he'd hidden his disappointment well. Before they'd set off this morning, she'd made an excuse to run back into the flat and check, but the bomb was evidently coming with them. And all this talk of rings seemed loaded with unspoken meaning that she was keen to steer clear of.

'I think it's brave of her not to marry a man just because he asks her or it looks good on paper. It's brave to hold out, pause and take a breath. She always realised that something wasn't right and she changed her mind. I wish my parents had done the same; they would have been a lot happier, a lot sooner.'

'Well, I don't,' Stephen said, taking his eyes off the road for a second to smile at her. 'If they had, I wouldn't have you. I just hope this latest poor sod knows what he's getting himself into with Joanna. Still, I suppose if he survives Christmas with the four of you girls in one piece, then he's pretty much capable of surviving anything.'

'We're not that bad, are we?' Lydia asked him, although she knew that, when she and her friends were all together, they seemed to simultaneously regress about ten years and drown out any other noise within a five-mile vicinity, each one clamouring to be heard above the others, just as it used to be on a daily basis in their overcrowded student house.

'No.' Stephen looked a little chastened. 'No, you are not bad at all, not even Joanna, I suppose. It's just . . .

it's just that I thought this year it would be different, no family, no friends, just you and me. That was how I pictured it.'

'I know, and that would have been lovely, it really, truly would,' Lydia said, suddenly consumed by guilt at her deliberate decision to avoid spending anything that could be described as 'potential romantic proposal time' alone with Stephen, just in case he popped the question and she wasn't ready to answer yet.

Here he was, sulking because she'd persuaded him to let them spend Christmas with her friends, but little did he know that she was doing this for him. Far better for her to be able to answer confidently when he finally proposed to her, rather than, 'Um, well . . . the thing is, I'm not sure, can you give me a month or year or two to mull it over?' Most of all, before Stephen produced that beautiful ring, Lydia wanted more than anything to have talked herself into saying yes.

Yes, because Stephen was certainly handsome, with his Nordic good looks, pale blond hair, light blue eyes and square manly jaw, and he would make a splendid contribution to the attractive children Lydia had vaguely pictured herself having one day. Yes, because he was genuinely a nice man, the kind of man who cared about what happened in the world and worked to make it a better place. But, most importantly, yes, because she loved him.

This hesitation wasn't at all like Lydia. When it

came to love, she usually rushed in where even fools turned back. After all, she'd met Stephen out of the blue, allowing herself to free fall into a relationship with him without a second thought, and she'd been content enough with their relationship for over a year. So why pull up short now?

Perhaps it was the memory of her mother's face, staring unseeingly at the burnt turkey languishing in the sink on the day her dad had finally left home, that was putting her off making that final commitment to one man. Or the string of boyfriends Mum had brought home, in the years before she'd finally met Greg. It seemed at the time like there was a new one sitting at the head of the table every Christmas, while her mum fawned over him with unseemly gratitude, expecting Lydia to treat him like a member of their tiny, disjointed family. Her mum had always been so sure that the next one was *the one*, that this time she would be happy. In reality, though, it had taken her a great deal of broken eggs to make her omelette, and if her mother never knew when she was making her latest monumental mistake, then how would Lydia?

If she were being strictly honest, though, Lydia knew that it was her more immediate past that was holding her back. Not least of all the fact that, when she'd first met Stephen, she had been horribly, utterly – and very dramatically – on the rebound.

Chapter Two

Lydia had met Stephen on a breast cancer charity fun run. She hadn't wanted to go on a fun run, because as far as Lydia was concerned, the words 'fun' and 'run' never, ever belonged in the same sentence. In fact, on that very day, she had made plans to take herself to Selfridges to spend far too much money on a pair of shoes she would never wear, but which, knowing they were there, even in a box in her cupboard, would made her feel better. It was her usual time-honoured tradition of getting over break-ups. Less fattening than drowning herself in the vat of Ben & Jerry's ice-cream that would otherwise be needed to take her mind off her troubles, and a ploy that had never let her down so far.

Alex, however, had had other plans for her. Good, sensible, tell-it-how-it-is Alex, who even now was also heading up the M6 in her husband David's ancient VW Golf. Back then, Alex had told Lydia that healing and self-worth were not to be found in the bottom of a Jimmy Choo box, and that doing something good for other people was the key to soothing Lydia's bruised, if not quite broken, heart. Besides, David had escaped by going to speak at some ancient history convention in Rome, and she needed someone to thrash. Lydia hadn't been totally sure she agreed with her best friend on this, but one thing she had learned in all the years of knowing Alex was that you never said no to her.

Alex was a good person in every respect. She ate well, and exercised daily, running about thirty miles a week, relentlessly pounding the streets of London in every spare minute. She cooked from scratch – actual vegetables and fruit – not meals that she heated up in a microwave to eat in bed. Since graduation, she'd worked as a corporate fundraiser for a breast cancer research charity, basically frightening rich businessmen into giving her their money, a cause close to her heart as the disease had robbed her of her own mother in their final year at college.

Those had perhaps been Alex's darkest days, when grief had worn her to a mere shadow of herself, and all she'd wanted to do was go home to a father who could barely help himself and had no idea how to comfort his bewildered, angry daughter. In those first awful months, Lydia had sat up with Alex every night, sometimes all night, holding her friend while she cried, talking when she wanted to, not talking when she didn't. Downing cheap wine, matching each other glass for glass, and putting on inches with every shared bar of Galaxy. It wasn't that Joanna and Katy hadn't been there for Alex too, they had, but the severity of her loss seemed to scare them a little; they were afraid they would do or say the wrong thing.

Lydia, though, knew something of what it was like to lose for ever the very person you couldn't imagine living without. Even though she still had both her parents, clinging on to what remnants of family she had left had sometimes felt like a full-scale battle. Alex had lost her mum, and she could never get her back, but Lydia knew exactly what her dear friend had had to do to make sure she didn't lose herself in the process. Together with Joanna and Katy, she had kept Alex together, kept her focused on her studies, told her to remember how happy her mother would be to see her graduate, and to keep going come what may. It had been a difficult final year, but when the four of them finally flung their mortar boards in the air on that July afternoon, Alex had taken Lydia aside and thanked her for never letting her go, for helping her have the guts to make her mother proud. And from that moment, Lydia had watched her friend go from strength to strength.

A six-foot-tall Amazonian of a woman, Alex embodied the term formidable; throwing herself out of planes or charging up mountains was all in a day's work for her, as long as she was being sponsored to do it. And with her wedding day only a few months away, she had gone into exercise overdrive, demanding that Lydia, her chief bridesmaid, join her for at least some of the torture. So when all Lydia had to do was a piddling little 5K, as Alex described it, to help find a cure for the disease that had killed her mother, it was frankly impossible, and would have been fruitless, even to attempt to refuse. Dutifully, Lydia had donned a pink T-shirt and a feather boa, got as many colleagues as she could to sponsor her, and lined up with an assortment of runners, variously wearing fairy wings and cow costumes, for what she anticipated was going to be the worst hour of her life.

And then she had caught Stephen smiling at her. Far too handsome to be straight, was Lydia's first thought, admittedly not helped by fact that he was wearing a neon pink tutu and tiara. His face was friendly and open, though, the kind of face that was hard not to like. He looked, Lydia remembered thinking, uncomplicated.

The starting gun had sounded, and predictably Alex shot off like a rocket into the wild blue yonder, leaving Lydia floundering in her wake, desperately wishing she'd worn her brand new trainers at least once before attempting to run in them. It was a hot day and, as she'd suspected, her training programme of taking the stairs instead of the lift was not quite up to scratch. Just as she was considering ducking out to a Starbucks she'd spotted outside the park, the handsome man in the tutu jogged back and started running alongside her before saying hello.

'You suit pink,' he said, managing a relaxed grin as he easily kept pace with her. Suddenly Lydia was regretting her decision to apply full make-up that morning; she could practically feel her mascara travelling down her cheeks, and probably looked like a drunk transvestite, but perhaps that was why he was talking to her.

'So do you,' she tentatively, nodding at the tutu.

'I know.' Stephen laughed. 'But the guys at work said they'd double their sponsorship money if I wore it, so what I could do? They say that only a real man can wear pink, don't they? Well, I figure that this must make me the manliest man in the world! The tiara's my own, though.'

Lydia laughed too. 'Seriously, it's such an important charity, I'm more than happy to make a fool of myself, if it helps.' He continued, 'Although if I'd known a stunning girl like you was going to be here, I might have thought twice.'

'Oh . . . really? Well, um, yes – it is a very important charity.' Lydia had nodded, supposing that already being the same shade as a post box was, in this instance, a good thing, as he wouldn't be able to tell she was blushing.

'Have you lost someone to breast cancer?' Stephen asked her. 'I lost my aunt, when I was younger. I was devastated. She was the definition of a cool aunt, I could talk to her about anything, she always inspired me – I still miss her every day.'

'No, not me, not personally,' Lydia said. 'But my best

friend, Alex, the one up there at the front, she lost her mum when we were at university. It almost destroyed her. I wouldn't normally . . .' Just in time, Lydia stopped herself from saying 'ever do anything like this, I'm far too lazy', and instead finished with, '. . . let her do anything without me. Skydiving, abseiling – you name it, we've done it. Together. We're a team. A fundraising team of good deeds. Plus, I'm scared of her.' Lydia smiled brightly at Stephen. It was then that she noticed his ice-blue eyes, sparkling with laughter.

'You must be a very good person to have on side,' he said.

'Oh, I am, I'm a barrister. I'm like the Wonder Woman of the legal world, helping the needy, putting away the baddies.' Lydia remembered feeling delighted at how impressed Stephen was by her claim.

'Really? I'm a solicitor, actually. I do divorce, family law, mainly to pay the bills. But I also do as much legal aid as I can, representing asylum seekers, travellers, homeless people – you know, the sort of people who never have anyone on their side. I just think it's so important to stick up for those people who so often don't have a voice, don't you?'

'Oh, yes,' Lydia said. 'Yes, I do too.'

They had jogged on in silence for a few minutes, while the sun rose in the sky, the August heat intensifying as the day wore on. Lydia found herself wondering if Stephen would notice her checking her face in the compact she'd slid into her pocket, desperate to know exactly how bad she looked, with her make-up sliding inexorably south and her thick hair plastered with sweat to her head. None of her usual weapons of seduction were available to her. Alex had insisted she take off her favourite plunge bra and put on a proper sports bra, and not even she had thought about running 5k in the sort of killer heels that made the best of her legs. Which was why she had been surprised and delighted by what Stephen said next.

'Er . . . would you, you know, like to go for a drink afterwards? Doesn't matter if you don't, no worries,' he told her, awkwardly backtracking, which made it all the more charming.

'Oh . . . um.' After the heart-wrenching end to her last entanglement, Lydia had promised herself at least a year without men, to get her head straight. But it was such a nice day, and Stephen seemed so sweet, it would be churlish to refuse. 'I would, thank you. But look at me – I'm all sweaty and bleugh.' Lydia pulled a face.

'You look great to me,' Stephen said, with simple, easy charm. 'But if you'd prefer it, I could meet you somewhere later? After we've both had a chance to spruce up.' As the finishing line finally came into sight, they'd made arrangements to meet at a pub halfway between their respective homes, exchanging casual goodbyes just as Alex thundered across the field, looking as fresh a daisy, to question her.

'Did you just pull on a fun run?' Alex had demanded, half in admiration, half in horror, as if flirting might have somehow undermined the charitable act.

'No! Yes!' Lydia caved in instantly under her scrutiny. 'Did you see him? He's lovely.'

'You are such a tart,' Alex chided her mildly. 'Seriously, Lyds – aren't you supposed to be heartbroken?'

'I am, but what's the point in moping about?' Lydia waved at Stephen as he walked away. 'I could do with a nice, uncomplicated man to take my mind off things, and anyway, you met your soon-to-be-husband on a walk across Siberia!' Lydia reminded her, thinking of sweet, shy David, who didn't seem like enough man for a woman like Alex, but who somehow clearly was, as she had never been happier.

'Well, it was cold, and he had a better sleeping bag than me.' Alex smiled fondly. 'So has this fun run made you feel better than shallow, pointless retail therapy?'

'I would say that, on this one and only occasion, yes, the impossible has been achieved,' Lydia was forced to concur.

'Half marathon in Leeds next week?'

'Not even if you promise me George Clooney at the finish line!'

Married by Christmas

Scarlett Bailey

EBURY
PRESS

The Proposal

The sun was just about setting as Anna Carter and her boyfriend Tom Collins finally reached the summit of Ivanhoe Beacon, the tallest point of the Chilterns. Tom's parents' overly enthusiastic Labradors charged around their legs in a series of haphazard circles before Napoleon caught the scent of a rabbit, and Nelson chased after him, both of them barking so loudly that any chance of actually catching one was obliterated by the din.

'I'm worried about that jumper I got your gran, now,' Anna said, her breath misting in the cold air, as she looked out over the stunning view of the Buckinghamshire valley, bathed in coppery gold, which stretched out below them. It was a perfect Christmas scene – snow globe worthy – of the village, gilt-edged with snow, the spire of the tiny jewel of a church sparkling in the crook of the hill. 'I mean yes, pastel pink is a good colour for a lady of a certain age, and it will go so nicely with her hair and her eyes, but what if she thinks I'm being patronising, what if she thinks that *I* think that all old ladies wear pink, and that I don't see her as person, just as a walking – tastefully dressed for her age – corpse?'

'A what?' Tom exclaimed, laughing, as he rubbed his frozen hands together, then checking his pockets once again, probably for his gloves, Anna assumed, although he still neglected to put them on. 'Granny may be eighty-nine, but the very last thing she is is a walking corpse! She was challenging Dad to a drinking game when we left to walk the dogs. She will certainly outlive us all, and she *loves* pink. You worry too much, Anna. She will adore your gift, just as much as she adores you. And if she doesn't she will say she does and exchange it in the New Year like most sensible people do. Everything will be fine.'

'But it won't be fine, will it?' Anna protested, looking at Tom, who in the dying golden light, his reddish hair shining and his cheeks ruddy from the cold, looked like a particularly handsome fallen angel, a person who was born to be good, but couldn't quite help getting into the occasional spot of trouble. 'This is our first Christmas together, my first Christmas getting to know your family. I want them to like me, and to know how much thought I've put into their gifts and that I've got it exactly right, so that they . . . you know, like me and don't secretly discuss why on earth *you* are going out with *me* whenever I'm not in the room. It's Christmas, it's *got* to be perfect.'

'Why do people put so much pressure on themselves at this time of year?' Tom asked her, shaking his head, genuinely bewildered by all the fuss. 'It's just another day, another big dinner and a load of money down the drain. Really, it's no big deal.' His grin faded as he watched Anna's face fall. 'What? What have I said? I was trying to make you feel better!'

'It's just . . .' Anna hesitated, as she struggled to find the right words. 'Look, I know it's silly, and frivolous, but to me . . . when I was a little kid, Christmas was the one time of year when everything seemed shiny and . . . exciting and magical and just for those one or two days everything was fine. And I suppose I'll always feel that way. This is my favourite time of year and I don't want that to change because I've killed your family with salmonella or offended your granny with the wrong jumper. This is the time of year when good things are meant to happen.'

'It is?' Tom put his arms around Anna and pulled her into a slightly awkward hug. Given that she was wearing his mother's ski jacket, which was made for someone a good deal taller and rounder than she was, at that moment, she most precisely resembled a duvet. 'Because as far as I'm concerned the good thing has happened already when I met you. And besides, my family already love you. How could they not? You arrived laden down with colour co-ordinated gifts, each wrapped in a different paper for every guest, you've volunteered to cook Christmas lunch for fourteen, a job my mother hates, as it very much interferes with her sherry drinking, *and* you've made my mother's only

428 • *Scarlett Bailey*

son a very happy and altogether much more organised man, who no longer forgets everyone's birthday, not even the dogs'.'

Anna looked up into his eyes apologetically. 'I know I'm a nightmare. I'm controlling and overanxious and constantly organising everything that moves. I'm sorry.'

'You're not a nightmare.' Tom grinned fondly at her, touching her rose-frosted cheek with the back of his frozen hand. 'You're extremely high maintenance, but you are not a nightmare.'

'It's just . . . it's just . . .' Anna gazed out across the valley, the twinkle of faraway headlights dipping and disappearing between hedgerows, as the whole world went home to be with loved ones on Christmas Eve.

'It's just, you're the sort of girl who likes things the way you like them,' Tom spoke for her. 'And I sort of like that about you, even though you do colour co-ordinate my pants.'

'I just think you know where you are with colour co-ordination. Particularly when it comes to scheduling when to do laundry, you get to cerise and you know it's time to put a wash on . . .' Anna began, before she broke into a chuckle. 'Sorry again.'

'You are *my* perfect girl, Anna, any time of the year,' Tom told her fondly, with more than a touch of pride. 'Even your imperfections are perfect.'

'Thank you.' Anna leaned her cheek into his hand. 'It

is so nice that you get me . . . What imperfections?'

Tom laughed, tossing his head back so that the very last remnants of the sun bathed his face in amber light.

'Oh you know: the endless list making, the constant diary co-ordination, the way you break into my phone and put reminders in my planner for me . . .'

'I don't break into your phone! You don't have a password on your phone. I keep telling you to get one. I even made a list of difficult-to-hack passwords and set a reminder for you to look at it on your . . . phone.'

The two burst into laughter. Anna playfully pushed Tom away and found herself backing into one of the dogs, who for some reason had made it his business to be tangled up in every available pair of legs he came across; Tom's grandmother said she was convinced he was dead set on getting her a hip replacement,

'Dog!' Anna yelled, giggling. 'Don't stand about, run!'

Tom grinned as Anna took off through the snow, Nelson barking and leaping excitedly at her heels, eventually bringing her to the ground in a good-natured tackle, which quickly became rather amorous on the part of the dog.

'Tom!' Anna shrieked and giggled at once as, pinioned to the ground, she suffered Nelson's enthusiastic attempts at a French kiss. 'Come here and defend my honour!'

Tom hauled the sizeable animal off Anna and threw an imaginary stick for him to chase – a ruse Nelson almost always fell for, even though he was now almost five. Tom knelt down in the snow next to Anna, who looked happier and more relaxed than he'd ever seen her, with her blonde hair fanned out around her, her eyes sparkling with mirth.

'I love you, Anna,' he said, rather more seriously than he had ever said it before, which was a total of thirty-nine times since the first time six months ago, Anna happened to know. (And had made a note in her diary in case she should ever forget.)

'What's wrong?' she asked, suddenly anxious as he helped pull her up out of the snow and on to her feet, just in time before Nelson got back from his ill-fated mission. The dog fixed his eyes on Tom, his tail wagging crazily until he threw another stick.

'Nothing,' Tom said. 'It's just, just then I realised that it's really true. I really do love you.' He smiled happily, but Anna frowned.

'So before then, before that moment all the other thir– times that you said you loved me you weren't really sure?'

'Yes. No. Oh God, Anna!' Tom rolled his eyes. 'Stop analysing everything I say, I'm trying to be romantic here!'

'Sorry.' Anna was contrite. 'Proceed.'

Tom took a breath. 'Well, I can't just be romantic on command, that's not something you set a reminder for in my diary, is it?'

Shaking her head, Anna made a mental note to delete the reminder she'd set for 13 February at the first available opportunity.

'I love you too,' she said, testing the words on her tongue. Tom was the very first man she had ever said them to, and they still felt unfamiliar and a little alien, like they weren't words that were ever meant for her.

'Do you?' Tom asked her, taking her hands in his and looking into her eyes. Anna was surprised to see her confident self-assured boyfriend looking suddenly nervous and uncertain.

'Of course I do,' Anna said gently, smiling at him. 'How could I not? Have you met you?'

'You're not that forthcoming with the romance yourself, you know,' Tom said. 'Most girls I've known have been so needy and "I love you, do you love me", but not you.'

'Really?' Anna was genuinely surprised, but then again she supposed she hadn't needed to make a list for how many times she said the three little words in question. 'Well, I do. I do love you Tom. It's just that I've never had anybody to say it to before, so I suppose I'm not familiar with the etiquette.'

'That's so you.' Tom smiled. '"Not familiar with the etiquette".'

'Oh, sorry again—'

Tom stopped Anna before she could say more. 'Stop

saying sorry for the things I love about you, otherwise I might have to change my mind.'

'Your mind about what?' Anna asked him, intrigued and then alarmed.

'I've been trying to tell you something since we got up here,' Tom said, pleased that he finally had Anna's full attention.

'Why?' she asked him anxiously. 'Because all I'm saying is if you were planning to dump me you should have done it before I arrived at your parents' house for Christmas. I bought a goose, Tom, a goose. There is a dead goose the size of a whale in the chest freezer in your garage. It would be exceptionally rude of you to dump a girl who's preparing to feed your family for the next month—'

'Were you there when I was talking about how much I love you?' Tom interrupted her. 'You know, about five seconds ago. Stop it, Anna! I'm not dumping you!'

'What then?' Anna asked him. 'Have you got a sexually transmitted disease?'

'What!' Tom shook his head in despair. 'You know what, I'm just going to do this.'

Anna stood watching as Tom fumbled in his pockets again, this time producing a small box, which he opened to reveal a respectably sized diamond ring, of at least a carat, glowing faintly in the dying winter sunlight.

'Oh!' Anna said, clasping her hands over her mouth.

'Good.' Tom nodded at her self-imposed gag. 'Now

keep your hands there until I've finished.'

Wide-eyed, Anna nodded as Tom dropped to his knees.

'Anna Carter, the moment I saw you when you opened the door at our friend Liv's birthday party eight months ago, the moment I set eyes on you, I knew you were the one for me. You are the funniest, kindest, most beautiful, sweetest, most compulsively obsessive and overanxious person I know. And, as previously mentioned, I love you. And even though I am certain that Anna Carter organising a wedding is going to be one of the single most terrifying things I have ever witnessed – or experienced – and may in fact bring about the end of the world as we know it, I am prepared to risk it. Which is why I want to ask you, will you marry me?'

Anna stared at him, her hands still clamped over her mouth.

'Now is the time when you say something,' Tom prompted her, 'especially as I've got a horrible feeling I've knelt in sheep's poo.'

'A full year before my deadline too,' Anna said, happily releasing her hands and gasping in a breath of icy air.

'Pardon?' Tom asked her.

'My life plan,' Anna explained, referring to the wine-red ring-bound notebook of mostly lists that she kept constantly at her side. She wrote in it every night, ticking off the things she had done, adding the things she needed to do. It included at its very back her life plan. Tom was familiar with it; he was one of the few people she had ever felt brave enough to show it to, a couple of months into their relationship when he still thought her controlling and obsessive traits were kooky and cute. And although it had made him scratch his head and look confused, he had not run, half naked, out of the door when he'd read her plan for a fairy-tale Christmas wedding, complete with an illustration of the dress, which she'd done aged nine. The plan was simple: married by age thirty-one, two children by thirty-five and a million-pound house in Chiswick to go with them. Which had been reason enough for Anna to decide to be in love with him then and there.

'Oh yes,' Tom said, clearly a little disappointed, if not surprised by her reaction. 'So that's a good thing, right?'

'Totally brilliant,' Anna said, looking at the ring some more, not quite able to bring herself to touch it. 'Completely wonderful in every way, Tom.'

'So you are going to say yes?' Tom asked. 'And I am going to be able to get up out of the sheep's poo, before the dogs come back and Nelson tries to have sex with me?'

'Oh yes!' Anna laughed, her eyes glittering with tears of joy. 'Yes, I say yes. Yes, Tom Collins, I will marry you.'

'Thank God for that,' Tom said, clambering to his feet, just as the Labradors skidded cheerfully to a halt at his heels. He added proudly, 'Try it on; I stole one of your dress rings when you were in the bath and traced round it.'

Anna slipped the ring on, where it sat, perfectly at home. Perhaps it was a fraction too big, but it was a neat square-cut diamond, in a simple platinum setting – exactly her taste.

'What are you thinking?' Tom asked, slipping an arm around her thickly padded waist and kissing her on the ear.

'I'm thinking there's an awful lot I've got to do if we're going to be married by next Christmas,' Anna said.

Almost One Year Later

Chapter One

Something was not quite right, Liv thought, as she watched Tom squirming in his pale gold upholstered Queen Anne chair while Anna fretted. Anna was dressed as immaculately as ever, her blonde hair tied in a chignon at the nape of her neck, her taupe patent leather heels exactly the same shade as her skirt suit. Liv thought – as she often did – that Anna looked like a cross between Grace Kelly and Marilyn Monroe, though she had been as careful as ever to attempt to hide her bombshell curves behind sophisticated clothes. Anna always worried that people would think she was nothing more than a dumb blonde, but it was a foolish person indeed that made the assumption.

Liv glanced down at her own pair of grubby Converse and wondered, not for the first time in her life, how it was Anna always managed to look like a princess in waiting, no matter what the occasion, while Liv always looked – as her mother had persisted in telling her fondly, since she was about five years old – like she had been dragged through a hedge backwards. Really it should have been the other way around. Anna was the one who had turned up at school halfway through the autumn term, aged nine, having been taken into care and placed in a local kids' home. While Liv's family was like one out of a storybook: her parents owned a large detached house with a big garden, were kind and loving and would do anything for her. Liv had grown up with the sure and certain knowledge that she would almost always get whatever she asked Santa for (except for the pet python – she never did get that).

Liv still remembered vividly the day that Anna had arrived. Before the new girl had been brought into the class, their teacher had given them a long speech about sparrows. It had been something to do with a flock of brown sparrows, who one day were joined by a single white sparrow, who, because it was a bit different and not brown, they eventually pecked to death, for reasons that were decidedly unclear. Neither Liv nor any of her other classmates could work out what this possibly had to do with them, until eventually their weary and sparrow-pecked teacher came straight out with the news that Anna was living in a children's home. Thirty nine-year-olds had all but rubbed their hands together with glee as they anticipated the arrival of their new disenfranchised victim, who was bound to be a target for torment if ever there was one. But when Anna arrived she hadn't been anything like what they were expecting, even then, fresh from all she had been through.

Yes, her uniform was worn out and second-hand, and her shoes had clearly been bought from a supermarket, but with her long golden hair rippling down her back, Anna had stood tall and proud before them, as Miss Healy introduced her, radiating a mixture of sadness and dignity that had made all the boys fall in love with her at once and all the girls want to be her best friend. Why Anna had picked Liv for the latter position, Liv still didn't know. Liv had never looked like a storybook princess. At age nine, her thick, unruly dark-brown hair had been cut short and spiky like a boy's by her own stubby nail-bitten hands, after deciding she longer wished to brush her hair. Her school uniform was always awry and her expensive shoes always scuffed two minutes out of the box. Yet she would be eternally glad that Anna had chosen her to be her friend. That morning at break the two of them had formed an instant and indestructible bond, which had lasted their whole lives since, eventually resulting in them becoming more like sisters. Chalk and cheese they might be, but Liv knew Anna would do anything for her, and she would do the same for her friend, no matter what it cost her. Which was why Tom's strange and distinctly un-Tom-like behaviour today worried her deeply. The wedding was imminent. If anything were to go wrong now, well, Liv was sure that Anna would never recover.

As Anna waited, tapping one perfectly manicured forefinger on the arm of her chair, for the venue's flower arranger to present her with her vision for the table arrangements, Liv knew that Tom's discomfort wouldn't have escaped her notice. And that as they sat here, in the very room where in a little over a week's time they would all be toasting Anna and Tom's union, she was more than aware that Tom looked restless, anxious, like he had somewhere much more important to be. Which didn't make sense, Liv thought, uneasily. Tom adored Anna. He had done since the moment he'd set eyes on her, around eighteen months ago when Liv had invited her new friend from her kick-boxing class to her birthday party. And it was hardly surprising – most men, when first confronted with Anna's mass of thick golden hair, her curvy figure and long legs, were usually blown away. Then when they got to know her they'd find she had intellect and humour in equal abundance. But then soon after that, that she was obsessively organised and a little bit controlling. Actually extremely controlling. Not that it was Anna's fault really. It was her way of adjusting to the chaos of her childhood, Liv understood that, but until Tom there had never been a man in Anna's life who got it.

Tom though had stuck around, and the more he had gotten to know Anna, the more he liked her. Anna's lists, her plans, her constant striving for perfection and her need to control almost everything around her, frightened most men off within weeks, despite how beautiful she was. And if she'd been asked to put money on it, Liv would have thought that sporty, but super easy-going and relaxed Tom would have been running a mile from her obsessive compulsive friend within weeks. Instead, he'd seemed intrigued by her, in turn fascinated and amused. Gradually, Liv had watched her new friend fall in love with her oldest and best friend. Aware that their lives were about to change for ever, Liv had done her best to conceal her mixed emotions as Anna and Tom grew ever closer, knowing that if anyone deserved a man like Tom, it was Anna. They were so good together, everybody thought so. So why did Tom now seem so distracted so near the wedding?

'So,' Jean the florist was telling Anna, as she opened a rather dog-eared and aged-looking photo album. 'For a Christmas wedding, my brides usually love this combination of holly, ivy and mistletoe displayed in this fishbowl vase. It looks very, very festive and yet modern and chic.'

It was Liv's turn to squirm as she watched Anna stare blankly at a photograph of someone else's wedding.

'I don't think,' Anna said very slowly and sweetly, 'that flowers in fishbowls are *quite* for me, not that they are not lovely for some people. It's just that if you remember my email, sent to you on the eighteenth of November at fifteen forty-eight, you'll recall that I asked for roses? Big fat red roses?' Anna unleashed her best smile, reserved for the people that were testing her compulsive need to have everything exactly the way she wanted it the very most. 'Here, let me give you a copy, because sometimes those pesky little emails just wander off and go missing, don't they?' Anna produced her wedding folder, an orange highlighter pen from her special highlighter-pen pocket in her bag, and retrieved a copy of said email from the dated files marked 'Correspondence (Venue)' which she passed to Jean. 'So let's just go through this, shall we? As you can see, it's composed in easy-to-read bullet points . . .'

Jean blinked at Anna, and closed her photo album with a distinct slap, clearly offended that her trademark 'festive plants in fishbowls' weren't considered to be up to standard. This was her fault, Liv thought, momentarily distracted from Tom's odd behaviour by Anna's anxiety. Not that Anna's face wasn't a picture of serenity. But Liv knew the signs and knew the murderous thoughts that were almost certainly running through Anna's head. She should have made her delegate more.

'You can't try and do everything,' Liv had told her the day Anna had broken the news of the wedding. It was last New Year's Eve. Liv had got back to the flat first, glad to have escaped her lovely, but energy-zapping family, and to finally be back home with a precious week off work to do nothing but watch bad TV and eat the poor quality junk food that she would never in a million years dream of admitting she loved. She'd just put the kettle on, and lined up a family-sized bag of Wotsits, when Anna let herself in the door. For once she had been without Tom.

'Happy New Year!' Anna had said, bounding into the kitchen. 'How's the family, did they miss me? I missed them. Tom's family is lovely, but it's an awful chore having to be on my best behaviour for all those days and not reorganise the kitchen or colour code their airing cupboard.' Liv had been about to respond when Anna had hugged her literally off her feet and spun her round. 'Why am I wittering on, Liv . . . this is going to be the best year ever because . . . Oh Liv! I'm getting married! To Tom! He asked me to marry him and it wasn't a joke or anything, he meant it and everything and I said yes!'

'Wow!' Liv had said, her eyes widening as the news slowly sunk in and she got a breath back. 'Wow, Anna. Wow.'

'Are you pleased?' Anna had asked her, not able to fail to notice the distinct lack of enthusiasm in her 'wows.'

'I am, of course I am,' Liv said, willing herself to catch up with the news. 'It's just . . . Oh that's amazing news. I'm so happy for you. You're going to be married! To Tom!'

The two women had hugged again, and the second time Liv put on a much better show of being pleased, because this was Anna, and she wanted to be pleased for Anna.

'I know,' Anna had said, skipping a tiny bit. 'And there is so much to do! Think of the lists! And the pie charts, and I'm certainly going to need a spreadsheet and maybe a PowerPoint presentation!' She rubbed her hands together in glee. 'I'm going to need millions of Post-it notes, all the colours!'

Immediately, Anna set about making lists, sitting on the living-room floor of the flat they shared, with a newly bought spiral-bound notebook and a set of coloured biros, which she must have picked up on the way home for just this purpose.

'We're supposed to be going out, remember? Dancing? Bringing in the New Year? Not making lists that can easily wait until tomorrow,' Liv had said, a touch petulantly. 'Especially as this will be our last *ever* single girl New Year, Anna.'

'I know, and we will, I promise. But just let me make a pre-list. A list of lists, please, Liv. You know how excited I get by a new notebook.'

Sighing, Liv had sat down on the floor next to her friend, crossing her legs, noticing a hole in the seam on the inside thigh of her leggings, and tugging at it to make it a bit bigger.

'I'm really pleased for you and everything,' she'd said, despite the heavy weight that was descending steadily downwards in her chest.

'But?' Anna looked up at her, her pen hovering mid-air.

'But what?' Liv asked.

'That sentence was definitely going to end in a "but",'

Anna said. "'I'm really pleased for you and everything but . . ." But what? Please, please, don't say you're not happy for me and you don't love Tom, because if you don't approve you realise I can't marry him, don't you? Your disapproval could seriously ruin my life, here.'

Liv had sighed, picking up the blue biro and slotting the lid of the green one onto it, just because she knew it would drive Anna mad.

Honestly, she couldn't quite make sense of her own feelings at that moment, and although Anna was quite right, there was a 'but', a massive huge 'but', it wasn't exactly one that she could communicate then, or indeed ever now that Anna and Tom were forever. Because you didn't do that, you didn't tell your best friend moments after they told you they were getting married that you were really pleased for them and everything BUT you'd been secretly in love with their fiancé since the first moment you'd set eyes on him, weeks before he'd even met Anna. Or that you'd only invited him to your birthday party, and made a fool of yourself by wearing an actual dress, because you'd rather hoped that it would be you he'd be kissing passionately on the sofa at ten to two the next morning, and not your flatmate and best friend. (And the person who had always best fitted the description of soulmate.) No, you definitely did not add that particular 'but' to the end of that particular sentence in response to that particular announcement. Not unless you were OK for life as you knew it to end for ever and ever less than sixty seconds later.

Liv really had done her best to get rid of her feelings for Tom as he became more and more of an integral part of Anna's life, really she had. She had told herself it was just another silly futile crush in a long line of silly futile crushes, exactly like the time she'd decided she was in love with Marcus upstairs, even though Marcus upstairs was living very happily and very monogamously with his life partner, Brian. But the truth was the more Liv got to know Tom, the deeper and more hopeless her affections became.

And now it felt like she was losing both the people she most cared about in the world for ever and there was nothing for it but to keep her chin up, have a stiff upper lip, be the kind of best friend that Anna always was to her and continue to let Tom treat her like one of the blokes down the pub, even ever so occasionally giving her short dark hair an affectionate ruffle, like she was his kid brother. There really was nothing else for it but to ride it out until the ache in her heart finally faded, only it was now almost a year on and Liv still felt exactly the same.

'But . . .' Liv had said heavily last New Year's Eve. 'If you take on organising every aspect of your own wedding with the same crazy controlling freakery you do everything else, you *will* literally explode. Take it as read that I'll help you. You just need to concentrate on the things that really matter. Like getting drunk with your oldest friend in about an hour's time?'

'It *all* matters!' Anna had said, distracted. 'Right, blue for the dress, green for the venue, red for flowers, black for catering, or do you think pink for the dress?'

'Er, we are caterers,' Liv reminded her. 'I'll cater your wedding. I might even give you a discount.'

'But you are the chief bridesmaid!' Anna had exclaimed. 'You can't be cooking in puffed sleeves and an Empire line dress!'

'Firstly,' Liv had said, 'thank you for asking me, I'm honoured, and, secondly, over my dead body will there be puffed sleeves and, thirdly, I will plan your menus, I will pay for it, I will prep it and then we can let our loyal staff cook it for you, and come to the evening do. It can be the Simple Pleasures wedding gift to you; after all, without all your hard work I'd still be doing Sunday roasts in a pub.'

'Nonsense,' Anna said. 'You are a cooking genius. It's only a matter of time before the world truly recognises your talent.'

'Which is why you'd be a fool not to let me at least take catering off your hands. Who else in the world knows you like I do?'

Anna had crawled across the floor and hugged her. 'Thank you. I'm so happy,' she'd said, beaming. 'I'm not used to being this happy. Normally when I'm happy something always goes wrong. Sometimes I think it's better not to be happy, and then you are never disappointed. Oh God, what if everything goes wrong?'

'Anna! Nothing will go wrong,' Liv had reassured her. 'Tom is one of the good guys. And he really loves you, anyone can see that. Now please put away your pens and your lists and let's go out and have some fun! For one thing I've only got twelve months to find a date to your wedding.'

'OK,' Anna had relented. 'But re the catering, could you do me a menu by the end of the week, and can we have monthly updates to check on progress?'

'Anna, it's not even January . . .' Liv began, knowing it was pointless to argue.

'I know, but can we?' Anna asked her.

'Yes, we can. And for God's sakes, get a florist to do your flowers. What the hell do you know about flower arranging?'

Famous for being one of the few people in the world that Anna listened to, Liv had made her concede control of the reception flowers to the venue florist, saying she might as well make full use of the services she was paying for. And so this moment of supreme awkwardness was in fact all Liv's fault.

'So as you can see,' Anna said, ever so politely, biting her lip, 'I want roses, deep, dark red roses, fat ones, old-fashioned fat roses, with dark green glossy leaves, a hand-tied natural-looking bunch of those every three seating places and, in between, petals scattered across the table, and candles, exactly the same colour red, alternating with the flowers. So that's not a problem, is it? To have it like that, *exactly* like that?'

'Give the woman a break,' Tom said, shaking his head, getting up suddenly and pacing to the full-length window, where he looked out across the grounds. Liv winced as Anna's head snapped round to watch him, her blue eyes full of concern. That's what all this nonsense to do with the flowers was about. She was trying to get Tom interested, to get him to take part. But for the last week or so he'd been anything but, all his apparent joy in his forthcoming nuptials seemingly seeping away. And Anna being Anna didn't know how to ask him what was wrong, so instead she went into crazy Anna overdrive.

'Look,' Liv said, leaning forwards and smiling pleasantly at Jean, 'you can get the fat roses, can't you? In that shade of red, and the candles, can't you? That's easy these days, right?'

'Yes, I can. I was just offering an alternative,' Jean said, clearly still a little wounded. 'That's what I'm here for, to offer ideas . . .'

'I know.' Liv smiled warmly. She leaned forwards and added with a conspiratorial air, 'And your alternatives *are* lovely, just not what Anna has in mind. Anna has had her table arrangements in mind since nineteen ninety-one. And you, of all people, know what brides are like, right? Mental.'

Jean said nothing, but her expression indicated that she'd seen more than one Bridezilla in her time.

'Also about the specific type of ribbo—' Anna began to interrupt, but Liv held her hand up to stop her, the only person in the entire world who could get away with doing that.

'The thing that is so brilliant about you Jean, is that you do know more about this than anyone, so who better for Anna to trust her table-setting dreams to than you?' Jean thought for a moment, and seemed unable to come up with any names. 'So, we know we can leave you to do everything as per the email, down to the last letter, and everything will be just fine. It will be more than fine, it will be a dream come true. A dream that *you* made come true.' Jean nodded and smiled, her hurt feelings instantly healed by a little of Liv's diplomacy. 'Great, now I need to have a look at your kitchens, and have a chat to your chef about your equipment, see if there's anything I need to bring with us for the day. OK?'

'Perfectly fine,' Jean said pleasantly, smiling at Anna, whose eyes were fixed on the back of Tom's shoulders. 'I must warn you that Chef is not thrilled at being ousted from his own kitchen for the wedding.'

'Well,' Liv said as she got up, touching Anna briefly on the arm. 'Chef can comfort himself with the knowledge that not catering this particular wedding will almost certainly extend his life by at least ten years.'

Liv paused, leaning close to her friend.

'Anna,' she said, 'just try to relax, darling. If you don't, all these months and years of planning will have been for nothing. It will all go by in a flash and you won't have noticed any of it, not even the reindeer-pulled sleigh that's taking you to the church, which you somehow managed to get Whipsnade Zoo to lend you for the morning.'

'It wasn't that hard. They don't open on Christmas Eve, I gave a considerable amount of money to the Save the Tiger fund and I'm paying the reindeer keeper an extra bonus. Everyone is happy, even the reindeer, who get more of their favourite feed. And I know, that's what everyone says, about it all flying past, but it won't for me. I've made a list of times when I have to pause and take stock: just before the ceremony, during the vows, speeches, photos, first dance etc. I'll be making mental memories!'

'Are there any other kind?' Liv asked her fondly.

Anna smiled at Jean. 'Thank you. I don't mean to be so demanding. It's the nerves, you know. And I always expect the worst, it's a bad habit of mine.' Anna glanced anxiously at Tom.

'Hey, Tom!' Liv succeeded in getting him to turn back from the window. 'Restrain your bride while I go and check out the kitchen, OK?' she said. She met and held his gaze for several seconds, attempting to psychically add the message *And at least look like you're having a good time* to the end of it, but Tom only stared at her blankly. It was clear that his mind had been elsewhere, somewhere very different from talking about wedding flowers. But where, or with whom and why?

That was the question that worried Liv.

Later that evening, after a long bath, and a large glass of red, Anna looked at Tom as he lay on his bed staring at the spot on the wall just above the TV. He'd said he had to go back to his place tonight, he had a big meeting in the morning, and Anna had accompanied him, unthinking. But now she was getting the distinct impression that he hadn't really wanted her to come.

'Hello,' she said pleasantly as she buttoned up her cream linen pyjamas and got into bed. 'Hello there? Anyone in?'

Tom smiled, albeit half-heartedly, and held out his right arm to her, which Anna gratefully scrambled into, resting her head against his chest and listening to the steady beat of his heart under his white T-shirt for a few moments.

For a while they had always gone to bed naked, or started out with clothes on, which during the course of their progress to bed would be discarded across the flat. Later, when Tom had drifted off, Anna would get up, pick up the clothes, hang, fold and pop them in the laundry as required, seeing it as a triumph of nature over nurture that she was able to be spontaneous even to that extent. But recently – was it recently? – a few months ago perhaps, they had started going to bed in nightclothes. And one night they had gone to bed without even kissing each other goodnight. Anna, who, before Tom, had limited experience of relationships that lasted longer than the seven days it normally took her to do some poor man's head in, wasn't sure if this was a normal thing, this cooling-off period, this calming down of passion. She would have asked Liv, but Liv had made her swear, soon after she started seeing Tom, not to tell her about anything she and Tom got up to in the bedroom.

'Why not?' Anna asked her, bemused. 'Finally, I have something to tell you and you don't want to hear it, why?'

'Because . . .' Liv had squirmed, looking like a restless little girl. 'Because it's been two years since I've had a proper boyfriend and, happy as I am for you, one of the main reasons I like you is because you always had a worse sex life than me. Now you have somehow lucked into a really great one, I don't need to further heighten my personal inadequacies by hearing about it!'

'That's not the main reason you like me!' Anna protested. 'We met when we were nine! The main reason you like me is because I do all your laundry and pair your socks. Oh please, Liv. Who am I going to ask about sex if not you?'

'Um.' Liv bit her lip, her dark eyes narrowing. 'You could try Mum? Call her. She's constantly trying to talk to *me* about sex. "How much sex have you had, Olivia?" "Are you having any sex, Olivia?" "Are you sure you aren't gay, Olivia? You know we wouldn't mind at all. Ask your brother, he's completely gay and Daddy and I love him just as much, Olivia!" You know, all the things that mums are not supposed to ask their daughters unless they want to mentally damage them for life. Give Mum a call, she adores *you*. *You* are her favourite.'

'I think I know why you haven't had a boyfriend for two years,' Anna had said, gently. 'Not because you aren't beautiful. With those massive brown eyes, and incredible skin and that kick-boxing-toned body of yours, you are stunning. And not because you seem to insist on wearing boys' clothes, and no make-up and having a hairstyle that looks rather like you accidentally wandered into a lawnmower. It's because you behave like every man you meet is your mate, the bloke you want to go for a pint with. You need some mystery, some allure, some waxing, some eyeliner and some . . .'

'Deep seated psychological flaws?' Liv countered with a smile. 'It does seem to have worked for you. Being mental.'

'I'm just saying, you don't realise how gorgeous you are,' Anna said.

'Thank you.' Liv had hugged her. 'But you still can't talk to me about your sex life. And that's final.'

And so Anna had gone on a journey of discovery with Tom without the aid of her best friend's opinion, on which she usually relied on so heavily, even secretly making a list of sex things that she liked, and sex things that she thought Tom might like and doing her best to check them off every time they made love. Had the honeymoon period been too short, had Tom lost interest in her already? Had she lost interest in him? After all, if it wasn't for his strangeness recently she would have been perfectly happy to curl up with her head on his chest and drift off to sleep and not mind at all that they hadn't done anything on either of her lists in more than two weeks. Perhaps, Anna found herself wondering ever so quietly, almost in secret from herself, marrying a man with whom the fires of passion had already died out could be considered, in some quarters, a mistake, but she quickly hushed that particular thought and filed it away mentally in her secret but overstuffed drawer labelled 'Now You Are Just Being Insane'.

Things that had been going so well, and so right, couldn't just suddenly go so wrong. Could they?

'What's up Tom?' Anna asked him quietly, after several seconds of silence during which they both pretended to watch TV.

'Up?' Tom asked vaguely.

'Today at the Manor, you seemed really uncomfortable. Have you got cold feet? If you tell me now that you've got cold feet, then perhaps I will need only ten years of therapy, prescription drugs and alcohol abuse to recover.'

'Me?' Tom hugged her a little closer. 'Why would I have got cold feet? I'm marrying you, the singularly most perfect woman I have ever encountered in my life. The only woman in the world who irons her PJs before getting into bed and, most importantly of all, the woman that I love.' He kissed the top of her head reassuringly, but Anna noticed the forefinger of his left hand tapping insistently under the covers.

'Look,' she said, sitting up away from him and pushing her mass of hair off her face. 'If you've changed your mind about marrying me, I completely understand. I am a terrible pain the arse. I know that. And you, you are a catch, Tom. Six foot two, with that body and those arms, and that chest . . . You've got a good job, you're kind and funny. You could marry any girl you wanted. So if you've changed your mind about me, even though it will kill me, and I will never recover and will live the rest of my life utterly heartbroken parading around in my spectacularly expensive wedding dress, which by the way cannot be returned as it's already had one set of alterations, like some modern day Miss Havisham until I eventually wither away and die, I *will* understand.'

Finally, Tom looked at her and the expression that Anna saw there didn't do anything to reassure her. It was one of uncertainty and something else, something she couldn't quite pin down. 'I still want to marry you, Anna, nothing's changed, I *promise* you.' He clicked off the TV, leaving the room in soothing darkness. 'Now come on, come here and give me a cuddle. I've got a six a.m. start in the morning and I need to get some sleep.'

But something had changed, Anna thought anxiously, as she lay awake staring into the dark, as Tom's breathing eventually relaxed and evened out. Tom had changed and for the life of her Anna couldn't work out why.

ALSO BY SCARLETT BAILEY:

SANTA MAYBE

Amy Tucker is single. So single in fact she hasn't had a man in her room for three years and her idea of a good time is buying new kitchenware at Ikea. So when she wakes up on Christmas Eve to find a strange man at the end of her bed, she is more than surprised.

Least of all, when the beautiful man claims to be Santa and has sexy stubble to rival George Clooney.

Santa whisks Amy on an exciting and unforgettable journey around the world through time and space. But can he really make Amy's Christmas dreams come true?

Available on ebook now.